TO HAVE
AND
TO HOAX

TO HAVE AND TO HOAX

A Novel

MARTHA WATERS

ATRIA PAPERBACK

New York   London   Toronto   Sydney   New Delhi

ATRIA
PAPERBACK

An Imprint of Simon & Schuster, Inc.
1230 Avenue of the Americas
New York, NY 10020

First Atria Paperback edition April 2020

ATRIA PAPERBACK and colophon are trademarks of Simon & Schuster, Inc.

For information about special discounts for bulk purchases, please contact Simon & Schuster Special Sales at 1-866-506-1949 or business@simonandschuster.com.

The Simon & Schuster Speakers Bureau can bring authors to your live event. For more information or to book an event, contact the Simon & Schuster Speakers Bureau at 1-866-248-3049 or visit our website at www.simonspeakers.com.

Interior design by A. Kathryn Barrett

Manufactured in the United States of America

1   3   5   7   9   10   8   6   4   2

Library of Congress Cataloging-in-Publication Data

Names: Waters, Martha, 1988– author.
Title: To have and to hoax : a novel / Martha Waters.
Description: First Atria Paperback edition. |
New York : Atria Paperback, 2020.
Identifiers: LCCN 2019031862 (print) | LCCN 2019031863 (ebook) |
ISBN 9781982136116 (trade paperback) | ISBN 9781982136123 (ebook)
Subjects: GSAFD: Regency fiction. | Love stories.
Classification: LCC PS3623.A8689 T6 2020 (print) | LCC PS3623.A8689 (ebook) |
DDC 813/.6—dc23
LC record available at https://lccn.loc.gov/2019031862
LC ebook record available at https://lccn.loc.gov/2019031863

ISBN 978-1-9821-3611-6
ISBN 978-1-9821-3612-3 (ebook)

For my parents, who took me to Jane Austen's house.
And for Jillian, Corinne, Eleanor, and Elizabeth—
future heroines of their own stories.

Prologue

May 1812

Lady Violet Grey, eighteen years old, fair of face and figure, with a respectable fortune and unimpeachable bloodline, had every advantage a young lady of good society could possibly desire—except, according to her mother, one tragically absent trait: a suitably ladylike sense of meekness.

"Curiosity, my dear, will take you nowhere," Lady Worthington had admonished her daughter more than once over the course of Violet's interminable years of adolescence. "Curiosity will lead you to balconies! And Ruin!"

Ruin.

While Violet had no objection to the word in the context of, say, the Parthenon in Greece—a place that she would have loved to visit, had she not been an English girl of good family and fortune—she had come to loathe it beyond all reason when it was employed in the context of young ladies such as herself. So frequently did her mother use the word to warn against Violet's unsuitable behavior that she had come to imagine it always with a capital *R*. One visited ruins; one was Ruined.

And if Lady Worthington's constant admonitions were anything to judge by, Violet was at particular risk of succumbing to this most undesirable state. When Lady Worthington discovered a book of scandalous poetry Violet had secreted from the family library, she warned of Ruin. When she discovered Violet writing a letter to the editor of the *Arts and Sciences Review* with a question regarding the discovery of a comet in France, she warned of Ruin. ("But I was going to send it under a gentleman's pseudonym!" Violet protested as her mother tore the letter into shreds.) All in all, it would seem—according to Lady Worthington—that Ruin was lurking around every corner.

It was, in short, alarming.

Or at least it would have been alarming to anyone but Violet.

For Violet, however, these constant admonitions, which only increased in frequency during the months leading up to her presentation at court and her first London Season, made her curious about what, precisely, Ruin entailed. Her mother, usually irritatingly verbose on the subject, became oddly closemouthed about the specifics when Violet pressed her on the matter. Violet had asked her two closest friends, Diana Bourne and Lady Emily Turner, but they seemed similarly uninformed. She began a slow search of the library at Worth Hall, the Worthingtons' country estate, but was whisked away to London for dress fittings before she had made much headway.

It was, therefore, with a frustrating lack of knowledge that Violet began her first Season. And it was rather disappointing when, a few weeks into the Season, she found herself on that most forbidden of edifices—a balcony—in the process of most likely being Ruined, and she realized that it wasn't quite as exciting as she'd imagined.

The gentleman who was attempting the Ruining, Jeremy Overington, Marquess of Willingham and notorious rakehell, was not entirely unknown to her, given that he was the closest friend of the elder brother of Violet's own best friend, Diana. In fact, Violet had vivid memories of Penvale regaling herself, Diana, and Emily with tales of Lord Willingham's exploits upon his visits home from Eton. Violet had not, however, seen Lord Willingham in several years, until this very month, when she had made her debut in London society.

Willingham was handsome to be sure, if one found golden hair, blue eyes, and perfectly fitted breeches appealing (which Violet, like any proper English girl, naturally did). He was rather witty, too, if one found verbal sparring enjoyable (which Violet, unlike many proper English girls, also did). And, this very evening at the Montgomery ball, Violet had learned that he was quick to turn a waltz with a young lady into an opportunity to waltz said young lady straight out onto a darkened balcony.

Violet was rather surprised by this turn of events—moments before, they had been chatting idly of her impressions of London, whirling around beneath the chandeliers, bathed in romantic candlelight, and now here they were, alone but for each other, the orchestra music muffled by the French doors that led back into the ballroom. From here, events progressed quickly. She couldn't quite say how it had happened, but one moment Jeremy was asking her, laughter in his voice, if this was the first time she'd been lured onto a balcony, and the next his mouth was covering hers.

Which brought her to her present condition of being Ruined. And yet—and yet. Violet had always been given the impression—by many books she had clandestinely read, certainly not by her mother—that Ruination was a rather enjoyable experience. Why else would a lady risk everything for a few fleeting moments? And yet, Violet could not, in perfect honesty, say that she found her own Ruin to be as enjoyable as she might have hoped.

3

To be sure, Lord Willingham's arms were strong as they clasped her to his chest, which itself was reassuringly firm as it pressed against her. And yes, he smelled pleasantly of bergamot, and his mouth moved over hers with an ease that spoke of years of experience, and yet.

And yet.

Violet found herself feeling curiously detached—while one part of her concentrated on the immediate activity at hand, lifting one hand to curl cautiously behind Willingham's neck, her eyes shut tight, some corner of her mind couldn't help being distracted by the chill in the evening air, the slight discomfort in her neck that came from keeping her face tilted relentlessly upward, and the possibility that she heard footsteps approaching them on the terrace.

A moment later, she realized with horror that she *did* in fact hear footsteps, and that they were accompanied by a decidedly masculine voice.

"Jeremy, you're losing your touch," the man said, causing Willingham to whip around, attempting to shield Violet from view. "I thought you at least knew to find a darker corner of a balcony for your liaisons."

The owner of the voice stepped into a shaft of light, and Violet's first impression was that he was the most handsome man she'd ever seen. She always thought girls in books were idiotic when they made that declaration—how was it possible, after all, that in a split second of staring at one man's face, a lady should decide that said face was more appealing than that of every member of the male sex she'd ever encountered in her years upon the earth? It was utterly illogical. Absurd.

And yet, in that moment, Violet apparently became absurd herself, for nothing could shake her certainty of that impression. The stranger was tall and broad-shouldered and appeared no older than Lord Willingham, who Violet knew had been down from Oxford for only a couple of Seasons. His hair, even darker than Violet's own, appeared black in the dim light. His eyes were a vivid, startling green, and as his gaze met Violet's over Lord Willingham's shoulder, she felt a thrill course through her—an awareness of his physical proximity, and of the appreciation in his eyes as he took her in. He moved with a compact, athletic grace, and she had a sudden thought that she would love to see this man on the back of a horse. She had a vivid mental image of her own mother's face if she could have heard this thought—somehow Lady Worthington would find it indecent, though she wasn't precisely certain why—and had to clap a hand over her mouth to stifle her laugh, unnaturally loud in the relative quiet of the balcony.

At this noise, the newcomer's gaze focused more sharply upon her, and his eyes widened. Violet was gripped with a wild, fleeting hope that he was as struck by her own beauty as she was by his. Even her mother, after all, was occasionally forced to temper her criticism with a grudging admission that Violet was "pretty enough to let the rest be overlooked, we hope"—"the rest" being all the aspects of Violet's character that made her *herself*, of course.

However, this romantic notion was quickly dispelled by the expression of anger that flitted across the stranger's face as he looked at her.

"Jeremy," he said, redirecting his attention to Lord Willingham, who stood protectively in front of her, doing a rather poor job at blocking her from the other gentleman's view, "this is too far."

"You've said that before, old boy, and yet it never quite seems to be the case," Lord Willingham said, his voice lazy. Violet, however, could feel the tension radiating off his body.

"When I encountered my father and he told me I might find you out here with a woman in need of rescue, I thought he must be mistaken. I expected the lady in question to be a widow, perhaps, or at the very least an unfaithful wife—not a girl." The stranger's green eyes flashed as he spoke, and despite the fact that he had not raised his voice, Violet could not help but think that this was a man many would think twice about provoking. She, however, was a thoroughly contrary creature by nature, and therefore naturally found the prospect of doing so quite enticing.

"Audley, don't get your drawers in a twist," Lord Willingham drawled, and Violet realized that this stranger was Lord James Audley, the second son of the Duke of Dovington and the third corner of the inseparable triangle that comprised himself, Lord Willingham, and Penvale. They had all been at Eton together, followed by Oxford. For all the time she had spent with Diana and Penvale, she had never met Lord James before.

"You're the only one who's seen us, so there's no cause for alarm," Lord Willingham continued, and Violet resisted the urge to roll her eyes with great difficulty. *How entirely like a man*, she thought—of course there was no cause for *his* alarm, as he was a man and could do whatever he liked. She, on the other hand, was in rather more of a pickle. She tried to remember what Penvale had said about Lord James over the years—was he a discreet sort? It was a difficult question to answer, considering Penvale's stories from school had usually involved frogs in beds and other things that boys, inexplicably, seemed to find so vastly amusing. Really, it was enough to cast in grave doubt the intellect of the entire sex.

"I could just as well have been someone else, and the lady's reputation would have been ruined," Lord James said, his voice steady but his tone growing chillier by the word. "I can't believe you've sunk to seducing virgins at balls."

Violet felt a wave of embarrassment mingled with anger wash over her, and before she could think better of it, she stepped out from behind the shadow of Lord Willingham's shoulder to stare directly into Lord James's arresting eyes.

"The virgin in question can hear you, sir," she said stiffly. "And she would certainly appreciate your discretion in this matter."

Lord James's eyes narrowed. "Then in the future, perhaps she ought to consider not taking strolls on dark balconies in the company of gentlemen with questionable reputations." He jerked his head roughly in Lord Willingham's direction, but his gaze never left Violet's.

Even as another wave of anger rushed through her, Violet felt curiously breathless as she found herself caught in that green gaze, as though her corset had been laced too tightly (which was entirely possible). Nor could she bring herself to break eye contact with him.

"I was overheated in the ballroom," she said, giving him her best demure-miss smile. "The marquess was kind enough to escort me out here for a moment of fresh air."

"Was he?" A dark eyebrow was raised. "Very gentlemanly of him." His tone turned mock thoughtful. "Odd, though, that when I encountered the pair of you, he seemed to be doing more to limit your intake of fresh air than to aid it."

Violet felt her cheeks warming, but she refused to be cowed. She wasn't sure what it was about this man that made her so desperately want to best him in conversation, but she could not bring herself to look away, to quietly murmur an excuse and request an escort back to the ballroom.

"I daresay Lord Willingham is behaving far more like a gentleman than you are at the moment, my lord," she countered. "I wasn't aware that it was the act of a gentleman to make ladies feel uncomfortable." She refused to allow him to see her discomfort, though; like any well-bred young lady, she had impeccable posture, and she resisted the impulse to shrink in the face of such an embarrassing conversation.

"Forgive me," Lord James said, and his eyes softened a fraction, though there was no regret in his voice. "I didn't realize you felt uncomfortable. You certainly give no sign of it." His tone was sardonic, but there was a trace of something like admiration in the words.

"It is my first Season, my lord," she said, considering batting her eyelashes but abandoning the idea in favor of a look of wide-eyed innocence. "I'm afraid this is all rather new to me." She was worried that she might have overdone it when Lord James's expression hardened slightly at the words, but it seemed that something she had said, rather than her simpering, was the cause of his change in demeanor.

"Christ, Jeremy," he muttered, shooting an angry look at Willingham. "Can't you at least find the ones who have been out for a few Seasons, who know what to expect from you?"

"Apparently not," Willingham said cheerfully. "The temptation was simply too great." He flashed a devilish grin at Violet, who had to work very hard to stop herself smiling back. It was easy to see why he had charmed so many a wife and widow. "Since I am so irrevocable a scoundrel as not to be trusted with innocent ladies, perhaps, Audley, you might do me the favor of escorting Lady Violet back inside? After a few minutes have elapsed, of course. For propriety's sake." This last was uttered in a tone of great drama that Violet was almost certain was employed merely to irritate Lord James—successfully, it would seem. His expression did not change, but she detected the further stiffening of his body, as though he were reaching the limits of his patience.

Lord Willingham meant, of course, that it would be entirely scandalous for Violet to reappear with him after so lengthy an interlude in his company; if she were to reappear with a different gentlemen, any gossipy society matrons in attendance were less likely to realize how long she and Willingham had been alone on the balcony—or, better yet, would forget just which gentleman she had disappeared with in the first place.

Lord James, however, was still frowning. "I fail to see how the lady's reemergence on my arm is any less scandalous than if she were to appear on yours," he said, and Violet could not help bristling at the reluctance in his tone. She had never considered herself to be unreasonably vain, but no lady rejoiced at the idea that a gentleman would be so hesitant to spend a few minutes in her company.

Lord Willingham laughed. "Audley, let's not fool ourselves. Everyone knows that you are a gentleman of honor who would never besmirch the reputation of an innocent young lady, whilst I am one step away from being barred from decent ballrooms." He stepped back, as though he were a participant in a duel ceding victory to his opponent, and sketched an elaborate bow before Violet. It was so woefully difficult to find a gentleman with a true appreciation for the art of bowing. "Lady Violet Grey, may I present Lord James Audley? He shall see you safely back into the warm embrace of society."

"Where are you going?" Violet asked.

"To find a drink." This reply was made with considerable enthusiasm—indeed, Violet thought, the most enthusiasm Lord Willingham had yet displayed in her company.

And then he was gone, leaving Lord James staring openmouthed after him, his impassive facade shattered at last, seemingly rendered speechless with indignation.

"That bloody bastard," he muttered, apparently forgetting that he was standing in the presence of a young lady whose innocence he had so lately been proclaiming. Violet, naturally, was delighted by his coarse language; it seemed like the type a villain in a scandalous novel might use and, furthermore, she'd been harboring hopes of hearing a man swear before her for years. She filed away this particular epithet for future consideration and use—out of earshot of her mother, of course.

For his part, Lord James seemed to belatedly recollect her presence. Despite his agitation, and the fact that he was clearly still somewhat distracted by Lord Willingham's abrupt departure, his attention worked its curious magic upon her once more. She grasped for the words to describe the sensation and found herself lacking—the closest she could come was some vague sense that, when he looked at her, he saw her more clearly and fully than anyone ever had before.

It was unsettling. And irritating.

"I apologize," he said stiffly, and Violet blinked, momentarily failing to realize that the apology was for his language, not the uncomfortable awareness she had experienced under his scrutiny. "That was quite rude of me."

"Oh, please don't," Violet said carelessly. "Or, rather, don't apologize for swearing. If you should like to apologize for implying that you find my company less than desirous, or for the fact that you spoke about me as if I wasn't there, as though I were a recalcitrant child, then I should be quite eager to hear that."

His eyes narrowed. "You're quite bold, considering we've never even been properly introduced."

"Nonsense. What do you call what Lord Willingham just did?"

"Wiggle his way out of a tight spot," Lord James said darkly. He gave her an assessing look. "So you're Lady Violet Grey, then. Penvale's spoken of you."

Violet gave him her most charming smile. "All good things, I expect?"

"He said he once caught you and his sister swimming in the lake in your chemises," Lord James said shortly. His mouth quirked up, lessening the effect of his severely furrowed brow, and he added, "So I suppose it's a matter of opinion. For example, I doubt your mother would consider that to be a good thing; to an eighteen-year-old lad, however, I must confess it was rather intriguing."

"My lord, I do think it rather early in our acquaintance for you to be discussing my undergarments," Violet said, grinning at him. A startled laugh escaped him before he seemed to realize it was happening, and it made her like him more.

"At what point would that be considered appropriate, then? I'm not entirely knowledgeable about the intricacies of etiquette."

Was he ... *flirting* with her?

"Certainly not until we've danced at least twice," Violet said firmly. And was *she* flirting in return?

"I see," he said, mock somberly.

"After all, I have very delicate sensibilities that you are at risk of offending," she added, and was rewarded with a quick flash of a smile in the darkness. It quite transformed his face, for all that it was so fleeting. She felt, absurdly, in that moment that she would have done a great deal to receive another one of his smiles.

"I rather think you're more at risk of offending mine, all things considered," he replied dryly. At this mention of the circumstances under which Violet had been discovered, she felt herself blush. It was maddening.

"My lord," she said stiffly, "I would ask you to please not mention—"

"You need not even ask," he interrupted. "I wouldn't." He didn't elaborate further, but she believed him instantly.

"I can't imagine what you must think of me," Violet said, giving a laugh that she hoped would pass for casual and worldly, as though she were frequently found embracing gentlemen on balconies at balls. Her heart pounded heavily in her chest, though, and she realized in a moment of clarity that she did, in fact, care what Lord James Audley thought of her, despite having made his acquaintance a mere five minutes earlier. It was rather vexing, considering that she prided herself—much to her mother's dismay—on not giving a farthing for anyone's opinion but her own.

She realized that somehow, without her noticing, he had moved closer. She found herself being forced to crane her neck upward at a sharper angle than she had moments before, and Lord James's broad shoulders blocked out some of the light emanating from the ballroom behind them. They were standing entirely in the shadows now, and even had someone chanced to wander onto the balcony at that moment, the interloper would have been hard-pressed to see them in their current position. The thought made her feel curiously breathless.

"I think that you're the most interesting young lady I've met so far this Season," he responded, without a trace of mockery on his face or in his voice. Why was it that *interesting* seemed like the nicest thing that any gentleman had ever said to her? Why was *interesting* on his lips so vastly preferable to *beautiful* or *charming* or *amusing*, all compliments that had already been paid her this Season?

His eyes caught hers and held them, and her heart began to race even more quickly, until she felt certain that he must be able to hear it, too, so loudly did it pound in her ears. Was this normal? Should she summon a physician? In everything she'd ever read about courting, there had been no mention of a moonlit scene on a balcony concluding with a swoon due to some sort of malady of the heart.

"I'm certain my mother would be appalled if she heard you say that," Violet managed, forcing a laugh, still not breaking their gaze. "She's always worried that I'm too interesting for my own good."

He smiled again, just a flash before it vanished, and Violet once more had the curious sensation that everything around them dimmed in comparison to the brightness of that smile. Even after it was gone, its presence somehow lingered, making the sharp-angled intensity of his face less severe, more welcoming. It was as though once she'd seen that smile on his face, she could never forget the impression it had left.

"Well, I think you're just interesting enough for *my* own good." He took a step forward and extended his hand.

"Lady Violet," he said, "would you do me the honor of this dance?"

"Here?" Violet asked with a laugh. "On a balcony? Alone?" There was, after all, a perfectly good ballroom a few feet away—one to which he was supposed to be escorting her, in fact.

"I actually thought we would go back indoors," he said, his mouth quirking up the slightest bit at the side. "But . . ." He hesitated, and Violet knew that he felt it, too, this pull between them. She didn't want to return to a noisy, crowded ballroom and discuss the weather with him.

"You can still hear the music," she said before she could convince herself not to, and it was true—she could catch strains of music filtering out through the French doors, spreading through the cool night air around them.

"Yes, you can," he agreed, so quickly that she nearly laughed aloud. "Please say you'll dance with me," he added, taking yet another step forward, and by now he was standing far too close for propriety. Violet tilted her head back and looked at him, finding herself caught in the intensity of that green gaze yet again. The word *please* sounded incredibly appealing on his lips.

"If I must dance with you twice before any discussion of your undergarments can ensue," he added, "I had better not waste any time— it's a conversation I suddenly find myself quite desperate to have."

A startled laugh burst out of Violet and he seized the opportunity to sweep her into his arms—she had always thought the expression a bit absurd when encountered in a novel and yet there, on that balcony, on that particular moonlit night, it seemed entirely accurate.

Violet had danced with gentlemen before, of course, and until this moment she would have said that she had enjoyed those dances thoroughly. Some had been better than others, naturally—such was the way of life, her mother had once noted with a heavy sigh—but on the whole, Violet would have considered herself a lady who liked dancing.

But now, waltzing around on a balcony in the arms of a man she barely knew, she realized that all of those previous dances had been mere flickering candle flames compared to this one, which blazed like the sun. His arms were strong around her, turning her deftly in time with the music. This close, she could smell the particular scent that clung to him, some combination of freshly pressed linen and shaving soap and the faint note of spirits—brandy, perhaps? Whatever it was, the mixture was thoroughly intoxicating. Wild, mad thoughts flitted through her head: would it be strange to press her nose to his immaculately pressed jacket and sniff?

She decided that yes, it would.

She looked up at his impossibly handsome face as they slowly rotated, her eyes catching and holding his. His smile had not made a reappearance, but she could somehow sense its presence in his eyes, in the way he looked down at her. It made her feel warm and itchy in a way that she could not precisely explain, but which was not at all unpleasant.

Over the past weeks of the Season, Violet had danced many dances, spoken to many gentlemen, worn many beautiful gowns—but it was here, in a not-particularly-spectacular evening gown of blush-pink silk (which, in her opinion, didn't flatter her complexion), on a secluded balcony, that Violet found herself at last thinking, *Yes, this.*

"You know, this might be the most enjoyable ten minutes I've spent at a ball all year," Lord James said, eerily echoing Violet's own thoughts.

"I can hardly believe that," Violet said lightly, attempting to ignore the thrill that had gone through her at the words. "Gentlemen are allowed to engage in all sorts of activities that are unsuitable for young ladies, some of which I imagine must be more enjoyable than standing outdoors on a rather chilly evening."

"True," he agreed. "And yet, I find myself with a strong preference for this evening's company."

She looked up at him then, as they turned slowly about the balcony, his hand warm and steady in her own, the other burning through layers of fabric at her back.

"Lady Violet," he said, halting abruptly, "I'm going to take you inside now, before I do something I regret."

"Oh?" Violet said, unable to suppress a note of disappointment in her voice. Instead of releasing her, he pulled her closer to him, the warmth of her body drawn to that of his like a moth to a flame.

"Well, *actually*," he said, gazing down at her, "I'm not certain I'd regret it at all. But since I do try to distinguish myself from the Jeremy Overingtons of the world, I don't make it a habit to kiss young ladies on balconies." He reached his hand up, relinquishing his hold on her waist to brush it against her cheek, then take one of her dark curls between his thumb and forefinger. Violet felt rooted to the ground—had the ballroom caught fire at that moment, she doubted even that would have spurred her to movement.

But, as she discovered a moment later, the sound of her mother's voice proved more effective than any blazing inferno.

"*Violet Grey!*" came Lady Worthington's shrill cry, horror and disapproval warring for precedence in her tone. Lord James dropped his hand immediately, and Violet took two hasty steps back, but it was too late.

They had been seen.

Lady Worthington swept toward them, the feathered headdress she wore atop her head quivering with indignation. She was still a very handsome woman, not yet forty, though Violet thought she often dressed as though she were far older. In this moment, her beauty was put to its full intimidating effect—fair cheeks blazing with color, blue eyes sparkling with anger. She looked from Violet to Lord James and back again, a single glance communicating more than words possibly could have. Violet braced herself for a blistering attack, but found her mother's first words aimed at the gentleman of the party, not herself.

"Lord James Audley, I believe." It was not truly a question; Lady Worthington had *Debrett's* memorized, as Violet knew only too well.

"You presume correctly, my lady," Lord James said with a courteous bow.

"Well, my lord," Lady Worthington said, and Violet winced at the sharp edge to her voice, "I assume you won't mind telling me what, precisely, you were doing on this balcony with my daughter?"

Lord James held Lady Worthington's gaze briefly, then broke it, casting his eyes to Violet's. He looked at her for a long moment, and she knew—somehow, she just *knew*—what the next words out of his mouth would be, much as she longed to prevent them.

"As it happens, your ladyship," he said, still every inch the proper gentleman, "I was just getting around to proposing."

One

Violet Audley had mastered many skills in her five years of marriage but, to her everlasting dismay, pouring tea was not one of them.

"Really, Violet," said Diana, Lady Templeton, reaching for the teapot. "Allow me." Given Diana's disinclination to exert herself when it was not strictly necessary, this was an indication of dire straits indeed.

"Thank you," Violet said gratefully, relinquishing the teapot and reclining slightly against the green-and-gold settee upon which she was seated. "I'm sure the maids will appreciate one less tea stain to mop up later."

"You must keep them busy in that regard," said Emily with a smile, accepting the teacup that Diana handed her, filled to the brim with unsweetened, undiluted tea. Violet had always found it rather amusing that Lady Emily Turner, the most beautiful debutante of their year, the most prim and proper and sweet of all English roses, preferred her tea plain and bitter.

"That's quite enough commentary on my tea-pouring skills, thank you," Violet said, watching as Diana dropped a lump of sugar and a splash of milk into the cup before handing it to her. Diana began to prepare a cup for herself.

"That's one thing you must miss about Audley," Diana said casually. "Didn't he pour tea for you, when you two were . . . friendlier?" The final word was laced with the delicate sarcasm at which Diana so excelled, and Violet stiffened—as she so often did at the mention of her husband's name.

"He did, on occasion," she replied, taking a large sip of tea and instantly regretting it, given that the contents of her teacup were scalding. However, perhaps fortunately, Diana seemed to mistake Violet's watering eyes and flushed cheeks for a response to the mention of James and the painful memories associated with him, rather than a reaction to the sensations associated with nearly burning the roof of her mouth off, and she desisted.

"Speaking of romantic entanglements," Diana said, taking a placid sip of her own tea and redirecting her sharp gaze from Violet—still sputtering—to Emily. "Have you seen your attentive Mr. Cartham lately?"

It was Emily's turn to flush now, and she was unfortunate enough to have set her teacup down already, giving her no chance of escape. Within moments, however, she assumed her usual mask of calm and poise. Violet had always thought that it was this mask that made Emily so attractive to the gentlemen of the *ton*. To be sure, she was lovely— golden curls, deep blue eyes, lily-white skin, curved in all the correct places—but it could be argued that Diana, with her hazel eyes and honey-blond locks and impressive bosom, was equally enticing, and she had certainly received less interest than Emily had during their first Season . . . at least from gentlemen with matrimony on their minds. Diana had received any number of offers of a more indecent nature.

Diana, like Violet, made no effort to mask her spirit or her sharp intelligence or, additionally, her frustration with the position of a woman of good background but not especially large fortune who was flung upon the marriage mart. Emily, though her frustrations were similar to Diana's (for Violet was the only one of the three whose dowry had been considered truly impressive), was so good at adopting an air of meek agreeability that men seemed unable to resist.

Until, of course, they learned precisely how little blunt Emily's father, the Marquess of Rowanbridge, had to his name. Then Emily became somewhat more resistible.

"He still has not returned from his trip to New York," Emily said in response to Violet's question about Mr. Cartham. "Apparently his mother's health was not so dire as he thought when he departed, and her decline was a lengthier event than he anticipated." She seemed to inject the level of concern appropriate for a lady speaking of her suitor's dying mother, but Violet was not fooled. "In any case, I received a letter from him yesterday noting his soon departure from America, so I expect he should return within a matter of days."

"Bother," Diana muttered, setting her teacup down with a clatter. "That means your reprieve will soon be over, then."

"Indeed," Emily murmured.

Silence momentarily descended upon the room, each of the three ladies reflecting on the unwelcome return of Mr. Oswald Cartham, an American by birth, owner these ten years past of Cartham's, one of the most notorious gaming hells in London. Cartham was in his mid-thirties, rich as Croesus, and, for the past three years, Emily's most persistent suitor.

He was also utterly odious.

It was rather absurd, Violet thought idly, staring into her teacup at the cloudy liquid it contained. Three ladies, all considered among the prettier girls to be presented at court upon their debut five years earlier, all from old aristocratic families of impeccable lineage and respectability.

And all utterly miserable in love.

There was Emily, whose father's debts at Cartham's meant that he had no choice but to allow the man's unwelcome attentions toward his daughter until he could scrape together the funds he owed.

There was Diana, who had been so desperate to flee the home of her aunt and uncle, where she had resided since her parents died—her mother in childbirth, and her father of apoplexy soon after—when she had been only five years old. She'd held no illusions about marrying for love; all she wanted was freedom, and she had seized it by marrying a man thirty years her senior, who had left her a widow at the age of twenty-one.

And then there was Violet. Violet of the impetuous love match. Violet, who had married James Audley a mere four weeks into their acquaintance, thoroughly scandalizing polite society. Violet, who in those four weeks had fallen head over heels in love with the man who had proposed to her—in front of her mother!—on that darkened balcony. Violet, who had been eighteen, infatuated, swept up by her young, dashing, impossibly handsome husband. Violet, who now . . . well.

The less said about Violet and James, the better.

It was uncanny timing, then, that at the precise moment that Violet was occupied with these utterly gloomy thoughts—about her husband, Diana's late one, and Emily's lack of one—that her butler, Wooton, appeared in the doorway of the drawing room, a platter balanced on his hands and a single letter placed in the center of the platter.

"My lady," he said, bowing without allowing the tray to drop so much as a millimeter. Even Violet's mother would have found no fault. "A note just arrived for you from Viscount Penvale."

"For me?" Violet asked, startled. "Not for Lady Templeton?"

"No, my lady," Wooton said. "It is very plainly addressed to you."

"Thank you, Wooton," Violet said, rising from the settee and taking the note from him. "That will be all."

"My lady." Another bow, and he was gone.

"Why on earth would my brother be writing to you?" Diana asked idly.

"I don't know," Violet replied, opening the missive, which appeared to have been hastily scrawled—Penvale's handwriting was barely legible.

15 July
Audley House

Lady James,

I write to inform you that your husband was thrown from his horse this morning whilst attempting to ride a particularly feisty stallion. The fall knocked him unconscious, and he has yet to regain his senses. A physician has been sent for, and Willingham and I remain by his side, anxiously awaiting his recovery. I will, of course, continue to keep you apprised of his condition, but I felt that you would wish to learn of this incident as soon as possible, and thought your husband would wish the same.

Yours, etc.
Penvale

Unconscious. The word echoed in Violet's mind as she stared down at Penvale's missive. She flipped the paper over, desperately hoping for more information than the scant few sentences that had been provided to her, but there was nothing.

"Violet?" Emily asked, and Violet looked up, startled; for a moment, she had forgotten that she was not alone. "Is everything quite all right?"

"No," Violet said, her voice sounding strange to her own ears. "That is, I don't quite know. James was thrown from his horse yesterday and knocked unconscious."

"Good lord!" Diana said, springing up suddenly. With a few quick strides, she crossed to where Violet was standing and snatched the letter from her. Scanning it quickly, she gave an unladylike snort. "Typical of my brother. Just enough information to thoroughly worry you, but nothing that might actually be of use."

Violet barely heard her. "I must go," she said, scarcely aware of the words leaving her mouth. "I must go to Brook Vale."

Brook Vale was a picturesque village in Kent and the seat of the Duke of Dovington, the title that was currently held by James's father. Although Brook Vale Park was the family seat, James had been bequeathed Audley House, on the opposite side of the village, upon his marriage to Violet. The house itself was of modest size when compared with the country estate of the duke, but Audley House's true value was in the attached stables, which were spectacular, stocked with a host of steeds of impressive bloodlines, contenders in all the major races each year. James's not-insubstantial annual income, an inheritance from his mother, was heavily augmented by the sale of those horses, the fees paid by other owners for the right to breed with his stallions, and race winnings.

It was all, on the surface, an entirely advantageous arrangement.

Violet hated those stables' very existence.

"Now wait, Violet—"

Violet ignored Diana. "I must depart at once. What if James is still unconscious? Or—or—" She couldn't bear to give voice to her thoughts in that instant—it was utterly impossible to think of her maddening, energetic husband as being anything other than in the best of health. She glanced up at Emily, who was studying her with a compassionate gaze.

"Of course you must go," Emily said briskly, standing up. She rang for Wooton, who reappeared a moment later.

"Wooton, Lady James must depart at once for Audley House," Emily announced.

"Indeed, my lady?" Wooton inquired, casting a look in Violet's direction that in a less well-trained butler would have been characterized as inquisitive.

"Yes," Violet managed. "It would seem that Lord James has had some sort of riding accident, and I would like to go see him immediately."

Wooton's impassive expression was betrayed by a slight furrowing of the brow—tricky to notice in such a heavily wrinkled face—that seemed to indicate concern. "I will have Price prepare a trunk for you immediately, my lady."

"Thank you, Wooton," Violet said distractedly, and turned back to Emily and Diana. "If you'll excuse me, I should like to speak to Price myself, inform her that I only need the barest necessities—"

"Of course," Emily said calmly, taking two steps forward to seize Violet's hand. "Dear Violet, do send word as soon as you know more about Lord James's condition."

"I'm certain he's fine," Diana said, then added with an attempt at her usual humor, "After all, I know I've heard you lament his hard head in the past."

23

"Thank you," Violet said, attempting a smile and managing no more than a wobble of the mouth. "I'm certain it's—well—" For once, words failed her, and she could do no more than bid her friends farewell and make her way to her bedchamber.

Once she arrived there, she found Price, her lady's maid, in a frenzy of activity, flitting about with various articles of clothing in her hands.

"Only pack for a couple of days, Price," Violet said upon entering the room. "If Lord James is well, I shall return to London immediately, and if not . . ." She trailed off, then shook her head vehemently, trying not to dwell on the prospect. "If his condition is serious, I will send word for more of my things to be sent along posthaste."

"Yes, my lady," Price said, bobbing a curtsey and resuming her frenetic pace. Violet retreated to her neatly made bed, upon which she lay down in the precise center, staring up at the canopy above. She was conscious as she never had been before of the rhythm of her heart in her chest, its pace still accelerated even as she lay entirely still. She couldn't remove the image from her mind of James lying in the mud, a horse's hooves dancing precariously near his head.

That head of his—one she had held in her hands, and kissed, and, more recently, wanted to scream at until her throat was raw—contained everything that made him James. Those green eyes, capable of conveying or masking great feeling, as he wished. The mouth she had kissed so many countless times in their first year of marriage, and not at all since then. And that mind—that clever, infuriating mind. She was angry with him—she had been angry with him for years. But she was not prepared for how devastating she would find the prospect of any harm befalling him.

In the first year of their marriage, before their awful falling-out, she'd pleaded with him to be careful at the stables—he enjoyed riding, but the attention he devoted to Audley House's stables verged on obsessive, a product of his desire to prove himself to his father, and the idea of him injuring himself for such an absurd reason had worried her as much as it had irritated her. He had largely ignored her concerns, refusing to delegate tasks at the stables that could easily be performed by a groom, and spending long hours poring over the books despite having a perfectly competent steward in his employ. She'd tried to bite her tongue at times, not wishing to nag, but there had been occasions when she could not resist raising the issue—after a week that involved two separate trips to Kent to check on the stables, for instance, or a morning when he appeared wearily at the breakfast table after working late into the night.

She asked him to step back a bit from the stables; she told him he had nothing to prove to his father. He, however, insisted that he wished to make a success of the stables for her sake, for the sake of their future children—which inevitably led to a quarrel. A quarrel followed shortly by a reconciliation, but still, a quarrel. Even now, Violet's hackles rose at the memory of this—of his inability to trust her to know her own mind. His inability to trust that she would love him even without the income of the (wildly lucrative, it must be said) stables.

And, of course, at the time, James had spent far less time at the stables than he did now.

Furthermore, given the current state of noncommunication between them, it had been a long time since Violet had reminded him to be careful.

Four years, if one wanted to be precise.

Violet could, in truth, offer the exact date of her last conversation with James before the event that had come to be known, in her head, as The Argument. She gave it the honor of capital letters because although it was not by any stretch the first argument they'd had in their marriage, none of their previous spats had rivaled it for passion—or for lasting damage.

She could still remember lying in bed with him that last morning, her head resting on his bare shoulder as his arm curved around her back, keeping her tucked firmly against his side. She had revisited the memory of that morning so many times that it was growing frayed at the edges, some of the details becoming confused in her mind—had it really been raining, or was the sound of raindrops a detail that she had fabricated?

In any case, she had learned from nearly four years of experience that to dwell too long upon this was to sink into melancholy. Which brought her back to her present circumstances: lying on her bed, contemplating a man who could, at this exact moment, very well be—

No. Violet quite simply refused to even consider it. James was fine—he had to be fine—because if he wasn't, that would mean that the past four years would be the end of their story, not a mere rough stretch in the middle. And somewhere, deep down, without even admitting it to herself, Violet had always assumed it would be the latter.

So, instead of allowing herself to grow maudlin, she allowed herself to grow angry. Here she was, about to tear off after a man who would barely speak to her, who had injured himself by taking a foolish, unnecessary risk—something she had asked him repeatedly to refrain from doing. Something he did to prove himself to a man whose good opinion, in Violet's mind, was scarcely worth having.

Who was *she*, after all, to demand such a sacrifice? Merely his wife, of course. And now she was the one about to be inconvenienced by a day of travel, all because her tiresome husband wouldn't listen to her. If he was not dead of some horrid head injury, she had half a mind to give him one herself once she arrived.

And with that comforting thought, she rose from the bed and made ready to depart.

Two

Lord James Audley had a devil of a headache.

"Of course you do," Viscount Penvale said from his spot across from him at the breakfast table at Audley House. "You were knocked unconscious by a fall from a horse yesterday. Even your thick head can't bounce back from that so quickly."

"True, true," added the Marquess of Willingham, himself seated a few chairs down from Penvale, busily applying liberal amounts of jam to a piece of toast. "Especially when you're not as young as you once were, old boy." Apparently satisfied with his jam-to-bread ratio, he shoved half the piece of toast into his mouth with considerable enthusiasm.

James divided a glare between the two of them, stirring milk into his tea with more vigor than was strictly necessary. "I'm twenty-eight," he informed them icily, setting aside his spoon. "And last I checked, Jeremy, you had two months on me—do I detect the sound of your own ancient bones creaking?"

"Can't say I hear it myself," Willingham—Jeremy—said cheerfully around his mouthful of toast.

"In a bit of a temper this morning, are we?" Penvale asked, applying himself to an egg with great interest. "Not greeting the world with our usual sunny disposition?"

"*We*," James pronounced through gritted teeth, "were knocked unconscious yesterday, and awoke in a sickbed, where we had weak tea forced down our throat. And *we* still feel as though a blacksmith is hammering away at our skull. So *we*"—he speared a sausage with great force—"are not, perhaps, in the mood for your chatter this morning."

A rather gratifying silence fell at this announcement, during which time James chewed his sausage. Although he wished for few of his father's personality traits, the Duke of Dovington's ability to silence a room was one he was grateful for. Even his very closest friends knew better than to poke at him when he addressed them in that tone. Long experience had taught Penvale and Jeremy that doing so would yield no information, and could even, on rare occasions, end in fisticuffs.

"So, back to London today, Penvale?" Jeremy asked, carefully ignoring James as he spoke.

"Quite. You as well?"

"I thought so."

"I'm coming, too," James said, setting down his fork with a clatter. He managed to avoid wincing at the sound, but only just.

"I thought you planned to stay for another few days," Penvale said cautiously.

"I did," James replied, reaching for his teacup. "But I want to tell Worthington in person that his damned horse is probably going to murder the next person who attempts to ride it."

"Wilson did attempt to tell you that before you got on the horse's back," Penvale pointed out. Wilson was James's stablemaster at Audley House.

"I know," James said ruefully. "I really don't know what I was thinking."

"Do you think it odd," Jeremy said with an air of casual unconcern that instantly set James on his guard, "that you are far more willing to speak to Worthington than you are to speak to his daughter?"

"No," James said shortly, using the tone he reserved for whenever Violet was mentioned—one that clearly indicated that further inquiries would not be welcomed. Generally this worked well for him; after fifteen years of friendship, Penvale and Jeremy did not expect much—or anything at all, really—in the way of heartfelt confessions from James. This morning, however, was clearly destined to be the most irritating of recent memory, because Jeremy, for once, took no notice of his tone.

"Does *he* find it strange that when he asks you how his daughter is, you cannot give him any sort of reply with certainty?"

"He *might*," James said shortly, "if it ever occurred to him to ask such a question, which it of course does not." Because Worthington was an ass. A benign ass, it was true—he had given his daughter a generous dowry and left the rest of her needs to his wife—but still an ass. James knew enough about neglectful fathers to know that Violet had minded her father's lack of attention, even if she'd never said as much.

"But don't you think—" Jeremy began, clearly with a death wish.

"Jeremy," Penvale said warningly as James opened his mouth to snap back at Jeremy. "Didn't the physician instruct us not to upset him?"

This merely had the effect of worsening James's temper. "I am not a child, nor am I in my dotage," he said. "So I would appreciate it if you were to refrain from discussing me as though I weren't here, as you sit at my breakfast table, eating my food."

Most men would have subsided at this—James's demeanor of icy calm had, on numerous occasions, proved quite effective at ending an argument—but, unfortunately, Penvale and Jeremy had known him for far too long to be intimidated.

"Are you certain you wish to journey back to London with us?" Penvale asked. "Perhaps you had better rest for another day—that fall yesterday was nothing to take lightly."

"I'm going back to London today, whether you want me to or not," James said precisely, taking a sip of his tea. A shaft of morning sunlight streamed through the windows, burnishing Jeremy's golden hair. Jeremy stared across the table at James with an eyebrow raised, toast in hand, and in the silence that followed, James became fully aware of the extent to which he sounded like a petulant child. He heaved a sigh, then set down his teacup with a clatter.

"My damned head aches, and I just want to sleep in my own bed," he said, leaning forward to meet Penvale's and Jeremy's eyes in turn.

"You have a bed here that, last I checked, belongs to you as well," Jeremy pointed out.

"It's not the same," James said shortly, and shoved his chair back from the table as he rose. Logically, he knew that Jeremy was correct; Audley House was his, along with everything within it, including the beds. He had some frightfully official-looking paperwork buried somewhere in a drawer in his study back in London to prove it. But he could never quite manage to shake the feeling he had when he was here—the feeling that his father was nearby. And, of course, there was the other damned fact: that here in the country, Violet wasn't.

"I'm going to pack," he said. "We'll depart in an hour."

Without another word, he strode from the room.

It was absurd, he reflected as he climbed the stairs. Ludicrous, really. It had been four years since he and Violet had shared a bed. In London, he slept in his bedchamber and she in hers, separated by a wall, a dressing room, a connecting door, another dressing room, another wall, and four years' worth of cold silences. And yet he still slept easier knowing that she was under the same roof. It was just the sort of sentimental nonsense that, prior to his marriage, he would have had no time for.

Of course, before his marriage, he wouldn't have thought himself the sort of man to let one argument with one woman ruin four long years of his life.

And yet he had.

Violet had refused to accompany him on any of his trips to Brook Vale since the day of their argument—a day he had taken to referring to, in the privacy of his own head, as the *Die Horribilis*. Each time he departed, he asked her, with his usual politeness—with the voice that he *knew* made him sound like an ass, even as he was using it—whether she would like to accompany him. Take a bit of the clean country air. Et cetera. Her answer was always no.

And James was always disappointed and relieved in almost equal measure.

He shouldn't have minded. She hated those stables—he'd lost count of the number of times she had told him that she wished he'd spend less time at them, leave the day-to-day running of them to his—entirely competent—staff. They were hardly in dire financial straits, not with her dowry and his inheritance—it wasn't as though they needed to worry about his inattention to the minutiae of the stables' operation sending them into ruin.

It had always irritated him that she couldn't see that all those hours spent at the stables were, in large part, for her. That he had to prove to her, to his father, to *himself* that he was the sort of man who could make something. Manage something. He'd had no title to offer her other than a courtesy title; he wasn't responsible for the running of the dukedom, like his brother would one day be. But he somehow felt that these stables gave him a purpose, and in so doing made him worthy of her. He wanted to be better than whatever feckless, idle, perhaps better titled aristocrat she would have married if she hadn't met him on that balcony, and that she never understood this had therefore been a constant source of friction.

So why he was disappointed not to have her there, to be spared her disapproving looks and cutting remarks, was a mystery to him.

But the fact remained that he never slept as well at Audley House as he did at their residence in town.

By early evening, they were nearly back to town. The weather was fine, all sunshine and blue skies and puffy white clouds, making the confinement of the carriage all the more intolerable. Outside, James could see the rolling green hills and woods of southern England and, patriotic man that he was, could not help but feel a surge of love for his homeland. One's marital troubles were undoubtedly distracting, but still: God save the king, et cetera.

It had been dry weather of late, meaning the roads were in good condition and the group was making excellent time. Opposite him in the carriage, Jeremy was slumped in a corner, attempting to nap—no doubt hampered in his efforts by the frequent jostling of the conveyance. Penvale was seated next to James, his nose buried in a dense tome about water management on country estates.

"You haven't got a country estate," James pointed out pleasantly. His head was starting to throb again, damn it.

Penvale glanced up and cast him a narrow look. "I will someday."

"Even if you raise the blunt," James said frankly, knowing he was pushing Penvale but unable to help himself, "do you think your uncle will really sell?"

"If I make him a good enough offer," Penvale said shortly, and returned his attention to his reading. James did not needle him further; given his own disinclination to discuss matters of a personal nature with his friends, he could not fault Penvale for turning closemouthed on this particular subject.

Penvale had been merely ten years old when his parents had died and he had inherited his title. The family estate had been in so much debt that there had been no choice but to sell it to cover the death duties, as it was unentailed—and the most eager prospective buyer had been his father's younger brother, from whom the late Lord Penvale had been estranged his entire adult life, and who had made his fortune with the East India Company. Penvale and his sister had been sent to Hampshire to live with their mother's sister and her husband—on an estate a mere handful of miles from Violet's father's. Diana and Violet had been friends ever since.

Penvale had spent his entire adult life obsessed with reuniting his title with its ancestral land. He had always been eerily lucky at the gaming tables, but instead of spending his winnings on wine and women, he'd hoarded his blunt like a miser, even going so far as to speculate on stocks—thus engaging in an activity abhorrent to all but the most desperate gentlemen—to increase his fortune. He didn't take kindly to questions about the likelihood of his uncle selling the estate back to him.

James felt the carriage slow and, leaning forward to peer out the window, saw that they were entering the yard of a coaching inn, where they could switch out their team of horses for a fresh set and, more importantly, get out of this blasted carriage for a moment.

The wheels had barely stopped turning when he opened the door and leaped to the ground, startling the footman reaching for the door handle. Glancing over his shoulder, he watched Penvale drop his book onto his recently vacated seat and give Jeremy a none-too-gentle pat on the shoulder to awaken him before he, too, alighted. James took a few steps toward the door of the inn, then stopped in his tracks as he saw a familiar carriage waiting for its passenger to return.

A *very* familiar carriage.

Unless he was very much mistaken—and James prided himself on rarely being mistaken—the well-sprung carriage that stood so serenely outside the inn was his very own. He and his friends had taken Jeremy's carriage to Brook Vale so that he might leave Violet with her own, but such an arrangement had been made with thoughts of her needing to visit her modiste, or the circulating library—not Kent.

Penvale stumbled to a halt behind James.

"What is it? Audley?"

"Unless the fall has got me more out of sorts than I suspected," James said, more calmly than he felt, "that is my carriage standing there. And unless it has been stolen—in which case this is a piece of very good fortune indeed—that would mean that my wife is here somewhere."

Rather than the swift intake of breath or the surprised exclamation that James might have expected, Penvale swore: "Bloody buggering Christ. I shouldn't have sent that damn letter."

James turned to fully face his friend, his eyebrows raised. "I beg your pardon?"

Penvale looked unusually shifty as he stood before James. Penvale usually had an air of lazy, lethal calm—one that his sister shared—but at the moment he looked like nothing so much as a nervous schoolboy, his hazel eyes apologetic as they met James's green ones. "I might have . . . sent your wife a note when you had your accident yesterday."

James strove to keep his voice even. "Oh?"

"And, well . . ." Penvale ran a hand through his hair, looking desperately around the inn yard as though hoping to find someone to rescue him. "You woke up nearly as soon as I'd sent it. And I might have forgotten to send her a second letter informing her that you weren't dying."

James opened his mouth to respond, but before he could get a word out, Jeremy's voice rang out from where he was standing by their carriage, having just emerged. "Darling Lady James! What on earth are you doing here?"

With a sinking feeling of dread, James turned to see—of course it was Violet. She was standing in the doorway of the inn, dressed in a plain frock for traveling, her hair in slight disorder, as though she had dressed in a great hurry that morning. No doubt she had, he reminded himself, given that she had received a letter informing her—well, James didn't know what precisely Penvale had written in that blasted letter, but he had no doubt that whatever it was had been sufficient to cause concern.

Her face was very pale as she stood there, staring at him, her brown eyes wide, dark tendrils of hair framing her face in a way that he found enticing rather than unkempt. It made him, entirely inappropriately, wish to kiss her.

But then, James always wished to kiss her. The kissing had never been the problem. It was the talking that seemed to give them trouble.

He took a step forward, dimly registering that she was likely in a state of shock at seeing him so suddenly standing before her, healthy and well, when Penvale's missive had doubtless made it sound as though he were knocking at death's door.

"Violet," he said, and as he heard his own voice, he registered that the note of hesitation it contained made him sound stiff.

"You . . . Penvale's note . . ." She seemed to struggle for words, un-usual for a woman who loved to talk as much as Violet did. Never mind that she didn't share most of her words with James anymore; he still heard her sometimes, as he passed by the drawing room while she had her friends to tea, chattering away much as she ever had. He was always torn, on those occasions, between the desire to smile at the familiar sound of her voice and the desire to punch something.

The course of true love ne'er did run smooth, naturally, but James rather thought that his path had been unnecessarily choppy. When sitting through a particularly icily silent meal, he thought of another set of famous words more applicable to his life.

Marry in haste, repent at leisure.

These thoughts—or fragmented versions of them—flitted through his mind in an instant as he watched Violet make a valiant effort to regain her composure. She looked weary and shocked and travel-mussed, a far cry from the oh-so-elegant young miss he had met on that balcony five years ago, and yet she was still the most beautiful thing he had ever seen. He tried to hate her for it, but couldn't quite get there.

A moment later, however, hating her seemed to require consider-ably less effort, given that she recovered enough to take several rapid steps forward, raise her hand, and slap him across the face with im-pressive force.

"Jesus—" He bit off the rest of what would have been a truly foul curse and raised a hand to his cheek, which felt hot beneath his fin-gers. His wife was not a terribly physically imposing woman, but she was stronger than she looked. "Violet—"

"How dare you," she said, her voice shaking with more emotion than he had heard from her in quite some time. "How dare you stand there so ... so ..." She seemed to struggle to find a word to adequately convey the severity of his crime.

"Healthily?" he asked acidly, lowering his hand from his still-smarting cheek. "I do apologize, my dear wife, if my continued existence proves an inconvenience to you."

Her eyes flashed dangerously. "What's *inconvenient* is receiving a note from your *friend* over there . . ." She jerked her head in the direction of Penvale; James risked a quick glance over his shoulder, and saw both Penvale and Jeremy watching himself and Violet with a mixture of amusement and apprehension. James was touched by their concern for his continued well-being, as it was a concern he shared quite earnestly.

Violet was speaking again. "... making it sound as though you were about to be laid out in a coffin. And when you consider that I've been expecting to receive a note like this every time you set foot in those blasted stables, climbing on top of some horse you've no business sitting on, it's not surprising that I was a touch worried." Her voice was positively dripping with scorn. It seemed she was not yet finished. "And yet, when I hasten to your side, what do I find in the midst of my journey but *you*, my allegedly ailing husband, standing before me as though you haven't a care in the world?" James opened his mouth to respond, but closed it again hastily. It was common knowledge that it was best not to interrupt Violet in the midst of one of her rants.

"In fact," she continued, "if we hadn't happened to be at this inn at the same time, I would have arrived at Audley House to find it empty! Is this your idea of a joke? Have you decided to up the ante beyond merely ignoring me, and are now going to start sending me on wild-goose chases across all of England instead?"

She fell silent, breathing heavily in a way that was most distracting to any man with a measure of appreciation for the female bosom—and James was certainly such a man. He determined, after a moment, that she expected some sort of response from him at last.

He was silent a moment longer, not because he had nothing to say, but rather because it was so difficult to know precisely where to start. Should he begin by pointing out that making it a quarter of the way from London to Kent could hardly be counted as a journey across England? Or perhaps by drawing her attention to the fact that, as far as the art of ignoring one's spouse went, he was merely an amateur aping the true master who sat across the table from him at dinner each night?

In the end, however, he chose to begin with the most obvious point. "I didn't know Penvale sent you the blasted note."

She gave an unladylike snort, which should have been wildly unattractive but somehow wasn't.

"It is rather hard, you see," he said with what he considered to be admirable patience, "to keep track of with whom, precisely, one's friends are corresponding when one is unconscious."

Her eyes narrowed further, a sure sign of trouble, but James didn't care. He felt reckless, alive, the way he always had when they had argued during the first year of their marriage. The way he hadn't felt in years.

"So you really were injured, then?" she asked skeptically, and James expected he only had moments before she turned to call for a physician to perform a full physical examination to verify his claim.

"I was," he said hastily, hoping to avoid such an occurrence—he'd had quite enough of physicians in the past day. "Your father's new stallion threw me from the saddle and knocked me unconscious." He should probably have been embarrassed to admit it, but he wasn't—he was a good horseman under ordinary circumstances, but that horse was deranged.

"And once you regained consciousness, it didn't occur to your *friend*"—she pronounced the word as she might say *your pet cockroach*—"to alert me to the fact that you were not, in fact, steps away from death?"

"I can't really say," James said, trying to suppress his own irritation and not entirely succeeding, "as I know nothing about what possessed him to write to you in the first place."

As soon as the words were out of his mouth, he knew they had been a mistake. Violet's eyes flashed, and he had to resist the urge to take a step back.

"Oh, of course," she said in a lethally quiet voice. "How silly of someone to alert a wife to her husband's possible demise. How ridiculous!" She cackled, the sound totally foreign compared to her usual laugh—not that her laugh was a sound James had heard much over the past four years.

"I merely meant he shouldn't have alarmed you unnecessarily," he said impatiently, waving his hand dismissively. "There was no need to worry you without cause." He spared a moment's thought for the very appealing fantasy of choking Penvale. It seemed a fair payment.

"And if he hadn't written to me," Violet said heatedly, "I expect I never would have heard about this little accident at all! Which is exactly how you'd like things, I expect. You'd never imagine my delicate female sensibilities could possibly handle the trauma." Her voice was so sharp that he was half surprised the words didn't draw blood as she flung them at him.

"There's nothing to tell!" James said, belatedly realizing that he had raised his voice. He cast a glance around and was relieved to note that no one in the inn yard—with the irritating exception of Jeremy and Penvale, of course—was paying them much heed. Clearly the grooms and travelers had better things to do with their afternoon than gape at a pair of bickering aristocrats. James agreed, considering that he himself had better things to do than *be* one of the aforementioned bickering aristocrats.

Violet crossed both of her arms over her chest in a way that managed to do extremely distracting things to her bosom. James spared a moment to be grateful that she was not wearing a more revealing frock, if only for the sake of his ability to concentrate.

"How often has this happened to you, then?" Violet asked, eyeing him with great scrutiny. "If you're in the habit of receiving head injuries without informing me, should I assume this is an everyday occurrence for you?" She spoke as though he had *asked* the bloody horse to throw him.

"This is the first time it has happened in recent memory, madam," he said through gritted teeth, his arms stiff and straight at his sides as he fought against his sudden desire to give her a good shaking. He made an effort to lower his voice, if only for the sake of making himself unintelligible to a certain viscount and marquess a few feet away.

"I'm not sure I believe you," Violet said with a delicate sniff. "And if this *isn't* the first such accident you've had, who knows what sort of damage you've done to your mental capacity?" She gave him an assessing look. "I mean . . . should I *really* trust you with the family finances, James, if it's possible that you've gone soft in the head?"

James's hand flexed of its own accord, but somehow, miraculously, his voice was still even. "I believe, my lady, that my mental state remains as undiminished as it ever was."

Violet arched a dark brow. "I will, of course, take you at your word, since I have no other choice . . ." She trailed off, an expression of carefully calculated skepticism on her face that spoke volumes. It was a look, he knew, that was calibrated to annoy him—and it worked. He hated that she knew him so well; he hated that he had once allowed her to get close enough to him to now use this knowledge as a weapon.

"Damn it, Violet," he began.

"I don't want to hear anything else from you," she said, and looked over his shoulder at Jeremy and Penvale. "Penvale," she called, raising her voice slightly, "next time he's enough of a fool to climb onto the back of a horse that my father told me just last week was unbreakable, please wait to notify me until you're certain about whether he'll live or die. I should hate to make a habit of exhausting the horses unnecessarily in mad dashes across the country."

She stepped neatly past James as she spoke, taking quick, tidy steps toward her—*his*, damn it!—carriage.

"London to Kent isn't across the country!" James called after her in frustration, unable to remain silent but equally unable to muster a better parting shot than that. "And you didn't even make it halfway!"

Violet spared him one last, scornful look over her shoulder before climbing into the carriage and disappearing.

"Not your best effort, old chap," Jeremy said, having appeared at James's side as he watched Violet walk away. "Bit embarrassing, really."

"Get in the carriage," James demanded. "Then take me to London, and never speak of this again." He paused a moment, considering. "Actually, first, get me a damn drink."

"That," said Jeremy, clapping him on the shoulder, "is the most sense you've made all day."

Three

By the time her carriage rolled to a halt in front of their house on Curzon Street late that evening, Violet was so tired that the edge had worn off her anger. The events of the day floated through her mind as she made her way into the house and then up the stairs toward her bedchamber, but she couldn't focus on any of them. While her conviction that she was in the right had not weakened in the slightest, she found herself so exhausted that she cared little for anything beyond the prospect of a bath, followed shortly by bed.

The next morning, however, Violet awoke feeling considerably more energized. She could tell by the light streaming through the windows that it was not terribly late, and after she had rung for Price and sat down at her dressing table to brush her hair, she found herself wondering whether she would find her husband at the breakfast table.

If he had returned home at all, that was. She assumed he had, but he might have been so irritated after their meeting at the coaching inn that he returned to Audley House.

Not that the man had any cause to be annoyed, Violet fumed. It had been infuriating enough when he'd accepted the stables as a wedding gift from his father without so much as a word to her until several days into their marriage, and worse still when she'd discovered that on days he spent at the stables or holed up in his study going over the figures, he met her at the dinner table in a prickly mood. Previously, however, her frustration had only ever slid into true anger when he tried to insist to her that the work he did at the stables was for *her*, for them—as though only he was aware of what she truly wanted.

She could not, no matter how many times they squabbled about it, understand why he dedicated such obsessive attention to the running of the stables at Audley House. To be sure, she knew her husband enjoyed a good ride in the park or across his estate as much as the next man, but James was not naturally inclined to spend an afternoon at Tattersalls eyeing and endlessly debating the latest horseflesh. And while he was undoubtedly excellent with figures—and had indeed seen revenues from the stables increase under his stewardship—she could not understand why he refused to hand over some of the responsibility to others, and any debate with him on the subject tended to only provoke her ire.

However, the events of yesterday had proved nothing if not her husband's unique ability to send her rage spiraling to new heights. She would have admired him for it had she not been so preoccupied by her desire to stab him with a fork in a delicate area. Repeatedly.

Cutlery-related violence, however, could not be enacted without the presence of its victim, and by the time she had dressed and descended to breakfast, James had apparently left. It was only after discreetly inquiring of Price as she was dressing that Violet had learned that he had in fact returned home the night before. She didn't know why she had expected this morning to be any different than usual. She frequently took breakfast in bed in order to reduce the number of times she and James must meet across a table in a given day, and even when she did come down, he often departed before her for his morning ride in Hyde Park. He liked to ride early, well before the fashionable hour at which the *ton* descended upon the park in hordes.

Once upon a time, Violet had accompanied him on some of those rides—she could remember vividly the peculiar quality of the light on the trees on those mornings, and the crispness of the air cutting through the warmth of her riding habit. The strength of the horse beneath her, and the strange elation, sense of *life*, that came from being out and about when much of the world—or, rather, much of *their* world—still slumbered, recovering from the previous evening's excesses.

So, too, could Violet recall the precise shade of pink the wind colored her husband's cheeks, making him look boyish and far younger than he usually did. Of course, she thought with an odd sort of pang, James had been little more than a boy when they had married. Twenty-three. Older than her own tender age of eighteen, to be sure, but only a couple of years removed from Oxford. So young to be married.

And yet, they had been happy.

For the most part.

And now they were . . .

Well, the truth was that Violet wasn't quite sure what they were. She would not have said they were happy, not by a mile, and yet calling it mere unhappiness seemed an oversimplification. As if the word couldn't quite encompass the multifaceted complexity of their existence these days. She felt, at times, in a state of suspense, waiting for their marriage to resolve itself one way or another—for them to go back to their old ways or to move on entirely, take up lovers, resign themselves to a future of politesse but never passion.

Violet was so occupied by her thoughts that she had been spreading butter on the same piece of toast for the past few minutes; the bread in question was growing soggy. She shook her head, then took a bite.

There was no time for lovesick musings; she cringed at the fact that she had even *thought* the word *lovesick*. Because she was certainly not that. She had read enough to know that the drippy, lovesick girls in novels were without exception frightfully dull, regardless of the fact that they were frequently the heroines of their stories. Violet refused to count herself among their ranks—particularly since doing so would bring her dangerously close to an uncomfortable admission about her feelings for her not-so-beloved husband.

After she had picked away at her breakfast for a suitable amount of time, Violet retreated to the library, as she so frequently did when she found herself at loose ends. The library was her favorite room in the house. She had not seen it until the afternoon of her wedding; when she and James had arrived at the house after their wedding breakfast, she'd teased him that he might have saved the effort of courting her by just showing her this room.

"It wasn't a terrible amount of effort, courting you," James had said, with the satisfaction of a newly married man who had experienced an exceptionally short engagement without the inconvenience of a trip to Scotland. "You were quite willing."

"I didn't have much choice, did I?" Violet said, arching her brows at him. "Given that Mother was standing there observing the entire thing?" She hesitated a fraction of a second, then added, "You didn't have much choice, either."

Brief as that hesitation was, James must have heard it, for the smug grin faded from his face almost instantly, replaced by a look of intense focus. He dropped her hand, which he had been holding in his own, and instead stepped closer to her, seizing her shoulders in a grip firm enough to prevent escape, but not forceful enough to hurt. "Violet."

Something in his tone had her eyes flicking up to meet his immediately. He dropped one of her shoulders to cup her cheek in his hand, and she turned her face into his palm, relishing the contact.

"I would've made the same choice, even if your mother hadn't caught us." His voice was quiet, intent, and she heard the truth in every word he spoke. "Admittedly, it might have taken a bit longer"—his mouth quirked up slightly, and she answered him with a weak smile of her own—"but I have no doubt that we would still have found ourselves here, in this library, and probably having a far more interesting conversation."

He finished speaking, but he did not drop his hands, nor did he break his gaze. He was so very handsome, she thought, as she thought nearly every time she looked at him—tall, broad-shouldered, his dark hair slightly mussed by her own fingers on the carriage ride over, his vivid green eyes staring unblinkingly into her own. And she loved him. And he had told her exactly what she needed to hear.

"I'm glad we agree, then," she told him, attempting to inject her usual note of airiness into her tone; whether or not she was successful, she was not entirely certain, but he pulled her into his arms all the same.

After that, not much was said for quite a while.

And the library got a very thorough inspection.

Now, standing in the same room recalling that moment, Violet swallowed and pushed the thought back. Regardless of the fact that the library was now used strictly for studious pursuits, rather than amorous ones, it was still a lovely room. The walls were papered a dark green, the carpets were deep red, and it was full of settees and armchairs, none of them terribly new, which meant that they were all exceedingly comfortable. The windows along one wall were large, offering a view of the garden behind the house, but the true beauty of the room was in the books. Floor-to-ceiling bookshelves lined three of the walls and, most importantly to Violet's mind, these books were not for show. They were worn, with cracked spines and peeling letters.

"My father's library at Brook Vale Park is full of books he's never read," James had told her once as they sat curled up upon one of the settees. "So as soon as I bought this house, I set about filling it with all the books I read and loved, regardless of whether they made for the most impressive collection."

"That explains the collection of Grimm I found yesterday, then," Violet said with a grin, nestling closer to him. "Not the most serious or literary volumes."

"Quite," James said dryly, but then had said very little else for some time to follow. Violet was once particularly good at silencing him, in a number of thoroughly enjoyable ways.

Once.

This morning, however, Violet did not find the library to be the sanctuary it so frequently was. She felt . . . anxious. She couldn't settle to one thing. It was Thursday, meaning that she had nothing on her schedule for the day until a musicale hosted by the Countess of Kilbourne much later that evening. Upon her return the previous evening, she had instructed Wooton to tell callers that she was not at home, assuming that she would be exhausted from her whirlwind travels. She was rather regretting that now—it was still early, and the empty hours seemed to stretch out endlessly before her.

Boredom was something with which Violet had little experience, though certainly not for lack of trying on the part of good society. Any occupation more strenuous than needlework was frowned upon in well-bred ladies—and Violet, despite her best efforts to thwart her mother over the years, was certainly that. So while many of the paths that she might have enjoyed had she been a gentleman were closed to her, she had managed, thanks to a fair bit of craftiness, to keep herself well enough occupied. While her mother had despaired of the hours she spent holed up with her books ("You'll develop a squint! What man will marry a lady who squints?"), she would have been considerably firmer in her disapproval had she known that, in addition to the improving novels that Violet kept placed strategically, and oh so visibly, about her bedchamber and the drawing room, her daughter was also reading every scientific text and volume of poetry she could get her hands on. She would have been even more appalled to learn how much time Violet spent composing poetry of her own, and writing letters to the editors of scientific journals—under a pseudonym, of course. She was bold, but she was not insane.

Upon her marriage, Violet had been able to engage in these activities openly within her own home, this small amount of freedom almost dizzying at first. James had been greatly amused to learn of her wide and varied interests, and had on more than one occasion offered to attempt to publish her poetry for her, but she had declined.

"It's not rubbish, but it's not brilliant, either," she had explained to him once. "I think I'm far too interested in too many things to excel at one single pursuit."

He had smiled at her, touching his hand to her cheek, but she could see he didn't truly understand—he, with his brilliant mind for mathematics, could not comprehend a mind like Violet's, built for dabbling.

In any case, she had, on more than one occasion over the past four years, spared a moment's gratitude for her ceaseless and wide-ranging curiosity; it was what had kept her sane in a marriage that had become so dissatisfying.

In the first year of her marriage, of course, it hadn't mattered much.

James had been home quite frequently then, sometimes stopping by in the middle of the day for no other reason than to see her. Now, he spent much of his day out of the house—she gathered, from fragments of conversation she overheard, that he had frequent meetings with his man of business about the finances of the stables at Audley House, and she assumed he was as reluctant as he had ever been to delegate any of that responsibility. He still journeyed to Kent frequently—sometimes at a rate of once or twice a week, depending on what was afoot at the stables at a particular time of year. Once, it would have bothered her; now, of course, it scarcely made much difference, since even when he was home, he was often locked away in his study for hours on end, attending to the never-ending series of tasks that required his attention as a landowner and the holder of a fortune in horseflesh. At least, she assumed that was what he was doing. It wasn't as though he ever told her himself.

This thought served to reignite some of her anger of the previous afternoon, as she recalled once again the feeling of looking up as she stepped out the door of the Blue Dove to see him standing there, perfectly healthy, staring at her with an expression of shock that she was certain must have mirrored her own. It was bad enough that it hadn't even occurred to Penvale to write to tell her of James's improved condition—although, she was forced to admit, she had dashed off in such a hurry after receiving his first note that she likely would have missed it. But that her husband—her *husband!*—had seemed disgruntled that Penvale had written at all . . . It was . . . well . . .

Intolerable.

Yes, it was intolerable. And Violet wasn't going to stand for it any longer.

She turned to her writing desk, which was set before one of the windows, and retrieved a blank sheet of paper and a pen and ink.

She scrawled a hasty note, then made a copy of it on another sheet of paper, and threw down her pen.

Turning on her heel, she swept out of the library, startling a footman who was passing.

"John!" she said, holding out the two missives. "See that these are delivered to Lady Templeton and Lady Emily Turner with all necessary haste." He bowed and made as if to turn. "And John," she added, causing him to freeze in his tracks, "see that Mrs. Willis has a particularly fine tea prepared this afternoon. We shall be three, and we shall be hungry."

As Violet had expected, both Diana and Emily were exceedingly prompt in their arrival that afternoon. They entered the drawing room within moments of one another with similarly inquisitive expressions.

"Please, take a seat," Violet said, standing to greet them. "And thank you for responding to my urgent summons."

"It's not as though I had much else to do," Diana said, honestly if not flatteringly. She smoothed the skirts of her green afternoon gown before sinking with her usual languor onto a settee.

"I cherish your friendship as well," Violet said sweetly. She paused as Anna, one of the maids, entered with a lavish tea service. "Thank you, Anna, that will be all—and would you be so good as to close the door on your way out?" This done, Violet leaned forward to pour.

"Violet, what on earth is this all about?" Diana asked impatiently the moment the door snicked shut. "I am judging based on your attire that you haven't joined me in the ranks of widows?"

Violet shot a reproving glance at Diana, who was wont to take the idea of a dead husband rather more lightly than was perhaps proper.

"No," Violet said, splashing tea into the saucer of the first cup. Emily wordlessly reached over and removed the teapot from her grip. She proceeded to pour three cups. "James has apparently made a full recovery from his accident."

"Well, that's good news, isn't it?" Emily asked, handing around the other two teacups before taking a sip of the unadulterated contents of her own cup.

"No," Violet said grumpily, doling milk and sugar into the other two cups.

"You would look lovely in black, though," Diana said, before quailing under Emily's glare. Emily had a glare that proved remarkably effective on the rare occasions she employed it.

"As I was saying," Violet said, and Diana fell silent, "I'm a bit . . ." She trailed off, searching for the most appropriate adjective. Selecting one at random, she continued. ". . . perturbed to learn that my own dear husband is *irritated* by the fact that his wife was alerted to his possible deathblow."

Diana raised one expressive eyebrow.

"We crossed paths on the road, you see. In Kent. We happened to be at the same coaching inn. He was rather surprised, shall we say, to see me, and not terribly pleased when he learned Penvale had written to me of his injury."

"Men," Diana pronounced, shaking her head.

"Quite," Violet said, taking a sip of her tea but barely tasting it. She wished it were socially acceptable for a lady to invite one's friends over for an afternoon brandy instead. She didn't even particularly *like* brandy, though she had partaken of it a couple of times with James in private, early in their marriage. However, she thought it likely that a splash of brandy would soothe her far more than tea at the moment.

"My point, however," she continued, "is that I've had enough." She sat up straighter in her chair, stiffening her spine in acknowledgment of her own proclamation. "I cannot bear to live like this any longer."

"You can come live with me," Diana offered at once. "I've an enormous house all to myself. I think the servants all find me rather pathetic."

"I'm not going anywhere," Violet said, and Diana slumped. "But I plan to take action. If James thinks so little of my place in his life that he believes I don't have the right to know whether he's alive or dead, then I think it's only fair to let him know what that feels like."

"What do you mean?" Emily asked, lowering her teacup.

"I'm going to turn the tables on him," Violet announced. She had given this plan a great deal of thought in the hours before Diana and Emily had arrived. "Let's see how he likes it when *I* take ill and he doesn't learn about it immediately." She took a sip of tea with great satisfaction, as Diana and Emily exchanged a covert look of skepticism.

"Violet," said Emily slowly, clearly pondering how best to phrase whatever was to come next. "Don't you think that you and Lord James"—Emily was always very conscious of titles—"might be overdue for a conversation?"

"I cannot think of anything that sounds less appealing." Violet avoided both her friends' eyes under the guise of carefully selecting a scone from the tea service.

"I agree with Emily," Diana said unexpectedly. "It's been four years of this nonsense, and I've held my tongue"—Violet snorted—"*for the most part*," Diana added hastily, "but if you've now stooped to the level of childish tricks, then I think this has gone on quite long enough."

"You don't understand—" Violet began, but Diana cut her off.

"Of course we don't," she said severely. "Because you've never told us anything about what this foolish argument was about in the first place."

This was, in fact, the truth. In the days following that horrible morning, Violet had been too distraught to say much of anything to her friends. She'd been sleeping in her own bedchamber for the first time in her marriage, and she missed James's warm presence beside her in the bed at night. She missed his surprise midday arrivals at the house, the feeling of his strong arms unexpectedly sliding around her as she sat reading or writing in the library, the scratch of stubble as he pressed a warm kiss to her neck. She missed the heat of his kisses, the feel of his bare skin sliding against her own.

She had even missed their arguments, infuriating as they were. Marriage to James was many things, but placid was not always one of them. They had quarreled frequently during their first year of wedded bliss—so frequently she thought bitterly in those long days immediately after their separation, that she ought to have seen this coming. And yet, they had always made up—often in spectacularly enjoyable fashion. Until now.

In short, she was miserable. And by the time she became slightly less miserable, and began to just get on with it, she had no desire to discuss the events of that day. Every time she thought about it she felt hurt and betrayed all over again, the sting of James's lack of trust in her, his inability to overcome the first instance of his faith in her being tested, as biting as it had been on that first morning, and the thought of sharing the story of their argument sounded as appealing as pouring lemon juice onto a paper cut. Meaning that no one—not her two closest friends, not her mother (perish the thought), no one—knew the reasons for her falling-out with James. Except, she supposed, for James's father. He'd likely worked it out quite easily. But since she, like James, made it a practice to have as little contact with the duke as possible, it was never a subject that had been broached.

"I don't wish to discuss it," Violet said, her voice sounding stiff even to her own ears.

"But, Violet, it's been four years now," Diana protested. "If you'd just tell us what the bastard's done, I should feel much better able to adjust my own behavior accordingly. I never know whether I should be moderately cold or if I should give him the cut direct. I shall feel wretched if he's done something beyond the pale and I've been making polite conversation with him for years."

"Carry on with your conversations," Violet said, cutting off Diana's flow of chatter once the latter paused for breath. Avoiding Diana's hawkish gaze, she instead looked at Emily, who was surveying her with a peculiar expression on her face, one that she hoped very much wasn't pity.

"You loved him once, Violet," Emily said quietly. "Don't you want to fight for it, rather than play foolish games?" She paused, then added in a small voice, "I would."

Violet looked at her friend, who had spent the past five Seasons catering to the whims of her foolish parents, who had watched both of her dearest friends marry while she remained, as ever, Lady Emily Turner, the prim, proper, and terribly virginal marquess's daughter. And Violet realized in a sudden moment of clarity that in Emily's eyes, it must seem extremely foolish of Violet to have allowed a great love match to wither and die. If only repairing the damage were so simple. If only it were as easy as walking up to her husband one morning and declaring a truce.

But it wasn't. It was not just the four years of silent meals and stiff conversations that divided them, but the knowledge Violet held, deep within herself, that her husband didn't trust her—her love, her faith in him, her knowledge of her own heart.

However, she said none of this. Instead, she said simply, "It's too late, Emily. I can't mend four years of damage. But I *can* show the man that I'm not something to be casually discarded."

"Ah," Diana said, as though something had become immediately clear to her. "Are you going to become enceinte?"

"Considering we don't share a bedchamber anymore, I'm not sure how I'd go about doing so."

"Oh, Violet, you can be frightfully naive for a married woman," Diana said impatiently. "I didn't mean that *Audley* would be your partner in this endeavor. I was thinking more of planting a cuckoo in the nest."

"You want her to *take a lover?*" Emily hissed, looking about frantically as though the walls had ears—which, considering the number of servants in the house, it was entirely possible that they did.

"She'd hardly be the first unhappily married woman of the *ton* to do so," Diana said. She shrugged. "I've been thinking of taking one myself."

"Diana . . . you . . ." Words seemed to fail Emily entirely, and she subsided into a sort of distressed sputtering.

"Diana, please do stop trying to shock Emily," Violet said.

"It's not my fault that her virgin sensibilities make it so easy." Diana leaned back against the settee. As ever, she managed to make bad posture look seductive in a way that Violet could never quite manage.

"In any case, Diana, your husband is dead, so I daresay the circumstances are a bit different." Seeing Diana open her mouth, no doubt with some new scheme to share, Violet waved her to silence. "I do appreciate your . . . er . . . helpful suggestions, but I have something else in mind already."

"Oh?" Diana sat back up again. "Do tell."

And, leaning forward conspiratorially, Violet did.

Four

James was having an extremely dissatisfying day.

For the second morning in a row, he had left the house early, before Violet was awake, assuming she had little desire to see him at the breakfast table in light of their most recent conversation. Although, he reminded himself firmly, it was *his* bloody breakfast table, and he could damn well use it as he saw fit, whenever he very well pleased.

In theory.

In practice, he was more or less hiding from his own wife. It was thoroughly embarrassing. Discretion was the better part of valor and all that rot, though, and he found the idea of another argument in the same vein as their last one to be extremely trying.

Yes, better to give her a few days to cool off before resuming the normal *froideur* of their dinners. Dinnertime in the Curzon Street house tended to be just shy of unbearable, in truth. Nothing terribly outrageous, of course—no blistering rows or other such unseemly displays of feeling. They were English, for God's sake. But the reality was somehow worse—sitting across the table from Violet, always painfully beautiful in her evening gowns, her low-cut bodices a hellish temptation for a man who'd had nothing more than his hand for company in bed these past four years. And the silence—the silence was the worst. Violet, who could rarely cease her chatter long enough to take a breath, so full of life and ideas and curiosity about everything, everywhere—to sit across from her in silence was worse than any argument could have been.

The only thing that made these dinners tolerable was the strength of his cellars, in truth—if he one day squandered his entire fortune on rare vintages, he would lay the blame entirely at Violet's feet. One could not sit across from her in silence without fortification.

With that less-than-pleasing thought in mind, James had spent yesterday and much of today meeting with his man of business and his solicitors. This was the aspect of owning the stables he had once enjoyed the most—the horse chatter at Tattersalls, less so. He loved to ride—loved the feel of being on horseback, loved the clarity of mind his morning rides afforded him—but he wasn't the sort to willingly spend an hour debating the merits of a particular filly. However, of late, even the cool logic of the Audley House finances had lost its appeal. What had once been satisfying—taking a task assigned to him by his father and performing it better than the duke could possibly have expected—had lost some of its allure as time wore on. He wouldn't admit it to anyone—not when he had fought with Violet so often over this very issue—but he was beginning to wish the stables occupied rather less of his time.

The stables at Audley House had been a wedding present. "Getting too old for it myself," his father had said on James's wedding day. And James—who had prided himself on the distance he had created between himself and his father, who hated the mere thought of being reliant on the duke in any way—had found himself powerless to resist. Because of Violet. He was about to marry Violet Grey—Violet Grey! A rather hasty wedding, it was true, but this was all to James's liking.

Those ten minutes on that balcony had been the most fortuitous of his life. While he'd planned for them to live in the house on Curzon Street on which he'd spent a chunk of his inheritance from his mother, he loved the idea of being able to offer her a country house as well.

The fact was, he'd been twenty-three and foolish, and he'd have agreed to just about anything if it offered him the chance to make Violet happier.

James had surprised himself with his own competence at managing the stables—and this fact was deeply satisfying to him. He was good at mathematics—not a genius, but very good. He excelled at working out the finances of the stables, maximizing their profits. He didn't find the buying and selling of horseflesh to be particularly fascinating—he found, in truth, poring over the books related to the home farm at Audley House to be far more interesting—but it was certainly not beyond his abilities. The time spent in the stables—an issue that had caused no small amount of friction between himself and his wife in their happier days—also quickly grew old. But he was determined to make a success of it—to prove to his father that he could, to show Violet that he could lay the world at her feet.

He immersed himself in every aspect of the running of the stables, and it was, if he were to be honest, not entirely satisfying—except for each time he was able to reply to an inquiry from his father with an informed report of his success. That made it all worth it. Or so he had always told himself.

Now, five years older and no longer blinded by an absurd school-boy lust for Violet, he saw matters differently than he had at the time of his marriage. He knew now—had realized it soon after the wedding, really—that his father was just hedging his bets. The Duke of Dovington left nothing to chance. If there was the slightest possibility that West, his elder brother and the heir, wouldn't be able to carry on the family line, then it only made sense to ensure that the younger son—who was about to marry a nubile young lady—was well provided for, since *his* son might very well be duke someday. Of course, James reflected wryly, his father had never been much worried about hedging his bets before—it was West's curricle accident, an event that had taken place not long before James had met Violet, that had suddenly made the duke worry for the future of the dukedom. This accident had seriously wounded West and killed Jeremy's elder brother—against whom West had been racing—and had apparently given the duke rather a fright about the future of the Audley line.

The fact that James and Violet now seemed extremely unlikely to produce an heir was perhaps the only thing James found at all positive about his current arrangement with his wife. He had always had a sense of vicious satisfaction in thwarting his father's plans.

In any case, James now found himself the owner of a successful set of stables, which mercifully kept him occupied enough to ensure that he didn't spend his days merely reading newspapers at his club, manufacturing excuses not to return home. It was hardly a substitute for a loving, happy, fulfilling marriage—or even for a project he felt more passion for—but it was better than nothing, he supposed. And yet, today he didn't find his work as distracting as he usually did. Everything seemed to frustrate him; he felt as though he were crawling out of his skin, and he didn't know why.

No. That was a lie. He knew perfectly well why. He couldn't get his damned encounter with Violet out of his head.

It was galling that a woman whose bed he hadn't visited in four years, with whom he routinely carried on conversations of five or fewer sentences, could destroy his calm like this. It had always been this way, though, from the first night he had met her. James had always prided himself on his cool head, his ability to distance himself from any situation, to not let others get under his skin. It was a skill he had perfected out of necessity, during the long, lonely years of his childhood at Brook Vale Park. Prior to meeting Violet, he had kept himself at a distance from others, even his closest friends. It was lonely, at times, but it was certainly less frustrating, less likely to end in hurt.

Violet, however, had waltzed into his life and upended it. And he had let her—hadn't even minded, because he had been so besotted. Looking back, with the benefit of five years' distance and experience, he could see how unutterably foolish he had been. *This* was why he had never let himself get close to a woman, prior to Violet—and look what it had led to. A wife who had at the first opportunity lied to him, plotted against him; a wife whom he'd fought with—bloody *shouted* at, for Christ's sake—and with whom he now shared long, unpleasantly silent dinners. It had been satisfying, somehow, to see her own icy demeanor shattered for once. Some men would have dreaded an angry wife; James found he vastly preferred it to an indifferent one.

In any case, after a day filled with thoughts like these running through his head, he returned home in the afternoon, drawn by some vague unformed hope that perhaps Violet would be sitting down to a late midday meal and he could join her. No doubt it would result in another bloody argument, but he found the prospect oddly enticing. He'd fought with her often enough, after all, even if he was a bit out of practice.

He snorted in derision when he caught himself thinking this—had he really sunk to the point that arguing with his wife seemed like a pleasant way to pass a meal?

Apparently, he had.

This was what marriage did to a man.

However, when he arrived home, he was informed by Wooton that Lady James had not come down from her bedroom all day.

"Is she ill?" James asked, frowning. Violet was never one to laze about like a lady of leisure, despite the fact that that was, strictly speaking, exactly what she was. She was one of the most energetic people he knew, male or female.

"Price said that her ladyship has not been feeling well since her return from the country," Wooton said, and though there was no hint of reproach in his voice, James stiffened slightly all the same. Damn Wooton. He had been his father's butler throughout James's childhood, and had done the unthinkable—left the employ of a duke to serve a lowly second son—upon James's marriage. James himself had barely been able to fathom it, though he knew Wooton had always had a fondness for him. Indeed, he had displayed far more concern for James's well-being during his boyhood than his own father had, though Wooton's concern was usually expressed in a stern, unyielding, butlerish sort of way. Sometimes, he thought Wooton forgot that he was a fully grown man, and not the lonely boy he had once been.

In any case, when James had returned home late the night before last, Wooton had been waiting by the door, as always, causing James a slight pang of guilt for keeping him up. A ridiculous emotion to feel for one's butler, to be sure, but Wooton was not as young as he once was—though had James been asked to pinpoint precisely how old Wooton *was*, he was not at all certain he would have been able to give an answer with any measure of accuracy.

Wooton hadn't said much upon his arrival beyond a curt, "I am glad to see your lordship in one piece," and yet James had felt three different sorts of censure from that one remark—for his recklessness, for the unnecessary worry he had caused Violet, and for allowing her to travel halfway to Kent and back without his escort.

Not, James felt like informing Wooton, that Violet would have welcomed his escort on her return to London. In fact, he was relatively certain that had he entered that carriage with her, he would not have emerged in one piece. However, he had not said this—it had been a long day, but he had not yet sunk to the level of having to explain himself to his servants. Even Wooton.

Now, however, James could sense all the unspoken words Wooton was holding back—little wonder that the lady of the house should fall ill after hours of worry and uncomfortable carriage travel. Again, James was tempted to tell his butler that Violet was a sturdy sort, and that he'd never known her to be unduly troubled by carriage travel before, but he knew that all he would receive from the man would be a bland, "Of course, my lord," so he refrained.

"I shall pay her a visit," he said to Wooton, handing him his coat, hat, and gloves, and walking decisively toward the stairs. Glancing over his shoulder quickly as he began to ascend the steps, he was satisfied to see a fleeting expression of surprise flick across Wooton's face. If nothing else, today he had managed to cause his butler to express an emotion, however briefly—any self-respecting Englishman could feel proud of such an accomplishment.

His steps slowed, however, as he approached Violet's door, and he hesitated. Should he knock, or go right in? He didn't wish to disturb her if she was asleep, but the idea of walking uninvited into her bedchamber, as though the past four years hadn't happened . . . No. He rapped softly on the door.

After a moment, Violet's voice: "Enter."

Upon opening the door, the first thing that hit him was the smell. The entire damn room smelled like Violet. It made sense, of course—she slept here, for Christ's sake—but it still caught him off guard, the strength of the scent. Violet smelled wonderful. It was hard to say what exactly her scent was—something floral and warm and uniquely *Violet*, though not *actual* violets—but he had spent the past four long years catching mere whiffs of it across the dinner table, and it was overwhelming to be surrounded by it once more. He felt like a starving man who'd been led out of the desert and sat before the most sumptuous feast he'd ever had in his life.

He gave himself a stern, internal shake. Was he going senile? Surely he was young for that.

He was distracted from these less-than-comforting thoughts, however, by the sight of Violet herself. She was sitting in an armchair by the fireplace, a shawl wrapped around her shoulders, a book lying open on her lap. She was watching him with a wary gaze.

"Violet," he said, his voice more formal by far than it had been on the night they met. "How are you feeling?"

She gave a faint cough, then hastily stifled it before responding. "Passable, thank you." Her voice was equally formal, and he guessed that she was still angry about their ordeal earlier in the week.

"Wooton said you're not feeling well," he said, taking a couple of steps forward. The curtains were pulled, dimming the light in the room, but he could see by the flickering light of the fire that she was dressed in a blue morning gown, though she had not gone to the trouble of dressing her hair, which lay in a thick braid over one shoulder. It made her look very young—very like the eighteen-year-old girl he had fallen in love with, in fact.

Had *thought* he'd fallen in love with, he reminded himself sternly.

It wouldn't do to allow one dratted hairstyle to make him go soft in the head.

"Yes," she said, giving another small cough. "I've been feeling a bit poorly since my return from the country"—*she*, at least, made no effort to disguise the note of reproach in her voice—"but I'm certain it's nothing to worry overmuch about. I shall be right as rain in another day, I expect."

James gazed at her intently, pondering—it was unlike Violet to admit to illness until she was delirious with fever. She shifted in her chair as he continued to look at her, her cheeks flushing slightly, causing the book on her lap to fall to the floor with a soft thud.

"What are you reading?" James asked, hastening to pick up the volume before she could lean down to do so for herself. He straightened and flipped the book in his hand so that he could peer at the spine. He read the title, then flicked an amused glance at his wife, whose cheeks appeared to be reddening further.

"*Childe Harold?*" he asked, handing the book back to her. "Please correct me if my memory is failing me in my advanced age, but did you not once call Byron a 'floppy-haired fool'?"

"I may have," Violet admitted, setting the volume aside on the small table next to her chair. "But I thought I might as well see what all the fuss is about. It's quite good, actually," she said reluctantly, rather as she might admit that Napoleon's coat was attractive. "Though I still think he's a bit of an idiot. All that carrying on with Caro Lamb." She sniffed disdainfully, and James had to suppress an urge to grin.

"I think he's rather an idiot myself," James said, and Violet's gaze met his, and for a moment it was as though no time had passed. She was enjoying herself—for a moment, just a moment, he could see it plain as anything. There was the look in her beautiful brown eyes that he used to see each time they really got into it about history or literature or anything else they used to debate—the keen interest, the intelligence that polite society found unseemly in a woman. It was one of the things James loved best about her.

Had loved best.

That sobering addendum brought him back to himself, and to his reason for looking in on her. "If you are fit enough to discuss Byron, then I suppose I can rest easy that I don't need to summon a physician for you?"

"Oh!" Violet said with a start, and an odd expression crossed her face, though it was gone before James could identify it. "No! That is, yes. That is . . ." She waved her hand, clearly attempting—unsuccessfully— to appear casual. "I shall consult a physician if I am not feeling better soon. You need not concern yourself, my lord."

And just like that, the distance was back between them. For a moment, as they had discussed Byron, it had felt like it used to, before everything went wrong in their marriage. But just as quickly, with the words *my lord*, the past four years reinserted themselves. And it was all the more frustrating for the fact that, for a moment, he'd forgotten how things stood.

"Very well," he said impatiently, angry at her for ruining the moment—for ruining things in the first place, he thought furiously. "If you have no need of my assistance, then I shall take my leave of you." He hated the sound of his own voice when he was speaking to her, sometimes—never did he sound like so much of a prig as when he was conversing with his own wife.

He reminded himself, as he so often did, that he was not the party at fault in this mess—he had reacted as any man would have upon learning his own wife had manipulated him in so appalling a fashion.

The fact that he had to remind himself of this fact at all was itself a dangerous sign—for a good while after their last, final argument, he'd been too angry to think clearly. He'd never needed reminding then.

"I require nothing of you," Violet said softly, in response to his last statement. And for a moment James wanted to shake her, to demand that she ask something, *anything* of him—he was her husband, after all, for better or for worse.

But, of course, he could not say that to her. So instead he bowed, and said nothing more at all.

⚜

Violet's plan was proving to be more complicated than she had anticipated.

"Of course it is," Diana said impatiently the next day as she, Violet, and Emily reclined in Diana's barouche outside Gunter's. "I do believe my exact words to you when you confessed this idea were, 'Have you lost your mind?'"

"And I assured you that I had done no such thing," Violet said, pausing to take a bite of her ice. It was a warm day, and Berkeley Square was packed with carriages and curricles full of other ladies similarly enjoying ices in the sunshine. Violet spotted at least three different clusters of ladies that she knew, but she did no more than nod in acknowledgment upon catching their eyes. She did not wish to be disturbed.

"However," she conceded, "this is presenting some difficulties. Do you think your physician would be willing to lie to the son of a duke?"

Diana and Emily both blinked at her, Emily with a spoon suspended halfway to her mouth.

"It's just that if I'm going to maintain this ruse, I'll eventually need a physician to say that I'm truly ill, and I know James's physician won't do it. So I need to find someone else."

"And you don't think he'll find it suspicious that you're suddenly consulting a different physician?" Emily asked skeptically.

"I shall just tell him that I want someone who has nothing to do with the Audley family," Violet said, waving a spoon dismissively. "He won't question me overmuch after I tell him that."

"What a pleasant time the two of you must have of it," Diana said, shaking her head. "Tell me, at mealtimes, do you slice your meat with great gusto whilst staring at your husband menacingly across the table?"

"Only on special occasions," Violet said, refusing to rise to the bait. "But the fact remains, if I want to give James what for, I'll need a physician at some point."

"Or someone who *looks* like a physician," Emily said thoughtfully, surprising Violet—she had rather expected Emily to be the one who objected more strenuously to all this.

"What do you mean?"

"Well, you'll struggle to find a physician willing to lie to a lady's husband, especially when the husband in question is the second son of a duke," Emily said. She took a bite of her ice. "So you might be better served by finding someone who could pose as a physician."

"What, an actor?" Violet asked, raising an eyebrow.

"Certainly not," Emily said, blushing. "The very idea! It would be most inappropriate for a lady of your breeding to even be in the company of an actor, there's no one who—"

"Wait," Diana said, her eyes lighting up. "There's one actor whose company would be acceptable."

"Who?" Emily asked, her tone highly skeptical. "Violet's reputation would be compromised if she were seen in the company of anyone involved with the theater. And it's not as though actors tend to frequent Wednesday nights at Almack's."

"Lucky them," Violet murmured.

"That's where you're wrong," Diana said gleefully. "There's one who does. Well," she amended, "probably not Almack's, because no one in their right mind would *choose* to go there. But there is one person involved with the theater who has entrée to places we can reach him."

Violet leaned forward, intrigued. "Diana, I do believe your penchant for gossip is finally proving useful."

"Indeed," Diana said smugly. "I take it you two do not recall the scandal of the Marquess of Eastvale's son?"

Violet took a thoughtful bite of ice. The name sounded familiar, somehow—beyond the routine familiarity every member of the aristocracy had with the families listed in *Debrett's*. What was it? She gasped.

"Julian Belfry?" she asked. "Oh, Diana, you *are* brilliant at times, I must admit."

"Who is Julian Belfry?" Emily asked, frowning.

"Don't you recall the story?" Violet asked. "It was a few years ago—during your second Season, perhaps? He's the second son of a marquess and instead of joining the military or the clergy—"

"Or raising a stable full of horses," Diana added dryly.

"—he started his own theater with the inheritance left him by a relative. I don't recall all the precise details," Violet said, waving her hand impatiently. "But it was quite a scandal—his father hasn't spoken his name since the day he received word of the purchase of the theater. He was a couple of years ahead of James and Penvale and Jeremy at

Oxford," she said, and then her face fell as a realization dawned on her. "Oh, but Diana, he won't do at all! James knows him! He'll see through any ruse in an instant."

"Are they closely acquainted?" Diana asked.

"No," Violet said, drawing out the syllable as she thought, trying to recall mentions of him James had made in passing. "I don't know that they were ever particularly intimate."

"And Belfry is supposed to be quite the actor, isn't he?" Diana pressed. "Performs in many of the productions at his own theater? It's all part of the scandal surrounding him, is it not?"

"Well, yes—"

"Then I don't think it will be a problem," Diana said dismissively. "Any actor worth his salt must be possessed of a few clever costumes—and men never see anything other than they're expecting to. Audley won't notice a thing."

"Much as it pains me to admit this, James isn't *entirely* unintelligent," Violet said. "I don't know if this will work."

"Well, do you have a better idea?" Diana asked impatiently.

"Not at present," Violet admitted.

"Then it's worth a try, I say."

"It's rather easy for you to say, when you won't be the one running the risk of being caught out by your husband in a blatant lie," Violet said peevishly.

In response to this, Diana played her trump card. She placed a hand dramatically upon her breast, heaving a deep sigh. "Of course, you are correct," she said mournfully. "What wouldn't I give to have my own dear husband here, primed to serve as the target of such a scheme?" She blinked as though fighting back tears, though her eyes looked suspiciously clear. "But of course, I am a widow now, and must live vicariously though my beloved friends to fill my long, sorrowful days—"

"Enough," Violet said, feeling it best to interrupt before Diana really got into the spirit of the thing. "I'll do it, I'll do it. But if this all goes disastrously awry, I shall be laying the blame squarely at your feet."

"Fair enough," Diana said, serenely taking a bite of ice, all traces of emotion suddenly, mysteriously absent.

"How do you intend to contact him?" Emily asked curiously— she had been observing without commenting for several minutes now. "Sending a letter seems rather risky, and it's not as though you can just show up at his theater . . ."

"I think," Diana said slowly, "that my useless brother may for once prove to be beneficial to me."

❧

"I can't believe I let you convince me to do this," Penvale said for at least the third time in the past five minutes. It was dinnertime the following evening. The day before, they had proceeded directly from Gunter's to Diana's home, where they had sent a frantic note to Penvale at his club. He had appeared less than an hour later, looking mildly alarmed, but his expression had rapidly changed to one of irritation upon joining them in Diana's elegantly appointed sitting room and learning what was being asked of him.

"Hauled out of my own club," he continued, setting down his drink and beginning to stride back and forth from one end of the room to the other. "Forced to lure a man I barely know to my sister's house, and obliged to phrase it all in such a way that he no doubt thinks she's interested in having some sort of liaison with him—"

"Who says I'm not?" Diana asked, smiling innocently at her brother. "I'm a widow, after all, and I've been distressingly well-behaved since Templeton died." She heaved a heavy sigh, which had the result of displaying her impressive bosom to even greater advantage in her evening gown of crimson silk; Violet personally thought Diana might have saved the effort for the gentleman whose favor they would shortly be attempting to curry.

"Good lord, Diana," Penvale said severely, giving his sister a stern look. "You might do well to look for someone a bit less notorious, at the very least. You're new to this business, after all."

"Yes," Diana said, batting her eyelashes. "And I've a lot of lost time to make up."

Penvale retrieved his drink and took another hearty swallow. "I regret this already."

"Well, it's too late for that," Violet said briskly, although privately she was beginning to have a few misgivings. Diana's idea had sounded so reasonable in the bright sunshine outside Gunter's, safely ensconced in her barouche, all this seeming more like a game than anything else. Now, however, she was beginning to feel rather foolish. Her plan to trick James into fretting over her health had seemed perfectly acceptable when she had fabricated it a couple of days before, stewing in her own anger, but now that she would be forced to confess it to a perfect stranger, she was not feeling quite so certain.

Penvale's reaction upon learning of her scheme had not been encouraging.

"I am feigning a case of consumption," she had informed him, with as much dignity as she could muster, when it had become apparent that some sort of explanation would be required to ensure his cooperation.

"You're *what?*" he had asked incredulously, staring at Violet as though she had grown another head.

"I am teaching him a lesson," Violet said. "It's all down to you anyway, Penvale. Your bloody note started all of this fuss."

"Had I known how much trouble that letter would cause me, I should have stood stoic and penless even had Audley been bleeding to death before me," he muttered.

"That is a charming sentiment indeed," Violet said. "But in any case, I am going to show my husband exactly what it felt like to stand in that coaching yard and have him tell me it was none of my concern whether he lived or died." She crossed her arms, her confidence bolstered by a wave of renewed indignation. "Men!"

Penvale had put up a few more protestations, of course, as men are wont to do, but when Violet had finally informed him that she would be doing this with or without his consent—and with all sorts of whispered threats from Diana when Penvale threatened to inform James of their plans—he had agreed, albeit with bad grace.

From there, things with Lord Julian Belfry had advanced rather more rapidly than she'd expected. They'd summoned Penvale in order to ask him if he could extend a dinner invitation to Belfry when next he saw him. Penvale, however, informed them that he'd been playing cards with the man at White's—"before I was so *irritatingly* forced to depart"—and that if he were permitted to go back about his business, he could no doubt make the invitation that very afternoon. Another couple of hours later, and a note from Penvale had arrived, informing them that Lord Julian Belfry would be pleased to dine with Lady Templeton the very next evening, should the invitation stand.

Fortunately, Diana had already planned to have Violet and Penvale for dinner that same evening, and it was little trouble to inform her cook that one more would be joining them. So it was that at eight o'clock the following day, Violet found herself in Diana's sitting room, awaiting the arrival of the man she hoped would assist her.

"What did Audley say when his supposedly ill wife set off for a dinner party?" Penvale asked wryly. He ran a hand through his hair, which was the exact same honeyed shade as Diana's. He was a very handsome man, tall and fit and broad of shoulder, though Violet had never paid him that much attention growing up. He had been Diana's exasperating elder brother, never an object of her romantic fantasies. And that was just as well—while he was not so much of a libertine as Jeremy (but then, who was?), he still seemed to display little interest in matrimony.

"I had already told him I wouldn't be home to dine tonight, as I'd be dining with Diana, so I think he arranged to eat at his club. I told him I was feeling much improved this morning, when I saw him at breakfast. But of course, I took care not to seem *too* healthy." She gave a slight cough, then another, hoping to give the appearance of fragility and weakness. The effect was spoiled a moment later when she realized that she had forgotten to tuck a handkerchief in her sleeve.

"Blast," she muttered, patting her arm vainly in the hope that one would materialize.

"A truly convincing performance," Penvale said darkly. "I can't believe Audley thought for a moment you were truly ill."

"I did try a bit harder with him, you see," Violet protested, abandoning the futile search for the elusive scrap of linen.

She was spared further editorial remarks by Wright, Diana's butler, who materialized in the doorway of the sitting room. "Lord Julian Belfry," he announced solemnly.

Violet's first thought was that she understood perfectly well why

Lord Julian should have found success on the stage. The man was devastatingly handsome. His hair was so dark a shade of brown as to be indiscernible from black, cut a bit too long for fashion, which gave him an appealingly rakish air. His eyes were a vivid blue, his face comprised of the strong bones and fine angles that marked him, unmistakably, as an aristocrat.

Beside her, Diana inhaled softly. "Good lord," she murmured. Violet couldn't disagree.

"Belfry," Penvale said, moving forward to shake the man's hand. "Good to see you again."

"Your invitation was too intriguing to turn down," Lord Julian responded, his gaze flicking over Violet and Diana with interest. Diana stood carefully so as to display her figure to its best advantage. Violet resisted the urge to roll her eyes.

"Lady James Audley, Lady Templeton, may I present Lord Julian Belfry?" Penvale said, and to his credit he did not allow any of his exasperation to make its way into his voice.

"Ladies," Lord Julian said, moving forward to bend first over Violet's hand, then Diana's. "It is truly a crime that two such lovely specimens of English beauty are only now being brought to my attention." He had a reputation as a womanizer, and in this instant, Violet understood why.

"Specimens, sir?" Violet asked, raising an eyebrow. "You make us sound like organisms to be studied under a microscope."

Diana shot her a quelling look. "I am certain Lord Julian did not intend to give offense," she said.

"I didn't say I was offended," Violet said. "I was merely commenting on his interesting word choice."

"Lady James," Lord Julian said, straightening and staring at her with frank amusement. "It seems that everything I have heard about you is true."

"As I cannot begin to imagine what that might be, I shall choose to take this as a compliment," Violet said lightly. This was a lie—she had a very good idea of what he might have heard about her from other members of the *ton*. She had never made it a habit to maintain a demure silence; in fact, as her mother so often reminded her, it was very fortunate indeed that she had managed to—in Lady Worthington's parlance—"snatch up" James in her first Season, because good looks didn't make up for oddity; men didn't want a woman who spoke her mind or read scandalous books, et cetera.

Et cetera.

Et cetera.

In any case, Violet had never been terribly bothered by it—and the fact was, slightly odd habits in a lady married to the son of a duke were far more permissible than in an unmarried miss, so she had never particularly felt the scorn of society. But she knew people did whisper. It was actually rather refreshing to meet someone like Lord Julian who addressed this matter head on.

"As well you should," he said by way of reply, and grinned at her so charmingly that she could not help but smile back.

At that moment, the dinner gong sounded. Penvale escorted Violet into the dining room, allowing Lord Julian to fall back and take Diana's arm, in utter disregard for the proper dinner entrance etiquette. Violet glanced over her shoulder and saw the two of them eyeing one another appraisingly. She felt rather as though she were at an auction.

Dinner itself was a slightly awkward affair—Penvale did his best to keep conversation afloat (for he could be charming when he tried), and Diana was all flirtatious invitation (indeed, Violet thought she might be taking on this role with a bit too much enthusiasm), but throughout the meal, Violet sensed an underlying strain. Lord Julian clearly wondered why he had been invited, and as the footmen cleared away the final course before withdrawing, Violet decided that the time had come to speak up.

"Lord Julian," she said, and he focused that unwavering blue gaze on her instantly. It was absurd, she thought. Men shouldn't be that handsome. "It was good of you to accept Lord Penvale's invitation on such short notice, and I know you must be rather . . ." She faltered, searching for the proper adjective.

"Intrigued?" he suggested, a hint of laughter in his voice. Violet bit back a smile.

"Indeed," she said primly, folding her napkin precisely and placing it on the table before her. "The truth is, I am in need of some assistance and I think you are just the man to provide it."

"Lady James, I must confess, you have roused my curiosity," he said, with a faint, suggestive pause before the last word.

Considering it best to ignore this, she continued. "I have an acting job for which I would like to hire you. It is . . . rather outside your usual line of work, and might pose some difficulties, but I was at a loss when considering to whom I could possibly turn."

"What sort of acting job?" he asked, his tone casual, but Violet could sense his interest, could somehow feel the energy emanating from him.

"I should like you to pose as my personal physician," she stated. "I am in the midst of a slight disagreement with my husband, and I need to convince him that I am extremely ill. He won't believe my ruse for long if I refuse to consult a physician, so I have need of someone to pose as one who will visit me to give a dire prognosis."

"What sort of prognosis did you have in mind?" he asked dryly.

"Consumption," Violet said, as simply as if she were announcing her jam preference at the breakfast table.

Lord Julian stared, as if determining whether she spoke in earnest.

"I see," he said at last, although he sounded very dubious indeed. "I must confess, I am at a loss for words."

"With excitement, owing to your eagerness to assist me?" Violet ventured hopefully.

"Ah, no. It is more that I find myself unsure of where, precisely, to begin in my attempt to explain to you the foolishness of this plan."

"Save your breath, Belfry, I've already tried," Penvale said, taking a large sip from his wineglass.

"To begin, I believe the recommended treatment for consumption often involves a prolonged journey to a sanitarium in the Alps, or some other godforsaken Continental patch of nature, which I presume is a bit more lengthy a recovery than you have in mind."

"Yes, but—"

"Secondly, I cannot imagine any man in his right mind reacting with anything other than anger upon discovering that he has been duped in so spectacular a fashion by his own wife, meaning that I cannot believe that this scheme will result in anything other than Audley slapping a glove in my face. And, alas, I fear I'm growing rather old for dueling."

"Then I suggest you don't let on that it's you," Violet said. "I was under the impression that you were a rather skilled actor. Or is your reputation inflated?" She could see that he was preparing to reject her, and hoped that pricking at his pride would motivate him where nothing else would.

Lord Julian, however, merely looked amused. "Well, my lady," he replied lazily, leaning back in his chair, "as tempting as it is to assist you in this entirely half-baked scheme of yours, I'm afraid it shan't be possible for a number of reasons. The most noteworthy being that I am acquainted with your husband, and therefore cannot possibly hope to pass myself off as an unknown physician."

"Surely any good actor is adept at costuming himself," Diana noted. Her silence apparently had its limits.

"This is true," Lord Julian acknowledged reluctantly.

"Then it should be no trouble for you to do as I ask," Violet said.

"I see no reason to play a role in your little marital game," Lord Julian announced.

"It's not—" Violet protested, but Lord Julian continued as though she hadn't said anything.

"I've no great admiration for the institution of marriage, so please believe me, my lady, when I tell you that my objections do not stem from a concern about the felicity of your and Audley's union. However, I see no possible advantage to me, and the mild possibility that your husband shall ask me to meet him with pistols at dawn. That is a risk I am willing to take only for the sake of more . . . pleasurable results, shall we say." He took another sip of wine, then leaned back in his chair, as though he were a chess player awaiting her next move.

"I am willing to pay you for your time, of course," Violet said stiffly—she generally scorned aristocratic mores, and yet she could not make herself comfortable speaking of pecuniary matters.

"I do not require your blunt, my lady." Lord Julian sounded amused.

"Well, surely there must be something I can offer," Violet said desperately. Lord Julian's gaze raked her slowly, making her cheeks warm, and then his eyes shifted to Diana, whose figure he perused with similar thoroughness. After a moment, however, he straightened in his seat, his manner at once more businesslike. While Violet was relieved that she seemed not to have drawn his interest, she felt Diana stiffen imperceptibly next to her. Diana was used to men finding her hopelessly alluring, allowing her the pleasure of rejecting them.

"There is one thing you can give me," Lord Julian conceded after another long moment of silence.

"And what is that?" Violet asked, torn between curiosity and wariness.

"Your presence," he said. "At my theater." Violet wasn't certain what she had been expecting, but it hadn't been this. She exchanged a glance with Diana, hoping her shock didn't show too plainly on her face. Diana, for her part, also looked surprised, though she hid her confusion fairly well, betraying it only by the slightest wrinkling of her brow.

"I understood your theater to be very successful," Violet said. Indeed, the Belfry, as Lord Julian's theater was aptly named, was frequently whispered of among members of the *ton*. While it was not seen as entirely respectable, Belfry's aristocratic connections had enabled him to obtain a limited patent to stage drama during the summer months, and she knew that it was quite popular among aristocrats who wished to take their mistresses for an evening's entertainment without running the risk of encountering their wives' friends. She had, in her darker moments, wondered if James had ever squired a mistress there himself. She had no reason to believe he'd been unfaithful—but four years was a terribly long time.

"It is," Belfry conceded, without a hint of modesty. "And it nets a pretty sum for me, make no mistake. But I've lately become a touch restless. I should like to test myself a bit. I want to elevate the overall tenor of my theater, and for that, I need respectable ladies to attend my shows."

"Why would you wish for that?" Violet asked blankly, causing Belfry to grin and Penvale to make an odd choking noise that Violet believed was the sound that resulted from a meeting of laughter and claret. But her question was genuine. The Belfry had carved out a rather nice niche for itself in London society: a space designed by and for the aristocracy, but with a distinctly masculine bent. It was, as Jeremy had once said admiringly, as though a gentleman's club had been transformed into a theater.

"I love my theater, Lady James," Lord Julian said, and he was uncommonly serious as he spoke, his gaze meeting hers directly without a hint of mockery or teasing. "I am proud of the productions we put on, but I also believe that we can do better—but we won't do so, and I won't attract truly top-notch talent, until the theater is seen as an institution as respectable and lofty as Covent Garden and Drury Lane, and I am licensed to perform serious drama, as those theaters are. I need men to bring their wives to my shows, not their mistresses, and I don't know how to convince them to do so other than to lead by example.

"So, I will take part in your little ruse—I shall put on false whiskers and mumble to your husband about your delicate state, and look very grim and concerned. But I shall do so only if you give me my word that you and Lady Templeton will attend one of my productions. Soon. And bring as many of your friends as you can."

"Well," Violet said slowly. It would be terribly scandalous to attend a show at the Belfry—she could already hear her mother's screeches echoing in her ears—but she found the prospect somewhat appealing. As it so frequently did, Violet's curiosity got the better of her.

"This is my final offer," Lord Julian added, seeming to mistake her hesitation for an imminent denial. "Do we have a deal?"

Violet's mind raced as she pondered the logistics—she would have to convince James to escort her, and that would be tricky in and of itself. And she needed to bring friends? Respectable friends? She thought of all the married ladies of her acquaintance; to a one, they were far too concerned with their reputations to consider attending. But then her thoughts turned to Emily—Emily, who was still unwed, but who had two married friends who were perfectly capable of serving as chaperones, especially if Emily's mother was somewhat misled as to their destination.

"I'll see your respectable wives, and raise you an eligible miss," Violet said, making up her mind all at once.

"We have a deal, then?" Lord Julian asked, setting down his glass. He now gazed at her keenly, his blue eyes intent.

"Yes," Violet said firmly, lifting her own glass in a silent toast. "I believe we do."

Five

When James returned home at midday the next day, after yet another early-morning departure, he would have been hard-pressed to explain even to himself why he did so. He had plenty with which to occupy himself this afternoon, and yet all morning thoughts of his wife had not been far from his mind. He couldn't possibly seize on any reasonable explanation for it, other than her illness of the previous week—which had apparently been naught but a trifle, as she'd been up and about as usual the following morning. But still, it had made him take more than his usual notice of her. All day, he'd had the image of her sitting by the fire, her hair in a girlish plait; mentally, he lingered on the soft swell of her breasts beneath the fabric of her gown, imagining how they would have felt in his hands.

It was disturbing; he had spent four years cultivating a carefully maintained coolness where Violet was concerned, and yet a faint cough and a fluttering handkerchief seemed enough to undo a composure that had been years in the crafting.

James was surprised, upon arriving in Curzon Street, to see the door open as he approached his home, and Wooton's anxious face peeking round the wood, clearly looking for him. While James prided himself on having a well-trained staff, this degree of anticipation of his arrival seemed a bit excessive.

"My lord," Wooton called as soon as James was within earshot. "I am glad you are returned." This was alarming in the extreme; James could count on one hand the number of times he had ever heard Wooton's voice containing emotion.

"What has happened?" James asked, mounting the steps and entering the house.

"A physician is here, my lord."

"Worth?" James demanded, naming the physician he had consulted when in town since the days of his boyhood.

"No, my lord. A man called Briggs, I believe, and unknown to me," Wooton said, and he gave James a significant sort of stare that made James take a second, longer look at his butler.

"Where is this Briggs, then?" he asked impatiently.

"I believe he is with Lady James—"

"You are sadly mistaken in your belief, my good man," came a voice from the stairs. "As I am now here."

James turned to the stairs and saw a gentleman of indeterminate years descending toward him. He was tall and broad of shoulder, dressed in plain black, carrying a case in one hand. He had a set of bushy gray whiskers that covered much of his face, and his eyes were hidden behind a thick pair of spectacles, but as he drew nearer, James could see that his skin was largely unlined, and he thought that this Briggs might be a fair bit younger than he appeared upon first glance.

"I've just been visiting her ladyship," Briggs said after offering an exquisitely correct bow. There was nothing at all untoward in his behavior, so why did James, suddenly and without reason, wish to punch him in the face?

"Indeed?" James asked, arching a brow, pleased to hear that his voice sounded calm, regardless of his inner turmoil.

"Yes," Briggs said, nodding. "She reports that she has been feeling poorly for some time now, and summoned me on the recommendation of her friend Lady Templeton."

James relaxed his posture an infinitesimal amount; if Diana used the man, he must not be an utter quack.

"I was unaware that her ladyship was still unwell," James said. "But I am glad she summoned you, regardless. Did you make any sort of diagnosis?"

"I am not precisely certain, my lord, and I of course do not wish to cause undue alarm—"

James's stomach dropped unpleasantly. Violet was fine, he told himself; she was only three-and-twenty, for Christ's sake. Nothing short of childbirth would slow her down—and that seemed an unlikely prospect at any time in the near future, given the current state of affairs between them.

"Out with it, man," he said curtly, and even to his own ears his voice did not sound entirely steady.

"Yes, my lord," Briggs said, bobbing another irritating bow. "I am not precisely certain, given her symptoms, but it did seem to me somewhat possible that her ladyship ... well ... her ladyship might be in the early stages of consumption."

If James made any reply, he was not conscious of it; indeed, he could hear nothing over the sound of the roaring in his own ears, as he all at once felt unsteady on his own feet. He reached out, for the first time in his life, for something to lean on. He, who prided himself on relying on nothing and no one, found himself grasping the banister quite gratefully, clinging to its reassuring firmness and strength. He felt an uncharacteristic wish to turn to someone, to seek their reassurance that all would be well. And yet, the idea of actually doing so—whether that someone be his brother, or Penvale and Jeremy, or even the presumably knowledgeable physician before him—felt so foreign to him as to be inconceivable.

Vaguely, he became aware that Briggs was staring at him, an unreadable expression upon his face; as James took a second look at said face, something niggled at the back of his mind, something familiar, just out of reach.

"I will take my leave of you now, my lord," Briggs said, his voice sounding as though it were coming from a great distance. "I have another pressing appointment, and I must not keep the lady in question waiting. But I should be happy to answer any of your . . . er . . . questions at a later date. Let me give you my card."

Briggs fumbled in his case, extracting a card and pressing it into James's unresisting fingers. With a last long, concerned glance and another bow, he made his departure.

The sound of the door closing behind Briggs had the effect of bringing James back to himself; he was suddenly moving, without recalling instructing his feet to do so, crossing the brief space of the entryway, Wooton opening the door even as he approached. He stood, blinking in the sunlight, opening his mouth to shout after Briggs—but Briggs was gone.

Or, rather, Briggs as he had been a moment before was gone. In his place, striding away down Curzon Street, was a man holding a set of false whiskers in one hand, a physician's case in the other, energetically making his way toward a waiting carriage.

James glanced down at the card in his hand, and his suspicions were confirmed. The elaborately engraved card read LORD JULIAN BELFRY.

Violet heard the footsteps on the stairs and sprang into action. She tightly screwed on the lid to her ink bottle and wiped her pen with a handkerchief, then hastily shoved both, along with the sheet of paper upon which she had been writing, into a drawer of her bedside table. She had just flung herself back against her pillows, folding her hands calmly atop the blankets that covered her, when she noticed an alarming splotch of ink on her index finger. She rolled over and frantically opened the drawer once more, grabbing the ink-stained handkerchief and scrubbing at her finger. She had, after all, supposedly just been examined by a doctor while lying docilely abed, and therefore could not afford any suspiciously fresh ink spots—the result of a highly emotional letter to the editor of *Ackermann's Repository* about a planned exhibition of the Elgin Marbles in the British Museum.

Shoving the handkerchief under her pillow, she forced herself to recline calmly, as any true invalid would. She had been lying abed in a state of some anxiety for quite a while now; Lord Julian had arrived that morning, as they had arranged, and lingered in her room until James returned home. He had brought along a sheaf of papers, which Violet thought might have been a script, and had spent a quiet few hours perusing them, occasionally muttering to himself. She had written three letters, read a volume of scandalous poetry, read the latest issue of *Ackermann's Repository*, and begun writing another letter. It was exactly what she would have been doing on any other day, but being forced to do it from the confines of her bed—since she had to keep up appearances, for the sake of any servants who might wander in—had made it inexpressibly more tedious. It had never occurred to her how dull a life of espionage must be at times, and she was very grateful that James had returned home early today.

Lord Julian had sprung into action as soon as they'd heard James's voice downstairs—they had kept her bedchamber door cracked for just this purpose—and had vanished out the door, false whiskers in place, before Violet could offer so much as a thank-you.

She hadn't been able to catch any of the conversation downstairs, had heard only muted male voices, but she heard James's footsteps now, loud and clear, and it occurred to her that she would recognize his tread anywhere. She knew the precise weight of his footfalls, the length of his strides, and she tried not to contemplate the number of evenings she had lain abed, listening to those footsteps passing by her bedroom door on the way to his own.

Her own door flung open with a bang, not at all like the quiet knock he had offered just days before. She firmly resisted the temptation to fuss with her hair. She was supposed to be *ill*, for heaven's sake.

James stalked into the room, reaching behind himself to shut the door, thankfully with less force than he had employed in opening it. His dark hair was in slight disarray, as though he had run a hand through it roughly, as she knew he was wont to do when frustrated or upset. She felt a sudden, piercing desire to smooth it for him, and her heart clenched at the thought, even as she gave herself a stern mental shake. She was supposed to be punishing the man, not soothing him.

There was an odd look on his face as he approached her bedside— assessing. He seemed to be sizing her up, perusing her from head to toe and back again. His green eyes were glittering, and there was more color in his cheeks than usual. She lifted her chin, waiting for him to speak first, and casually laced her hands so that the telltale ink-stained finger was hidden.

"Why the devil was there a physician leaving the house as I arrived?" he barked, coming to a halt approximately a foot away from her. "Wooton said he had been here for some time."

"You asked me to speak to a physician," Violet replied.

"I suppose it was too much to ask that you perhaps inform your husband before doing so?" He phrased it like a question, but did not wait for a response before halving the distance between them and seizing her hand. Most unfortunately, it was the hand with the ink-stained finger.

"I wasn't aware that such courtesies were expected between us these days," she said, hoping to distract him from the noticeable dark stain. His only reaction was an involuntary squeezing of the hand he now held firmly between his. Or *not* so involuntary, as it transpired. He flipped her hand over so her palm faced upward atop his own and began poking at it with no great finesse.

"Might I ask what you are doing?" she asked, reining in her temper with some effort. The pokes were not as gentle as they might have been. And was the ink stain visible? From this angle, likely not—but she thought it best to bring an end to these proceedings as quickly as possible.

"Checking your pulse," came the curt reply, as the hand palpitations continued.

"I think you've missed it a bit," she said dryly, as his hand inched up her inner arm.

"Yes, well, I'm not a trained physician." Was it her imagination, or was there extra emphasis on those last words?

"I know," she said, yanking her arm out of his grasp. "That's why I consulted one."

He paused a moment, eyeing her, his expression inscrutable. She thought longingly of the days when his every thought and idea had seemed to rest openly on his face when he looked at her, secrets that were hers for the taking laid bare. The fact that he hid so much of himself away from everyone else had made it feel even more special, like a gift he offered to her alone.

"And what did this physician have to say, precisely?"

She looked at him for a long moment—hadn't Lord Julian spoken to him? Had something gone amiss downstairs? She thought quickly, then hedged. "He had a good many things to say."

"What sorts of things?" he asked with deadly calm, sitting carefully down on the edge of her bed. The bed was large enough that he still was not touching her, but she braced herself with one hand to ensure that she did not accidentally roll toward the depression he had created.

"Well," she said, drawing the word into several syllables, "he seemed very interested in my lungs."

"In your lungs, or the breasts that cover them?" he asked darkly.

Violet sputtered.

His eyes, which had been fixed for a moment on the assets in question, flicked to her face. "What I meant to say," he added hastily, clearly attempting to salvage the situation, "is that I can't have a lecherous doctor treating my wife."

Violet nearly snorted. Lord Julian had barely looked at her in the time he'd been in the room, so engrossed had he been in the script in his hand; he had occasionally summoned one of the servants to bring hot water or tea, for the sake of appearances, and had at one point taken a dramatic trip to the library to consult some sort of medical text. Or so he told Wooton, who had lurked in the hallway like an anxious mother hen. Violet had never seen him so fussed.

"I don't think that Briggs had lechery in mind, my dear husband," Violet said, resisting the impulse to bat her eyelashes at him. "He was rather elderly."

"Was he?" James looked at her closely, and she felt that she was being tested, somehow, though she couldn't quite tell what exactly he wished—or didn't wish—her to say.

"He was," she confirmed, her mind on Lord Julian's absurd set of false whiskers. "You saw him, I trust? Or is your eyesight failing now, as your own age advances?" She was testing him, too, and she knew she shouldn't, but something about him had always made her want to prod at his stiff exterior until it shattered. His jaw tensed and, glancing down, she saw his hand drumming a pattern on the counterpane, one of his few tells.

"What did the doctor say, Violet?" The words were terse and clearly enunciated.

"Didn't he tell you? Or did you not speak to him?" She was hesitating, and she wasn't certain why. Hadn't she looked forward to the chance to see the look on his face when he learned of her supposed illness? Wasn't this the revenge that she had wanted? And yet, it was proving less satisfying than she had expected. James was behaving so very strangely, and she found difficulty summoning the words.

It was one thing to concoct a (thoroughly half-baked, to use Lord Julian's words) scheme; it was quite another to lie to the face of the man she had once promised before God and a church full of people to love and cherish. She'd mentally crossed her fingers when she'd gotten to the bit about obeying, but the rest of the vows she had meant wholeheartedly. The fact that for the past four years he had believed her to be (at best) a liar by omission and (at worst) conniving and manipulative did not make the telling of this lie any easier. She didn't relish the idea of being as untrustworthy as he had unfairly believed her to be.

"I did speak to him," James said, his expression unreadable. "But I was rather curious to hear what he told you."

"Well," Violet said again, "as I said, he was very interested in—"

"Your lungs, yes, I know," James said, and she was perversely pleased to hear the note of impatience in his voice. As ever, she counted it a victory whenever she managed to crack his cool facade, even for a moment.

"Consumption!" Violet burst out, and then clapped her hand over her mouth as though doing so would somehow take back the word that lingered between them. She hastily turned this movement into a small coughing fit—not one of her best, though, if she were to offer an honest evaluation of her performance.

"Yes," James said after her coughs had subsided. His tone was odd, and she gave him a long look. He met her gaze evenly, and she felt trapped, pinned to the pillows behind her by its strength. "Well," he said, standing up, his manner suddenly businesslike, "I suppose if this physician of yours is to be believed, then we had better start packing our bags."

This was not the reaction Violet had been expecting.

"I beg your pardon?"

"Our bags," James said slowly, enunciating each word clearly. "I don't suppose you plan to travel in that nightgown, lovely as it is?" Violet sat up straight, and his eyes dropped to her breasts. She was tempted to cross her arms over her chest, but the heat of his gaze kept them still at her sides. She chanced a quick glance down, wondering what had caught his attention, and realized that her sudden motion had caused the thin fabric to press against her chest in interesting ways. She leaned back slightly, letting him look his fill. She was not above admitting that it was thoroughly gratifying.

"You were saying?" she asked after a moment, feeling that this had gone on quite long enough. Although she had to admit, it considerably soothed her ego—she had wondered more than once if James had found comfort in someone else's arms during the years of their estrangement, but this seemed a tick in the box of evidence in the negative. Breasts were all very well, but no man who was enjoying bedsport on a regular basis looked at a pair with such an expression of wistful longing.

He wrenched his eyes away from the sight and blinked twice to refocus his attention on her face.

"Packing?" she prodded gently.

"Ah, yes." He took a step back, and his voice had returned to its usual distant tone. "Packing. You see, I understand that on the Continent they have sanitariums that offer rest cures for consumption, so it seems that we should pack your bags and make arrangements to leave immediately."

"To go where?" Violet asked warily.

"Switzerland."

"Switzerland!" She shoved back the blankets that covered her—it was too bloody warm in this room, anyway—and came up onto her knees. "I'm not going to Switzerland!"

"If this physician of yours is correct, and you have consumption, then I don't see that you have much choice." James looked around the room thoughtfully. "Shall I ring for Price immediately, or would you like to take a nap first? I know it's been a trying day for you." He reached out, placed a hand on her forehead. "And you *are* starting to feel feverish."

Violet swatted his hand away; playing the invalid was all well and good, but she was hardly prepared to be carted off to some patch of grass on the Continent. "I certainly am not! I'm just warm from being trapped in bed all day in the middle of the summer."

He *tsk*ed once, now reaching out to press the back of his hand against her cheek. "That's what you would say if you *were* truly feverish, so I don't know that I should trust your word in this regard." He paused, looking at her thoughtfully. Unlike when he'd been evaluating her a moment before, there was nothing remotely amorous in his eyes now.

"I am not going to bloody Switzerland!" Violet half shrieked. Belatedly remembering she was supposed to be ill, she offered a sort of hacking swoon that resulted in a not-terribly-graceful collapse back onto her pillows.

"I'm not certain I should respect your wishes in this case," James said, eyeing her with a show of concern. "Switzerland's supposed to be very healthy. All that Alpine air. And the goats."

"Goats?" Violet repeated blankly.

"Goats," James confirmed with a nod. "They're healthy sorts of creatures, aren't they?"

"Er," Violet said, words momentarily failing her.

"If Switzerland is good enough for a goat, it's good enough for you," he declared grandly.

"How very romantic," she murmured, privately wondering if perhaps an *actual* physician should be summoned to examine him. "But I don't have the slightest desire to go to Switzerland, goats or no. I'm certain that it's very lovely, but I don't think that's quite necessary yet."

"Well, a second physician certainly is." His tone was flat, and any trace of lightness that she might have seen in him was suddenly absent. He crossed his arms over his chest, and the only wildly inappropriate thought she seemed capable of summoning was that his doing so did very enticing things to the muscles in his arms.

"James, I don't want another physician," she said, only slightly belatedly. She sat up straight again, and again his eyes dropped to her chest. She really must find a different nightgown to wear, she determined—or perhaps not, on second thought, given the wicked light that gleamed in his eyes as he looked at her. "I do not feel terribly poorly, truly," she added before adding a faint cough as punctuation. She didn't want to be bedridden—and she certainly didn't want an actual physician to come and tell him she was perfectly healthy—but it wouldn't do to seem *too* much recovered.

"Briggs seemed to think that my condition would vary wildly by the day," she improvised, hoping that James knew nothing at all about the course of the illness, and cursing her own foolishness in not doing a bit of research. "He said there was no reason I shouldn't carry on with my usual activities on the days I felt up to it."

"You're in bed," he pointed out. "In the middle of the day. Clearly, you don't feel up to much of anything. Unless this is an invitation?" he added, and, to her fury, she found herself blushing. Her mind was instantly filled with memories she had done her best to suppress over the past four years, so as not to drive herself mad. Memories of bare skin, entangled limbs, the warmth of James's mouth on unspeakable parts of her body.

"I'm a bit fatigued, is all," she managed, and before she even realized what she was doing, she had reached out to place a hand over his own. He froze, his eyes looking down at their hands.

It was not that she had never touched him over the course of the past four years. A polite bow and a formal kiss on the hand were not uncommon, and he had helped her in and out of many a carriage. But those were scripted touches, ones deemed acceptable—even necessary—by society. This was sudden, unplanned, for them and them alone.

And it still felt so *right*.

Before she could think better of it and remove her hand, he had turned his palm-up, capturing hers in the grasp of his much larger hand. His grip was firm, his skin very warm against her own. She didn't dare look up at his face, instead directing her comments to their linked fingers.

"I'm certain I shall be feeling better in the morning, so there's no need to concern yourself overmuch. In fact, Diana has invited us to the theater with her tomorrow, and I should like to attend."

"The theater?" he repeated slowly, and she risked a glance upward, to find that she was being surveyed with a narrow-eyed gaze. He looked . . . suspicious. Suspicious was not good. "A bloody physician has just told you you have consumption and you want to go to the *theater?*"

"Well," Violet hedged, thinking fast—or at least, as fast as was possible when half of her attention was still devoted to the feeling of his hand clutching hers. "It's *tomorrow*, not today. And I do think I am improving already."

"This is ridiculous," he said, dropping her hand. "I am going to send for Worth at once for a second opinion, and then, if he confirms this quack's diagnosis, we can consult with him on a plan of treatment."

"Considering how my concerns and wishes were not given any thought during your recent health scare," she said through gritted teeth, "I find it a bit rich that you are attempting to be so high-handed about all of this."

He stilled, and gave her a long look that she could not interpret. She refused to be the one to break first, though, and met his eyes evenly. His green gaze traveled the length of her body, leaving a trail of heat in its wake; Violet found herself feeling exposed, vulnerable, as though every secret and desire within her were laid bare for his perusal. She was irritated to find that she would very much like him to do considerably more than look at her. With his slightly mussed hair, the color still high in his cheeks from fresh air, he was dangerously enticing.

"I see," he said at last, and there was something in the way he said it that she did not like at all, though at the very least it dragged her thoughts away from the lustful direction they had veered toward. He swore under his breath. "This is why men refuse to marry. It's not worth the bloody trouble."

"And those charming words, spoken at the bedside of your beloved wife, are the reason that I am disinclined to take your concerns into account, my lord," Violet said, an edge to her voice.

"I am leaving," he announced abruptly.

Violet sniffed. "As you wish."

"I've better things to do with my day than trade words with an unreasonable harpy."

"I wonder that men find marriage such a trial," she mused aloud. "It seems to me that ladies have far more to complain about, if this is the treatment we are to expect from our husbands." She sounded vaguely like Mrs. Bennet from *Pride and Prejudice*—a novel she had thoroughly enjoyed—but believed herself justified.

He took his leave of her with an impossibly short bow. If he allowed the door to bang shut behind him with perhaps more force than was strictly necessary—well, she supposed that every gentleman had his limits.

Six

That evening, James visited his club and proceeded to get very, very drunk. Never had he been so grateful that Penvale and Jeremy did not have wives to return home to at a reasonable hour, because they took to this activity with great enthusiasm.

It began with a brandy—or two or three—in the drawing room at White's. They then took themselves to the gaming tables, where Penvale won a tidy sum off of both Jeremy and James. There was more brandy, and a bottle of claret, before James declared himself done. He might be drunk, and he might be *extremely* angry with his wife, but that did not mean that he wished to lose so much money that he had to pawn her jewels.

Thus it was, at some ungodly hour of the morning, that the three men found themselves back in armchairs before the fire, sharing a bottle of Madeira, as James stared gloomily into the flickering flames before him.

"All right, Audley," Jeremy said suddenly, breaking what had been a momentary peaceful silence. "You smell like a distillery, so out with it. What's sent you into your cups?"

"Matrimony," James said succinctly, taking a hearty gulp of his drink. He peered into his glass. Was it empty again already? This seemed to be happening more and more quickly as the evening wore on.

"Ah," said Jeremy knowingly, leaning forward to rest his elbows on his knees. "Precisely why I haven't the slightest interest in the institution."

"Yes, well," James said darkly, continuing to stare unseeingly down into his empty glass, "I do have to give that wife of mine credit. She has outdone herself when it comes to creating new ways to make my life difficult."

"What's she done now?" Penvale asked, and James didn't think he was imagining the wariness in Penvale's voice.

Some dim part of his mind registered that sober James, or perhaps even moderately intoxicated James, would prevaricate at this point, or back away entirely from any discussion of anything to do with himself and Violet. However, excessive-amounts-of-brandy-and-wine James had a loose tongue, and little desire to mince words. "Caught consumption."

Jeremy choked on his drink. "Excuse me?" he managed, after his wheezing had subsided.

"Or at least, that's what she'd like me to believe," James continued, feeling a fresh surge of anger as he spoke. It had been devastating, four years prior, to learn that he had misplaced his trust in a woman who, as it turned out, would keep vital information from him. He, who had been so slow to trust in the past, had felt like a fool for being taken in by a pretty face and a charming laugh. Now, on his seeing further evidence of her duplicity, the pain was absent—but the anger was just as strong.

"She's been acting oddly the last couple of days, and I return home yesterday to find some charlatan of a physician leaving the premises who informs me that she might or might not have consumption, he's not quite certain." James could hear the sarcasm in his own voice as he finished speaking.

"How do you know he was a charlatan?" Jeremy asked.

James thought of the calling card with Belfry's name on it, still sitting in one of his coat pockets. "Trust me," he said. "I know." His friends, recognizing the tone that he adopted when he would not be pushed further on a given topic, didn't protest. He redirected his bleary gaze toward Penvale, who had, until this point, remained largely silent. "And it's your bloody fault for that letter, you ass."

Penvale didn't even blink. "According to my sister, everything usually is." His tone was the weary one of a man accustomed to a lifetime of unfair accusations.

"Your sister," James said, pausing, a thought occurring to him. "I'll bet she knows all about this. Don't suppose you've plans to see her anytime soon?"

"As a matter of fact, I'm engaged to escort her to the theater tomorrow," Penvale said, with all the cheer of a man facing the gallows.

James frowned. "Violet mentioned the theater tomorrow, too." Then, suddenly, the pieces fell into place. "She didn't mention which one, though. Covent Garden? Drury Lane?" he queried innocently, knowing perfectly well what Penvale's answer would be.

"No," Penvale said, shaking his head. "The Belfry."

Jeremy, who had been slouched back in his chair, swirling the contents of his glass around, sat up so quickly that some of the liquid sloshed over the side of the glass and onto his immaculately pressed breeches. "The Belfry?" he said, sounding more like an anxious mama than James would have believed possible. "You can't take ladies to the Belfry, have you gone mad?"

Penvale seemed to be considering his words with care. "Diana was recently introduced to Julian Belfry. He extended the invitation."

"I'll bet he did," Jeremy muttered, with more feeling than James would have expected.

"She asked Violet to come, too, for the sake of appearances," Penvale explained. He slumped back slightly in his chair, raising his glass to his lips in a gesture of practiced indolence that was reminiscent of his sister—Penvale and Lady Templeton both shared a particular lazy grace.

"And apparently I shall be accompanying Violet, also for the sake of appearances," James said wryly. He leaned his head back against his chair, staring unseeingly up at the ornate ceiling of White's. His mind was full of conflicting desires: the desire to catch Violet out in her lie in the most embarrassing way possible; the desire to learn how the hell Julian Belfry had gotten tangled up in all of this; the desire to tear off that bloody sheer nightgown she'd had on earlier and drag his tongue over every inch of the body that lay—

It was this enticing thought that was occupying most of his mental energy when he was dragged out of the reverie by the sound of Jeremy's voice.

"West! Fancy a drink, old chap?"

James raised his head. Sure enough, his elder brother stood before them, regarding James in particular with an expression that was a mixture of amusement and disapproval.

"West," James said shortly.

"James," his brother replied. "Rough evening?"

"Not at all," James said coldly, sitting up straighter in his chair.

West raised an eyebrow. James returned the gesture.

He could remember happier days, when conversations with his brother had not always felt like some sort of silent battle. When they'd been children, the duke had largely ignored James, focusing his attention and energies on his eldest son and heir, West. The young Marquess of Weston, it was understood, was the one the family pinned its hopes on. The future duke and steward of the land. The continuation of a long line of dukes. It was West who spent long days riding about the estate with the duke, while James was left behind in the care of a nurse or, later, a tutor.

His father's motives for favoring West had not been particularly clear at the time to a boy who had spent his entire life in a large house in the country without anything in the way of fatherly affection—and not much of the brotherly sort, either, given West's frequent absence. He had been sent to Eton, where Jeremy and Penvale had become brothers of a sort to him, and it was only after he'd taken up residence in London after finishing university that he and West had formed any sort of friendship. As an adult, James had come to realize that in some ways he, and not his brother, had received the better end of the deal in regard to their father.

The aforementioned friendship had faltered when his marriage had. Immediately on the heels of his argument with Violet, James—admittedly in a rather prickly mood—had quarreled with West, ostensibly over the management of the Audley House stables, but more broadly over their father's role in his life, his marriage, and his relationship with his brother.

Their conversations in the recent past had been less warm than they once had been.

"West, have you plans for tomorrow evening?" Jeremy asked, interrupting James's line of thought.

West refocused his attention from his brother. "Nothing specific."

"Come to the Belfry with us then. We're bringing the ladies," Jeremy added in a conspiratorial whisper.

West stilled, looking suddenly and without warning very ducal. His gloves, which he had been slapping lightly against one of his thighs, ceased moving, and everything about him—from his perfectly tied neckcloth to the shine on his shoes—screamed disapproval. "The ladies?" he repeated in a deceptively mild tone. He shifted the walking stick he had used ever since the curricle accident from his side to his front, bracing it with both hands.

"Just my sister and Violet," Penvale added quickly, but this did not seem to mollify West in the least. His dark gaze left Penvale and Jeremy and refocused on James with greater intensity. James and his brother shared a striking physical resemblance: both were tall and broad of shoulder, with similarly disheveled dark curls and memorably green eyes. From a distance, the only difference between them was the slight limp that had plagued West's gait since the age of twenty-four.

"How can you possibly be considering escorting your wife to a place like the Belfry?" West asked, giving James a glimpse of the formidable duke he would one day become. His voice was mild, and he was careful to speak quietly enough to ensure that no one beyond Penvale and Jeremy overheard them, but James could sense the anger lurking behind his words.

James rose, feeling this was a conversation for which he would like to be at eye level with his brother. "If you must know, my wife asked me to escort her," he said evenly, hoping that he was giving nothing away through his tone. Other than Violet, West had always been the person best able to see through his cool demeanor.

"On friendly terms with her again?" West asked, arching a brow.

James's fist clenched, but he merely said, "No."

West broke first. "Do what you want, James." He shifted his cane back into one hand and took a step back. "I assume this is the latest parry in your never-ending war." He nodded at Jeremy and Penvale in turn and turned back to James for one final parting shot. "I suppose I shall see you at the Belfry tomorrow, then."

"But—"

"If you're determined to risk your wife's reputation rather than have any sort of honest conversation with her, then I suppose, for the sake of the family, I shall have to join you to control the damage." And with that, he made an unhurried exit.

"Bastard," James muttered, staring after him a moment before dropping back into his chair.

Jeremy watched West's exit from the room with interest. "How does he manage to make a limp look so elegant?" he wondered aloud to no one in particular.

"Shall I cripple you, to give you some practice?" James asked pleasantly.

"If this is what marriage does to a man's temper, I shall continue to avoid it," Jeremy shot back.

James sank back into his chair and generously refilled his glass from the bottle of Madeira at hand. He took a healthy sip.

"What are you going to do, Audley?" Jeremy asked more quietly, his tone uncommonly serious.

James rolled his head to the side to look at his friends. "I'm going to play her game," he said decisively, taking another sip from his glass. The room was beginning to look fuzzy around the edges, and he knew he would have a devil of a headache in the morning, but he couldn't bring himself to care at the moment. "And if that requires going to Julian Belfry's bloody theater, then so be it."

There was nothing, Violet reflected the following evening, quite so satisfying as a well-thought-out plan, executed perfectly.

Or so she imagined. She would not know from personal experience. Her own plan, as it were, was proving to be slightly more frustrating than anticipated.

She had awoken that morning, eager to feign a brilliant recovery from the previous day's illness, but no sooner had she rung her bell to summon Price than she received a visit from her husband. Unlike the previous afternoon, however, he had not lingered; he had merely hovered in the doorway, informing her that he was leaving for his morning ride and that he had given strict instructions to the servants to ensure that she remained abed all day.

"To preserve your strength," he said solemnly, and then had departed, so quickly that the pillow she had flung to the floor in consternation and the unladylike oath she had uttered had been observed by no one.

The day that had followed had been dissatisfying, to put it politely.

To put it impolitely, she had felt like throwing herself out the bloody window.

One day in bed, particularly when one is, in fact, in the pink of health, is tiresome; two days confined are nearly intolerable. Prior to her "illness," she had been engaged in cataloguing the complete contents of the library in preparation for a complete reorganization. She couldn't very well spend her entire day on a ladder in the library, but she had already read all of the most recent editions of the periodicals to which she subscribed and written enough letters to the editor that she felt a satisfying sense of accomplishment, and yet still the hours stretched ahead of her. She picked up and set aside a dozen books in turn. She even, in a fit of desperation, penned a note to her mother, inviting her to tea the following day. And still, it was only midmorning.

Deciding there was only so much one could tolerate, she rang for Price. At the request she made, her lady's maid's calm demeanor slipped for a moment—but only a moment. She then offered a curtsey and a calm "Yes, my lady," as though this request were nothing out of the ordinary. Violet, pleased, leaned back against her pillows and waited.

By late afternoon, she had a pleasing routine worked out. Price would bring her a stack of books—only a few at a time, in case she were observed by Wooton or one of the footmen—and Violet, using the makeshift desk she had created for herself (her tea tray, cleared of its china), would scribble away at the stack of papers that currently comprised her catalogue. While she was working, Price would remove any books with which she was finished, return them to the library, and reappear with a fresh stack. It was perhaps not ideal, but it was certainly better than twiddling her thumbs and reading *Pamela* for the tenth time.

At some point in the afternoon, she detected voices in the entry-way downstairs, and she leapt to her feet, nearly upsetting her ink bottle in the process. She shoved the catalogue, pen, and ink back into her bedside table drawer, but what to do with the books? They wouldn't fit, and judging by the pace of the footsteps, she had no time to scamper to her desk, which she had resisted using in the event that a maid came in unannounced and should see her sitting there rather than languishing piteously in her bed. She didn't *think* James would stoop so low as to have the servants spy on her, but she supposed she couldn't be too careful. Lacking any other options, she buried the remaining three books underneath her pillows and flung herself back into bed, noting with satisfaction that she had managed to avoid any ink splotches. She picked up the closest thing to hand—the *Lady's*

Monthly Museum, which she had left nearby to be utilized in the event of just such an emergency—and affected an air of great interest in its contents as she heard a firm knock at her door.

"Enter," she called, idly flicking a page. She avoided looking up, leaning forward to focus on the rather maudlin bit of poetry on the page before her.

There was a rather loud throat-clearing from the direction of the doorway.

Violet turned another page.

"Violet."

She looked up innocently.

"Yes?"

James was standing in the doorway, his tall form leaning slightly against the doorframe. He was dressed for riding, and her eyes could not help dropping to admire the clinging cut of his buckskin breeches. His jacket was a dark, dark green, which served to make his eyes stand out even more vividly. Her heartbeat quickened at the sight of him, in spite of their estrangement, just as it had when she was eighteen and so very foolishly in love.

He was staring at her with an unreadable expression. Violet arched a brow.

"Are you feeling improved this evening?" he asked at last, not moving from his position by the door.

"Quite," Violet said, flipping shut her magazine and casting it aside. She batted her eyelashes sickeningly. "No doubt owing to following your wise counsel to remain in bed, my lord and master."

Something flashed across his face at her sarcasm, so quickly that she could not identify it before it was gone. "Still feeling well enough for the theater this evening, then?"

"Indeed," Violet said, sitting up straighter. "Diana sent word that she and Penvale would come collect us in her carriage, so we might all attend together."

"We have a perfectly good carriage of our own."

"But it's more *fun* to all arrive together, don't you think?"

"To be squeezed so that we can barely breathe, you mean?"

"Don't be churlish." Violet folded her arms across her chest to indicate that she was done with the discussion. James threw his hands in the air and departed, muttering something about not bothering to have his valet press his breeches if he were going to be packed so tightly into a conveyance that he would have to sit on Penvale's lap. Violet jumped out of bed and began her evening preparations.

So it was that she now found herself mere inches from her husband as Diana's carriage rattled across the cobblestone streets of London. They had entered the carriage some minutes before to find Emily sitting beside Diana instead of Penvale

"Penvale has abandoned me to the ladies, I see," James remarked as he entered, having already handed Violet in.

"He and Willingham elected to travel separately when it transpired that I needed his seat for Emily," Diana said serenely.

"And how, exactly, did you induce your mother to allow you to come?" Violet asked Emily as she settled her skirts around herself.

"Diana can be very persuasive," Emily said with a small smile.

"Lady Rowanbridge was unconvinced of my suitability as a chaperone," Diana said disdainfully. "But when she learned that you and Audley would be not just attending but in the very carriage with us, she decided that it was acceptable." She coughed delicately. "I may have taken your suggestion, Violet, and misled her as to which precise theater it is that we will be attending."

Emily's and Diana's presence went some way toward lightening the atmosphere inside the carriage, which would otherwise have been rife with tension between husband and wife. This was not an entirely new experience for Violet—after all, she and James had had precious little to say to each other for the past four years, but they had taken a fair number of carriage rides together—and yet somehow the silence between them tonight felt entirely different from their usual cool ones. She felt . . . *aware* of him in a way that she had not in some time. It was not, of course, that she had ever ceased to find him handsome, or that she had not tossed and turned on more than one night, imagining him sleeping one room away, her mind lingering entirely too long on the question of whether he still slept naked—a question that no respectable lady should devote so much thought to, of course. But Violet felt that she never had been entirely respectable, particularly where James was concerned. When she had descended the stairs tonight and seen him awaiting her, immaculately dressed in black and white evening clothes, she had wanted to rip his carefully tied cravat from his throat and lick him.

So: not respectable.

"I was surprised you asked me to the theater this evening," Emily said, breaking the silence. "I thought you loathed *Romeo and Juliet*, Violet." Emily looked much as she always did, which was to say, beautiful. Her golden hair was pulled back neatly, and she was dressed in an evening gown of pale blue silk, the neckline modest enough to be entirely correct for an unmarried lady, and yet offering the slightest tantalizing glimpse of creamy skin.

Next to her, Violet felt rather more daring. She had been extremely irritated as she dressed, still thinking about James's orders to keep her confined to her room all day, and had purposefully selected a dress that was several years old, one that he had laughingly told her she shouldn't wear for anyone but him. In fact, this was the first time Violet *had* worn it before anyone other than her husband—she had bought it for the purpose of dining à deux on the terrace, as they used to do on summer evenings in the early days of their marriage, and it featured a bodice that was daring enough to ensure that they had never once finished their meal before becoming distracted by more pressing physical hungers.

Now, sitting in the carriage, she smoothed the violet silk over her knees, casting a quick glance at James as she did so. Her traitorous heart thumped a quick beat. There was not a single gentleman of the *ton* whose appearance was not improved by the elegance of a well-tailored jacket and a perfectly tied neckcloth, but none of them, as far as Violet was concerned, could match James. His dark hair was combed back, leaving nothing to distract from the strong lines of his face, his arresting eyes.

Why, Violet wondered in a moment of self-pity, did he have to be so hopelessly beautiful? So beautiful that she still caught her breath sometimes, wondering that she had once caught his attention? It would be so much easier to nurse her anger, to keep it burning hot and bright, if she were not still, on some level, the same besotted girl she had been when she met him.

Violet was dimly aware of Diana responding to Emily's comment, but she scarcely heard her, so distracted was she by the man beside her. James had been gazing out the window of the carriage, but he suddenly glanced at her as though drawn by her eyes on him.

"I'm pleased to see you looking so well, darling," he said, and there was a sardonic note to the term of endearment that Violet didn't like. "Do let me know if you begin feeling unwell at any point in the evening, and I shall endeavor to remove you from our box before you commence coughing over all of our companions."

Violet narrowed her eyes. He looked at her evenly, without blinking, and she found herself unable to look away. She knew he was angry with her over her refusal to summon another physician, and yet some part of her thrilled to hear the edge in his tone. She hadn't realized, until the past few days, how much she had missed hearing something, *anything*, in his voice other than cool politeness. He seemed likely to throttle her at any moment, it was true, but somehow this didn't concern her as much as it perhaps should have.

"Thank you, my lord," she said in a voice of calculated sweetness. "I did bring a handkerchief along with me, so I think I shall be able to manage. Your concern is much appreciated, but—" She paused to stifle a carefully calibrated cough in her sleeve. "—I received plenty of advice and wisdom from Dr. Briggs, and it rather renders your contribution unnecessary."

A muscle in James's jaw twitched, and for a moment he was silent. Opposite Violet, Emily shifted, clearly uncomfortable.

Before Emily could intervene with some sort of polite inquiry to break the tension, James spoke again. "Very well, darling," he said, his eyes still on Violet. "I shan't trouble myself a moment more about you, then."

He returned his gaze to the carriage window, and Violet felt suddenly oddly discontent. *That* wasn't what she wanted at all.

She hadn't long to stew over his words, however, for the carriage soon slowed to a halt and the door was opened. James exited first, then stood waiting, his hand outstretched. This contact—the touch dictated by politeness when entering and exiting a carriage—was often the only physical contact Violet and James had for weeks at a time. Even through the fabric of her gloves and his, she could feel the warmth of his hand, its steady strength. She should not have been so comforted by it.

A moment later, however, the contact was broken as James unceremoniously dropped her hand and reached up to help Emily down in turn—with rather more gallantry, Violet noticed.

"It is a shame Mr. Cartham was unable to join us this evening," James said to Emily, his tone indicating that he felt just the opposite. "But I see it has worked in my favor, as I now have two ladies on my arm, rather than just one."

He extended his other arm to Violet without looking at her, his attention still focused on Emily and her murmured reply, and Violet took it with bad grace. She would have liked nothing better than to drop his arm and storm ahead of him into the theater unescorted—well, no. She would have liked that, it is true, but she could think of several things she would have enjoyed doing even more. Near the top of that list was stabbing James's well-muscled, perfectly garbed arm with a letter opener.

However, bloodshed did have an odd way of spoiling an evening—and seemed like behavior ill befitting a sometimes-invalid. She paused to spare an idle thought for a time when James had not treated her as though she were a rather inconvenient and recalcitrant sheep, and allowed him to escort her and Emily into the theater, Diana trailing behind them on the arm of her brother, who had arrived directly in their wake.

The Belfry, despite its scandalous reputation, was a beautiful theater, both outside and within. The building Lord Julian had selected was an elegant neoclassical concoction near Haymarket, and Violet could not help but stare admiringly at the columns framing the entrance as James swept her between them. Inside, the Belfry was even more impressive, sumptuously appointed in velvet and silk in varying shades of blue and green. It wasn't at all what she had been imagining—she had had in her mind something akin to a tawdry imitation of a brothel—and she now better understood why Lord Julian was so determined to make the establishment respectable. Such a space deserved a more illustrious crowd than dissolute aristocrats and their mistresses.

At the moment, however, that was who surrounded them. Violet recognized half a dozen men she knew, viscounts and earls and, heavens, even a marquess, but not a single one was with the woman she was accustomed to seeing him escort. She tried very hard to seem worldly and bored, but she was, in fact, slightly shocked. She knew, of course, that fidelity was hardly universal among the *ton*, and that love matches such as hers were exceedingly rare, but to see the evidence of these gentlemen's extramarital activities was another thing entirely.

She had married for love—well, love, and because she'd been compromised—but that was a decidedly less romantic explanation, and one that she generally chose to ignore. She and James had discussed it more than once, and he had told her that even had they not been discovered on that balcony, he would likely have proposed within a fortnight.

"Truly? A fortnight?" Violet had asked on the first occasion upon which this had been discussed.

"At most," James said with a masculine grin. He leaned toward her to place a lingering kiss upon her lips, one Violet felt from her head to her toes.

She and James had made a hash of their supposedly great love match in the end—but that first year had been often glorious. Lazy mornings in bed. Long hours together in the library. Evenings out at the theater and musicales, making occasional eye contact and sharing the knowledge of what delights awaited them upon their return home.

Oh, how she missed it.

Yes, she would admit that much—she could not, *would* not admit to missing James himself, but she was not too proud to admit that she missed what they'd had, what their marriage had once been. It had not been perfect by any stretch of the imagination—James had often infuriated her almost beyond bearing, and yet they had always managed to make it up. Until one day they couldn't.

Now, standing here in this beautiful theater, surrounded by men with women who were not their wives, she suffered a small pang of uncertainty. Had James come here before? It had been four years since they had shared a bed; had he truly remained celibate that entire time? She had always assumed he had, had assumed that he was as miserable as she. Had that been naiveté?

James, with his usual abysmal timing, chose that moment to speak to her.

"Try not to look so shocked, darling, it's very unfashionable."

Violet resisted the temptation to grind her slipper into his foot. Instead, she smiled sweetly up at him and said, "I'm not shocked at all, my lord. I'm taking notes."

She felt the arm beneath her hand stiffen, and a surge of triumph raced through her. *Point to Violet.*

James gave her a narrow look but said nothing more, instead turning back to Emily to respond to some unheard inquiry. As he spoke, Emily gazed past him to Violet, raising an eyebrow inquisitively. Violet smiled back at her.

As they made their way to the box that Lord Julian had reserved for them, Violet could not help but be aware that they were attracting some attention. She had expected this to some degree, of course—three gently bred ladies, one of them unmarried, could not attend a theater with a reputation like the Belfry's without arousing some notice—but she wondered if they had miscalculated by inviting Emily along. She and Diana had thought merely to give Emily an evening out without her mother watching her like a hawk, or the odious Mr. Cartham's unwelcome attentions, but she was now second-guessing this decision. Emily was unmarried, and easily shocked. Who knew what the sight of this blatant parade of mistresses would do to her delicate sensibilities?

"Did you see that lady's bodice?" Emily hissed gleefully at Violet as James led them down the green-carpeted hallway that housed the theater's most exclusive boxes. "I don't know how she even *moved*." She cast a not-terribly-surreptitious glance back over her shoulder. "I should like to ask her how it manages to stay up," she added thoughtfully. "Her modiste must be very clever."

"*Emily*," Violet said severely, at the same time that James made an odd choking sound that, after a moment, Violet realized was a barely suppressed laugh.

"I do not think that *lady* is the appropriate word to use to describe that woman, Lady Emily," he said a moment later, having somehow managed to school his features into a somber expression.

"Yes, yes, my lord, I do realize she's a doxy," Emily said impatiently, waving her hand as though this distinction were too insignificant to even warrant her notice. "But that gown was some sort of scientific marvel. I should dearly love to see how it was made."

"Well," Violet said, "I expect she shall be taking it off with a fair amount of haste at some point in the next few hours, so perhaps you could follow her and the viscount and snatch it away whilst they are in the midst of a passionate embrace." For a fleeting moment, James caught her glance, the lines around his eyes crinkling slightly in amusement. In that instant, it was as though the past four years had never happened, as though they were still in the habit of sharing private jokes, of allowing their eyes to meet across a crowded room and reveling in the knowledge that they understood one another better than anyone else.

It was just a moment, however, and then Violet averted her gaze.

They arrived at their box at last, and were followed in by Penvale, Diana, and Jeremy, who were close on their heels.

"Emily, darling, I can still scarcely believe you are here," Diana said gleefully, dropping her brother's arm as soon as the door to the box closed behind them.

"Nor can I," Emily admitted. "You're very convincing, I must say."

"Your mother shall have an absolute fit if she ever finds out," Diana said cheerfully.

"And your reputation could be harmed," Violet added, more seriously.

Emily's mouth quirked up at the corners in a smile that Violet wasn't sure she'd ever seen before. "I know. And I find myself not terribly bothered by either prospect."

At this juncture, Penvale and Jeremy performed the requisite bows and hand kisses before engaging James in conversation, and Violet could not help but be strangely aware of their presence behind her, all of her nerves sensitized. It was as though her very skin was attuned to James's proximity, in a way it hadn't been since the early days of their marriage.

No doubt it was a simple result of having seen him more often than usual of late, she told herself firmly.

". . . that dress, Violet," Diana was saying, and Violet started, realizing she hadn't been attending to anything her friends were saying.

"I'm sorry?" she asked, a trifle guiltily.

"I *said*," Diana said patiently, "that I don't believe I've ever seen you wear that dress before." She cast it an approving glance. "I must say, I do like it."

"Of course you do." Diana's own gown, which was a deep shade of green with intricate beadwork on the sleeves, was as daring as Violet's own—and yet Violet knew it to be far from the most scandalous dress in Diana's wardrobe. She had to admit that the effect was enticing, however—Diana's impressive bosom was displayed to great effect, and the green of the gown brought out the green flecks in her lovely hazel eyes. Violet wondered if this was for the benefit of Lord Julian. He had not been as taken in by her charms as men tended to be upon meeting Diana, and yet she could certainly be stubborn. If she had truly decided to take a lover at last, Violet wasn't sure how well she liked Lord Julian's chances in the face of Diana's resolve.

Further conversation was forestalled by the arrival of Lord Julian himself. He was, just as he had been at Diana's dinner, very handsome; the black and white of evening attire suited him as well as it did any man, and he wore his clothes well, with the air of confidence that is natural to a man who has been told since birth that he is special, favored above other men. Even when a man cast off that world, as Lord Julian had done, the confidence seemed to linger.

"Audley," he said, shaking James's hand easily, showing no sign of even remote discomfort. "I've not seen you in an age, I don't think."

"Belfry," James said, and there was something ever so slightly *odd* about his voice as he spoke. Violet looked at him sharply, but there was nothing unusual in his expression—not that that was saying much, of course. "It was good of you to invite us." Was Violet imagining the wryness to his tone?

Lord Julian shrugged lazily as he shook Penvale's and Jeremy's hands in turn. "I ran into Penvale at dinner the other day," he said, which was true enough, as things stood. "He mentioned that he still saw a fair amount of yourself and Willingham, and I thought you chaps might enjoy an evening out. Especially with such lovely company," he said, flashing a winning smile at Violet, Diana, and Emily. "I don't believe we've been introduced," Lord Julian added, and Violet had to fight hard to suppress a smile.

"My wife, Lady James," James said, stepping back toward Violet and touching her elbow lightly. In the early days of their marriage, he had always included her first name as well as her courtesy title when introducing her, unlike most gentlemen of the *ton*—not that any gentleman would be so bold, or rude, to refer to her with such familiarity, but James had done so nonetheless. It was a small breach of social norms, but one that Violet hadn't realized she'd appreciated until he'd ceased doing so.

"And this is my sister, Lady Templeton," Penvale added, with a lazy nod toward Diana. Not that it was necessary—even if Diana and Lord Julian hadn't already met, it would have been obvious which lady was Penvale's relation.

"And their friend Lady Emily Turner," James finished. Lord Julian, who had bowed over Violet's and Diana's hands in turn, redirected his attention toward Emily, who had lurked slightly in the shadows, escaping his interest until now. He paused for a brief second before bowing over her hand.

"Lady Emily," he said, straightening. "I believe we have an acquaintance in common."

"Indeed, sir?" Emily's voice was, as ever, carefully calibrated—not so warm as to seem overfamiliar, not so cool as to seem rude.

"Indeed. A Mr. Cartham, I believe, counts himself among your many admirers?" Violet detected a distinct note of distaste in Lord Julian's tone at the name, though there was nothing in his expression to betray what his opinion of Cartham might be.

At the sound of Cartham's name, Emily stiffened almost imperceptibly—Violet wasn't even certain that Lord Julian noticed. She dearly wished in that moment that the rules of etiquette allowed her to jab an unmarried man she had purportedly just met in the mid-section.

"Yes," Emily said, her tone one of polite disinterest. "I am indeed acquainted with Mr. Cartham, though my admirers are not so numerous as you seem to believe, my lord. I fear you have been badly misinformed."

"I am never that, Lady Emily," Lord Julian replied, and Violet watched him with renewed interest. There was something in his manner that struck her as odd; the intensity of his gaze on Emily was out of proportion to anything Violet would expect of a gentleman being introduced to a lady. His expression undoubtedly held appreciation for Emily's charms, but there was something else, something apprais-ing in the way he looked at her that Violet felt must somehow be related to his apparent familiarity with—and possible distaste for—Mr. Cartham.

"But," he added, as though he, too, became suddenly aware of the oddness of the moment, "the reports of your beauty, I am pleased to see, are not exaggerated in the least."

"You are very kind, my lord," Emily said demurely, but she con-tinued to look at him curiously even as Lord Julian redirected his attention to the group at large, with something in her gaze that Violet couldn't quite translate. Appreciation of his appearance, certainly—any lady with a pulse would have felt as much. But curiosity, too—and it was unusual for Emily to allow anything as telling as curiosity to show on her face, given her usually perfect composure.

"I hope that you enjoy the show this evening—it's a production of *Romeo and Juliet* that I'm quite pleased with, if I may be perfectly honest."

"Are you not performing in the play, my lord?" Diana asked.

"No." He shook his head. "We are in the midst of preparations for an upcoming production of *Macbeth* that I shall be performing in instead, and that has occupied much of my time."

"A far better choice, in any case," Violet said briskly. "There is no play quite so silly as *Romeo and Juliet*."

"Darling," James said dryly, "I am not entirely certain one can ignore the silliness of a production that involves three witches surrounding a cauldron in the woods."

"*Macbeth* has atmosphere," Violet said airily. "*Romeo and Juliet* is a melodramatic cautionary tale warning against the dangers of jumping to conclusions." The group stared at her. "Not that we're not terribly grateful for the invitation, Lord Julian," she added hastily.

"Quite," Lord Julian said dryly, but he flashed her a quick grin to assure her that he hadn't taken offense. It was a potent weapon, that grin.

Further conversation was forestalled by the dimming of the lights, indicating that it was time to take their seats. Violet found herself positioned between her husband and Lord Julian, with Emily on Lord Julian's other side. As she leaned past James to ask a question of Penvale, who was on his other side, she caught sight of James casting a scrutinizing look over her shoulder toward something she couldn't see.

She glanced behind her, only to discover that what had caught James's attention was the sight of Lord Julian engaging Emily in conversation, their voices so low as to be nearly inaudible.

After a brief moment of panic that James's attention to Lord Julian was evidence of some suspicion on his part, Violet relaxed, realizing that James must be concerned for Emily's virtue—a fair consideration, given Lord Julian's reputation. She frowned slightly, wishing he would set his sights on Diana instead—she would be a far more appropriate and willing source of entertainment for a gentleman such as himself.

With these thoughts to occupy her, she paid little attention to the action occurring onstage, and it seemed as though mere moments had passed when intermission arrived.

"And how have you found the play thus far, Lady James?" Lord Julian inquired as they all rose from their seats.

"Most illuminating," Violet said untruthfully. She was fairly certain that the actors playing Romeo and Juliet could waltz into this very box and she wouldn't be able to recognize them, so little had she attended to the proceedings onstage.

"And what of you, Belfry?" James asked abruptly over Violet's shoulder. She twisted her head around to stare at him—his tone was so curt as to border on rude. James was many things, but coolly polite was almost always one of them. "How did you find the performances?"

"I think the actor playing Romeo is overplaying the love scene, but otherwise, I've no complaints."

"Of course," James said, though Violet had the distinct impression that he hadn't taken a word of Lord Julian's reply. "I just thought it would be interesting to hear your opinion, as an actor. After all, you must play so many interesting roles."

"Darling," Violet said through gritted teeth, reaching back to press her slipper down upon his shoe. "I'm certain you don't mean to interrogate Lord Julian at his own theater. In this lovely box, which he so kindly invited us to use."

James smiled down at her blandly. "Of course not, my dear. And such a kind, generous invitation it was, too."

Lord Julian gave them both a pleasant smile. "I must beg you to excuse me—there is a matter I need to attend to during intermission."

As soon as he had left the box, Violet rounded on her husband.

"What is wrong with you?" she whispered.

Before James had the chance to reply, however, the door to the box opened once more. Violet turned, expecting Lord Julian had forgotten something before he left, but instead, to her surprise, James's brother West stood in the entrance.

"West!" she cried, moving past her husband with her hand outstretched. A genuine smile crossed his face at the sight of her, making him appear several years younger and even more like her own husband. The resemblance between the two brothers was stronger than usual, as they were wearing nearly identical evening kit. West leaned his cane against the wall to take Violet's hand.

"Violet, darling," he said, and in a tone entirely different from the one James employed when he used that particular term of endearment. "You're looking well." From just behind her, she heard the sound of a derisive snort; she shot a glance over her shoulder, only to see James watching her with a look of bland geniality that she was not fooled by for a moment. Not wishing to cause a scene, however, she turned back to West.

"I could say the same for you," she said, dropping his hands and stepping back to give him an appraising once-over. Completely aside from West's handsome face, his height, his broad shoulders, there was something simply so entirely *masculine* about him that Violet had no trouble at all understanding why every eligible and not-so-eligible lady in London paused whenever he entered a room. There had not been so much as a whiff of rumor about a mistress surrounding him since before his curricle accident, however; the *ton* seemed divided on whether he was merely uncommonly discreet, or whether to view him as something of a romantic figure, mired in the tragedy of his past. The latter speculation was, in Violet's opinion, unforgivably maudlin, but she did know that he'd had a tendre for a particular lady of the *ton* before his accident—a lady who had married shortly after said accident, in fact.

"West," James said, joining them and reaching out to shake his brother's hand. "What are you doing here?"

"Did you forget that I told you just yesterday that I would be here?" West asked pleasantly. "You were rather in your cups, so I suppose I should make allowances for your memory."

Violet looked sharply at her husband. James liked to drink, of course, as any gentleman of the *ton* did, but she had never seen him outright drunk—though she supposed, on reflection, that he could be foxed at his club all the time, and she'd never know a thing about it. The thought upset her.

"I recollect perfectly, thank you," James said, a definite edge to his voice. "I thought you were joking."

"And why would you possibly have assumed that?"

Violet knew nothing of the source of their tension, but deciding that some sort of intervention was necessary, she quickly said, "West, you must come to dinner sometime soon. We should be happy to have you. Wouldn't we, darling?" she asked James, batting her eyelashes at him.

He narrowed his eyes.

She, still batting, narrowed hers in return.

"Is something in your eye, Violet?" West asked politely.

She gave him a radiant smile. "Not at all. But you'll come to dinner?"

"I'm not sure he should," James said slowly.

"Whyever not?"

"Well," he said solemnly, "I'm not certain your health would permit such an ordeal as playing the hostess."

"Are you ill, Violet?" West inquired, looking concerned. How nice it would be to have her *husband* look at her with such an expression, rather than the look of vague boredom that currently marked his handsome features.

"It's nothing at all," Violet said airily, waving a hand. "A mere trifling cough."

"That kept you abed for two days," James said.

"No," Violet said, smiling dazzlingly at him. "It kept me abed for *one* day. You kept me abed for the second."

There was a beat of silence. Violet's face heated to such a degree that she was certain one could fry an egg on it—not that she knew what was involved in frying an egg. But a great deal of heat was required, she would imagine.

Then, to her utmost astonishment, James slid an arm around her waist, pinning her to his side. It was wildly inappropriate, of course; her mother likely would have swooned had she been present. (But wasn't that always the case?) She looked up and met his gaze and saw, in the crinkles around his eyes, the telltale signs of barely suppressed mirth.

"I appreciate your concern for my fragile ego," he said, "but there's no need to lie about my stamina." He lowered his voice then, speaking so softly that she did not think even West, closest to them, could hear. "It's impressive enough without embellishment, as I believe you know."

Violet leaned closer as well, their faces now mere inches apart. "I am going to stab you with a hairpin if you do not remove your arm from my waist."

Even as she spoke, however, she could feel it pulsing between them: that wild, reckless energy that had always seemed to draw them together, from the very first evening on that balcony. She imagined herself throwing propriety to the wind and sliding her arms around his neck, dragging his mouth down to her own. The mere thought sent heat crawling up her neck, and she hoped the dim lighting within the box would conceal the telltale flush upon her cheeks.

"Ahem," West said extremely dryly.

Violet took a quick step away from James, breaking his hold upon her person.

"Yes, well, I am feeling much improved," she said quickly, as though nothing at all out of the ordinary had disrupted their conversation.

"I should be feeling the same, were I permitted to enjoy an evening out without a nursemaid dogging my steps." James's tone was bland, but there was a razor-sharp edge underlying it, and Violet was mildly shocked at his rudeness to West. She risked a glance at her brother-in-law and saw that, far from looking offended, West was eyeing his younger brother speculatively. She would have given a fair amount of coin to have been a fly on the wall at White's whenever they had met there, but as a lady, she could not even be respectably seen in a carriage on St. James's, much less within the walls of White's itself.

"Would you like to join us, West?" Violet asked. "We've plenty of seats." This was certainly true—Lord Julian's box was spacious, and luxuriously appointed.

West refocused his attention on her, offering her a warm smile. "I should be delighted, Violet. Thank you."

And so it was that Violet passed the remainder of the play seated between her husband and his brother, aware of the tension simmering between them, and yet unaware of its underlying cause.

All in all, it was a thoroughly vexing evening.

Seven

"*What the blazes is going on?*"

The following morning, James had awoken at dawn. He had taken his usual early-morning ride in Hyde Park, but the crisp air and sunlight had failed to have their usual invigorating effect upon him. He had returned to Curzon Street only to be informed by Wooton that Lady James was feeling poorly again, and had requested a breakfast tray be sent up to her. James had been strongly tempted to burst into her room again and demand some sort of an explanation, but he held off. He did not entirely understand the game that Violet was playing, but he knew that he did not want to play his next hand without careful consideration.

A reasonable man might simply confront her with the facts as he understood them: she was not ill; she had somehow hoodwinked a dissolute aristocrat into pretending to be her doctor; this was all some sort of misguided attempt to get his attention. Well, if that was her goal, she had thoroughly succeeded; he had not spent so much mental energy on his wife in years. He had a sneaking suspicion that confronting her would lead to a screaming row, and he liked to at least understand what he was rowing about before getting himself ensnared in one.

He directed his coachman to an address on Duke Street. *Marriage*, he thought, with great disgust. It had its definite advantages, to be sure, but he was beginning to believe that even his favorite evenings spent in bed with Violet had not quite been worth all this trouble.

But then, there'd been that one occasion, on the dining room table...

Lost in happy reminiscences, he was at his destination before he'd expected, and mere moments later he found himself being shown into a masculine drawing room, with walls papered in dark burgundy and filled with heavy oak furniture, by a surprised-looking servant. James assumed the man's confusion was owing to the unfashionably early hour but discovered, upon entering the room, that the servant's surprise was likely due to the fact that, despite the hour, James was not Lord Julian's first visitor of the morning.

"Penvale." James's voice was flat, but he found himself less shocked than he should have been. He waited for the door to close behind the footman, who had assured him that Lord Julian would be down shortly.

"Audley." Penvale, who had been slumped in an armchair, stood up hastily. He pasted onto his face a look of practiced innocence, but James had known the man long enough to see through it. It was eerily reminiscent of the look Penvale had given the authorities at Eton upon being questioned about the sudden appearance of several impressively large toads in the bed of a particularly loathed classmate.

"Fancy seeing you here." James strolled into the room, examining a painting of a horse rearing on its hind legs and trying to keep his temper in check. "I wouldn't expect to find you out of bed at this hour— it's not even noon yet."

Penvale remained silent. James continued toward the fireplace, resting his arm upon the mantel above the empty hearth.

"I expect it would be too much of a coincidence for you to be paying a simple social call on Belfry at"—James checked the grandfather clock upon the wall—"ten past eleven in the morning."

Behind him, Penvale heaved a great sigh. After nearly twenty years of friendship, James was familiar with that sigh, and felt a surge of triumph: it was a sigh of resignation.

"What do you want to know?"

James turned. Penvale glanced up at him.

"What the deuce is going on?" he demanded.

"I'm going to need you to be a bit more specific." Penvale tugged at his collar.

"Well," James said pleasantly, "let me see. Specifically, could you tell me why Julian Belfry showed up at my house masquerading as a physician, informed me my wife had consumption, and then departed?"

Penvale dropped back down into his seat. "When did you learn Belfry was the physician?"

"I don't know," James said, mock thoughtful. "Perhaps when he dropped his card into my hand upon departing?"

Penvale's head shot up. "You knew it was him from the beginning? Why didn't you say so yesterday?" He paused. "And what the bloody hell is Belfry playing at? Violet shall eviscerate him when she finds out."

"I've little interest in understanding the workings of Julian Belfry's mind," James said shortly. "Though I've half a mind to call him out—the bastard visited my wife in her bedchamber. Christ." He felt a surge of anger at the thought. A small, unwelcome part of him asked him what right he had to anger—after all, he'd spent the better part of four years doing his best to ignore Violet. Did that not mean he forfeited some of his right to husbandly outrage? "I'm more interested in learning what,

133

precisely, my darling wife thinks she's doing." He speared Penvale with a glance. "And how it is that you've found yourself mixed up in it all."

"The answer to that should be obvious." Penvale's tone was dark.

James hazarded a guess. "Your sister?"

"She wouldn't leave me alone until I agreed to arrange a meeting between Belfry and your wife."

"She's your younger sister. I would have thought you could manage to outwit her now that you've achieved the age of eight-and-twenty."

"That is mere proof that you don't have a sister," Penvale replied.

James began to pace. "So—and please correct me if I am wrong— you are telling me that you were bullied by a couple of young ladies."

Penvale paused. James could practically see the wheels in his mind turning, weighing his options, the potential loss of dignity that would result from admitting to being bested by his sister and his best friend's wife, and then—

"Yes," Penvale said, more cheerfully now. "That's about the shape of it."

James resisted, with great effort, the urge to seize Penvale by the neckcloth and shake him. He had always thought that his distrust of others was a sign of his own strength; the relatively few people he allowed into his inner circle must somehow be inherently more worthy. But it had transpired that first Violet, and now Penvale, had lied by omission; he seemed to be a less astute judge of character than he had thought. And yet, the revelation of Penvale's complicity in this wild scheme did not send him into the towering rage he might have expected; rather, the involvement of one of his best friends merely made him curious to learn more about what was afoot. For the first time, he wondered if a single lie was perhaps not the unforgivable betrayal he had once believed it to be.

"I would be most gratified," he said, enunciating every word clearly, "if you would tell me, in clear and concise fashion, what the hell is going on."

"Allow me to assist you, then," came an amused voice from behind them, and James and Penvale turned. Belfry was leaning in the doorway at the entrance to the room. He was clothed in a simple shirt and breeches, a scarlet banyan completing the ensemble. His dark hair was tousled, and his eyes were bleary. He had the look of a man who had recently awoken from a rough night—and who had enjoyed every minute of it.

"Belfry," James said shortly.

Belfry offered him a bow that went beyond the bounds of what politeness required and veered dangerously close to mockery. One of James's palms curled into a fist at his side, but he was resolved, as always, to keep his temper, at least until he gained the information he sought.

After that? Well. He made no promises. Every gentleman had his limits.

"I'm touched by your eagerness to call upon me," Belfry said, pushing off from the doorjamb and sauntering into the room. "But I must ask whether it was necessary to do so at such an hour." He paused at the sideboard, considered the decanter sitting there, then seemed to think better of it and continued his progress into the room.

"I can assure you, Belfry, I'd rather be anywhere than here at the moment," James said shortly. "But, you see, when a man discovers another man visiting his wife in her bedchamber, he suddenly finds himself with some questions that need answering."

"Does he?" Belfry flung himself onto a chaise. "I should think that it would all be rather obvious." He did not smile, but James suspected that Belfry was trying to bait him.

"Why did you call upon my wife?"

"Why does a man ever call upon a lady?"

"Give it up, Belfry. You gave me your damned card. A man caught out in an improper liaison doesn't usually leave behind his calling card."

"Did I?" Belfry widened his eyes, and tapped his chin. "Must have been a mistake on my part."

Keeping one's temper was all very well, but there were times, James decided in an instant, when action was called for. He crossed the room in three great strides and seized the fabric of Belfry's banyan, hauling him into a sitting position upon the chaise. James leaned close, his eyes locking with the other man's.

"Tell me what is afoot," he said with deadly calm, "or I shall ask you to meet me with pistols at dawn."

"I believe, as the challenged party, I would have the right to select the weapon," Belfry said, but when James's grip tightened, he sighed. "All right, let me go, you bloody madman." He slumped back against the chaise when James loosened his hands, and surveyed James with some degree of irritation.

"I was invited, apropos of nothing, to dine with your friend here"—Belfry jerked his chin in Penvale's direction—"at his sister's house. I accepted. At said dinner party, your wife requested that I show up at your home disguised as a physician and make some sort of dark prognosis. I declined, naturally. She was persistent. I'm sure that doesn't surprise you?"

It did not.

"Not having any desire to remain trapped at that dinner table for the rest of my natural life, I eventually agreed, provided she and Lady Templeton agreed to attend a show at the Belfry. I'm trying to attract a more respectable clientele."

"Why did you give me your card, then?" James was genuinely curious. "I wouldn't have recognized you under all that fur you had plastered onto your face."

"I dislike being managed by women," Belfry said, crossing one knee over the other. Even clad in a banyan, barefoot, dark hair mussed, he looked like a prince.

"I strongly advise you not to marry, then," James suggested.

"No need to tell me that," Belfry said with a thin smile. He gave James an assessing look. "I also thought, based on your reaction to my news, that your wife might have rather misjudged you."

"What do you mean by that?" James asked. It was galling to have a man he barely knew making judgments about the state of his marriage. Belfry merely smirked.

"What are you going to do, Audley?" This was Penvale, who was eyeing James warily. As well he should be, considering the role he had played in this entire bloody mess. "Speak to Violet, I hope?"

James gave him a tight grin. "Something to that effect."

⬦

Cataloguing a library from the confines of a bedchamber was no easy task, Violet reflected. She had thought that after the excitement of last night's outing, a day of relapse might be called for, and had thrown herself into the role with great enthusiasm, especially since it had given her an excuse to revoke the invitation to tea she had extended to her mother the day before. She'd had all of her meals delivered to her chamber on trays, and had spent no small amount of time selecting the most innocent- and virginal-looking of her chemises—invalids, of course, being entirely excluded from the realm of earthly pleasures. She had braided her hair, then unbraided it, allowing it to flow over her shoulders in dark waves. She had practiced her cough several times, until she thought that she had it calibrated to a perfect degree of frailty.

And then she had taken to her bed and rung for Price. She did not think she was imagining the look of weary resignation that flickered over her maid's face when she repeated her request of the day before. Violet supposed Price had better things to do than spend her day hauling small stacks of books up and down the stairs. However, she—Violet—*also* had more important work to do than reading improper novels in bed, and to do this work, she needed Price's assistance.

And so Violet had set to work again. However, the work gave her less satisfaction than it had done before. Productivity was all well and good when one had the freedom to roam about the house when necessary; after hours and hours of nothing but books, papers, and a tea tray for company, she was growing a bit . . . well . . . restless. She was discovering that there was a vast difference between being an invalid when one was truly ill and being an invalid in the full bloom of health. And while some society ladies did nothing more strenuous than lift a teapot each day, Violet was not one of them. A day in bed did not suit her, to say nothing of *three* days in bed in a row.

In a brief moment of weakness, she wondered if this plan of hers was not, in truth, an entirely disastrous idea. James was proving overall to be a less doting and devoted attendee at her sickbed than she would have wished. In her mind, she'd had vague fantasies of a dimly lit room, herself lying prone beneath the bed linens, her face pale. Sitting at her bedside was the worried husband, a tragic, romantic figure who clutched her hand and mopped her brow and proclaimed that she had never been more beautiful than she was in that precise moment, at the point of expiring.

Of course, Violet found upon closer examination of this fantasy that neither participant remotely resembled herself or James. Which, in turn, might explain why none of this was going precisely to plan.

It was as she was pondering how soon would be too soon to appear downstairs, fully clothed and miraculously on the mend, that there was a light tapping at her bedroom door. She started at the sound.

"Bugger," she muttered. She had been so engrossed in her fantasies of freedom that she hadn't heard footsteps approaching in the hallway. While Violet rather prided herself on never losing her head, there was no denying that there was a slight panic to her motions as she hastily yanked a blanket over the books on her tray, just as the door opened and James walked in.

Violet's heart—treasonous organ that it was—immediately picked up its pace. Why, oh why, did he have to be so handsome? He was dressed in fawn-colored breeches and a dark blue coat. His dark curls were slightly mussed, as though he'd been outdoors. It was as though, whenever he walked into a room, something primal within her cried out to him, and some part of him answered.

It was, as ever, thoroughly unnerving.

And, most unsettling of all, at the moment his full attention was focused entirely on her.

With effort, she resisted the urge to pull the bedclothes up to her neck. She was a married woman, she reminded herself, not an innocent girl of sixteen. There was no need to cower in the presence of a man—not just any man, but her *husband*. He had, after all, seen her naked on any number of occasions. Recalling the rather large number of such occasions—and the creative locations in which some of them had occurred—brought warmth to her cheeks, which she hoped James would mistake for fever.

Wait. Was fever a symptom of consumption?

Drat. She had no idea.

"Violet," he said, bowing slightly before shutting the door behind him.

"James." She watched warily as he approached the bed with purpose. He reminded her of a graceful predator in the wild, stalking his prey. A lion, perhaps, or a tiger. There was something catlike about his movements.

"When I returned home and Wooton informed me that you were ill once again, I knew I must come see you immediately." He stopped at her bedside, close enough for her to catch a whiff of his scent—a combination of sandalwood and soap. She tried not to admire the way his coat fit across his broad shoulders. "How are you feeling?" He reached out and seized her hand, and she allowed herself one moment of weakness in which to savor the warmth of his grasp, the comfort it conveyed.

"A bit better," she said weakly, then coughed. "Certainly less poorly than I was feeling this morning." She smiled at him, allowing the corners of her mouth to tremble a bit, as though she were merely putting on a brave face. This was not entirely an act—she had risked death by boredom today, which she felt was brave in its own way.

"Good, good," James muttered, though Violet was not certain he had listened to her words as carefully as he ought. There was something rather . . . *odd* . . . in his eyes, and he was lavishing a perhaps undue amount of attention upon the hand he held so tightly in his own. It was a bit disconcerting, after the woefully inadequate displays of concern he had offered until this point. Violet was immediately suspicious.

He sat down beside her on the bed, then immediately leaped to his feet once more. Violet watched him, perplexed, before she realized the cause of his sudden motion: the feeling of several sturdy leatherbound books beneath the bedspread. He reached underneath the counterpane and retrieved one of the offending volumes.

"Er," Violet said.

He quirked an eyebrow at her.

"You see," she said, improvising hastily, "I felt my mind growing— er—*disordered*, and so I felt that reading something familiar and comforting might make me less confused." It was, as even Violet would admit, not her best work. She was supposed to have *consumption*, for heaven's sake; she wasn't a mad old maiden aunt who wandered about the house at all hours of the night in confusion.

"I see," James said, then peered at the spine. "And you found *Agricultural Innovations of Shropshire, 1700–1800* to be just the sort of comfort read you were looking for?"

Drat. "Er," Violet said again, thinking quickly. "I thought it might include some sheep."

"Sheep?" James said blankly.

"Yes, sheep," she said with greater enthusiasm. If she was going to do the thing, she might as well get into the spirit of it. "You know, about hip height? Very woolly?"

"I understand what a sheep is," James said. Violet could practically see him grinding his teeth. "How, precisely, is this a source of comfort for you in your moment of need?"

"Sheep remind me of my childhood," Violet said mournfully. She heaved a great sigh, one that might have been more convincing had James not been perfectly well aware how eager she had been to escape her mother's clutches at the age of eighteen. "It wasn't all lovely, of course, but there were moments . . . walking through the gardens with Roland when he was a baby . . . seeing the sheep dotting the hills behind the house . . . all that baa-ing . . ." She trailed off, staring into the middle distance with a wistful expression.

"So adorable. So pudgy. With such fluffy hair." She sniffled.

"The sheep?" James asked.

"No, Roland!" Violet said with indignation. "He's a bit of a rotter as far as brothers go, especially now that he's at Oxford, but he was a darling baby."

This was in fact something of a stretch. Roland had been a very red, very fussy, very smelly baby. Violet, however, smiled a watery smile at her husband, as though barely able to refrain from bursting into tears.

James regarded her as though she'd entirely taken leave of her senses—which, Violet was forced to admit, was not an unfair reaction to the past three minutes of conversation.

"Well," he said as though he'd come to some sort of decision, placing the book down on the bedside table. "It is clear that you shouldn't leave this bed anytime soon."

"Er," Violet said, her mind racing. The words she was thinking at the moment were decidedly unladylike.

"Are you comfortable?" he asked, reaching behind her to plump her pillows. Violet caught her breath at his proximity—he hadn't touched her, and yet he was so close to her that if she were but to lean forward a hairsbreadth she could press her lips to the underside of his jaw. That decidedly unhelpful thought sent her heart racing once again. His scent was stronger at such close range, and she recalled how in the early days of their marriage she could tell as soon as he entered a room, no matter how crowded—as though she were somehow more attuned to his scent than to anyone else's. At first, she had thought it rather odd; after a while, however, it had merely been comforting, to look up in a room full of people and find his gaze unerringly, see those green eyes seeking out her own.

It had all been so . . . lovely. There was a great sense of peace that came from the knowledge that there was one person above all others who was always on her side.

Until, of course, he hadn't been.

Until he had chosen to believe the worst of her, of her motives for marrying him.

Until he had added her name to the long list of people that he could not trust. She understood to a certain extent why he had such difficulty trusting others—a childhood with the Duke of Dovington would have that effect on many men, she suspected. What she could not understand was why *she* had not been worthy of his trust. Why, four years ago, he had allowed a single argument to do such damage to a marriage that had been—to her, at least—so precious.

Her usual surge of anger came upon her, and she embraced it, finding it a relief after a few days spent in James's company, during which her defenses had lowered infinitesimally. This anger was a welcome reminder that before her was the man who had made her fall head over heels in love with him—and then pushed her away just as abruptly, making the past four years a misery.

Well, she was finished with all of that. She refused to allow one person to be the sole keeper of her happiness a moment longer.

So she would cough, and she would wheeze, and she would bring him to his knees—and then she would move on with her life.

It would be a bit easier to do so, of course, if the close proximity of his forearms to her person did not send her into a fit of swooning, but she was determined to be stronger than this traitorous body of hers.

Beginning now.

"I am quite comfortable, thank you," she said, a note of steel in her voice, and reached out with one hand to grasp one of his arms. "My pillows are entirely satisfactory."

"Of course," he murmured, the very picture of solicitousness as he withdrew his arms from behind her. The welcome space that was created between them was erased a moment later, however, when he sat back down on the edge of the bed. Mercifully, he managed to avoid either of the other two books that were somewhere under the bedspread.

"Did you require something else from me, husband?" she asked sweetly.

He raised an eyebrow; it made creases in his forehead that she found annoyingly endearing, and she quickly drew her eyes away from that treacherous terrain. She could afford no skin-wrinkle-induced moments of weakness.

"I am merely here to ensure that you are as comfortable as possible, in your weakened state. Especially as it seems that your mind may be going." Something about the way he said the word *comfortable* sent a shiver down her spine, despite the fact that the look on his face was one of bland concern. It was distracting—she realized that he was still speaking to her, though she hadn't been attending anything he'd said.

He raised a sardonic brow at her. "If I were a more easily offended man, I'd think you weren't paying attention."

"Funny, because I believe that the current status of our marriage is predicated on your being easily offended."

As soon as the words were out of Violet's mouth, she wished them back; she very nearly clapped a hand over her mouth, in fact. What on earth had possessed her? Over the past four years, she and James had developed a set of unwritten rules, and one of them was a refusal to acknowledge anything about the argument that had led to their current state of affairs. And, indeed, if Violet were being truthful, she knew that her words hadn't been entirely fair. James was not, in fact, an easily offended man—he was merely a distrustful one, and for reasons that she knew enough about to feel were valid, to a certain degree at least.

James arched a brow again. "It is always interesting to hear a revisionist view of history, my dear."

"Don't call me that," Violet said through gritted teeth. He had never once called her "my dear" in earnest—only ever in that horrible, vaguely sarcastic tone of his that she'd had so many occasions to hear over the past four years. She hated it. Sometimes, she knew without any doubt that the man she had once loved was still underneath there somewhere, if that layer of ice would only melt away—but when he used that tone with her, she found it nearly impossible to believe.

"Of course," James murmured. "I shouldn't wish to upset you in your fragile state of health."

"I'm not—" Violet began, then cut herself off hastily by feigning a coughing fit. It was just as well she wasn't prone to lying on a regular basis—it seemed that she was utterly inept at it. She allowed her coughs to subside, offering a weak, "Indeed."

"Quite." A pause, and then James said, his manner suddenly businesslike, "What can I do to assist you? More pillows?" He peered behind Violet's shoulder, as though to assess the current status of her cushioning. "Yes, more pillows, I think."

"I have eight pillows," Violet said, but James did not seem to hear her, given that he was already walking briskly toward the bellpull to ring for Price.

"Now," he said, turning back to her. "I believe you need some tea."

"I've already had tea."

"*More* tea. And some milky toast," he added. Was Violet imagining the slightly gleeful look in his eyes?

"I hate milky toast," she gritted out. "Passionately."

"Yes, I know," James said, adopting an expression that Violet assumed he meant to be apologetic but which wasn't quite successful. "But one must do what is necessary in the face of illness."

"I assure you, husband—"

"And broth!" Violet had never heard someone sound so delighted at the prospect of broth. James paused thoughtfully. "Perhaps I should be writing this down—I wouldn't wish to forget anything by the time Price arrives."

"Somehow, I think you'll manage," Violet said darkly under her breath. She had forgotten how sharp his ears were, however, for he shot her a grin at this—and her breath caught in her throat.

"More blankets," James said decisively. Her brief feeling of tenderness passed. "And perhaps a hot-water bottle or two." He stood with his hands on his lean hips, surveying her the way a general might survey his troops, his brow slightly furrowed, clearly deep in thought.

"It's July!" Violet wailed, forgetting entirely that she was supposed to be frail and weak.

"You're right." James paused, suddenly serious. He turned to the window, which was cracked slightly, letting in the warm breeze from the back garden. "This window needs to be closed—we can't have unhealthy airs waft in and weaken you further."

Violet narrowed her eyes at him, assessing. Something was . . . odd. This level of solicitousness should be gratifying, but it merely had the effect of thoroughly rousing her suspicions. It made no sense, his rapid-fire transition into a version of James that she had never seen before. Even in their happiest moments, he had never fussed over her like this. It had been one of the many things she had found so freeing about marriage, after years of her mother's ceaseless attentions. He had treated her like an adult, not like a recalcitrant child. He had made it perfectly clear that he saw her as his equal, and it had been ... liberating. Like taking a full breath of clean air after being trapped inside a smoky cupboard.

Nothing about that man squared with the behavior of the one currently fidgeting with her curtains. It was strange. Something wasn't right.

As she was contemplating this, he whirled around, a feverish glint in his eye that instantly had her on her guard. "I have realized," he said dramatically, "what you truly need."

She was nearly certain that she was not going to like the answer to her following question. "And what is that?"

"Your mother!" He rubbed his hands together, looking pleased with himself. "There is nothing like the warmth of a maternal embrace to set an invalid on the path to health."

Violet was temporarily struck dumb with horror. She scarcely knew where to begin. For a start, she had never received an embrace from Lady Worthington that could be deemed anything approaching warm—indeed, on the rare occasion the countess felt duty-bound to offer some show of physical affection to her only daughter, the resulting display more closely resembled a monarch offering a hand for a lowly peasant to kiss than any sort of moment of familial tenderness.

Furthermore, she was fairly certain that affectionate nursemaids did not result in consumptives miraculously finding themselves cured—indeed, if physical devotion had any effect at all on an invalid, she thought it likely some enterprising woman would have already had the brilliant idea of creating a combined brothel and hospital.

All of these logical questions, however, paled in importance compared to her strongest, most instinctive reaction: that she would rather have *actual* consumption than be forced to live under the same roof as her mother for even one night.

She could not, however, say *that* to her husband. Her husband, who was watching her with an uncharacteristically attentive look in his eye. She narrowed her eyes at him in return.

"What an ... unexpected idea," she offered.

He nodded. "I know you've had your differences with her, but who better than the woman who raised you to attend you in your moment of need?"

She smiled sweetly at him. "I'm afraid my childhood nurse lives in Somerset now, darling."

James waved a hand dismissively. "I'm not saying your mother was the most attentive parent, but this seems like a perfect opportunity to let her make up for lost time."

"I don't think . . ." Violet began, but a sound that would surely haunt her nightmares came emanating from the corridor just outside her bedroom: her mother's voice, outside her bedroom door.

"Where is my daughter?" the countess demanded; Violet would have thought it rather obvious where to find an invalid, but it occurred to her that her mother likely didn't know where her bedchamber was—Violet could count on one hand the number of times Lady Worthington had visited Curzon Street since Violet's marriage.

She must have received some sort of murmured direction from whichever beleaguered servant had the misfortune to be accompanying her, for a moment later the door was flung open and Lady Worthington stood in the doorway, looking for all the world as though she expected a round of applause for this performance of Loving Parent Rushing to Offspring's Bedside.

Violet groaned internally.

"What was that noise?" her mother demanded; apparently, that groan had not been internal at all. "I've never heard her make that noise before; surely it must be a symptom of her illness."

"Are you feeling any great discomfort?" James asked Violet solicitously, leaning over her to place a hand on her not-so-fevered brow. "As you will see, I took the liberty of inviting your mother to come attend to you. I would have asked you before doing so, but I thought that you would attempt to downplay the severity of your illness, so as not to put Lady Worthington to any trouble." His voice was solemn, but his eyes were teasing. And in that instant, he made her suspect that *he knew*.

She could not, of course, accuse him of anything within her mother's hearing. Instead, she said, "I hardly think I need such a fuss made."

James cupped her cheek and turned to look at Lady Worthington, who had made her way to Violet's bedside and was looking at Violet's rather tousled hair with an expression of vague distaste. "This is what I meant," he said to her mother. "My Violet. My flower. So courageous in the face of grievous illness."

Lady Worthington sniffed. "Audley, please don't become maudlin, or I may find myself in need of a physician as well." She looked at Violet, frowning. "You look flushed. Are you feverish?"

"I wish," Violet said honestly. "That might indicate that this was naught but a horrible nightmare."

"She must be feverish," Lady Worthington said to James.

"She clearly requires constant attention," James said earnestly. "I have been, naturally, as attentive as I can manage, but I thought a feminine presence . . ." He trailed off.

"Indeed," Lady Worthington said curtly, with the air of someone resolving herself to tackle an unpleasant task. "A sickbed is no place for a man, Audley. Leave it to me."

"Of course." James leaned forward to press a kiss to Violet's brow. "I will leave you in your mother's loving care."

I will murder you in your sleep for this, Violet attempted to say with her eyes as he gave her a limpid, loving, thoroughly sickening look. His lovesick smile slipped for a second, replaced momentarily by an entirely self-satisfied grin, and in that instant she knew two things beyond a doubt.

One, her eyes' message had been received.

Two, he undoubtedly knew that she wasn't ill.

Eight

It had, James reflected over a late luncheon the next afternoon, been a remarkably enjoyable day. The day before, he'd had to work very hard on several occasions to stifle his laughter at the expressions on Violet's face—which had ranged from incredulous to murderous—but on the whole, he'd put on a rather impressive performance. When he finally left his wife in her mother's care the previous afternoon, she'd been propped up by enough pillows to support an entire family, under a layer of bedclothes thick enough to ward off a Russian winter. Her mother had been patting her gingerly on the shoulder with an air of long-suffering weariness that implied that she expected to shortly be sainted for this effort. He wondered how long it had taken for Violet to convince her mother to leave—he had seen no sign of the countess at the dinner or breakfast tables, and an inquiry of Wooton confirmed that the countess had not occupied the room James had ordered prepared for her.

On his way out of the room he'd caught Price on the stairs with a stack of books in her hand, so he'd guessed that Violet was running some sort of elaborate scheme to continue her library cataloguing project from the confines of her bedchamber—it must have driven her mad to have her mother's visit interrupt her progress. In some ways, this was an improvement—at least now he could enter the library at any hour of the day without worrying about finding her there, filling the room with her scent, biting her lip in concentration as she scribbled away at her catalogue, her face as beautiful as it always was when she was deep in thought.

He'd been half expecting to find her up at dawn, or at least by the time he left for an early meeting with his man of business about a pending sale of a stallion. He shut himself away in his study for several hours with a neglected pile of correspondence, both stables related and personal, and when he grew peckish and rang for a footman to ask for a tray to be sent in, he learned that Violet still had not made an appearance outside of her bedchamber.

He allowed himself a brief moment of surprise as he accepted the tray placed before him on his desk, wondering at her lingering in bed, but promptly decided that she must have calculated that she could not reemerge, bright-eyed and in the full flush of health, without rousing his suspicions. He told himself that this was all the better—his trick had worked so well that she had now taken to punishing herself—but he could not deny the small voice within him that noted that tormenting Violet was considerably more entertaining when he was actually in her company.

He took a bite of bread—upon which he promptly choked, when Violet entered the room.

"Good afternoon, darling," she said sunnily, sinking into the chair facing his desk. She was dressed in a riding habit of midnight blue, her dark hair pulled neatly back from her face into some sort of elaborate braided concoction at her nape. She looked beautiful—and perfectly healthy.

His eyes narrowed.

Violet seemed not to notice. "Did you sleep well?" She reached forward and, without so much as a by-your-leave, poured a cup of tea, which she nudged toward him.

James, being rather occupied with the task of forcing air back into his lungs, took a moment to reply.

"Very," he finally managed, taking a healthy gulp of tea and watching as she prepared a cup for herself. He was amused to note that her inability to pour tea without at least a splash or two winding up in the saucer remained unchanged. "What are you—"

"Oh, I'm feeling much improved this afternoon," she said cheerfully, stirring sugar into her tea. The sound of the spoon against china was loud in the otherwise silent room. "My mother's visit really worked wonders—you were entirely correct in that regard. I can scarcely believe what a miraculous recovery I have made. But then, this is how Briggs said it might be, you see."

"Did he?"

"Oh, yes." She beamed at him, and he averted his eyes. Her face was radiant when she smiled, and he sternly reminded himself not to be distracted by a pair of sparkling eyes and uneven dimples—he had made that mistake five years earlier, and all he had gotten in exchange was a brief window of happiness, followed by a long period of regret. "One day bedridden, the next up and about as though nothing were at all the matter."

Despite the knowledge that she was lying to his face, James was nevertheless amused. She seemed to be taking an awful gamble that he knew nothing at all about the symptoms of consumption—which, admittedly, he didn't, but he'd never heard anything about the wild fluctuation in health associated with the disease.

"Interesting." He drew the word out slowly. "You know, darling, I can't help but think this isn't at all consistent with what I've read of consumption in the past." Which was nothing. But she didn't need to know that.

"Oh, James." She waved an airy hand as though he were being entirely foolish—was he imagining it, or did she seem more alert than normal? "I'm certain Dr. Briggs knows more about it than you do—or would you like to summon your own physician for a second opinion?"

She blinked at him innocently.

His eyes narrowed. What the bloody hell was going on? Did she know that he knew? But how could she possibly?—he'd only learned the truth for certain the previous day, and she'd not seen anyone but him and her mother in the interim.

Belatedly realizing that she was still awaiting his reply, he said slowly, "Yes, perhaps we shall. I'm certain Dr. Worth would like to make a thorough examination of you." And why, oh *why*, did discussion of a physician visiting Violet have to send such utterly lewd images into his mind? Never had the word *examination* sounded so . . . obscene. Clearly he was going slightly mad from lack of female contact.

Or, he amended hastily, entirely too much female contact of the non-nude variety.

"Anytime you wish, James," Violet said, raising an eyebrow as if they were playing chess and she was awaiting his countermove— which James had a sudden feeling was remarkably close to the truth.

Feeling it best to tread on safer ground, he asked, "When did your mother depart?"

"Yesterday afternoon, not too long after she arrived," Violet said, a note of satisfaction in her voice.

"How did you manage that?" he asked, impressed despite himself— Lady Worthington did not strike him as a woman easily dismissed.

"I told her that if she did not leave me be, I'd take to riding in breeches in a gentleman's saddle."

He bit back a smile with considerable effort. "I imagine she swooned from horror."

Violet smirked. "I think I should take it as a compliment that she believed me."

"Speaking of which," James said, "you're dressed for riding."

"Yes," she said, taking a sip of tea and casting a brief glance down at her riding habit. "Since I'm feeling so improved today, I thought I might take a ride in Hyde Park."

James had to hide another grin at this. Violet was a reasonably accomplished rider, but she was not horse-mad by any stretch of the imagination. Her desire to go riding could only be indicative of one thing: she was tired of being confined to her room.

"I don't know," he said slowly, pasting a concerned look on his face that he hoped was convincing. "I'm not certain the physician would think—"

"I'm getting on a bloody horse this afternoon whether you think it's a good idea or not," Violet said through gritted teeth, and James was surprised into silence. While Violet was certainly no shrinking, well, *violet*, swearing was still a bit much even from her, aside from the occasional muttered curse when she thought no one could hear. Although he supposed, upon a moment's reflection, that had *he* been confined to his bed for three days, he might have had a choice word or two to offer as well.

"I am going to drink my tea, and I am going to have a groom make Persephone ready, and then I am going to go riding in Hyde Park. I am entirely uninterested in your thoughts on the matter."

After this little speech, she dedicated her attention to the cup of tea at—or rather, in—hand, as though she'd never seen anything quite so fascinating, leaving James to make a valiant effort to force back the many questions that rose in his throat, begging to be voiced.

As was so often the case in matters concerning his wife, his willpower failed him.

"Do you recall our wedding day?" he asked, leaning back in his chair and lacing his hands over his stomach. Violet, he was pleased to see, choked slightly on her tea.

"With unfortunate clarity," she said once she had dislodged the liquid from her windpipe.

"Why unfortunate?" he asked, arching a brow.

Violet straightened in her seat. "It's difficult to think back so clearly on a day that was such a massive mistake."

A beat of silence. Then:

"A hit," he said coolly. "A palpable hit." He kept his voice bored and disinterested, hoping that it wasn't obvious that her barb had, in fact, landed. "I myself recollect it a bit differently."

"Not a mistake, then?"

"No," he said, his gaze steady on hers. He couldn't read the look in her dark eyes, but something flickered through them in response to that one word—was it relief? "It is safe to say that many mistakes have been made since, but I do not believe the events of that day can be counted among the tally." He spoke the words before he entirely knew what he was saying, but realized in an instant that they were true: despite everything, he did not regret marrying Violet. This knowledge felt like a sudden revelation, and one that he did not have the time to examine at present.

She cleared her throat.

"Why do you ask?"

Why *had* he asked? He mentally floundered for a moment, feeling rather as though he'd waded out into a marsh and was now seeking to find solid ground once more. Ah, yes, there it was. "I was merely curious," he said, "whether you remembered the part of the vows that mentioned obeying."

It was remarkable, really, how fast that soft look in her eyes vanished, likely not to be seen again for another four years. It was replaced by a flash of anger equally satisfying to observe, though in an entirely different way.

"Are you going to forbid me to ride in the park, then, husband?" she asked, her voice low and deadly. James knew that that was precisely what she wished him to do, if only so that she might have the pleasure of defying him.

"Not at all," he said, kicking one heel up to rest upon his desk. "I am merely going to come with you."

❦

Less than an hour later, James found himself cantering down Rotten Row, Violet at his side. It was not yet the five o'clock hour, meaning that the park wasn't bursting with aristocrats out to see and be seen the way it would be in a couple of hours, but the weather was fine enough that they were far from alone. Since entering the park, James had seen several acquaintances—men he knew from his club on horseback, married couples in phaetons, and a few clusters of ladies on foot, tiny dogs accompanying them, led by their footmen, of course, not by the ladies themselves.

He and Violet had been largely silent for the duration of their ride, offering little comment other than a few stilted remarks about the weather and their pace. It was so easy, when they were together, for him to weaken, to soak in the simple enjoyment of being in her company once more. But then there would be a moment like this, in which she stifled a cough in her sleeve that he was almost certain was feigned, and he would recollect all at once the game that was afoot, and he would be awash in anger once more. Anger and disappointment— disappointment that she was lying to him again, that she was proving to be just as deceitful as he had accused her of being all those years ago.

No, he amended. That wasn't fair, either. He'd been very angry that day, had felt very betrayed, and he'd be the first to admit—though never had he admitted this to Violet, he realized—that he'd spoken too harshly. Once his anger had cooled, he'd realized that he'd reacted some-what out of proportion to the facts. On the day of their argument, he had learned that she had been involved in her mother and his father's plot to meet him out on that damned balcony at that long-ago ball.

And it had stung—still did sting, if he were being entirely truthful. He had worked hard for his entire adult life, which at that point was admittedly relatively brief, to distance himself from his father, to be-come an independent man, in control of his own life and destiny. And yet, in a matter of such importance as his *marriage*, he had been ma-nipulated like a pawn on a chessboard. But now, with some distance, he could admit that his accusations of Violet that day—that she was a conniving girl who'd married him for his position—had been unfair. She had been eighteen, in her very first Season, and he knew from personal experience how domineering Lady Worthington could be. It stung that he had been deceived in such a fashion, but it was not so unforgivable as he had once believed.

No, what was unforgivable was her refusal to admit to her own complicity. She had first disavowed any knowledge of his father and her mother's scheme, before changing her story, claiming that she'd scarcely known about their ruse longer than he had. By that point, her words hadn't mattered; he didn't trust her to tell him the truth, and even if she were being honest now, the fact remained that she had still kept her knowledge secret from him, no matter the duration of her deception—and that her first instinct, upon being accused of doing so, was to lie. That was what maintained that rift between them, as far as he was concerned. Perhaps he was a fool, but he believed that by the time they had wed, Violet had truly come to love him—no one was as good an actress as all that. And he thought that he could have forgiven her for betraying his trust—once. But when she had lied in the face of discovery, had denied all knowledge of their parents' plotting—that was what he could not forgive.

And that was why this fresh deceit of hers, with its bloody coughing and swooning and malingering, was so damned irritating.

And he was determined to get even.

"Is Willingham planning to host his hunting party next month?" Violet broke into his thoughts, not looking at him as she spoke, keeping her attention focused firmly ahead of her. This gave James the luxury of admiring her profile, which was so lovely it made his heart clench. Her cheeks were flushed by the fresh air, and tiny wisps of dark hair had escaped her braids to curl against her fair cheeks and throat. He was suddenly possessed by so strong a desire to reach out and stroke his finger down her cheek that he tightened his fist around the reins, causing his horse to shy slightly at the pressure. He hastily loosened his grip and saw her glance sideways at him, still awaiting an answer.

"Yes," he said belatedly. "I believe he is. I trust you will be accompanying us, as usual?"

Violet's refusal to visit the country didn't extend to all country houses, merely their own; it was James's distinct impression that she had no objection to being at a country house party, full of friends, other ladies with whom she might converse—it was just the idea of visiting Audley House with only her husband for company that she found distasteful. She had accompanied him to Jeremy's estate each August for a visit that usually stretched at least a week longer than planned. For all his other faults, Jeremy was an excellent host, and his shooting parties were among the more coveted invitations among the *ton*.

Violet hesitated. "I don't know. I suppose it all depends on my health." She gave a small cough at the end of this sentence, stifling it so quickly that James might not have noticed it at all if he hadn't been looking.

Which she was clearly aware that he had been.

Had he been less annoyed, he might have been tempted to applaud.

"Of course," he said, striving to keep a note of sarcasm out of his voice. As was so often the case with Violet, however, his emotions were a bit closer to the surface than he liked this afternoon. "I shouldn't want you to suffer any sort of a relapse. Although," he added, as though giving the matter great thought, "I do wonder if the fresh country air might do you some good. Perhaps we would do better to depart London immediately—we could allow you to convalesce at Audley House and then join Jeremy in Wiltshire once you were feeling improved."

For the first time in his life, he wished he had a beard, if only so that he might stroke it thoughtfully. On second thought, however, that might be laying it on a bit thick.

"I don't believe I would find a stay at Audley House terribly restful," Violet replied. "It's rather difficult to rest peacefully when one is constantly worrying about one's husband breaking his neck on the back of an untrained horse, you see." Her spine was rigid and she did not look at him as she spoke, her gaze fixed on the path ahead of them. In profile, her expression appeared carefully blank, but he could tell that her jaw was clenched tightly.

"My dearest wife, you seem to have forgotten that I am not a man prone to making the same mistake twice."

She snorted then, the sound thoroughly unladylike.

"It seems to me that you are in fact a man prone to repeating the same mistake over and over again for his entire life." She gave him a sideways glance as if to measure his response, and James fought to keep his facial expression neutral.

"Meaning?" His tone was cool.

"Meaning," she said, and her voice was not as calm as it had been a moment before, "that if you are going to insist on losing faith in someone the moment you see the slightest possibility that they have wronged you, then you are going to have a very frustrating life."

"As opposed to my life as it is now, which is all sweetness and light?"

"If you already find your life frustrating, darling, I would suggest that you have only yourself to blame." She had gotten herself back under control, and this was delivered in a tone of perfect smoothness that he assumed was carefully calculated to enrage him.

He hated that she knew him so well—and that if her goal was to rattle him she was succeeding.

He reined in his horse sharply and reached out a hand to seize the reins of her horse as well. Persephone shied at the sudden firm touch, and reared ever so slightly on her hind legs. Violet was a competent horsewoman and adjusted her seat with ease, in no danger of falling.

And yet, that did not stop James's arm from reaching out, as if of its own volition, to wrap around her waist and steady her. She stiffened in surprise; he knew he should loosen his grip, but he found himself unable to do so. In the blink of an eye, Persephone had all four hooves planted firmly on solid ground once more. Violet was entirely secure within the saddle . . .

And still, James could not let go.

He was obsessed, suddenly, with the curve of her trim waist beneath his hand, the warmth of her skin even through the many layers of her clothing and his gloves. He was seized with a wild, reckless desire to reach out his other hand and lift her bodily onto his horse, to sit snug before him in the saddle, her back pressed against his chest and his arms tucked around her.

This fantasy lasted but a moment, but was so vivid that he dropped his arm from her waist as though he had been stung by a bee. Violet let the rough motion pass without comment. For once.

"I assume you had some reason for halting us so abruptly?" she remarked, and James, with great difficulty, brought his mind back to the conversation at hand. He raked a hand through his hair in frustration, and did not miss the way Violet's eyes followed the movement.

"If I find my life frustrating," he said after a moment, having gathered his wits as best he could, "I promise you that living in the same home as *you* does nothing to make it less so."

The words were harsh, and he very nearly regretted them—certainly would have if anything like hurt had flickered across Violet's expression. But her eyes narrowed and her mouth flattened into a thin line, and he felt the same rush that he always experienced whenever he succeeded in provoking her.

"Of course," she said stiffly. "Of course you give up on your marriage, on your relationship with West, but none of it is your fault. Of course."

James gave an internal howl of outrage—*give up? He* gave up? It was utter nonsense.

"I don't think my relationship with my brother is any of your concern." He sounded like a pompous ass, even to his own ears.

"Oh, of course not," Violet said. "What am I but your wife, after all? Or had you forgotten?"

"As if you'd let me," he muttered.

"Funny," she replied, her eyes flashing, "you seemed to have little difficulty doing so last week."

"Violet—"

"Of course it wouldn't even occur to you to send your wife a note that you'd been injured," she continued, ignoring him. "Silly me to even expect such a courtesy. After all, we wouldn't want your *wife* of all people to worry about you. Your *wife* who for years has been telling you that she wishes you'd leave the running of those stables to others. Your *wife* certainly doesn't have any right—"

"Enough about the bloody accident!" he shouted, more forcefully than he had intended. He glanced around quickly, but they were far enough away from other riders that no one seemed to have heard his outburst. Belatedly, he realized that they were still standing stock-still in the middle of the path, and he gave his horse a nudge with his heel, spurring him into motion. Violet followed suit, and they continued at a measured pace down the path, James uncomfortably aware that he had just raised his voice at a lady in public. He might roll his eyes at society and its many dictates, but he liked to think that he had some semblance of good manners.

Just not with his own wife.

He inhaled deeply. "I apologize that you were alarmed by Penvale's note," he said after a moment. "And I apologize for my words at the Blue Dove. I may have spoken . . . hastily."

Violet turned her head to look at him suspiciously, as though she suspected some sort of trap.

James exhaled in frustration. "For Christ's sake, I'm trying to apologize and the best you can do is blink at me like an owl?"

The corner of Violet's mouth twitched. "How flattering."

"A very attractive owl, of course."

Violet arched a brow. "Indeed?"

"Yes," James said, by now quite certain that continued speaking on his part would only lead to more trouble, and yet somehow unable to stop. "A very fine specimen—"

"Specimen?"

"—of owlishness—"

"Owlishness?"

"The best sort of owl, really." He managed to force his mouth shut, just barely resisting the temptation to clap a hand over it for good measure. He had *some* dignity left, after all.

"I can't believe you managed to convince me to marry you," Violet said after a moment's silence.

Just like that, the lightness of the moment vanished. "I seem to recall the situation being quite neatly managed," he said shortly.

Violet's face, which had been if not quite smiling then definitely amused, suddenly turned serious. "I know what you think you recall," she said, her gaze never leaving his. "And I know that you will never consider, for one second, that you might not have been the only one neatly managed that day."

James opened his mouth to respond, then hesitated a moment,

suddenly uncertain. He had nursed his anger on this issue for so long that he tended to reach for it instinctively; however, there was nothing in Violet's expression at the moment except sorrow, and it gave him pause. He searched for words, not entirely certain what he planned to say, but before he could speak, she let out a faint cough. A swell of anger rose within him, his doubts vanishing. Hadn't he just apologized for the bloody horse accident and his behavior following it? Did she still mean to continue with this ridiculous ruse?

It was infuriating, truly. And, furthermore, it was the perfect example of why he could not trust her. Did she realize that, he wondered? Did she see how perfectly she was proving him right?

Before he could make any sort of reply, he heard his name being called. Jeremy approached on horseback. And riding next to him was— James squinted, though he had a sinking feeling he already knew—

Oh, Christ. It was Sophie Wexham.

Although he supposed that she wasn't, in fact, Sophie Wexham anymore. She was Lady Fitzwilliam Bridewell. She was also a widow, and this was her first Season out of mourning.

A fact of which Jeremy had wasted no time in taking advantage.

James wasn't entirely certain how long they'd been carrying on together—a couple of months, he thought. In truth, he found it an odd match. The Sophie Wexham that he and West had known did not seem the type who would find Jeremy's brand of cheeky charm all that appealing.

But of course James hadn't spoken to her—other than to offer a bland pleasantry at a ball or musicale—in years. He had no idea how she had changed since her marriage or widowhood.

He wondered if she was still in love with his brother. For both their sakes, he rather hoped not.

As Jeremy and Lady Fitzwilliam drew closer, James and Violet reined in their mounts. "Is that—" Violet murmured under her breath.

"Indeed," James replied, equally quiet.

"Rather brazen of them to be out together on Rotten Row, isn't it?"

"They're on horseback, not in a closed carriage," James pointed out. Violet didn't even dignify this with a response, merely giving him a dubious look.

"Audley! Lady James!" Jeremy called as he drew up beside them. "How . . . unexpected." His tone was mild, but James could practically see the waves of curiosity rolling off him. James couldn't entirely blame him—to see himself and Violet out on what was, to all appearances, a cordial afternoon ride was highly unusual these days.

"Jeremy," James said. "Lady Fitzwilliam."

Lady Fitzwilliam was still every inch as beautiful as she'd been when James had first met her, at some London ball or another. She had golden curls and brown eyes and some of the longest eyelashes he had ever seen. Sitting easily atop her mount next to Jeremy, the sunlight streaming behind her, she looked glorious—and James gave hearty thanks that his brother was not there to see her. It would have been rather too much for West to bear, James suspected.

"Lord James," she murmured. "It's been quite a while, hasn't it?"

"Indeed it has, my lady," he agreed. "I do hope you'll allow me to express my condolences on your husband's passing."

"Thank you." Lady Fitzwilliam's lips pursed slightly, then softened back into their usual smooth curve.

"You must be pleased to be back out in society," Violet said.

"Yes," Lady Fitzwilliam said after the merest hesitation. "It's very . . . invigorating."

"Lord Willingham's company does tend to have that effect," James said dryly; the flush that swept over her face made him immediately regret his words. In truth, he was surprised to see her with Jeremy today—from what precious little Jeremy had told him, he'd been under the impression that their liaison was drawing to an end. Not that he was terribly surprised by that development—she really didn't seem at all in the usual line of Jeremy's lovers. She in fact seemed far more like someone James himself would take up with, were he the trysting sort.

And, just like that, he had an idea.

A brilliant idea.

A brilliant, *awful* idea.

Did he dare? He glanced sideways at his wife, the memory of her patently false cough echoing in his mind.

Oh, he did dare.

"My lady," he said, all of these thoughts coalescing within him in an instant. "Should you ever have need of anything, you know that you must call upon . . . us." He paused for a fraction of a second before saying the word *us*, just long enough for all present to realize that what he really meant was *me*.

Jeremy frowned at him.

Violet stiffened.

And Lady Fitzwilliam . . . She arched a brow, her gaze flicking between him and Violet lightning-fast. She must certainly have heard the rumors swirling about the state of their marriage—said rumors being quite numerous, of course. While one could never credit the *ton* with an extraordinary amount of collective intelligence, it could not help but notice when one of the great love matches of the past decade turned into a chilly marriage of cordial strangers instead.

"Thank you, my lord," Lady Fitzwilliam said after a moment, since it was, in truth, the only polite thing she could have said. Jeremy was still staring at James as though he were a particularly tricky puzzle that he was attempting to work out. James shot him a speaking glance—or, rather, he very much *hoped* it was a speaking glance. And he very much hoped that the message it spoke was, *I'll explain later, please don't make a fuss*, and not, *Please make a scene here in the middle of Hyde Park.*

Whatever message Jeremy took from said glance, it was enough to keep him silent. This in and of itself was quite an achievement. James felt rather pleased with himself.

And, feeling pleased with himself, he decided to test his luck.

"In fact," he proclaimed, "you should dine with us. Next week."

There was, of course, nothing so *very* improper about a dinner invitation—and yet, James did his best to make it so. He'd inched his horse forward as he spoke, making it so that Violet's view of Lady Fitzwilliam was blocked slightly by his shoulder. And his voice had dropped a register as he murmured the invitation, making it all seem rather more . . . intimate than it should have.

Out of the corner of his eye, he saw Lady Wheezle ride past in the company of a groom and turn her head to stare at their little tableau.

"I beg your pardon?" Lady Fitzwilliam asked, clearly perplexed by whatever undercurrents she detected between himself and Violet as he made this invitation.

"Dine with us," he repeated, flashing her the winning smile that had served him so well in his bachelor days, on the select occasions he had chosen to deploy it. "We could celebrate your reentry into society."

"When have you ever given a deuce for society?" Jeremy asked grumpily, his hands twitching on the reins he held. James was certain that, were they not in a public park, Jeremy would have reached across to lay an entirely inappropriate hand on some part of Lady Fitzwilliam's person, like an animal marking its territory. However, since they *were* in a public park, he contented himself with repeated fist-clenching.

"Darling," Violet cut in, and never had the word *darling* sounded more menacing, "I believe you're forgetting the state of my health."

"I assure you I wasn't," he said, turning to his wife. "After all, was it not you who insisted that we ride in the park this afternoon?" He blinked innocently at her.

Her eyes narrowed.

"I can't say how I shall be feeling next week," she said, and James nearly laughed aloud at the look on her face, which rather resembled that of someone who had just been served an extremely unpleasant dish by one she didn't wish to offend.

"If Lady James is unwell—" Lady Fitzwilliam started to say, but James and Violet both ignored her.

"Then let us assume you shall be perfectly well," James said, his eyes never once leaving his wife's face.

"But I can't say for certain that I *shall* be perfectly well."

James was dimly aware that Jeremy and Lady Fitzwilliam were watching this exchange with great interest, their heads bobbing back and forth as though they were spectators at a duel.

"Well then, let us choose to be optimistic." He gave her a thin smile.

"Funny," Violet said, "I've never known optimism to be a trait that you possessed in great abundance."

"Meaning you should be doubly glad that I am attempting to turn over a new leaf." He inched his mount closer to her as they spoke, and they were now in such proximity that he could have reached out and knocked his knee against hers. He'd meant only to intimidate her, but he realized belatedly that this might have been a mistake—this close, he could smell her skin, could practically feel the warmth radiating from her. Her cheeks were flushed—whether from anger or the exercise of their ride, he wasn't certain—and she looked so much the picture of health that he had to fight back the urge to laugh. She looked . . .

Radiant.

Yes, radiant. Her hair curled around her face, and her eyes sparked in that familiar way they did whenever he was arguing with her.

And in that moment, he wanted to kiss her so desperately that he nearly forgot that they were in the middle of Hyde Park, with Jeremy and Lady Fitzwilliam watching from a few paces away. His eyes caught hers and held, and the color of her cheeks deepened further under the intensity of his gaze. She bit her lip—he'd nearly forgotten that old habit of hers—but did not break their eye contact.

And James found that he was incapable of doing so as well.

She was infuriating, and he was still determined to best her at whatever this game was that they were playing—but he also wanted her more than he'd ever wanted any woman in his life.

Still. After five years. And there was no point in lying to himself about this fact any longer.

He wanted her, and he did not know how to have her. Christ, what a mess.

It was impossible to say how long this stalemate would have continued had Lady Fitzwilliam not broken the silence.

"I am certain that I wouldn't wish to impose if Lady James is feeling unwell."

"Lady James was just telling me this morning how improved she is," James said smoothly, wrenching his gaze away from his wife with great difficulty to refocus on Lady Fitzwilliam. Violet elbowed him in the ribs, which he ignored. "But regardless, Soph—Lady Fitzwilliam," he amended hastily, as though he hadn't intended to nearly address her by her Christian name, "my offer stands—please do call upon us if you should need any assistance of any sort." He urged his horse closer to Lady Fitzwilliam's, reaching up to take her hand in his own.

"Audley," Jeremy said, and James nearly laughed out loud at the strangled note in his voice. "Are you feeling quite the thing?"

"Never better, I assure you," James said cheerfully, allowing his thumb to stroke rather intimately across Lady Fitzwilliam's palm before he released her hand. He would have felt like a cad had she not continued to regard him with that questioning, suspicious look of hers—the one that told him she was not at all fooled by his rather blatant attempts at seduction. "I don't seem to have picked up Violet's little malady, much to my relief."

Next to him, Violet coughed. Unlike the noises she had been emitting of late, which James thought seemed carefully calibrated to achieve the perfect mix of frailty and feminine delicacy to play upon his sympathies, this was a violent cough indeed. More of a hack, really.

"Feeling all right?" he asked mildly once she had subsided.

"I was feeling considerably better five minutes ago," she said with a bland smile.

"Must be all the fresh air," James said wisely. "It might be a bit much for your fragile lungs."

"In that case, my lord, I should be exceedingly grateful if you were to escort me home."

"But of course," he said gallantly. He turned back to Lady Fitzwilliam and Jeremy, who were both regarding him as they would a madman. An affable madman, perhaps, but still a madman.

"Jeremy, Lady Fitzwilliam," he said, nodding to each in turn. "I'm afraid we must take our leave." He reached for Lady Fitzwilliam's hand once more, and she gave him a startled look as he bent down to press a quick kiss to the hand in question. "Lady Fitzwilliam," he murmured in intimate tones—intimate tones still loud enough to carry, "it has truly been a pleasure. One I look forward to repeating very soon." And with a cheeky grin, he turned his horse and took a few quick steps back to Violet's side. "Shall we?"

She did nothing but nod tightly—and proceeded to ignore him for the entire ride back to Curzon Street. She also, James noticed, failed to cough once.

Nine

"Have you quite lost your mind?" Jeremy demanded.

It was later the same evening, and Jeremy and James were seated in Jeremy's study—Jeremy at his desk, James lounging across from him in an armchair, brandy in hand. In truth, the study at Willingham House was not a room Jeremy frequented, and James was nearly certain that he had elected to receive him here as a show of authority. It would have been a more effective display if Jeremy had not looked so uncomfortable in the seat his father and brother had once occupied.

"Perhaps," James said, tilting the glass in his hand so that the liquid within caught the last rays of summer evening light streaming in through the windows. "I assume you are referring to our meeting in Hyde Park?"

"Of course I bloody am!" Jeremy exploded. Jeremy was mild-tempered in the extreme—he was rather famous for it, in truth. The trait had served him well—it was impossible that one could sleep with as many men's wives as Jeremy had without making some enemies, and James was certain that Jeremy's famous charm and good cheer were the only reason he hadn't yet been smothered in his bed.

"What the devil do you think you're about?" Jeremy continued, sitting up straighter behind his desk. His own glass of brandy was sitting untouched before him—a sure sign of how deadly serious he was. "Fawning all over Sophie like that—and in front of Violet, no less?"

"I was under the impression—from you yourself—that you and Lady Fitzwilliam were ending your liaison," James murmured.

"That's not the bloody point," Jeremy replied, which was his standard response in any situation in which he didn't want to acknowledge the truth of someone else's words. "I still want to know what the deuce you thought you were doing."

James shoved his chair back and stood, suddenly unable to bear the thought of sitting still a moment longer. He'd been filled with a sort of frenzied energy ever since he and Violet had left the park. He'd been unable to settle to any single task at home, despite the numerous ones that demanded his attention, and hadn't waited long before seizing his hat and gloves to visit Jeremy. Instead of calling for his horse or carriage, he'd walked to Jeremy's house in Fitzroy Square, the exercise doing little to calm the jangle of his nerves.

Besting one's wife, it seemed, was highly invigorating.

"I'm giving Violet a dose of her own medicine," he said, pacing back and forth across the length of the room. Jeremy was a marquess, so his study was larger than most, despite how infrequently it was used, and yet James still felt caged.

Jeremy leaned back in his chair. "Don't you think this has gone a bit far?"

"I apologized to her," James said, stopping his pacing to look Jeremy directly in the eye. It felt odd to admit something so personal aloud, even to as close a friend as Jeremy. He was accustomed to keeping everything of real significance held tightly within him; discussing anything of his conversation with Violet made him feel strange, slightly uncomfortable in his own skin. And yet, as soon as the words were uttered, more followed, almost without conscious thought. "I apologized to her for the incident with the blasted horse, and she is still lying to me."

"I see," Jeremy said, and James rather thought Jeremy *did* see, and that he pitied him. It was galling. However, they were Englishmen, and Englishmen certainly didn't sit about discussing their *feelings*, of all things. "So your new scheme is to pant over every widow you see until your wife becomes so enraged that she murders you in a jealous passion?" He lifted his glass to James in a mocking tribute. "Congratulations. I've no doubt the drama they pen about you will be performed before generations to come."

James took a hearty sip of his drink. "I've no plan at all," he admitted, dropping back into his chair. "Unless you consider needling her until she admits she's been lying to me a plan."

"You've likely caused a fair bit of gossip, and likely gained nothing for it," Jeremy pointed out. "We were hardly the only people in Hyde Park today. There were plenty of witnesses to you making an ass of yourself." He took a sip of brandy. "Don't you think it would be easier to just speak with her?" Jeremy's voice was uncommonly serious, his gaze direct. In that moment, he looked every inch the marquess, and not at all like the Jeremy that James had known for fifteen years—the devil-may-care rogue, the second son without a whit of responsibility. In the nearly six years since Jeremy's brother's death, James had seen flickers of this—hints of the man that Jeremy could perhaps be, if he were ever to dedicate his thoughts to matters more weighty than which young widow of the *ton* was the most desirable at any given moment. Usually, he found these glimpses comforting, an indication of the person that James had always known lurked within Jeremy, underneath all the flash and charm and merrymaking.

At the moment, however, he just found it dashed inconvenient, as he was the one bearing the brunt of Jeremy's attention.

"It's been four years," James reminded him. "I'm not sure we've much to say to one another after four years." A more accurate statement would be that they had entirely *too much* to say to one another after four years, but he didn't feel like sharing that sentiment with even his closest friend.

Jeremy opened his mouth, then closed it again. James could see the internal struggle taking place, could see how desperately Jeremy wished to ask questions. Seeming to give up the battle, he said, "If you would just *tell* me what your argument was all about—"

"No," James insisted, and something in his tone must had been thoroughly convincing, because Jeremy fell silent at once, which was entirely unlike him. James had no desire to discuss the events of that day, to share the conversation between his father and Violet that he had overheard. And he didn't care to pause long enough to examine *why* exactly he was so bent upon keeping the details of that day locked up within himself. A small voice in the very corner of his mind, one that was easily silenced, whispered that he feared someone telling him that he had been in the wrong four years ago. That was a possibility that he did not wish to consider. Because if he had been, then Violet's anger with him was every bit as justified as his with her. Perhaps even more so.

No. He could not bear to think on it. He merely avoided speaking of that day because no man liked to admit that he had been outmaneuvered. And four years ago, he had learned that the circumstances of his marriage had involved a good deal more maneuvering than he'd had any notion of.

"Fine," Jeremy said, settling even deeper into his chair like a petulant child. His posture was beginning to rival Penvale's for lazy indolence. "But you're being a bloody idiot, and I begin to wonder that Violet hasn't left you and taken up with the first dashing Italian to waltz across the Channel. For Christ's sake, Audley, do you know that Penvale and I didn't realize that you and Violet had stopped speaking for months after it happened?"

James frowned. "That can't be true."

"It's true," Jeremy said firmly. "We knew you were drinking yourself into a stupor on a nightly basis, but we'd no notion of the reason until Penvale finally resorted to asking that *sister* of his"—Jeremy said the word *sister* the way he might have said *succubus*—"and she told him what was afoot."

"It was none of your concern," James said.

"If you treat Violet this way, it's no wonder the two of you can barely hold a cordial conversation these days."

"Jeremy, enough." James suddenly felt a great deal more sympathy for the men who had challenged Jeremy to duels in the past. It was an appealing thought at the moment.

"Suit yourself, Audley," Jeremy said in a way that made James somehow feel that he had come out on the losing end of this conversation. "But I warn you, the gossip will continue if you keep this madness up."

James waved a hand dismissively. "There's nothing to gossip about," he said impatiently. "I hardly think a single conversation in the park is enough to whip the *ton* into a frenzy."

"Ha," Jeremy said, in the dark tones of a man who had had more than one irate husband threaten him with pistols at dawn after hearing the latest on-dit whispered in a ballroom. "You were practically falling all over yourself. And in front of me, no less." He attempted an air of wounded outrage, largely unsuccessfully.

"Might I remind you, Willingham," James said, and Jeremy looked up sharply at that—James almost never used Jeremy's title—"that I have known Lady Fitzwilliam longer than you have, and quite possibly better."

Jeremy eyed him for a moment.

"Then might I remind you, Audley, that all that business with your brother was six years ago, and the lady married in the interim."

James opened his mouth to reply, but Jeremy wasn't finished speaking.

"Might I also remind you that it's no good acting wounded on your brother's behalf, when you and West are barely on speaking terms these days."

"I hardly think that's any—"

"You never think anything is my concern," Jeremy cut in sharply. "Not if there's the least chance that you might be in the wrong. It's much easier to be tight-lipped about it and then no one has to tell you when you're being a bloody idiot."

"A bit of the pot calling the kettle black, isn't it?" James drawled, in a tone that he knew would irritate Jeremy further. "Or perhaps the pot calling the kettle a pot?"

"What exactly do you mean to do here?" Jeremy asked, leaning forward. Anger was etched into all the lines of his body, though James wasn't sure it would have been obvious to anyone other than himself or Penvale. "Flirt with Sophie at every turn? You'll destroy her reputation."

"Funny," James said, "I rather thought you were doing a perfectly good job of that already."

"We've been discreet," Jeremy said defensively, and James couldn't argue with that, because it was true. Jeremy was, in fact, usually discreet in his carryings-on with married ladies, and he had taken extra care with Lady Fitzwilliam these past few months. James had actually been a bit impressed by how little gossip swirled around their liaison.

At the moment, however, James was disinclined to be charitable. "Regardless, I hardly think that one conversation in Hyde Park compares to months of sharing a bed. Does West know about the two of you?" he asked, as though the thought had just now occurred to him.

"If he does, he's never spoken of it," Jeremy said tightly. "But I doubt he'd extend the same courtesy to you, were you to continue this ridiculous flirtation." He stood suddenly, a clear signal that he wished James to leave. "As you well know, Sophie and I are ending our liaison," he announced. "That was why we were in the park this afternoon—I meant to discuss it with her, before we encountered you and Violet. Afterward, she beat me to it. We don't suit—don't know why I ever thought we would, really." He looked at James evenly the entire time he spoke. "But I hold her in very high regard, and don't wish to see you make a fool of her out of some misguided attempt to convince yourself that you're not still in love with your wife."

James shoved his chair back and stood. "I'm not—"

"I don't want to hear it, Audley," Jeremy said wearily, and walked James to the door of his study. "But do have a care with your brother, by the by. If he catches wind of you sniffing round Sophie's skirts, there will be hell to pay."

❦

The devil of it was that Jeremy was correct. It had been years now— more than six—but his brother and Sophie Wexham had at one point been very much in love. Miss Wexham had been in her third Season when she'd met West, who had been twenty-four. *It must be a family failing*, James mused. *Falling disastrously in love at an inappropriately young age.*

Sophie Wexham was beautiful and clever, and had a dowry that made every fortune hunter of the *ton* look twice—but she had never quite taken, as James had once overheard one dowager say. Her bloodline was far too new—her family's title only stretched back one generation, and many of the older aristocratic families turned up their noses at Viscount Wexham and his daughters. The Marquess of Weston, as heir to the ancient and venerable duchy of Dovington, ought not to have looked twice at such an upstart chit.

But he had.

More than twice. They'd met at a musicale and had spent a good portion of the evening in whispered conversation about the crimes against Mozart being committed. One would think it difficult to fall in love while trying not to stuff one's fingers into one's ears, but West and Sophie seemed to have managed it. By the end of the evening, they were entirely in one another's thrall.

So it continued for the rest of that Season—they danced twice at every ball, West called on Sophie at her parents' town house with almost laughable frequency, and they went for long rides together in Hyde Park. A marriage seemed inevitable—there was even betting at White's as to when the engagement would be announced.

And then there had been West's curricle accident.

Such a silly thing to alter the course of one life and end another one.

West had impulsively challenged Jeremy's elder brother David, the Marquess of Willingham, to a race, during which the curricles over-turned on a sharp corner, killing David instantly and shattering West's leg. He was bedridden for months, and in the days following the accident had been gripped with a fever that had very nearly killed him.

When he was well enough to rejoin society—though society had a rather difficult time recognizing the formerly reckless and charming Marquess of Weston in the somber gentleman who had taken his place—it was to find that his beloved Sophie had married West's childhood friend Fitzwilliam Bridewell.

Three years later, Lord Fitzwilliam was dead—killed in battle on the Continent. Lady Fitzwilliam was a widow at the age of twenty-four. Through all of this—the six years that spanned West's long recovery, Sophie's marriage, her widowhood, her mourning, and her reentrance into society—James had never once heard his brother utter her name.

Until now.

"I would ask what the hell is wrong with you, but I'm certain there are too many correct responses to select only one."

James looked up—it was the following morning and he was at home in his study, his head full of numbers involving competing offers for a mare in his stables whose foals tended to grow into exceptionally fast runners. For a second, he merely blinked up at his brother, who stood in the doorway, hat and gloves in hand. It was such an incongruous sight, West here in his house, that for a moment he wasn't able to process it. By the time his mind had caught up with his eyes—something Violet had once remarked was uncommonly difficult for the entirety of the male species—West had crossed the room and was towering over him. James could sense waves of anger rolling off of him.

Christ. It was going to be that sort of day. First Jeremy last night, now West—he supposed that once he'd dealt with his brother, he should take himself upstairs and submit to whatever verbal lashing

Violet was no doubt saving for him. Might as well get it all over with at once. At least this time, he was the one sitting behind the desk.

"West," he said, rising respectfully—West was, after all, still his elder brother, and a future duke at that. "What can I do for you?"

"What is this nonsense I'm hearing about you at my club?" West demanded, crossing to the sideboard where James kept a decanter of brandy and several cut-glass tumblers. He raised the decanter, un-invited, and poured himself a healthy splash. He did not ask James if he cared for a drink as well.

"I'm not entirely certain I know what you mean," James said, though he in fact had a fairly good idea.

"It seems that you had a lengthy conversation with Lady Fitzwil-liam in the park yesterday," West said, his fastidiously correct use of Sophie's title making the words sound extra stiff.

"Do you have spies?" James asked.

West looked at him sharply over the rim of his glass as he took a sip of his drink. "The fact that I've already heard of this should indi-cate how much gossip there has been, James. I'm not some old biddy swapping the latest news over tea, you know. But a man displaying blatant interest in a woman who is known to be linked to his best friend—"

"Not widely known, I shouldn't think," James muttered, watch-ing his brother closely. It was clear that his suspicions had been correct—West likely knew every move Lady Fitzwilliam had taken in the years since they'd been close, even if he hadn't so much as ut-tered her name.

"Widely enough," West replied curtly, clearly in no mood for split-ting hairs. "James, I know that we've not been on the best of terms these past years"—an understatement, James thought, but West always had been polite—"but as your brother, I can no longer sit by and watch you make a mess of your life."

"Funny," James said acidly. "You didn't seem to mind overmuch when Father made a misery of it time and time again." This was a slight exaggeration—James hadn't been abused or mistreated, merely neglected. Now, as an adult, he realized that he had been rather lucky, all in all. As a boy of six, or eight, or ten, however, he'd been unable to see anything except a father whose love and attention were reserved solely for the elder brother he rarely saw, so much time did West spend in the duke's company.

"I have never claimed that Father was a particularly good parent," West replied, his eyes focusing intently on James.

"In fact, as I am certain you know, I do my best to avoid speaking to him whenever possible," West continued, his eyes never leaving James's. "So if you'd stop bloody punishing me for the fact that he's a piss-poor father, then perhaps we could have a proper conversation."

"I'm not punishing you for that," James said sharply. "You were a boy, you couldn't be expected to stop his favoring you. But I don't have to forgive you for meddling in my life as an adult."

"If you're referring to that bloody row we had—"

"What *else* would I be referring to?" James asked, exasperated. He was rapidly reaching the limits of his patience—it had hardly been a restful twenty-four hours.

"—then I don't know how else to make you see reason. You're being a fool, and you've been a fool for the past four years." West downed the rest of his drink in a single gulp, then crossed the room and set the empty tumbler down on James's desk with a decisive clunk.

"I told you this four years ago, and I shall say it again today," West said, leaning forward to fix James with his penetrating gaze. James, for all that he was a grown man of eight-and-twenty with a wife and a home of his own, felt very much like a younger brother in that moment. "You have made an utter mess of what started off as a brilliant marriage. You've allowed Father to guide everything you have or have not done for the entirety of your adult life, and you're making yourself miserable in the process. I don't mind much what you do with your own life—I can't very well stop you, though I do pity poor Violet. But leave Sophie out of this."

James barely managed to keep his expression neutral at the sound of West voicing Lady Fitzwilliam's name, nor did he miss the emotion in his brother's voice.

"Furthermore, you might consider the fact that I'm your brother, and it's permissible for me to have opinions about how you conduct yourself, and how you go about your life. You don't have to agree with me, or listen to me, but I'm allowed to voice them nonetheless. It's part of loving someone, James." He paused for a moment; when he spoke again, he had gotten himself under control, and his voice was once again cool and regulated. "When you're ready to act like a man and not a child, you know where to find me," West finished, tucking his hat under his arm and pulling on first one glove, then the other. "Until then . . ." He trailed off, clearly unsure how to conclude this heartwarming interlude of brotherly affection. "Until then," he repeated, more firmly this time, before striding from the room as abruptly as he had materialized, scarcely seeming to lean on his cane at all.

James sank back into his chair as West departed, thinking longingly of the virtues of a lengthy tour somewhere without wives, friends, or brothers. Somewhere remote. The Far East, perhaps. Or New South Wales. A criminal colony seemed preferable to London at the moment.

He glanced down at the papers spread across his desk, the numbers swimming before his eyes, and groaned softly. If he ever had a son, he decided in that moment, the first piece of fatherly advice he would ever give him would be to never marry. Wives were too bloody distracting.

"My lord?"

James looked up, startled. As if summoned by his thoughts, his own wife hovered in the doorway. He rose instantly, and she took a couple of steps into the room. She was dressed in a morning gown of white lawn, her hair slightly disheveled. He wondered if she had any idea how utterly tempting she looked standing there, her cheeks flushed, dark tendrils of hair curling about her face. Her gown was modest, but it somehow only made James more tempted to reach for the bodice, to tug it down and follow its path with his lips.

Forcing his unruly thoughts into order with some difficulty, he said, "Violet? Can I help you?"

"I saw that West was here," she said, walking toward one of the windows that bracketed James's desk. "It was an unusual enough occurrence that I thought to see what he wanted."

She spoke as though the answer he gave was not of terribly great interest to her, but he had one of the flashes he'd had of late—moments where suddenly he was twenty-three all over again and her every word and thought was visible to him, a book that only he could read. At the moment, she was desperately curious, but trying very hard not to show it.

It was all going according to plan—even West's visit, unexpected (and rather unpleasant) as it had been, could serve its own purpose.

"He just stopped by to say hello," James said, walking out from around the desk. Violet had stopped directly in front of the window, squinting into the late morning sunlight as she stared into the garden. She pretended not to notice his approach.

"Did he, now?" she murmured skeptically, not removing her gaze from the window, even as James took several steps closer, crowding her. "Odd, isn't it? He's not been in the habit of paying you calls much of late."

"I always thought you liked West," he said, watching her profile, gilded by sunlight. He told himself that he was staring to make her uncomfortable, but the truth was she was so lovely that he could not possibly have brought himself to look away. "I should have thought you'd be pleased that he paid a visit."

She did look up then, and he mentally congratulated himself on a well-placed hit. "I *do* like West," she said, her eyes sparking, and as she met his gaze full-on, he realized that he might have made a slight miscalculation. He'd meant to needle her, annoy her, but always maintain the upper ground—and yet, when she was looking at him like that, *really* looking at him without any of the distance that had spread between them, it was all he could do to keep his hands at his sides, to resist the temptation to reach out, pull her to him, and kiss her senseless.

She, however, seemed oblivious to his internal struggle, because she was still, as usual, speaking.

"But I don't believe for a second that his visit today was at all coincidental." A moment of silence fell, during which she glared at him furiously and he tried desperately not to notice the interesting things her angry breathing did to her bosom. It was covered in fabric, to be sure, but it was still moving in a very distracting fashion.

"What do you mean?" he managed.

"You know precisely what I mean," she said with quiet derision, and this was when James knew that she was very angry indeed. Angry Violet became noisy. Even angrier Violet became alarmingly quiet. "I am certain West stopped by because he heard of that shocking display in the park with Lady Fitzwilliam yesterday, and if you think for a second that I am going to allow you to ruin a respectable woman's reputation—"

"She's carrying on with Jeremy," James felt compelled to point out, though he knew that he hadn't much of a leg to stand on in terms of the rightness and wrongness of the matter. "Not exactly a pillar of respectability himself, you know."

"He has been uncommonly discreet," Violet said tersely. "I've heard only the slightest whisperings of any carryings-on between them— yesterday was the first time I've ever even seen them together. So please do not try to convince me that the lady's reputation was already in tatters. Jeremy has done nothing to ruin her, and has indeed gone out of his way to ensure that no damage has been done to her social standing. What *will* ruin her, however, is your making a spectacle of yourself in Hyde Park."

She paused for breath, and James, suddenly feeling like a rather great ass, opened his mouth to reply. Violet, however, had not finished speaking her piece.

"Furthermore," she continued, her gaze still holding his own, "the state of the lady's reputation is really a bit beside the point. The fact is, she is a person in her own right, and not an object of revenge. Did you spare a moment's consideration for that small fact? Did you even for a moment stop to think that she might have some rather strong feelings on being treated in such a fashion?" Her voice never rose louder than her normal speaking volume, but James felt every word like a physical blow.

She paused, eyeing him from head to toe. Her gaze was like a hot poker on his skin. "No," she said dismissively. "Of course you didn't. You are a man, and she is merely a woman."

In that instant, James felt like more of a cad than he ever had done in his entire twenty-eight years of life. He had always considered himself a gentleman, someone who respected women and treated them with the courtesy they deserved. He had always looked askance at men who belittled female intelligence, able to see their derision for what it truly was: insecurity. And yet, in less than a minute, Violet had shown him what an utter prick he was.

In truth, he had not given overly much consideration to Lady Fitzwilliam's feelings the day before; he had been able to tell from a quick glance at her face as he was speaking that she knew he was not serious in his flirtation, and that knowledge had been sufficient to ease his conscience. In that moment, it had been enough; now, however, he saw that it should not have been. She was a widow; she might or might not still be in love with his brother; and, beyond all that, she was a woman, with feelings and thoughts of her own. And he had treated her abominably.

Violet was right—and so was West, and so, God help him, was Jeremy. He sighed, scrubbing his hands over his face, suddenly exhausted by the entire bloody mess that he and Violet had created. At that moment, he would have given every shilling he possessed to go back a week and undo every word he had spoken to Violet outside that damn tavern.

Actually, he'd have liked to go back four years and undo every word he'd said to her that fateful morning when he had discovered her conversing with his father. At the time, all he'd felt was betrayal—betrayal at the hands of the person he'd trusted most in the world, the *only* person, in fact, that he had ever truly trusted with the deepest, most important parts of himself. Now it all seemed less important.

"Well?" Violet asked, her voice sharp. "Don't you have anything to say for yourself?"

James lowered his hands and looked at her. Her cheeks were flushed; a curl of dark hair lay against her neck, in striking contrast to the creamy perfection of the skin behind it.

He dragged his eyes upward, meeting her gaze directly. "I'm sorry."

She blinked. Under different circumstances, he would have found it amusing—she had clearly been preparing for a fight, and his capitulation had caught her completely by surprise. He watched as she clutched at the threads of her composure. "I—of course you are," she said, clearly attempting to put her best face forward. "As you should be."

He took a step closer to her, all but erasing the distance between them. "I will send Lady Fitzwilliam a note of apology today," he said. He noticed that at this proximity, she had to tilt her head back to look up at him as he spoke. It was one of the thousand tiny details he had unlearned about her over the past few years, now presented for him to memorize anew. "I owe her an apology in person, of course, but I would not risk her reputation by calling on her."

"A bit late for such consideration, don't you think?" Violet asked, her eyes narrow. He spared a moment's longing contemplation of the normally round shape of the eyes in question—he had found them narrowed upon his person so often of late that he had almost forgotten what they looked like in their natural state.

"Entirely," he conceded, and had the pleasure of watching her face register her surprise once again. "But as I cannot undo the past, I am merely going to do the best I can in the present."

It was then his turn to be surprised as, with absolutely no warning, she burst into laughter.

She raised a hand to cover her mouth, the move doing little to contain the peals of unladylike laughter. She took a step back from him, even as she seemed to be making largely futile attempts to contain her mirth.

"I'm sorry," she gasped, but was unable to say more as another fit of giggles overtook her. For his part, James found himself less irked at being laughed at than he might have expected. It had been so long since he had seen her laugh that he could only stand and drink in the sight, his eyes greedily consuming the details that had grown fuzzy in his memory.

She attempted speech once more. "You just seem so absurdly serious—it really all sounded a bit ridiculous . . ."

James was dimly aware that he was being mocked, but he seemed unable to be overly much bothered. And then, without really giving the matter much thought at all, he did the only thing that, in that precise moment, seemed at all reasonable—or perhaps even possible.

He kissed her.

And the moment his lips descended on hers, all reason fled.

The only vague thought that flitted through his head as his lips moved over hers was that he'd forgotten. He'd forgotten how soft her mouth was as it brushed against his own. She seemed momentarily startled by his kiss, her entire body freezing in the instant that he first touched her. But then, suddenly, it was as though she melted all at once, kissing him back with a fervor that matched his own. His tongue darted out, teasing at the corner of her mouth, and her lips parted. This, too, he had forgotten: the precise feeling of her tongue tangling with his own, the strength with which her hand moved to the back of his neck, cradling his head in her palm as she kissed him.

190

He slid both of his hands to her waist, pulling her more firmly against him. Each spot where their bodies touched felt suddenly alive, as though every single nerve was sparking at the friction. He could feel himself stiffening and, rather than stepping back to put some much-needed distance between them, he let his hands drift down to cup her bottom, keeping her pressed tightly against him so that there was no space between them, nothing but warmth and desire.

And here was yet another thing that he had forgotten: how perfectly their bodies fit together, her breasts crushed against his chest, her arms tangled around his neck, their heads tilted at just such an angle as to allow the kiss to stretch on endlessly, time seeming to stand still. He broke his mouth away from hers at last and moved lower, planting a series of soft kisses along the silky skin of her neck, the sound of her uneven breathing making his heart pound even faster.

"James," she moaned softly, and his tongue darted out to taste the hollow of her throat, flicking against the pulse that beat steadily there. She shivered, the small vibration rippling down her body like a wave, and slid her hands into his hair, pulling his mouth back up to her own. His mouth opened, her tongue darted inside, and he nearly groaned aloud it felt so good—it was all he could do to keep from sinking to the floor with her, hiking up her skirts and—

The sound of a throat clearing, with perhaps more force than was generally necessary to such an endeavor.

Violet broke the kiss with a gasp, whirling around to face the doorway, where Wooton stood, his face carefully impassive.

"My lady, your carriage is ready," he said, his tone neutral.

"I, yes, thank you, Wooton," Violet said, panting slightly. "I'll be along shortly."

"Very good, my lady," Wooton said and, with a perfect bow, exited the room.

James could have kissed his butler in that moment—needless to say, not a sentiment he had ever expected to experience. But who knew how far things might have gone had Wooton not interrupted? He ought to give the man a raise, really.

Because James was feeling deeply unsettled. How could it be that he still responded to Violet with such intensity? Why was it that a few stolen moments spent kissing his wife in his own study left him feeling more alive than he had in years? It was infuriating. Absurd. And so James did what he always did whenever he was feeling off-kilter, lacking the upper hand.

"I'd forgotten how easy it can be to silence you," he said, his tone deliberately even, just the slightest note of mockery lurking underneath.

It worked in an instant; Violet had turned to face him a moment before he spoke, and in that moment he had seen a hundred things in her face—uncertainty, amusement, lust. But as soon as the words left his mouth, her face closed, her gaze shuttering and the corners of her mouth turning down.

"And I'd forgotten what an ass you can be," she responded, her own voice clipped and remote. She turned on her heel without a further word and sailed from the room.

And James—despite having achieved exactly what he'd intended, despite having put some much-needed distance between them—was left feeling precisely as she had described him: like an ass.

Ten

"Violet," Diana said, rising from the chair upon which she was seated, dropping her paintbrush in the process. "This is a pleasant surprise."

"I needed to speak to you at once," Violet said as soon as Wright had closed the door behind her. "I apologize for arriving so early—it's barely past noon, but I knew you would be awake—"

"Not at all," Diana said, waving a lazy hand at a chair and sinking back onto her own. "Shall I ring for tea?"

"No," Violet said, not wanting the distraction, then paused, reconsidering. She liked to think she was a sensible person, and any sensible Englishwoman knew that life was more easily tackled with tea. "Well, perhaps a spot of tea wouldn't go amiss."

Diana rose again to ring the bell, and after a moment's murmured request to a maid, she resumed her place in her chair. They were not in her sitting room but in the solarium, Diana's favorite room of the house and, she often joked, the reason she had agreed to marry Lord Templeton in the first place.

At least, Violet *thought* she was joking. It was rather difficult to tell with Diana sometimes, and her motives for marrying the viscount had certainly been mercenary.

The room was littered with chairs and a couple of settees, all given a warm glow by the ample light flowing in through the windows that lined the walls and roof. Diana spent most of her mornings in this room, painting, as she had been doing when Violet interrupted her.

"Darling, what's all this about?" Diana asked after she had settled herself once more. "You don't look quite the thing at all."

Violet, who had perched on the edge of an armchair as she waited for Diana to resettle herself, barely able to contain her impatience, burst out, "I think James knows I'm not ill!"

Diana blinked once, twice, and Violet, with effort, relaxed her posture slightly, doing her best to attempt to look casual, rather than like an escapee from Bedlam.

"How could he possibly have found out?" Diana asked, waving a dismissive hand. "He's a man. They're sheep."

Now it was Violet's turn to blink. "Meaning . . . they follow each other?"

Diana sighed, impatient as always with anyone who couldn't quite keep up with her. "No, meaning their minds can only focus on about three things at once—and I'm quite certain your husband doesn't have the mental capacity to think overmuch about the symptoms of your malady."

"He did take a first at Oxford," Violet felt compelled to mention, out of some lingering sense of wifely loyalty. "He's not a complete idiot, you know."

"Oh yes, Audley's clever enough, as men go"—Diana's tone indicated that she had her doubts as to the extent that any man could, in fact, be considered clever—"but they're all the same. None of them question anything too terribly much. It's why in any real marriage the woman should pull all the strings."

"I pity your next husband," a voice sounded from the doorway. Startled, Violet turned in her seat, only to relax upon realizing that it was Penvale, leaning against the doorjamb. "I showed myself in," he said, pushing himself upward. At that moment, a maid bearing a heavily laden tea tray appeared behind him; he relieved her of her burden with a wink and a smile, making her blush and giggle as she bobbed a curtsey and departed.

"Really, Penvale," Diana said as he carefully set the tray down on the table before her. "Please don't send yet another one of my maids into a tizzy, you'll put her off her work."

Ignoring her, as he frequently did, her brother flung himself into a chair, then leaned forward to select a scone. "What's this about, then?" he asked after swallowing his first mouthful.

Diana, who had busied herself pouring cups of tea for them, didn't look up as she spoke. "Violet's concerned that Audley knows she's bamming him."

Violet, who had expected a denial from Penvale, instead merely received a snort of laughter. "Of course he does," he said.

"What?" Diana asked, freezing in the act of handing a cup of tea to Violet. "What on earth do you mean?"

"I mean," Penvale said, speaking with exaggerated slowness, "that Audley isn't a complete idiot, and he's perfectly capable of recognizing when he'd being lied to by his own wife." Penvale's tone wasn't reproachful, but Violet couldn't help stiffening all the same.

"When did he realize?" she asked.

"He recognized Belfry," Penvale said wearily, taking another hearty bite of scone, "as he was leaving your house that day." He cast a wry glance at his sister. "I realize you might find all this difficult to believe, given his man-size intellect."

Violet slumped in her chair. "I *knew* it," she said, feeling glum. She ought to feel relieved, she supposed, that she didn't have to attempt that ridiculous cough anymore, and yet instead she felt oddly bereft. It had been rather nice to have an excuse to speak with James, even if much of their conversation over the course of the past week had involved arguing.

And kissing.

Her lips tingled at the memory of the feeling of his mouth on hers, and she resisted the urge to press her hands to them with great effort. She felt rather irked with her traitorous body for choosing that precise moment to relive the scene in James's study, when she was so terribly annoyed with the man in question.

And yet, here she was.

"How did you realize?" Penvale asked curiously, having finished his scone and now redirecting his attention to the cup of tea his sister had handed him.

"He summoned my mother to nurse me back to health," Violet said darkly. "The man knows full well that ten minutes in her company is likely to force me to take to my bed, not cure me. And then there was that ridiculous scene in Hyde Park yesterday afternoon with Willingham and Lady Fitzwilliam," she said dismissively. "Absurd."

"I gather he and Jeremy quarreled about it."

"As well they might," Violet said severely. "It was frightful."

"Lady Wheezle was telling some sort of outlandish tale along those lines at Lady Markham's dinner party last night," Diana said. "The behavior she described sounded so wildly out of character for Audley that I didn't believe a word of it, and said as much to the entire table." She paused, heaving a dramatic sigh. "She probably won't invite me to her Venetian breakfast this year, but that seems a fair price to pay. Odious woman."

"She unfortunately more or less has the right of it," Violet said, turning to her. "James and I went riding yesterday. We encountered Jeremy and Lady Fitzwilliam Bridewell whilst we were out, and James made a cake of himself assuring the lady that he was at her . . . *service*, should she ever require it."

Diana's mouth fell open. "That bounder!"

"Quite." Violet took a sip of tea. "It was so out of character for him that I felt certain that he was doing it merely to irk me. Penvale has simply confirmed my suppositions."

"So you're speaking to him now?" Penvale asked hopefully, in the tones of a schoolboy who has been told that a particularly nasty assignment has been canceled.

"I most certainly am not," Violet announced, hoping that she did not blush and give herself away. Speaking—only as was necessary. Engaging in passionate embraces—well, rather. "I did give him a piece of my mind this morning before I left the house, though, I assure you."

"As well you should have," Diana said encouragingly.

"And now you shall leave all this in the past and carry on as normal?" Penvale asked, ever the optimist.

"Hmm," Violet said, tapping her chin, pretending to consider it. "No, I think not. I've a better idea."

❦

Lady Fitzwilliam Bridewell lived in a large house not far from Diana's. Although her late husband had only been a second son, her dowry had evidently been sufficient to keep them in lavish style, and to ensure her comfort after his death. Violet had lingered at Diana's for the rest of the morning, eating a meal with her after midday before finally departing in her carriage for her next social call. Upon arriving at Lady Fitzwilliam's, she was led by the butler into a small drawing room, where she sat, rather uncomfortably, on a well-upholstered armchair. What had seemed like a clever move in Diana's solarium now seemed a bit foolish.

Before she had further time to reconsider, however, the lady of the house appeared in the doorway. She was dressed simply in a gray afternoon gown—Violet knew that she was out of mourning, but this looked like one of her frocks from the months of half mourning that had concluded that period. Her golden hair was pulled back from her face into a simple knot at the nape of her neck, and her features bore an expression of polite curiosity.

"Lady James," Lady Fitzwilliam said, walking into the room. "What an unexpected pleasure." Her tone was wary, as well it might be—Violet had never spoken to her outside of a ballroom before, barring their meeting of the previous day, and she knew that for her to call upon Lady Fitzwilliam in her own home was curious indeed.

"Please, call me Violet," Violet said, abandoning all etiquette as she stood. Her mother would have fainted at this breach of propriety—but then, Lady Worthington tended to swoon at the slightest provocation. Violet secretly suspected that she laced her corsets tighter to ensure said swooning—though, valuing her life (or at least her ears), she had of course never voiced her suspicion to her mother.

"Then you must call me Sophie," was the reply, and Lady Fitzwilliam—Sophie—crossed the room to take Violet's hand and squeeze it lightly, seemingly unfazed by how highly irregular everything about this was. "Would you care for some tea?"

"No, thank you," Violet said, resuming her seat.

Sophie cast a quick glance around the room, as though reassuring herself that they were alone, then said, "Something stronger, perhaps? I've some brandy stowed away for special circumstances—and I rather suspect that this is going to be one."

Violet realized in an instant why West had been so taken with Sophie Wexham. On the surface, she was all that was prim and proper—her hair pulled neatly back, her trim figure clothed in an entirely appropriate gown—but there was clearly more to her that lurked just beneath the surface, and Violet found herself rather intrigued by what, precisely, that *more* might be.

"Yes, I think that might be just the thing," she said by way of reply, and Sophie shot her a pleased smile, rather as if she had sized Violet up correctly.

Sophie hastened to a sideboard and opened a cabinet, removing a decanter half full of brandy and two crystal tumblers. She poured a couple of fingers of brandy into each glass.

"Cheers," she said, offering Violet a glass.

"Cheers." Violet raised it in reply. She took a sip.

"So," Sophie said, selecting the armchair closest to Violet's own, "I presume you're here to discuss our meeting in the park yesterday." Her brown gaze was direct, holding Violet's own without blinking.

"I am, yes," Violet said. She paused, momentarily uncertain—she wasn't at all sure how to phrase her request. Being at a loss for words was not a condition she was terribly accustomed to. "I presume you are somewhat familiar with the rumors surrounding my marriage."

Sophie's mouth quirked up slightly. "I've heard some whisperings that you and Lord James are not as close as you once were."

"My husband and I married for love, but we were very young," Violet said bluntly. "We have discovered that we did not suit so well as we thought."

Sophie arched a golden brow. "It did not seem that way to me yesterday afternoon."

Violet lowered her glass, momentarily diverted from her purpose. "I beg your pardon?"

Sophie shrugged elegantly and took another sip of her drink. "You two seemed rather . . . connected. I assumed that was why he was so friendly with me, when Lord Willingham and I appeared. To make you jealous," she clarified, though Violet had taken her meaning.

"He and I are currently engaged in a bit of a . . . duel," Violet said, failing to find a more appropriate word.

"Indeed?" Sophie leaned forward slightly, clearly interested. "Do go on."

And so Violet did. She gave Sophie a somewhat condensed version of events, but thorough enough that by the time she had finished speaking, Sophie's eyebrows were near her hairline, creating small wrinkles in her normally smooth brow.

"And so that is what you stumbled upon in Hyde Park yesterday," Violet finished. "I apologize that my husband saw fit to drag you into this, and that he treated you so abominably in the process."

Sophie waved a dismissive hand in a gesture eerily reminiscent of Diana, though twenty minutes ago Violet would not have thought the two ladies similar in the least. "I assumed it was something like that," she said. "Well, not like what you have described, precisely, because I do not think my imagination rich enough to conjure that scenario." She took another sip of brandy, and Violet followed suit. "As it happens, I received a profusely apologetic letter from your husband just an hour or so ago."

Violet was impressed, though she supposed she shouldn't have expected anything less. James was a man who, once set upon a course of action, tended to see it through immediately.

"It all seemed rather out of character for Audley, truth be told—his behavior yesterday, I mean," Sophie amended. "Not the apology." She paused. "Although nothing you've told me sounds terribly *in* character for him. Except for the stubbornness, of course. That sounds exactly right."

It was interesting, Violet reflected, speaking to a woman who had known her husband longer than she had. Not as *well* as she had, of course, but still—before Violet had met James, before she had even had her first Season, West and Sophie had been courting. James would have been all of two-and-twenty at the time—a boy. A boy that Violet rather missed, much as it pained her to admit it.

"I thought, when I came here this afternoon, to ask you to play along with him," Violet said a bit hesitantly.

"What, flirt with him in turn?" Sophie's voice sounded amused, although it was with a straight face that she lifted her tumbler to her lips once again.

"Yes, rather. It would no doubt confuse and horrify him, and I'm irritated enough at the moment to relish the prospect."

"Has it ever occurred to you to speak to him instead?" Sophie asked, posing a question that Violet had considered on more than one occasion over the course of the past week.

"I can't," Violet said simply. "When we quarreled . . . well, I'm certain I'm not blameless, but the issues we quarreled over really have to do with him. They're all in his head."

She could practically see the curiosity radiating from Sophie's person, but of course she was entirely too well-bred to ask probing questions. And yet, Violet felt an almost painful desire to unburden herself. It had been four years, and she had never told anyone the story of that morning, which was really the story of the year that led to it. Diana, Emily, even her mother—they had all asked, of course. But she had never wished to speak of it—it felt like a betrayal of James, of her marriage and the secrets it held. And yet, here she was, with a woman she barely knew, and she found the words bubbling up within her so that she could barely contain them.

"We were very much in love when we married," she said, having made up her mind in an instant. "I was only eighteen, you know—it was early in my very first Season that James and I met."

"How did you meet?"

"At a ball—on a balcony, actually," Violet said, smiling at the memory. "But it was instant—I fell in love with him so fast, it made my head spin." She paused, thinking. "Of course, now I think it was merely infatuation at first—the real love came later, the more I grew to know him. But at the time, I thought that it was love at first sight, and he seemed to feel the same way. It was . . ." She paused, a lump rising in her throat at the memory. "It was wonderful.

"And we were happy at first, of course. James's father made a gift of Audley House as a wedding present—it was far more than James was expecting to receive from him. James has never wished to be dependent on his father, but I think he wanted to prove something to the duke—show him that he was capable of this task that he'd been set. I think he enjoyed the challenge of it, too, in some ways. He studied mathematics at university, you know, and there are quite a lot of numbers involved in running successful stables. So in some ways, he enjoyed it. But he was always doing it for the wrong reason, I felt— always looking over his shoulder at his father, as if to make sure the duke saw that he was managing, that he could be more than some mere afterthought of a second son.

"James and I quarreled about it, sometimes," Violet added, lost in memories. "I thought he spent far too much time on the stables—he would ride down to Kent once a week sometimes, despite employing a number of grooms. And when he was in London, he spent hours holed up going over the finances, despite having a man of business employed for that very purpose. But he would never listen to me. I think that he felt he had something to prove to *me*, too, which was ridiculous, but I could never convince him to see things that way. And other than that, things were so splendid—I kept myself busy, and James was always popping home at odd hours in the middle of the day to see me. It sounds frightfully silly now, but at the time, it was very romantic."

"It sounds lovely," Sophie said, and Violet looked up sharply, detecting a wistful note in her voice. She wondered what Sophie's marriage had been like—and what a marriage between Sophie and West could have been like instead. "But what happened?"

It was a question Violet had asked herself, on nights when she lay sleepless in her own bed, conscious of James in his own room, not so very far away and yet seemingly separated by miles and miles of space between them.

"We quarreled," she said simply, which was the truth and yet not even close to explaining what had happened. "We'd quarreled before, of course, but never quite like this—I don't know if it all just came to a head, or . . ." She trailed off, thinking. "No, I think it was his father's presence that made it so awful."

"The duke was there when you quarreled?" Sophie asked incredulously, and with a note of alarm in her voice that made Violet curious about what had happened between Sophie and West all those years ago.

"No, he'd left by then," Violet said. "But it was his presence that set everything off." She took a deep breath, thinking back to that long-ago morning.

"A couple of days before we quarreled, I had been to tea with my mother. She and I—" She broke off, searching for a delicate way of describing her relationship with Lady Worthington. "Don't always see eye to eye," she finished.

"I have met Lady Worthington on several occasions, and I must confess that does not entirely surprise me," Sophie said diplomatically.

"She was needling me about my marriage," Violet continued. "I had made some offhand comment about James in jest and she took offense. She said it wasn't my place to comment on my husband's activities"—she could feel herself growing irate just recounting this conversation—"and I told her that when I wished for her opinion on my marriage, I'd ask for it."

Sophie let out a laugh at that. "I take it that went over well?"

"As well as you'd imagine, I expect. She then informed me that my marriage wouldn't have come about at all if it wasn't for her—she was the one who found James and myself on a balcony at a ball and more or less forced him to propose," Violet explained. "So I naturally told her that we would have found ourselves in the same spot sooner or later regardless of whether she'd forced the issue." She paused. "That was when she told me that she and the duke were the only reason James had gone looking for me on the balcony in the first place."

Sophie's jaw dropped. "They staged your meeting."

Violet nodded. "Apparently my mother saw me leave with Lord

Willingham, and rather than coming and fetching me herself, she informed the duke, who sent James out as a sort of knight in shining armor. I suppose as soon as my mother saw Jeremy come back indoors she made her way out there as quickly as possible to intercept us." She paused. "I've never asked Jeremy about it, but she implied that she was the reason he'd escorted me out there in the first place. She can be quite intimidating when she wishes to be; even a rake like Jeremy would be cowed by her, and I wouldn't put it past her to send me out there like a lamb to slaughter, just waiting for James's rescue."

"I have to give your mother credit," Sophie said thoughtfully. "It doesn't seem as though it should have worked, and yet it did. You must have been angry."

"I was," Violet admitted. "And confused—I didn't know how to feel about it at all. I was so in love with James, and to now know that my happiness was owed to the machinations of my mother and his father—it made it all seem rather sordid." She sighed. "I wanted to discuss it with James, of course, but I was so muddled about it all that I didn't quite feel ready. I was concerned it would make him feel differently about our marriage—he has such a difficult relationship with his father, and I hesitated to confide something that would have made it worse . . ."

She leaned forward. "You must understand, I fully intended to tell him—and soon, at that. I just needed a bit more time."

"Of course." Sophie frowned. "I take it you didn't receive it?"

Violet shook her head. "This is where the duke comes in. I was at home a couple of mornings later, and the duke came to call. This in and of itself was unusual—James liked to avoid him as much as possible. I'd never met him without James before. I thought it was odd, but of course I couldn't refuse to see him. So I invited him in . . . and he started asking all sorts of . . ." Violet trailed off, searching for a delicate way to phrase it. "Personal questions," she finished.

Sophie stared at her, uncomprehending, for a moment, and Violet touched a hand quickly to her own midriff. Sophie's eyes widened, understanding. "He didn't," she said in rapt horror.

"He did," Violet confirmed. "Oh, he wasn't so brash as to come straight out and ask when I'd be providing his son with an heir, but he danced quite close to it."

"What did you say?"

"I told him that I didn't think it a conversation appropriate for the drawing room," Violet said, sniffing in remembered outrage. She recalled being quite pleased with her response at the time, thinking that for once she had managed a reply that even her mother would have approved of—for of course, Lady Worthington considered pregnancy and the marital activities that led to it to be unsuitable topics for any conversation. Ever. Suffice to say, given her mother's disinclination to discuss the topic, Violet's wedding night had been highly educational.

Violet had followed up this remark by asking a question of the duke.

"I don't know why you should ask me that question," she had said irritably. "My husband isn't your heir. I believe you have an elder son who perhaps is more deserving of your interrogation."

"My elder son is unlikely to ever provide me with an heir," the duke ground out, and Violet had looked at him blankly. Surely he wasn't saying that West preferred men? She'd read of such things, of course, in her study of the Greeks, and in some of the more illicit poetry she had stumbled across—she had even once asked James a series of questions about the mechanics involved, which had been possibly the only time she'd ever seen him blush—but West's reputation had always been that

of a rake about town, and she had heard the whisperings of the near-engagement with Miss Wexham a couple of years before . . .

"I don't understand why you should think that," she said, when the duke seemed disinclined to elaborate. "The marquess is only six-and-twenty, I believe? Rather young to be considering marriage, so I wouldn't despair that he hasn't yet taken a wife—"

"He will never take a wife," the duke cut in, enunciating each word so clearly that it sounded as though he were hacking them each off of a block of ice. "After that foolish accident, he seems to have been left with an injury that will prevent him from ever fathering children."

"He—oh!" Violet said, understanding dawning. Pity followed closely on its heels—how awful for West. She had grown quite fond of him over the past year—though she did wonder at James never mentioning something of this great a magnitude about his brother. Perhaps he felt it too delicate to discuss with his wife.

None of this, however, could she share with Sophie. Aside from the fact that it was highly inappropriate drawing room conversation, she had no idea what the depth of Sophie's feelings for West might still be—or any notion of what had passed between them in the past.

"He didn't take too kindly to my comment about the appropriateness of the conversation," she added, "and expressed some rather rude doubts about my suitability as James's wife. I hadn't intended to confront him before speaking to James of course, but at that point I rather lost my temper and told him I'd had quite enough of his interference in my marriage."

"I do wish I could have witnessed this," Sophie said somewhat dreamily. "I should so dearly love to see that man delivered a set-down . . ."

"Yes, well," Violet said, preening a bit before subsiding, "it didn't last long, I'm afraid. He wasted no time at all in informing me that he and my mother had interfered because neither of them had any confidence in their children's ability to make appropriate matches on our own."

"*I needed an heir for the dukedom, and my elder son was unable to comply,*" the duke said. "*And you—your mother was worried that you wouldn't take, I understand. How much easier to throw you two together than to leave it all to chance. You should be thanking me,*" the duke said smugly. "*It seems to me as though your happiness is entirely thanks to your mother and myself.*"

"*My mother said something similar just the other day as we were discussing this very matter,*" Violet said coldly. "*You may think yourselves some sort of strategic geniuses for working out how to take advantage of James's gentlemanly instincts, but—*"

The duke interrupted her with a laugh. "*It hardly was the work of a genius. It was really all too easy. My son is entirely too predictable—if he sees a maiden in distress, of course he will come to her rescue. I merely had to mention to him that I'd seen his friend with someone who might cause a bit of a headache for him to send him tearing out in pursuit. And of course, it was nothing at all to have your mother stumble across the two of you on the balcony. I really must congratulate you, my dear, for putting on such a thoroughly convincing performance. Your mother questioned how well it would work, but I—*"

"*You knew precisely how to manipulate me.*"

Violet and the duke both turned, startled, to the doorway, where James had appeared silently. Violet had been so caught up in the duke's tale that she hadn't noticed any noise from the mews heralding his return. She had never seen James look like this before—he was very still, his broad-shouldered form filling the doorway. His eyes were flicking back and forth between herself and his father, as though he couldn't quite decide whom to focus on. After a moment, however, his gaze settled on the duke.

"Well, congratulations, Father," James said, strolling into the room with a sort of studied casualness that Violet could see instantly was an act. "You win. You found me a bride with impeccable lineage, and you managed to keep your little secret until after all the papers were signed." He continued to advance toward the duke, not stopping until he was only a couple of feet from his father. "You haven't quite succeeded in your aim, though, since we've yet to provide you with an heir. Which I surmise is the reason you came to sniff around my wife today." There was the slightest tremble in his voice, which Violet recognized as a sign of just how angry he was.

The duke's expression grew hard as he surveyed his younger son. "Don't make a scene, James. If you can't keep your emotions in check, I don't think there's any point in my lingering." He rose, making as if to step past James, but James blocked his progress.

"I will never provide you with an heir," he said quietly, and while Violet knew—she knew—that it was just his anger speaking, the words were still like a dagger to her heart. Those were her future children he was disavowing. She knew he didn't mean it, but that didn't mean she wanted to hear it. "So your bloody scheme was all for naught." He took a step closer to his father. "Now get out of my house."

"You don't mean he thought you were involved somehow?" Sophie's brows knit together, and her tone of offended outrage on Violet's behalf was obliquely comforting.

"I mean precisely that," Violet said. "I made things worse because I panicked a bit, initially."

The door had scarcely closed behind the duke when James turned to *her. She wasn't sure what she hoped to see in his eyes—understanding, perhaps? A sense of shared anger? Love? Whatever she was looking for, she didn't find it, seeing instead a look of profound betrayal in those familiar green eyes.*

"James," she said quickly, before he could speak, "I knew nothing about this." This wasn't, of course, entirely true—she had known for close to two days, without telling him. But she was so eager to distance herself from their parents' actions that she spoke without thinking.

"Yes, you did," he said quietly. "I heard you. You just told him you'd been discussing it with your mother." His voice was relatively calm, but she could hear the accusatory note to it.

"I tried to tell him I'd only learned of it a couple of days prior," Violet said now. "But he . . . he didn't believe me. He couldn't fathom that I wouldn't have come to him directly upon learning of such a thing, and so he assumed I must have known for far longer—perhaps even been involved from the very outset." Her mind glossed over the memories of the hour that had followed the duke's departure that morning. There had been words—angry words—so many of them that they blended together in her mind, leaving only the impression of hurt feelings and a sense of irreparable damage done.

One sentence, however, stuck out in unfortunately vivid detail.

"I should have known better. What well-bred miss would go out onto a balcony with Jeremy, of all people? It's asking to be ruined."

And the worst of it was, even the memory of that still stung. Because she *had* gone out onto that balcony with Jeremy—not because she was part of the ludicrous scheme that her mother and James's father had cooked up, but because she had been eighteen and curious. And James had made the entire thing feel cheap and sordid.

That was one of the many things about that morning she could not forgive. Most of all, she could not forgive him for his distrust in her—she who had never given him any reason to doubt her. She who had just this once spoken overly hastily—who had just this once, and never before, kept information from him, and always with the intention of telling him the full truth. She who had entrusted her entire heart to him and had felt free, for the first time in her life, to be her true, honest self, without feeling the need to suppress any of the things about herself that her mother had insisted were so entirely unsuitable. For him to repay her by losing faith in her at the first provocation was a betrayal that she had at the time considered unforgivable.

Then there was the fact that when she had stormed out of the room in a fury, he had not followed. Had never followed. Had obviously not considered their marriage worth fighting for.

"Well," said Sophie, finishing the last of her brandy in one healthy and entirely improper gulp, "that is quite the tale."

"Isn't it just," Violet said, not managing to sound quite as matter-of-fact as she might have desired in that moment. To tell the truth, while unburdening herself of this story certainly made her feel lighter, somehow, it also made her feel rather glum.

Silence fell for a moment. Violet, lost in thoughts of that day four years past, watched as Sophie turned her empty tumbler in her hand, the crystal catching the afternoon sunlight streaming in through the windows. It was a small room but cozy, clearly well cared for. Violet wondered how many solitary hours Sophie had whiled away in here since her husband's death. She wondered if she ever got lonely. She then reflected—rather grimly—that her own existence over the past four years hadn't been that different from that of a widow, considering the amount of time she spent in her husband's company.

The thought was thoroughly galling.

Violet sat up straighter in her chair, her mind working more quickly now. What a fool she had been, she realized all at once. She was twenty-three years old and she had a husband she had once adored, who was living in the same house with her, eating at the same table, sleeping in a bedchamber that shared a connecting door with her own, and yet they barely even spoke. Sophie, meanwhile, lived here in this house, her days only slightly more solitary than Violet's own, but her parting from her husband had not been due to any lasting argument, but rather to the permanent separation of death.

She thought of that note from Penvale from the week before, and imagined an alternate scenario—one in which she had made it all the way to Audley House, only to find James dead. She thought of never being able to speak to him, touch him, kiss him again—and she felt empty. As if some critical, nameless part of her had died as well.

She had enacted this ruse to punish him for his neglect, for his distrust of her—and perhaps she had succeeded on some level. But she saw now—as perhaps she should have seen all along—that she had really done all of this because she still loved him, and she thought there was something between them worth fighting for.

Oh, to be sure, she was still thoroughly angry with him. He was still in the wrong when it came to their dispute the day of his father's visit—but perhaps instead of waiting four years for an apology, she should have taken that step forward to bridge the divide herself. She had been so *angry* at first, expecting him to take the first step, to grovel at her feet. And when that hadn't happened . . . she had done nothing.

She had done nothing to save their marriage, the relationship most precious to her. He had made a mistake, to be sure—one he still owed her an apology for—but she knew the man she had married. She knew how reluctant he was to entrust his heart to another. And she could imagine the sense of betrayal he must have felt that day, the entire foundation of his marriage having been proved to be based on his father's duplicity. She could imagine how it must have hurt him, to think that anything about her feelings for him might have been duplicitous, too.

He had been in the wrong, there was no doubt—but he was still worth fighting for. *They* were still worth fighting for.

Sophie was staring at her curiously. Violet realized how long the silence had lingered between them and smiled apologetically.

"I'm sorry. I was woolgathering."

Sophie waved a hand dismissively. "As was I. You gave me rather a lot to ponder, I must confess."

"I seem to have given *myself* rather a lot to ponder." Violet paused, then plunged on, an idea already taking form in her mind. "I felt rather foolish when I came here with my original intent."

"Of asking me to flirt with your husband?" Sophie sounded bemused.

"Quite." She couldn't even muster embarrassment anymore. "I was beginning to feel our game rather childish."

"I thought it was a duel?"

"So did I," Violet admitted. "But I'm beginning to see it's nothing more than a game. One that I intend to win, with your help."

Sophie leaned forward slightly. "In flirting with him? Or did you have something else in mind now?"

Violet picked up her own tumbler, still partially full, and downed its contents in a single, gasping gulp before setting it down on one of the spindly tables that seemingly littered all ladies' sitting rooms in England. "I thought I wanted to punish my husband. But more than that, I want to make him want me again."

Violet felt her cheeks warm at her own daring in speaking so frankly, but she might as well lay all of her cards on the table.

"I rather think he already does."

"But I think you might prove useful to my cause." Violet hesitated for a moment, as James's words—spoken to her once after he'd observed her convince Emily to smuggle three abandoned kittens from Violet's home (James was allergic) to her own, where she fostered them for the better part of a month before her mother discovered them—flitted into her mind.

You know, Violet, people will do as you ask even if you don't browbeat them into it.

Those words had, predictably, led to a rather spectacular row on their part—followed, Violet recalled, her cheeks heating, by a rather spectacular reconciliation on the Aubusson rug in the library—but she was forced to admit that there'd been some ring of truth in them.

"If, that is, you are willing," she amended hastily. "I already berated my husband once today for damaging your reputation; I wouldn't like to do the same, even inadvertently."

Sophie's mouth quirked up at the corners. "I rather think I've already damaged it myself, haven't I? Carrying on with a notorious rake like Lord Willingham does tend to create a bit of a scandal."

Violet was surprised to hear Sophie admit it so bluntly. "Not so very great a scandal," she said carefully. "I've only heard the faintest whisperings about it, in truth—Lord Willingham has been uncharacteristically discreet."

"In any case, that's all finished now," Sophie said.

"I don't mean to ask very much of you," Violet said. "I merely want to teach James one last lesson. I want him to realize that he wants me, just as I want him . . . and I want him to be afraid that I won't be waiting for him when he does."

"I really should stay out of this," Sophie replied, sounding as though she were enjoying herself thoroughly. "And yet, I'm compelled. Something about the idea of tormenting an Audley brother . . ." She trailed off for a moment, a dreamy expression upon her face. She then directed a steady gaze at Violet and leaned forward, intent. "Tell me what you have in mind."

Eleven

The Rocheford ball was one of the highlights of the end of the London Season—not that James had much time for it this year. He was still feeling distinctly rattled by his quarrels with West and Violet—and even more so by the distinct knowledge that they were in the right. Being correct was something he usually prided himself on, but in this case, he somehow felt that he'd come out in the wrong, and he wasn't entirely certain what to do about it.

He could say he was sorry, but James disregarded this idea almost instantly. He had already apologized to Violet for his behavior in the park—and for his conduct at the Blue Dove, for that matter. Anything more would be excessive. Although, if another apology ensured the chance to kiss Violet again . . .

He had tried to put that kiss out of his mind, but it was difficult. He was, after all, a healthy man of just eight-and-twenty who had been sleeping in an empty bed for far too long. As a result, he had spent much of the night reliving the taste of her, the smoothness of her tongue tangling with his own, the feeling of all of her soft curves pressed intimately against him.

He knew that much of society must assume that he had taken a mistress and was just remarkably discreet about it—it was certainly what he would have assumed of a man in his position. And yet, he never had. The idea had occurred to him—particularly on long nights when he was feeling particularly in want of feminine companionship. But he had never seriously entertained the idea, because the thought of bedding another woman after he had experienced the joy of making love to Violet was, quite simply, profoundly unappealing.

Jesus Christ. She had ruined him. Perhaps *she* should be apologizing to *him*.

And West . . .

Well, perhaps he *should* apologize to West. God knew that his life would be easier if he were engaged in only one long-standing row.

With all of this on his mind, James hardly placed the Rocheford ball high on his list of priorities the following morning when he awoke. He skipped his morning ride, having rather soured on Hyde Park, and instead dressed and headed to the breakfast table, not certain whether he hoped Violet would be there. The table was unoccupied, but midway through his meal, a footman delivered a note.

"From her ladyship," the footman clarified, although James recognized the handwriting immediately. He tore it open, not knowing what he expected—an apology? A stinging rebuke? A request for a damned physician to come examine her allegedly delicate lungs? But instead he found a simple reminder of the ball that evening, and a request that he be ready to escort her there at eight o'clock.

"Not too ill to go to a ball, I see," he muttered, crumpling the note in his hand. He was dimly aware that he was speaking to a plate of kippers and eggs, and spared a passing mournful thought for the shreds of his dignity.

Fortunately, he had enough business to keep him occupied for much of the day, though he often found his thoughts wandering to linger unhelpfully on the curve of Violet's cheek or the sound of her laugh. In truth, he had found it difficult to spare any attention for the business of the stables at Audley House of late. When he and Violet had first quarreled, the stables had been a welcome distraction, occupying his time and energy so that he could not linger overmuch on the ruins of his marriage. Now, however, he frequently found himself feeling an odd sort of disconnect from the business that consumed his life, motivated only by the vague desire to prove to his father that he could make a success of this endeavor.

Upon his return home, he lingered over a glass of brandy in the library, reading a lengthy letter from the estate agent at Audley House before finally, as the light filtering through the windows took on the particular rosy glow of evening, heading upstairs to dress for the night's entertainment.

At the appointed hour he was back downstairs, fully decked out in black and white evening attire, resisting the urge to tap his foot impatiently. After five years of marriage, he still failed to understand what precisely it was about women's toilettes that required so much bloody time.

He had made the mistake of voicing this question to Violet once. He had never done so again.

He was distracted by a clearing of the throat at the top of the stairs. He looked up and watched as the lady in question descended the staircase.

Magnificent seemed such a woefully inadequate adjective.

She wore a gown of midnight blue, the bodice cut low enough to draw his eye immediately to her décolletage—though, hell, perhaps his eye would have been drawn there anyway. He was, after all, a man. Even he, who knew nothing about ladies' fashions, could see that this dress had been lovingly tailored to nip at every curve of Violet's body.

Her dark hair was piled high in a gleaming mass atop her head, and her dark eyes seemed to burn out of the pale perfection of her face, her gaze never leaving his as she slowly descended.

He realized that his mouth was open, and he snapped it shut instantly. It was maddening that one woman should have so much sway over him, but some corner of his mind still capable of intelligent thought suggested that perhaps he should accept it as his lot in life, and merely enjoy it.

She descended the final step, then gave a tiny, delicate cough, and he rapidly amended his previous statement.

It was maddening that the woman who should hold him in thrall would be, of all the women in London, one as stubborn and infuriating as Violet.

Even as she fished a delicate, lace-edged handkerchief out of her bodice—and, damn it, she must have put it there on purpose, knowing that he'd be unable to tear his eyes away from this production—her gaze did not leave his face. She coughed into said handkerchief—which was currently the object of considerable envy on his part—and there was something knowing, something ever so slightly daring in her expression, and instantly, he knew.

He knew that *she* knew.

Or rather, he knew that she knew that he knew.

It was enough to give any man a headache, truly.

Given the events of the past week, he was not even entirely certain that he could be classified as sane any longer—sane men did not engage in lengthy wars of attrition with wives pretending to have illnesses with fluctuating degrees of severity—but, dash it, he knew this much: Violet knew that he knew that she wasn't really ill.

Her gaze was all practiced innocence, wide brown eyes framed by impossibly dark lashes—eyes that had once made him wish he was the poetic type, so that he could compose an ode to them.

"James," Violet said, taking a step toward him, a note of amusement in her voice.

James did not allow her the opportunity to say more. He took three quick steps forward, seized her by the waist, hauled her against him, and kissed her.

And, just as when he had kissed her the day before, his immediate thought was to wonder how, precisely, it was that he had gone for so long without doing so. Before he had met Violet, he would have said that he enjoyed kissing, that it was a diverting stop on the road to greater pleasures. But with Violet, kissing was not merely a stop along a well-trodden path. It was a destination all its own.

He could feel this kiss . . . well, *everywhere*. In the warmth of her skin, burning through the fabric of her dress where his hands gripped her waist. In the softness of her lips as he kissed them, his tongue darting out to trace their seam, slipping inside her mouth as she opened it with a slight gasp. In the softness of her breasts, pressed against his chest, making him itch to slide his hand up, cup them.

So he did.

Violet gasped into his mouth once more at the touch and pressed herself more firmly against his hand as he caressed the curve beneath his palm, his hands frustrated by the layers of fabric separating him from the warmth and smoothness of her bare skin. Their mouths grew desperate, tongues tangling, and Violet arched her neck with a low moan, allowing James access to the long, pale column of her throat, upon which he traced delicate designs with his tongue. In his breeches he was stiff and aching, and it was only with difficulty that he resisted the urge to roll his hips against hers.

Violet slid her hands into his hair and pulled his mouth back to her own, her lips possessing his with a frenzy and ardor that nearly undid him. It was as some vague corner of his mind began to wonder about retreating upstairs that she seemed to recall herself, tearing her mouth away from his.

"James," she said, and he was pleased to hear the slight pant in her voice, the unevenness of her breathing a sign of the same desire that coursed through him, setting his blood on fire, every nerve in his body jangling. "We can't," she said simply, and reached up a hand to smooth her hair, which had escaped from their interlude with remarkably little damage done.

"I apologize," he said, in tones of exaggerated politeness. "I was undone by your beauty." The words were not untrue, but he knew that Violet would take them for rank flattery and disregard them—which was, he told himself, all for the best. Better that she should never know what the sight of her in that gown did to him.

What the sight of her every day did to him.

He reminded himself, quite sternly, that she was leading him on a merry chase—reminded himself of the realization that had prompted the rash and most certainly unwise action of kissing her in the first place.

And yet, in that moment, with the taste of her still on his lips, he would have played hound to her fox quite happily for the rest of his days.

That was it. He had finally lost all reason and dignity whatsoever. This, apparently, was what marriage did to a man. Or, at the very least, marriage to Violet. He somehow thought that marriage to, say, Lady Emily Turner, would be an entirely different and altogether more restful experience.

As though sensing his thoughts, the source of his aggravation shot him a narrow look.

He adopted a look of practiced innocence, causing her gaze to narrow even further.

Despite the turmoil of his thoughts, despite his complete and utter inability to work out how the bloody hell he felt about his wife at any given moment, it was still all he could do to refrain from grinning at her, and he realized in a rush how much he had missed this—had missed teasing her, needling her.

Kissing her.

He offered his wife his arm, which she took graciously.

And yet, as he escorted her out to the carriage, as they rattled over the cobblestone streets of London, he could not stop his thoughts from returning to one simple truth:

He wished very badly to kiss her again.

The evening was a success, and they'd only just arrived.

Violet managed to resist congratulating herself with great difficulty—oh, very well, she didn't entirely resist, only so much could be expected from a lady—as she swept into the glittering Rocheford ballroom on her husband's arm.

She wasn't at all certain what had brought on such an ardent display from James as the one at the base of their staircase half an hour earlier, but she decided to call it a success nonetheless. Whatever his reasons for kissing her—and a small, easily distracted part of her couldn't help wishing that she knew what those reasons were, so that she might attempt to coax a repeat performance out of him—that he had done so was undeniable proof of that fact that she was so anxious to drive home:

He still wanted her. Quite desperately.

Now she only had to gently prod him into action. Fortunately, she had Sophie to help her in this regard.

The minor, insignificant fact that her traitorous body had responded to his kisses and caresses as kindling to a spark was immaterial. Of course she still wanted him. She had already admitted as much, had she not? That was not relevant to the matter at hand. She was there not to prove her own desire, but his.

To make him realize it—even if doing so required making him suffer a bit. And to make him rue the day he had ever thought he could suppress that desire, or forget it, or ignore it.

She scanned the ballroom as she and James entered. This ball would no doubt be given that highest of compliments tomorrow— being described as a terrible crush. In one quick survey of the room, Violet saw two dozen people she knew. Hundreds of candles glimmered in sconces on the wall and from chandeliers overhead, reflecting off the sparkling jewels at the throats and on the wrists of the ladies below. Along one wall was a long table groaning under the weight of bowls of punch and lemonade, and discreet servants circulated amongst the guests, offering the same on trays. Couples assembled on the dance floor, and the opening strains of a minuet could be heard.

Upon a second perusal of the room, however, she groaned quietly— one of the familiar faces she spotted was her mother's.

"Something wrong?" James murmured.

"My mother is here," she said in an undertone. "Over by the refreshment tables." Lady Worthington, dressed in a blue satin gown a few shades lighter than Violet's own, was chatting animatedly with Baroness Highgate, one of her mother's dearest friends and a notorious gossip. Violet could not think of a conversation she would less like to be a part of at the moment; she watched as Lady Worthington took a sip of lemonade and gave a polite smile.

"Fortunately for us, I see Jeremy and Penvale on the opposite side of the ballroom," James said, steering her firmly away from said refreshment tables. Violet prayed her mother hadn't heard their names announced, but she rather thought that might be too much to hope for. Lady Worthington had inconveniently good hearing.

"Audley," Penvale said as James and Violet approached. "Violet," he added, in a much lower tone of voice—Violet had given both Penvale and Jeremy leave to use her given name years ago, but this was scandalously familiar enough that they were quiet about doing so in public. "You're looking very . . . healthy," he added, giving her what she supposed he intended to be a look heavy with meaning.

Her eyes darted to James before she could stop herself, and she saw that he had adopted a deliberately bland expression. She looked back at Penvale and narrowed her eyes at him slightly.

"Yes," she said carefully, and heaved a dramatic sigh. "One does never know what to expect upon waking each morning, but I seem to be having one of my good days." She gave a sad little smile. "Who knows how long it will last, though? I suppose I should enjoy the time I've been blessed with."

She thought that she *might* have laid it on a touch thick, but, really, how long was James going to continue this charade? While her primary aim at the moment was forcing James to admit he still wanted her, she was petty enough to admit that she also found the prospect of needling James to the point of admitting she wasn't truly ill to be incredibly satisfying. She would wrench a confession out of the absurd man if it killed her.

Of course, the trouble was, as always, that James didn't *look* the least bit absurd. He looked so very, very handsome in his evening kit, the precise knot of his snowy white cravat keeping his chin at just such an angle so as to show off the devastating lines of his face. He just looked so very ... *male*. It was in the way his broad shoulders filled his coat, the manner in which the careful cut of his clothing did nothing to conceal the muscle and strength beneath them. He was standing there with that closed-off look on his face, the one that angered her more than she would have ever thought possible, and yet a significant portion of her mind was occupied by the distracting wish to fling her arms around him and claim him as her own.

She had observed dogs, on occasion, urinating on trees to mark their territory, and while her instincts had fortunately not yet reached *that* primitive level, she felt an unexpected sympathy with the desire.

Her rather ridiculous thoughts were interrupted by the unmistakable voice of Diana. "There you are! Emily and I have been looking for you since we arrived, and just look who we found along the way!"

The group turned as one to see Diana and Emily making a beeline for their corner, Sophie being tugged alongside them, her arm firmly linked through Diana's as though they were the dearest of friends, rather than passing acquaintances. Violet couldn't resist sneaking a glance at James as they approached. A look of suspicion crept across his face. He looked at Violet, and she shot him a quick, satisfied smile before stepping forward to greet her friends.

"Diana! Emily!" she said, seizing each of their hands in turn, as though she'd not seen them in weeks, rather than a day. "Sophie!" she added, turning her head slightly toward James as she spoke so that he would be unable to miss her use of Sophie's given name. "You look beautiful."

This much at least was true; no more of the muted colors of

mourning for Sophie. She was wearing a daringly cut gown of emerald green, her blond hair gleaming in the candlelight. Violet had never seen Sophie—in the years she had encountered her at society events—in a gown with a bodice so revealing. While Sophie was not particularly curvaceous, having a petite, trim figure, the cut of this dress could have made a stick look enticing. And Sophie was certainly not a stick.

Violet gave Sophie a quick, conspiratorial smile, then stepped back to allow the ladies to greet the gentlemen.

After kissing Diana's and Emily's hands in turn, James turned to Sophie. "Lady Fitzwilliam," he said, bowing over her hand, everything in his manner entirely correct. The flirtatiousness of the day before was entirely absent and Violet realized, with a slight pang, that he truly had taken her words to heart. She felt her resolve waver for a moment—she was beginning to feel slightly awful about what she was about to do. Or, to be more accurate, what *Sophie* was about to do.

"I feel I owe you an apology," James continued, straightening. "My behavior in the park was not that of a gentleman, and entirely inexcusable."

"Not at all, my lord," Sophie replied, and Violet nearly started, so entirely foreign was the seductive note that she heard in Sophie's voice. "There is nothing to apologize for."

James blinked. "Nonetheless," he said, his voice less assured, "I deeply regret any discomfort I may have caused—no lady deserves to be treated in such a fashion."

Sophie laughed, and the sound was tinkling, flirtatious, not at all like her natural laugh—and James knew it. His face was slowly draining of color.

"Lord James," Sophie continued as James struggled for words, "you're looking very well this evening."

"As are you, my lady," James managed gallantly, the expression on his face akin to that of an animal facing an unpredictable predator at close range. "It is an unexpected delight to see you again so soon."

"I assure you, my lord, the pleasure is all mine," Sophie purred—*purred*? Violet was impressed. In a different life, she thought, Sophie could have had a brilliant career on the stage.

In a feat of impressive timing, no sooner had this thought crossed her mind than she heard Penvale's name called; Lord Julian Belfry approached.

"My lord, I was not aware that you frequented these sorts of events," Diana said after Belfry had greeted each group member in turn and been introduced to Sophie.

"I don't, normally," Belfry said, looking extremely handsome—and extremely unconcerned by the whispers he had undoubtedly left in his wake as he cut across the ballroom. "However, I found myself lacking other plans for the evening, and I thought the company here might prove . . . entertaining." His tone was casual, but Violet didn't miss the unmistakable look of interest he cast in Emily's direction. Emily, looking so beautiful in a prim white dress with her shining golden curls that it was almost laughable, really. Emily, who—unless Violet was very mistaken—cast a look of her own in Belfry's direction, her cheeks coloring under his regard.

Violet looked at James at the precise second that he looked at her, an eyebrow arched, and for a moment they seemed to understand each other so perfectly that it was as though no time had passed, as though the past four years were a dream, as though it was the first year of their marriage once more, when Violet felt, even in a crowded room, that she and James were somehow alone together.

James broke eye contact first, his attention having been drawn by the sound of his own name.

". . . have heard that you are a skilled dancer," Sophie was saying, as Violet, too, directed her attention back to the group. "I should be absolutely *bereft* if you were to deny me the chance to experience your skill for myself." She gave James a rather assessing glance, one that clearly indicated that dancing was not the only one of his skills she would like to experience. Violet had to bite the inside of her cheek to refrain from laughing out loud at the look on her husband's face. She leaned closer—was he actually *blushing*?

"I would, of course, be honored if you would save me a spot on your dance card, Lady Fitzwilliam," James said, since it was really the only polite thing he *could* say under the circumstances. When a lady practically begged a man to dance with her, no gentleman could refuse her.

"Lovely," Sophie said brightly. "I think a waltz would do nicely, don't you? It's so . . . intimate." She hesitated ever so slightly before the last word. James cast a frantic look around the ballroom, tugging at his collar as though his cravat were knotted too tightly.

This was, Violet decided, the best evening she'd spent in years.

This was, James was utterly certain, the bloody worst evening he'd spent in years. He adjusted his collar again, feeling as though he couldn't get enough air in his lungs—and was it just him, or was the ballroom overwarm? He didn't know why the *ton* insisted on having these damned events in the middle of summer—who could possibly think it a good idea to cram hundreds of perfumed peacocks into a single room, along with hundreds of candles, during one of the warmest months of the year? He needed air. He needed a drink.

He needed Lady Fitzwilliam to remove her hand from his arm.

He felt like a boy of fourteen again, one with no experience of women, flustered by the first girl to cast an appraising look in his direction. This was a bloody disaster.

It was entirely his own fault.

What the hell had he been thinking, flirting so outrageously with Lady Fitzwilliam in Hyde Park? He'd thought, deep down, that West and Violet were correct, that his primary concern should be any potential damage he had done to her reputation, and he had felt like an utter cad once he'd come to his senses in this regard—but now, too late, he realized another danger.

That she might take him up on his implied offer.

He never would have expected it of her, in truth. He'd never thought her the slightest bit interested in him as anything other than West's studious younger brother, but apparently the years that had passed since he'd last seen her had had quite a transforming effect.

Unless . . .

He went cold as another unpleasant thought struck him.

He and his brother bore a strong physical resemblance—everyone commented on it. Could she possibly be setting her cap for him out of some desire to use him as a sort of stand-in for West? It was an appalling prospect—and not terribly flattering, at that.

He dimly registered that Lady Fitzwilliam was still speaking to him, but he interrupted her, manners be damned.

"Lemonade!" he burst out, sounding like an imbecile.

Lady Fitzwilliam blinked at him. Casting a quick glance at the surrounding group, he saw Penvale and Jeremy raise their eyebrows. Diana smirked. And Violet . . .

Violet looked as though she were trying hard not to laugh.

And that was when he knew. He knew that Violet was somehow behind this.

The realization did him little good at that precise moment, however, because he had just uttered the word *lemonade* aloud, apropos of nothing, and some faint part of his mind—the reasonable, rational part that, until the past fortnight, had usually made up the majority of his brain—realized that some elaboration upon this comment was likely required.

"It is very warm this evening," he said smoothly. "I thought a glass of lemonade might not go amiss. Don't you think, Lady Fitzwilliam?" He did not allow her the opportunity to respond. "Please allow me to fetch one for you. It would be a delight, I assure you."

Lady Fitzwilliam gave a sort of wistful little sigh. "How very thoughtful you are, my lord." Her hand tightened slightly on his arm. "And so capable. It is most . . . illustrative."

James had never realized that the word *illustrative* could contain such a wealth of illicit meaning. It was a rather—dare he say it?—illustrative moment.

That was it. He had finally taken leave of his senses.

"I shall fetch your lemonade, Lady Fitzwilliam," he said expansively, removing her hand from his person at last, but placing a gallant kiss upon it before releasing it. "The sooner I retrieve it, the sooner I may return to you." He turned to Violet. "Dearest wife. You are looking a bit pale. Would you like to walk with me to the refreshment tables? I think a bit of movement might do you some good."

"I should be happy to accompany Lady James on a turn about the room while you fetch her a lemonade," Belfry said with the merry air of one who was observing a particularly entertaining bit of theater. He let out a soft "oof!" as soon as he made this offer, and James was nearly—although not quite entirely—certain that Diana had elbowed him in the stomach.

"Come, wife," James said, taking Violet by the elbow and steering her away from the group before she quite seemed to realize what was happening.

"Let go of my elbow, you idiot," she hissed, shaking off his touch as soon as they began their slow progress across the crowded room. "Have you taken leave of your senses?"

"No," James said through gritted teeth, smiling at some of the curious glances being thrown at them as they walked. "But I'm wondering if you have."

"I don't know what you mean."

James snuck a sideways glance at Violet; her head was held high, her voice as lofty as that of a queen. It was maddening.

And maddeningly attractive.

With some effort, he focused on the matter at hand. "I know you invited Lady Fitzwilliam here tonight, so you needn't even pretend on that account."

"I am flattered that you think I have so much sway over Lady Rocheford that I should be able to control the guest list at her ball." Violet's tone was sweet, innocent, but James was unmoved.

"All right," he allowed. "But I don't for a second believe it was a coincidence that we met her so soon after arriving."

"James, we are at a *ball*. The entire point is to see and be seen."

"Ah, yes," James said mock thoughtfully. "And I could not help *seeing* that Lady Fitzwilliam was rather *friendly* this evening."

"Perhaps she took pity on you and thought to offer you the gift of female companionship, since you made your interest so blatantly obvious yesterday."

"It is strange that she seemed so patently disinterested in any sort of flirtation yesterday, and yet this evening seems to have had a change of heart," he said icily, pausing as they reached the refreshment table. He poured a glass of lemonade so hastily that some of the liquid sloshed onto the white linen tablecloth. He thrust the glass at Violet, then poured another one for himself—despite the fact that, not being a debutante himself, he couldn't recall ever having drunk the watered-down swill previously.

"Perhaps she had time to reconsider," Violet said, taking a careful sip, her tongue darting out to catch a drop from the corner of her mouth. How was it that the small pink tip of a perfectly ordinary tongue could be so mesmerizing? James couldn't tear his eyes away from it, nor could he ignore how desperately he wanted to be in close contact with that tongue once more.

"You're a reasonably handsome man," she added, "if one likes that sort of thing."

This, at least, was enough to draw his attention. "'That sort of thing'?" he inquired. Once he had poured a third glass of lemonade for Lady Fitzwilliam, they moved away from the table and began a slow circuit of the room, keeping close to the walls rather than taking the most direct path back across the dance floor, which was full of people milling about, as the orchestra was between sets.

"Oh, you know." Violet waved an airy hand. "Tall. Dark. Handsome. It's all right for some, I suppose, if you find that type terribly attractive."

"But you don't."

"I'm afraid your charms have rather faded for me, James."

He blinked. His *charms* had *faded*? It had to be simple male pride that accounted for the burst of indignation—indignation laced with some deeper, more potent emotion—that this statement provoked. "Perhaps it's merely been too long since you've sampled them," he managed.

"I don't see how *that* can be true," Violet said with a laugh—was it his imagination, or did that laugh sound slightly unsteady? "Or have you already forgotten our—er—*encounter* earlier this evening?"

James stopped dead in his tracks, forcing Violet to halt as well. All the teasing was gone from his voice as he said, "I've never forgotten anything about you, Violet. About us."

She blinked up at him. "Oh."

"Just so we are clear."

She blinked again, and then her face resumed its expression of archness. "Well then, my point remains."

"And which point was this?"

"That I'm not some girl of eighteen to be taken in by a handsome face and a few kisses." She kept her voice low, smiling blandly at an acquaintance they passed.

"So you *do* find me handsome," he said triumphantly. He tightened his grip on her arm.

She feigned disinterest—it was a decent charade, but he saw through it. At some point in the past fortnight, he had come to know her again—not in the way he once had, of course. But the part of him that had, from their first meeting, beat out a pulse of recognition had been awakened once more.

"The fact remains," she said, sniffing, "that it takes more than a couple of improper kisses to turn my head these days."

"Have my kisses been improper?"

Her cheeks heated under his gaze, and he mentally crowed. "They certainly have."

"How so?" he pressed, enjoying himself thoroughly. "Is it not proper for a husband to kiss his wife in the sanctity of his own home?"

"Well—"

"Now, I will grant you, had I kissed you somewhere in public, *that* would have been improper." He slowly drew her toward an alcove they were passing, shaded in part by a potted fern. "Had I led you into a dark corner of a crowded ballroom and pressed you against a wall, and kissed you with half the *ton* milling about a few feet away—*that* would have been improper." He had reached the alcove in question and turned her to face him, edging her back into it and blocking her from view of the crowd. He leaned forward, and her chin tilted up, her breath quickening.

"Had I kissed you in this alcove, again and again, with my hands in your hair and your skirts tangled about my legs and our bodies pressed together so tightly so that you could feel every inch of how badly I wanted you—" He rocked his hips forward slightly as he spoke, and she gasped in reply. Her dark eyes were heated with passion.

"Now *that* would have been improper," he said, leaning forward, hesitating so that their mouths were mere inches apart. His heart pounded in his chest, their uneven breaths meeting and mingling in the minimal space between them. He could practically feel the heat radiating from her skin, and his mind was already lost in detailed imaginings of precisely how soft her lips would feel beneath his.

He leaned forward even farther, making to close the gap between them—

"Lord James! Lady James!"

The voice was so unpleasantly familiar that all thoughts of seduction fled at once, any arousal doused so quickly that he might as well have had a bucket of cold water dumped on his head.

Resisting the urge to groan, James turned. Violet, who actually *did* groan, followed his suit.

It was Violet's mother.

Lady Worthington was, he supposed, an objectively attractive woman. She actually bore quite a strong resemblance to her daughter—the same dark hair, the same wide eyes, the same fair, unlined skin. Lady Worthington had to be past forty by now, but she was aging beautifully, offering a glimpse of how Violet would look when she was older. However, to James's mind, there was no comparison between the two. Everything that made Violet *Violet*—the quirk to her mouth when she was amused by something inappropriate, the sparkle in her eyes that made them look so vivid and alive—was entirely missing in her mother. It was as though Violet were an original work of art, and Lady Worthington a cold, emotionless copy created by an artist with much less skill.

And that was *before* she even opened her mouth.

"Lord James," the countess said, offering him her hand, which he bent over, brushing a kiss across her knuckles. "Lady James," she continued as James straightened, leaning forward to brush her cheek against her daughter's. James knew that Violet had told her mother that she would prefer that she continue to address her by her Christian name, rather than her courtesy title, but Lady Worthington was a stickler for propriety. Violet had married the son of a duke—not, it was true, the *first* son of a duke, as would certainly have been preferable, but the son of a duke nonetheless, and she would never, for an instant, forget this triumph, which had, of course, been of her own engineering.

"Mother," Violet said, and James was struck, as always, by the change that came over his wife whenever her mother was in the room. She seemed shrunken, paler, a slightly faded version of her usual self. He had suggested, early in their marriage, that Violet stand up to her mother, which had led to a fight. She had insisted that she did so, whereby he replied that needling her and truly defying her were not at all the same thing. They had argued in circles for at least an hour—and then, by the end of the evening, had made up in highly memorable fashion, as was their wont. James lingered on *that* particular memory—which had, he recalled, involved testing the strength of one of the armchairs in the library—but after a moment decided that, given the cut of his coat and breeches, it might be best not to linger on it too terribly long.

Fortunately, the sound of Lady Worthington's voice was sufficient to thwart any such pleasant reminiscences.

"I am pleased to see you two together this evening," Lady Worthington said, disapproval evident in every syllable that came from her lips. James wondered how much she had been able to see of their activities—or sad lack thereof—in the alcove before she had interrupted them. "It's lovely to see a wife where she belongs." She paused, giving James and Violet a significant look, as though they might not take her meaning. "At her husband's side," she clarified. She cast James a sympathetic smile, as though they were long-suffering partners in crime.

James could practically see the rage rolling off of Violet, and quickly spoke before she could. "It is funny you should think so, Lady Worthington," he said. "I've rather thought that, considering the great honor your daughter did me by agreeing to be my wife in the first place, the least I can do is dog her footsteps wherever she goes. I'm afraid I've been rather remiss in that matter."

Violet watched him with a curious expression.

"You and I shall have to agree to disagree, Lord James," Lady Worthington said icily.

"Something I'm certain James finds entirely acceptable," Violet put in, and James had to smother a smile. "Mother, it's been lovely to see you this evening—"

"I had something I particularly wished to discuss with you, Lady James," Lady Worthington said with a severe look at her daughter. "Come to tea tomorrow."

The invitation was, as was so often the case with Lady Worthington, a command, not a request.

"Of course," Violet murmured, dipping the shallowest curtsey she could offer without seeming openly rude.

"Lady Worthington, you must allow me to steal your daughter away now," James said. "I'm afraid her dance card is so full that she cannot afford to dawdle."

Lady Worthington opened her mouth to reply, but James had already taken Violet's arm once more and proceeded to steer her firmly away. Over his shoulder, he added, "Lady Worthington, next time you seek to scold my wife in a public place—or any place at all—I would advise you to reconsider."

And with that, he and Violet made their retreat.

"I'm very tempted to turn around to see what the look on her face is like, but I don't think I quite dare," Violet said, a note of distinct satisfaction in her voice.

"Probably best not to tempt fate," James agreed.

"Thank you," Violet said, so softly that he nearly missed it, a gentle squeeze of his arm accompanying her words. He placed his free hand over hers and squeezed it in return.

"You don't have to go to tea with her tomorrow, you know."

Violet sighed. "It's best just to go and let her say her bit."

James frowned, but further conversation was forestalled by the fact that they had rejoined their party, though it had been reduced in number. Jeremy, Penvale, and Lady Fitzwilliam stood in a loose circle, making idle conversation; just as Violet and James approached, a gentleman—the younger brother of the Earl of Dunreedie, if James wasn't mistaken—bowed to Diana and departed as she rejoined her friends. With a quick glance at her wrist, he could see that Diana's dance card was already nearly entirely full.

"Where is Emily?" Violet asked, draining the rest of her glass of lemonade. Without thinking, James reached out and took the empty glass from her, handing it to a passing footman before turning to Lady Fitzwilliam and offering her the full glass in his hand with what he hoped was a not-at-all-flirtatious bow.

"Dancing with Belfry," Diana said, in a tone of voice that James thought might be her attempt to sound casual. It was spoiled by the eager expression on her face.

"Is Mr. Cartham attending this evening?" Violet asked, craning her neck around to get a better look at the room. Even if Cartham were here, James thought, Violet would be lucky to spot him—it was quite a crush.

"I believe so, but I've yet to see him. I've instructed Penvale"—here Diana jerked her head at her brother, who was sipping a glass of champagne and looking bored—"to keep a sharp eye out for him, so that we might keep him away from Emily."

"Playing matchmaker, are we?" James asked.

Diana sniffed. "I don't think it's unreasonable of me to want to see Emily married to someone other than that vulgar boor."

"You sound frightfully snobbish, Diana," Penvale said, sounding amused. "Not such a rebel after all, are we?"

"You're making a mistake if you think to match Belfry with Lady

Emily," Jeremy added. "A less likely man to marry I've never seen. Haven't you heard anything of his reputation?"

"Mmm, yes," Diana said sweetly, giving Jeremy a saccharine smile. "But I didn't think it was any worse than yours, my lord."

Rather than look offended, Jeremy appeared amused. "Touché. And yet I've no intention of marrying, either, so my point remains."

"So you say," Diana said, sounding skeptical. "But need I remind you that you are a marquess? At some point, you'll have to produce an heir."

Jeremy shrugged. "I've a cousin who I've no doubt would be quite pleased to inherit. He has a very fertile wife, if I recall."

Diana tossed her head impatiently. "Don't be absurd. Of course you'll marry."

Jeremy shrugged again, and James was fairly certain he was doing so merely to irritate Diana. "If you say so. I've yet to meet a debutante I didn't find insufferable, so you'll forgive me for remaining unconvinced."

"You knew *me* when *I* was a debutante," Diana said through gritted teeth.

"Did I?" Jeremy asked in mock surprise. "Oh, I do believe you're right." He pointedly did *not* apologize, nor did he amend his previous statement.

Diana took a deep breath, in the manner of a parent dealing with a particularly stubborn toddler. "I'll wager you'll be married within the year. I could find you a bride in three snaps."

Jeremy laughed out loud, and James suspected that Jeremy and Diana had entirely forgotten the presence of the rest of the group, who were observing this interaction with some interest. "That would be money in my pocket, Lady Templeton."

"Then you'll take the wager?" Diana asked, a steely glint in her eye, and, seeing the alarmed look on Penvale's face at this, it suddenly struck James that Jeremy might be in over his head for once. It was rather enjoyable to witness. "And you'll allow me to send a parade of marriageable misses in your direction?"

"Why not?" Jeremy asked blithely. "I somehow think I'll be able to resist the temptation. What shall we make the bet?"

Diana paused, and James wondered for a brief moment if she was going to affect ladylike hesitation to deal with something so sordid as money.

"One hundred pounds." James blinked; that sum would pay the annual salaries of half of his household staff, for Christ's sake. He was beginning to wonder if Diana and Jeremy weren't taking this a bit far.

"Done," Jeremy said briskly, then extended his hand. "Shall we shake on it?"

Diana appeared momentarily startled—James was quite certain that no one had ever attempted to shake her hand before—but she took Jeremy's proffered hand.

"I shall spend my winnings on a glorious wedding gift for you," she said.

"Of course," Jeremy said, unconcerned. Out of the corner of his eye, James saw Violet and Lady Fitzwilliam exchange raised eyebrows.

"How would you feel about a swan centerpiece for your dining room table?" Diana asked.

"Lovely," Jeremy replied. "Since I don't expect to ever see such a thing."

"Right," said Penvale, seeming to seize upon the momentary cessation of hostilities to change the subject. "Shall we—"

The faint strains of a waltz began to filter throughout the room;

the previous set had ended while Jeremy and Diana were speaking, and Penvale was now interrupted by a gasp from Lady Fitzwilliam. He turned politely in her direction. "Yes, my lady? Is something wrong?"

"No, no, nothing at all," Lady Fitzwilliam replied, waving her hand quickly. "I merely . . . no, never mind."

"I assure you, my lady, we are all ears," James said, in as pleasant a voice as he could manage.

"It is only that I thought I heard the sounds of a waltz," Lady Fitzwilliam said with her best downcast look.

The rest of the party turned to look at James.

"Lady Fitzwilliam," he said as politely as he could, despite the fact that he felt rather like a cornered fox, "would you do me the very great honor of giving me this dance?"

"Oh," Lady Fitzwilliam said brightly, as though the idea had never occurred to her. "How very kind of you, Lord James." She took his proffered arm. "I do so love to dance the waltz, but of course I would never be so forward as to ask you myself . . . how *very* thoughtful you are." She stroked a finger down the length of his forearm in a disturbingly flirtatious way. James shot a glare at Violet, who looked as though she were biting the inside of her cheek to stop herself laughing.

This, James thought, not for the first time over the course of the past fortnight, was why men should never marry.

Twelve

Violet was not certain what it said about the state of her marriage—
or, perhaps, her social life—that watching her husband dance with
another woman was the most entertaining thing she'd experienced at
a ball in years.

James steered Sophie around the ballroom with the look of a man
faced with an unpleasant task who was determined to get it over and
done with, no matter the cost to him personally. Sophie, by contrast,
was leaning forward ever so slightly—not close enough to cause any
blatant gossip, as there was still a sliver of space between James and
herself, but certainly closer than either Emily or Diana had ever stood
when dancing with James before.

The evening was going perfectly according to plan. James appeared wildly uncomfortable with Sophie's advances, and his kiss at
home, and his seductive words just a few minutes before—blast her
horrible mother for interrupting *that* particular interlude!—seemed
to indicate that he desired her as much as she did him. And he didn't
like it one bit when she feigned indifference. Surely, all of this combined was enough to cause some sort of revelation in even the most
thickheaded, emotionally stunted of men—and James, fond of him
as she was, could not be said to possess a great deal of emotional

intelligence. But surely even *he* must be awakening to his own desire. For her. Now, in theory, all she had to do was wait for him to come to her.

Violet was drawn back from watching the entertaining tableau before her with a sharp "Lady James."

She turned, her hackles already going up at the distinct note of disapproval she heard in the voice summoning her, and found herself face-to-face with James's brother.

"West," she said, sagging slightly.

West's eyes, at the moment, were focused on her with an expression of more gravity than she had ever seen. In truth, Violet and West had always gotten on well—early in her marriage, when James and West had been closer, she had invited West to dinner often, and they would frequently dine à trois, West lingering late into the evening for drinks and discussion. The loss of this camaraderie was one of the many things she regretted about the past four years.

"I suppose you have something to do with this," West said. He jerked his head in the direction of the dance floor, where James and Sophie were currently waltzing near Diana and Belfry. Past them, weaving in and out of the other immaculately dressed couples on the dance floor, she spotted Penvale and Emily.

"I don't know what you mean," she said airily, but West was having none of it.

"I quarreled with my brother yesterday, and I don't wish to do the same with you," he said shortly. "But I'd greatly appreciate it if you two would leave others out of whatever twisted little game it is that you are playing."

Violet wished to object in outrage, to defend herself, but she wasn't certain that she could, in complete honesty. She and James both appeared aware that they were now playing a game, one that each of them seemed equally unwilling to concede.

"For the record," she said, "Lady Fitzwilliam was eager to assist me."

"I don't care a whit," West said with an anger that belied this statement. Violet wondered if Sophie had any idea of the feeling with which he still spoke of her. "She is a respectable widow, and she has no business risking her reputation for the sake of some petty revenge against my idiot brother. I don't deny that he likely deserves it," he added wryly, his tone softening somewhat. "But I have always thought rather highly of you, Violet, and I think you are above this."

In that moment, watching James dance with another woman, accompanied by the man who very well might still be in love with that woman, Violet reviewed her actions of the past fortnight. And, all at once, everything that had seemed calculated and clever suddenly seemed foolish and desperate.

"It has been so nice having him take notice of me once again," she said truthfully, in a very quiet voice. It hurt her pride considerably to admit this, and yet she somehow could not find it in herself to lie to this man who was, after all, her brother, if only by marriage. She did not like admitting weakness, much less a weakness that she felt to be somehow beneath her. It was far easier to pretend that she did not want James to notice her, that she did not care for her husband's opinion, that their whirlwind courtship and marriage had been no more than youthful foolishness and lust, nothing deeper.

But she had already realized that this was simply not true. And, all at once, she was tired of pretending otherwise.

"Violet," West said, looking at her evenly, "I do not know what it was that came between you and my brother. It's really none of my concern, after all. But I do think you are entirely incorrect to assume that he has only taken notice of you recently." Violet opened her mouth to reply, but West forestalled any protest. "He has never stopped noticing you," West said simply. "I doubt he ever will. I do not know what has broken between you, or whether it can be fixed, but I think the first step to take would be to stop lying to yourselves."

And, suddenly, Violet found herself quite at a loss for words. It was an unusual experience for her. She had no reply for West, because she knew, in a rush of feeling, that every word he had spoken was true.

Why was she watching her husband dance with another woman? Why was she attempting to trick and torment him into coming back to her? Why was she not taking matters into her own hands and demanding he dance with *her* instead?

"Thank you, West," she said suddenly, and before he could reply she was off, diving into the crowded dance floor, weaving this way and that among the waltzing couples, offering hasty apologies over her shoulder when she bumped into someone or other. She knew she was making a spectacle of herself, but she didn't much care at the moment.

Then James and Sophie were before her. A few minutes before, she would have taken pleasure in the expression of discomfort on James's face. Now, however, she barely noticed, instead reaching up and tapping her husband quite firmly on the shoulder—and *not* allowing herself to notice how very shapely and well-muscled said shoulder was.

James turned, startled, and Violet met his eyes straight-on, not blinking. "Would you mind if I cut in?"

James's eyebrows rose, and a smile flitted across his face—it was gone before it was ever truly there, but Violet had seen it, and it gave her a bit of courage. This was a commodity in which she was not usually lacking, but which she rather welcomed at the moment.

Sophie, for her part, looked equal parts amused and pleased. "I find myself suddenly fatigued," she said, placing a dramatic hand to her forehead. "I think I must find somewhere to sit down." Violet was vaguely conscious of the eyes of the surrounding dancers on them; several couples had stopped waltzing altogether to better watch this scene. Sophie, however, seemed unconcerned—she was quite a bit bolder than anyone gave her credit for, Violet realized. Without so much as a backward glance, she vanished into the crowd, her head held high, heedless of the whispers she left in her wake, leaving Violet and James alone.

So to speak. They were, of course, in the middle of a crowded dance floor—proving a bit of an obstacle to the other dancers at the moment, in fact, who were still watching them with a great deal of interest.

"Shall we?" James asked, extending a hand. Violet took it and allowed him to pull her close to him—closer, she noticed, than he had been standing to Sophie during their waltz.

She was conscious of everything about him—it felt as though every nerve had become sensitive to his presence. She smelled the familiar scent of him, sandalwood and soap and something indefinable but entirely *James*. She could feel the warmth of his hand at her back, seeming to sear her flesh despite the barriers of clothing and glove between their skin. She was standing so close to him that if she looked at his jaw—which she found herself doing, because the idea of looking into his eyes suddenly seemed impossible—she could see the faint trace of evening stubble there. While initially she was aware of the stares and whispers of the couples around them, the longer she danced in James's arms, the dimmer her consciousness of anything but him became.

After several paces, James said, "Oh, I'm sorry." Violet glanced up, startled, and he continued, the corner of his mouth quirking upward,

"Did you want to lead? You were the one who secured this dance with me, after all."

"If I were not in the middle of a dance floor," Violet informed him, with as much dignity as she could muster, "I think I would hit you with my fan right now."

"You didn't bring a fan."

"A mistake I shan't repeat in the future, I assure you."

"Of course not," James said gravely. "After all, think of all the uses you could find for a weapon at a ball. You could whack any gentlemen who attempt to lure you onto a balcony—oh, wait." He frowned, mock thoughtful. "If my memory serves me correctly—and I am getting up there in years, so please do correct me if I am wrong—"

"You're eight-and-twenty," Violet said, resisting the urge to grind her teeth.

"—but I seem to recall that you have a fondness for such interludes. But then, of course, if you were to see your husband dancing with another woman, one behaving in a rather forward manner, you could intervene—"

"James," Violet said warningly.

"—but no, you seem to enjoy throwing your husband into just those situations." He shook his head. "Perhaps that fan wouldn't be as useful as I initially thought."

"I should very much like to have it right now," Violet said acidly, "so that I might thrust it down your throat."

This time the smile lingered on James's face, and it was embarrassing—truly, just *absurd*—how the sight of it seemed to make Violet's heart swell. "I am a fortunate man indeed," he said dryly, the smile still in place, "to be the recipient of such loving tributes from my wife."

"I shall never ask a man to dance again," Violet muttered. "It makes you utterly insufferable."

"What was that, my darling?" he asked innocently. "I could not hear you over the sound of my own head swelling under such praise."

This time, Violet couldn't help it—she smiled, too. And it felt wonderful.

"Did you enjoy your waltz with Lady Fitzwilliam?" She smiled up at him with a look of innocent inquiry. "She seemed most . . ." She trailed off delicately. ". . . *enthusiastic.*"

"Yes, quite," he said dryly. "Though I suppose it's no more than I deserve."

Violet looked up sharply at that—the smile had faded from James's face, and he was looking at her intently. It wasn't quite an apology, but it was something—something that gave Violet reason to hope.

"I quite agree," she said lightly. "Though of course I was as shocked as you at the drastic turn in Lady Fitzwilliam's feelings for you." She sighed airily. "I suppose one never can predict the workings of the human heart and all its complexities."

"Violet." James's voice was stern, but she could detect a thread of amusement running through it. "Did one of your bloody poets say that?"

"No," Violet said, then admitted, "although it wouldn't be at all out of character for one of them."

"That idiot Byron would certainly spew some such nonsense," James muttered.

"We'll feel foolish if, after all our mockery, Lord Byron goes on to be considered one of the great poets of the ages," Violet said, mainly to annoy him.

"I think I shall have to eat my words about some things, but never about Byron."

"Shall we wager on it?"

"No," James said firmly. "I believe Jeremy and Lady Templeton have done enough wagering for all of us for the evening."

Violet laughed, and silence fell between them for a moment. Unlike their usual silences, however, this one wasn't strained or cold. It felt comfortable. Violet realized that here, in the middle of a crowded ballroom, enclosed within the circle of her husband's arms, she felt safer than she had in ages. Years, perhaps.

She only felt truly safe when James was there.

"James," she began hesitantly, "I've been thinking that perhaps you and I should talk."

She looked up at him as she said this, and he opened his mouth to reply, but before he could, the dance ended. They separated, and James bowed stiffly as Violet curtseyed. They stood awkwardly before one another for a moment, and James opened his mouth to reply once more, but before he could, they were interrupted.

"Audley," Penvale said, materializing at James's shoulder, "fancy a game of cards and a drink?" He was accompanied by Diana, who linked her arm through Violet's own.

"And *you* must come with me, darling," she said, already pulling Violet away from the gentlemen. Violet could do no more than wave helplessly to her husband as she was tugged along in Diana's wake, feeling oddly bereft. She couldn't recall the last time she and James had said so little and yet communicated so much with one another—and she would have given a considerable amount to know what he had been about to say when they were interrupted.

"Your timing is abominable," she grumbled as Diana led her to the refreshment table, where Emily was nursing a glass of lemonade in the company of—Violet gave an internal groan—the dreaded Mr. Cartham. Now Violet understood Diana's hurry.

"Emily was in need of rescue," Diana said. "And in any case, I had promised the next dance to Willingham and I needed an excuse to abandon him. The man is truly insufferable, do you know that? I don't know how your husband has tolerated him for all these years—although I suppose that, being men, they communicate largely through grunts and clinking glasses, so I'd wager Audley isn't aware of just how horrid the man is."

"Diana," Violet protested, laughing a bit, but before she could say more they had reached Emily and Mr. Cartham.

"Ladies," Mr. Cartham said in that oily voice of his. He was of middling height, with dark hair scraped back severely from his face, and harsh features. He was not a handsome man, and his face was further ruined by the smug expression he always wore in Emily's company. Violet didn't know how Emily could stand to be in the man's presence for more than two minutes—but she also knew that Emily had no choice in the matter. Taking a cursory glance about the room, she saw Lady Rowanbridge watching them carefully from where she held court amongst a swathe of society matrons. She looked anxious.

"Mr. Cartham," Diana said, her tone curt to the point of impoliteness. "I do apologize for depriving you of Lady Emily's lovely company, but I'm afraid I've a pressing need for her at the moment. It's a bit of an emergency, I'm afraid." She leaned forward conspiratorially, then played her trump card. "A ladies' problem."

Mr. Cartham might have made a fortune from his gambling hell; he might have been well-connected; and he might have—according to rumor—known his way around certain criminal elements of the

London underworld—but even he was not so foolhardy as to face the prospect of a "ladies' problem" with complete sangfroid.

"Of course," he said hastily, dropping Emily's arm as though it were a blazing-hot poker. "I relinquish her to your care."

"You are all that is magnanimous," Diana replied—Violet thought that, had they been characters in a novel, Diana would have been wielding a rapier and offering an elaborate courtly bow, somehow all while twirling her impressive moustache.

"What on earth was that about?" Emily asked as they darted out of the ballroom and into the corridor that lined it.

"We were saving you, of course," Diana said impatiently as they turned right and walked toward the ladies' retiring room, their footsteps muffled by the heavy carpet. "I couldn't allow you to languish in that man's company."

"Diana," Emily said, an uncharacteristic note of impatience in her voice, "it's entirely possible that I might have to marry Mr. Cartham someday—someday soon, in fact," she added, and Violet could not miss the hint of sadness in her voice. "I'm not getting any younger, you know."

"And you're still the most beautiful woman in any ballroom," Diana said loyally.

"That isn't the point," Emily insisted, and Violet and Diana looked at her in surprise. "I shall have to grow accustomed to the man at some time, and I can't do so if you are constantly conspiring to keep me from his company."

"Darling, his company makes you miserable," Diana said. She paused for a moment before adding, "And besides, I couldn't help but notice that you seemed to find Lord Julian Belfry's company rather enjoyable."

Emily blushed. "He asked me to dance, and my dance card wasn't full. It would have been the height of rudeness to refuse him."

"Yes, of course," Diana said with a grin. "I am certain that is the only reason you had for dancing with him—mere politeness."

"Lord Julian would be an entirely unsuitable candidate for marriage—" Emily began, but Diana cut her off with an incredulous laugh.

"More unsuitable than Mr. Cartham from heaven only knows where? I think not."

"*And*," Emily continued, as though Diana hadn't spoken, "he has given no indication that he has the slightest interest in matrimony."

"Well, of course not," Diana said impatiently. "Men never do have the slightest interest in matrimony, until they suddenly do."

While Violet thought that Diana might be sticking her nose where it didn't belong at the moment, even she was forced to privately acknowledge the truth of this statement. It had certainly proved true in her own case—James had once confessed to her that, prior to meeting her, he hadn't thought to marry until he was thirty. Instead, they were five years into their marriage, and he still had yet to achieve that lofty age.

"I don't wish to discuss this anymore, Diana," Emily concluded, a note of steel in her voice that Violet thought Diana would be wise not to ignore. Diana evidently had thoughts along the same lines, because as they slipped into the ladies' retiring room—which was mercifully unoccupied at the moment—she redirected her focus to Violet.

"You and Audley looked quite cozy," she said, sinking down onto a settee in the small sitting room. Violet sat down next to her and set about unbuttoning her gloves. It had been quite warm in the ballroom, and the temptation of air—even the overheated air of this small, stuffy room—on her bare skin was too great to resist.

"We were waltzing," she said shortly, stripping off first one glove, then the other. "Close proximity is one of the requirements of the dance, I believe."

"I do not know what I did to deserve such vexing friends," Diana announced to no one in particular. "It seems a cruel fate for one such as myself."

Violet let out a rather unladylike snort and exchanged an amused glance with Emily.

"For your information," she said, and Diana leaned forward eagerly, rather like a dog beneath a table hoping to receive scraps of food, "James and I were in the midst of a conversation that I think had real promise—until you and that brother of yours so rudely interrupted us."

Diana moaned dramatically, flinging a hand to her forehead as she leaned back against the cushions of the settee. "I shall never forgive Penvale," she said morosely. "Just think—if he had not been so determined to seize Audley for one of their masculine tête-à-têtes, you and Audley might have . . . I don't know . . ." She trailed off for a moment, seemingly trying to think of some suitably scandalous behavior. "*Kissed* on the ballroom floor," she finished dramatically.

"Are you sure you're not thinking of yourself?" Emily asked innocently, calmly fanning herself. "That seems rather more your style than Violet's."

"The point is," Violet said loudly, seeking to steer this conversation back on course, "I should rather like to continue that conversation. So I think I am going to do just that, if you will excuse me."

She stood without awaiting a reply, shoving her gloves into her reticule rather than putting them back on—her mother would probably deliver an ear-blistering lecture at the sight of such impropriety, so Violet made a mental note to exert even more effort than usual to avoid her. She did not reenter the ballroom, since she knew James would not be there; instead, she continued down the hallway, peering into each room she passed until she spotted James and his friends—Penvale, Jeremy, Belfry, and, to her surprise, West—around a table littered with glasses.

She hesitated, unsure whether James would welcome the interruption—but at that precise moment West looked up, noticed her, and arched a brow.

Violet was nothing if not quick to respond to a challenge, and she did just that. "James," she called, and the gentlemen looked in her direction as one, five heads craning around to register her presence in the doorway. There was a brief pause, then the cacophony of several chairs scraping the floor at once as their owners all rose respectfully.

"Please, do sit down," she said, taking a couple of steps into the room. "I just wished to have a word with my husband, if you can manage without him."

"Of course," James said promptly, dropping his cards without a second glance at them and offering his companions the barest of nods before joining her.

"Is something wrong?" he asked in a low voice, taking one of her hands in his own. He looked intently at her face, and Violet quickly smiled to reassure him.

"Everything is fine," she said. "I just wished to continue our conversation of earlier, and I didn't really wish to wait. If you'd rather finish your card game, however . . ." She trailed off and tried to assume a nonchalant air. She disliked vulnerability, and had too little faith in the fragile peace they were forging to display any now.

In truth, however, his reply mattered a great deal.

"I think the cards can wait," James said dryly, his mouth curving up a bit at the corners, and Violet felt a flash of warmth rush through her. James took her by the arm and led her from the room, then paused once they were in the corridor. "Do you want me to send for the carriage?" he asked. "Are you feeling unwell?"

There was a teasing glint in his eye. Violet let out a sickly cough without breaking eye contact with him. "My health is, of course, always delicate, but I think I can carry on."

"I am delighted to hear it." James led her across the hallway into a room directly opposite. He glanced in quickly, apparently ascertaining that it was empty, and then pulled Violet in behind him and shut the door. They were in the Rochefords' library—it was dimly lit, but Violet could see floor-to-ceiling bookshelves and some rather uncomfortable-looking armchairs. She wandered deeper into the room, surveying the volumes on the shelves. They did not look heavily worn.

"I doubt we'll be interrupted here," she said, opening a book whose spine cracked with the motion—it had never been touched. "An excellent choice."

"If memory serves, I recall it being little used," James said from behind her, and there was a strange note in his voice—strange enough that Violet set the book back on the shelf and turned to look at him inquiringly. "Have you forgotten?" he asked quietly, taking a couple of steps toward her.

"Forgotten—oh!" Violet said, and it all came back to her in a rush, her cheeks warming. The year she and James had met, the Rochefords had held their ball much earlier in the Season, before Violet and James had married. They had been engaged at the time, and had managed to sneak away together to the Rocheford library, where they'd been slightly naughty on one of the window seats.

"I wonder if that window seat is still here," Violet said, curiosity overtaking embarrassment, as it so often did with her.

"I can't imagine they've torn out a window seat in a two-hundred-year-old room," James said wryly, and followed her toward the windows in question. Violet could feel his presence behind her—the warmth of his body against her back raising the hairs at the nape of her neck and causing her arms to break out in gooseflesh.

They arrived at the window seat, and Violet flung herself down upon it. "We should have one of these installed in our library," she said, patting the cushions. "It's extremely comfortable."

"Whatever you wish," James said, but from the way he was looking at her, Violet wasn't at all sure that he had heard anything she had said. "What was it you wanted to speak about, Violet?"

"Um," Violet said, unaccountably nervous, "I enjoyed our waltz this evening."

She sounded inane, she knew.

"As did I," James said, stepping closer to her. She tilted her head back to peer up at him, his head framed by the dim light surrounding him. "Violet . . ." He hesitated, and Violet leaned forward. She could see some sort of internal war being waged within him, and in that instant she wished desperately that she could read his thoughts. When he spoke, however, his tone was guarded, and he merely said, "That can't be the only thing you wished to tell me."

"Oh," she said, striving to keep a note of disappointment out of her voice. "Er—did you enjoy your dance with Lady Fitzwilliam?" That, of course, hadn't been at all what she intended to ask him.

"It was invigorating," he said, raising an eyebrow at her in silent inquiry; he could clearly tell she was working herself up to something and was stalling a bit.

"I'm certain it was," she replied, resting an elbow upon the windowsill behind her. "I'm sorry my delicate health wouldn't permit me to dance as enthusiastically as I normally would."

She had noticed that somehow she had begun to use the ruse of her illness as a code—when she wished to say something else to him entirely, she mentioned her failing health. It was a lie they held together, both of them aware of its falseness, neither one admitting as much in words. Rather perversely, it had the effect of making her feel closer to him—and if *that* wasn't a sad commentary on the state of her marriage, then she didn't know what was.

"Ah yes," he said, leaning down and bracing his hands on the sill, allowing his arms to bracket her face. "And yet you felt well enough to suddenly interrupt the middle of a waltz?" He shook his head in mock astonishment. "Amazing."

"One never does cease to marvel at the wonders of the human body."

"Indeed," he said, and there was a dark promise in that single word that sent a delicious shiver up and down the length of her spine. She looked into his shadowed face, into the green eyes gazing so intently at her, and she reached out, very deliberately, and placed a single ungloved hand on his cheek.

He closed his eyes briefly at the feel of her hand on his skin, then opened them again—and, quite suddenly, she couldn't breathe. She sucked in an unsteady breath, but it felt as though she could not get enough air in her lungs. He leaned forward, giving her ample time to pull away, but she remained still.

He hesitated a fraction of an inch from her lips, giving her one last chance to stop him, but instead she leaned toward him, brushing her lips against his. And then, it was as if in doing so she had released him from a curse that bound him, for he bent down, seized her face in his hands, and took her mouth in a bruising kiss.

This kiss bore no resemblance to the chaste touch of lips of a moment before, and Violet relished its difference as she slid her hands up to cup the back of his head. Their mouths were hungry, his lips moving against hers in a frenzied dance, giving her no chance to so much as catch her breath. Violet parted her lips and let her tongue dart out to trace the seam of his lips, savoring the familiar taste of him as he opened his mouth in turn.

And, oh, she had forgotten how this felt—the wet heat of their mouths together, the growing warmth in various parts of her body to which she normally paid little attention. James reached out and slid a hand into her hair; Violet could feel the pins that held her coiffure in place falling to the seat cushions behind her. James cupped the back of her neck with one hand as he slid the other to her waist, pulling her to the edge of the window seat and into the cradle of his body as he dropped to his knees.

She let out a moan and they broke the kiss, each breathing heavily. She allowed her head to fall back against his hand at her neck, eyes staring unseeingly at the ceiling far above. James leaned forward and placed a kiss at the hollow of her throat, where she could feel her pulse pounding wildly. His tongue darted out to taste her, and she slid her hands into the thick locks of his hair, pulling his mouth back to her own.

She slid forward even farther until she was perched on the very edge of the window seat, her breasts brushing against the fabric of his coat. The hand that was clutching her waist began a slow journey north, cupping the weight of a breast, rubbing a finger across the hardening tip.

"James," she gasped, breaking the kiss again, but words failed her as he began to kiss a path along the side of her neck and onto the upper slopes of her breasts. His other hand released her head and reached down to tug at the bodice of her dress—not forcefully enough to tear the fabric, but with a persistence that, after a moment, was rewarded when first one breast, then the other, popped free of fabric and corset.

"Someone might come in," she said with what remained of her sanity in that moment, and James stilled at once, his head rising so that she could no longer feel the heat of his breath against her bare skin. He turned his head to peer over his shoulder, and Violet followed his glance. From their perch, Violet could not see the room's entrance.

"We're hidden from view of the door," James said, and Violet was pleased to hear that he was breathing rather heavily himself, his voice slightly uneven. "But if you're concerned—"

By way of reply, Violet leaned up and kissed him again, prompting a rumble of satisfaction from deep in his chest that she felt in her own body, pressed against him as she was.

"Lean back," he said, tearing his mouth away after a moment, and pushed against her waist with an inexorable pressure that resulted in Violet half reclining against the cushions of the window seat, her legs spread wantonly. James moved forward to fill the space she had vacated, and she could feel the evidence of his arousal pressing against her as he crouched between her legs. He raised his hands and practically tore his gloves off, flinging them over his shoulder without a backward glance. He bent his head and, without further preamble, took one of her breasts into his mouth, causing Violet to arch off the window seat, her body bowing in pleasure at the feeling of his lips and tongue on her sensitive skin.

Her head fell back on the pillows behind her and she slid her hands into his hair once more, keeping him cradled against her as he kissed and sucked. Violet felt as though she were on fire, the blood in her veins racing with a feverish heat. She gave a wanton arch of her hips against him, once, twice. He groaned in response and lifted his head, his eyes blazing, and the sight of him there, with his hair disheveled and his cheeks slightly flushed, his chin resting in the hollow between her bare breasts, was so intoxicating that Violet felt as though she might spontaneously combust.

The first year of their marriage had been one of love and lust, of desire, of a need and hunger that she had not previously known existed. And yet, nothing—*nothing*—could have prepared her for what she felt at this moment.

Had it been it simple deprivation? she wondered with the small part of her mind that was still capable of rational thought. Had four years of abstinence been enough to prompt this reaction? Yet she could not imagine feeling this desperate, frenzied desire for any man other than her husband. It was something specific to *them*, to Violet and James and Violet-and-James, impossible to define but here, crackling between them.

"I need you," she said, barely recognizing the throaty sound of her own voice, so much deeper than its normal register. "Now. Here."

"Are you certain?" he asked, even as his hand began a steady, sneaky slide up her bare calf under the voluminous skirts of her gown. In that moment, when he asked that question, even as Violet could feel the strength of his need pressed against her own body, she knew, without a doubt, how much she loved this man.

She nodded once by way of confirmation, and it was the only signal he needed, his hand continuing its journey up, up, over her knee and onto the silken skin of her thigh, moving ever closer to where she so desperately wished him to touch. He paused for a moment, as if sensing her own urgency and determined to thwart it, his thumb stroking a rough circle into the skin of her inner thigh.

"Are you enjoying yourself?" he asked innocently, a wicked grin curving at his lips even as his thumb continued its movements—so close and yet still so frustratingly far from where she wanted it.

"I might enjoy myself a bit more," she said a bit unsteadily, "if you would get to where you were going." She leaned forward then and placed a kiss at the base of his throat, then used her tongue to trace a slow path upward. A groan from James was her reward, and she finished her journey with a gentle kiss on his chin, leaning back to smile smugly at him.

"You do like to win, don't you?" he asked, but before she could answer his fingers touched her slick folds, and she fell back against the window seat with a moan that she just barely managed to stifle against the back of her hand. Said hand was torn away from her mouth a moment later and replaced by James's lips, kissing her with a frenzy that matched the rough movements of his hand below. His tongue slid into her mouth just as he slipped a single finger inside her, and Violet whimpered against his lips, her hands rising to clutch at his shoulders.

"James," she gasped against his mouth as his thumb rubbed a particularly delicate spot. She shoved her hands under his coat, pushing it from his shoulders, and James pulled back to shrug it off. Violet tugged his shirt from the waistband of his trousers, her fingers greedy for the feeling of his bare skin. She slipped her hands up under the fabric of his shirt, moving them over the muscled expanse of his abdomen before sliding them around to clutch once more at his strong back. He leaned forward and placed a series of kisses against her neck, while his fingers resumed their distracting rhythm beneath her skirts.

"Enough," she said, and reached forward to fumble with the placket of his breeches. He sucked in a breath as her fingers brushed against him, but a moment later the buttons were undone and he was spreading her legs, hooking them up and over his hips.

"Are you—"

"Don't ask me if I'm certain," she said, reaching up to twine her arms around his neck. She pressed her forehead against his, their faces so close together that all she could see was the intense green of his gaze burning into her own. "I am."

This was all the confirmation he needed, and with a flex of his hips he slid into her, the sensation enough to make Violet's back arch and another helpless moan escape from her lips.

"God . . . Violet . . ." he panted, then withdrew before sliding forward again with a powerful thrust. Violet buried her face in his neck, her arms still wrapped tightly around him, her lips sliding over his skin without much finesse or purpose.

He continued to thrust, her hips rising to meet his, and it was just like every time they had ever done this before—and yet somehow different, and better, and entirely new. If their kiss had been a conversation, then this was something else entirely—a bond that went beyond words, beyond thought. The world outside the window seat shrank and vanished, until Violet couldn't remember her anger, her hurt, her loneliness—she could barely remember her own name. All she could focus on was the feeling of James moving inside her, the delicious friction that accompanied every move he made, the warmth of his hand at her breast, his face buried in her hair, his lips forming unintelligible syllables against her scalp.

For the first time in a fortnight, Violet didn't care about revenge, about teaching anyone a lesson, about winning. She only cared about

James's hips flexing against her own, and her desire for him to never stop.

Soon, too soon, she felt a warmth rushing up within her, setting every nerve in her body jangling. James was close, too, she could tell—his thrusts were growing more erratic, his breathing heavier, and his hand had slid from her breast to clutch at her hips instead, pinning her to him as he moved ever more forcefully within her.

"Vi . . . Vi . . ." he panted, pulling his head back to look at her once more. She pulled his face down to her own, kissing him sloppily and desperately, her heart pounding in her chest.

She was close—so close—but not quite there.

"James," she moaned, arching against him with an inarticulate cry, and somehow, he understood. He let one of his hands glide down underneath her skirts, sliding it into the negligible space between them, and rubbed—not with the finesse she usually expected from him, but at that moment, Violet didn't care—once, twice, thrice . . .

She shut her eyes tight, her head falling back against the cushions as wave after wave of pleasure washed through her. She could feel herself clenching around him, and a moment later he was gone, too, groaning into her neck as he shuddered helplessly above and within her, the sound of his pleasure heightening her own.

And, for the first time in four years, she had the feeling she'd nearly forgotten: that there was nowhere else on earth she would rather be.

Thirteen

Violet couldn't have guessed how long they lay like that, her feet still hooked around his back, he still buried within her, his face pressed against her neck, her eyes screwed tightly shut. Eventually, however, she returned to herself and released her grip on him, allowing her legs to slide back down to the floor, her thighs protesting. The movement seemed to rouse James from his stupor, as he lifted his head at last, straightened up, and stood, his hands fumbling to refasten his breeches.

Feeling unaccountably shy, Violet blushed and looked away, suddenly very conscious of the fact that she was only half dressed in the library of a house that was not her own. She sat up, tugging her bodice into place, then raising her hands to her hair to ascertain the damage there. She fumbled around on the window seat cushions behind her, feeling for the pins that James had so cavalierly flung aside; finding them, she began shoving them haphazardly into her coiffure, attempting to restore some semblance of order.

"I don't know much about ladies' hair," James said, thrusting his arms into his coat and then dropping to his knees to hunt for his gloves, "but I don't think you'll be able to make that look the same as it did before." There was a faint note of satisfaction in his voice that made Violet simultaneously want to kiss and smack him.

"I know," she said. "But I have to try something—I can't go out looking like this."

"We'll sneak out before anyone sees us," he said, locating his gloves and pulling them on. He paused, looked at her. "Where are *your* gloves, by the by?"

"In my reticule."

"Ah."

A slightly awkward silence fell.

"Well," she said brightly, jumping to her feet. "Well."

James looked down at her. "Would you like to leave?"

"Yes," Violet said immediately. His gaze unnerved her; she had so much she still wanted to say to him, and yet in this moment no precise idea of how to get it out.

She opened her mouth to speak, sucking in a deep breath—and coughed.

Later, she would find it amusing how much trouble a single bit of dust could cause. They were in a library, after all—dust was rather to be expected, particularly when the library in question didn't seem to be as heavily used as James's and her own. In any case, this speck of dust caused her to cough once, twice—and by the time she had regained her composure, the smile had faded from James's face.

"I'd offer you a handkerchief," he said coldly, "but no doubt you've one tucked away in there somewhere for just this purpose."

Violet's mouth fell open. "I beg your pardon?"

He took her arm in a firm grip, attempting to lead her out of the library, but she resisted, digging her heels in and wrenching her arm free of his. James stopped, too, turning to her with his hands on his hips.

"Was all this just part of your game?" he asked, gesturing around him as though to encompass the library in general, the window seat in particular, and most especially the activities that had so recently taken place upon it. "Do you have a bloody plan written out somewhere? Does it tell you how often each day you should cough to raise my sympathies?" He took two steps closer to her, his cheeks flushed, eyes blazing. "Violet, *I know you don't have consumption.*"

He appeared to think he'd thrown some sort of gauntlet, as though she'd cower and retreat upon this revelation. She, however, was so angry that the words practically poured out of her as she took a step closer to him, so close that she had to tilt her head back to meet his eyes.

"I *know* you know, you bloody bastard!" She reached out and whacked at his chest. "I had a piece of *dust* in my throat! I'm so frightfully sorry," she added, sarcasm dripping from every word. "I didn't realize you were so sensitive to my health that a mere cough would unnerve you so."

James let out an incredulous laugh. "Says the woman who's spent a fortnight wandering about our house coughing whenever she's in earshot, summoning *an actor to pose as her physician?*"

"I suppose that's somehow more beyond the pale than a man flirting with the woman his brother once courted out of some misguided quest for revenge," Violet said mock thoughtfully. "How foolish of me not to realize that you, as ever, occupy the moral high ground."

"I apologized for that," James said stiffly, and Violet could practically see him sliding an aloof mask into place upon his face. And, all at once, she decided that she simply would not allow it.

"Yes, for *that,*" she said scathingly. She reached out a fist to pound upon his chest once again, but he caught her curled hand in his own viselike grip, refusing to release it. "Has it ever, even once, occurred to you to apologize to me for anything that's happened over the course of the past four years? Did it ever occur to you that I might like an *apology* for having my happiness destroyed?"

"I think there's plenty of blame to go around on that front." Despite the fact that he was standing mere inches away from her, that her hand was still caught in his grasp, that just a few minutes earlier he had been *inside* her, James suddenly seemed very, very far away. And then, just for a moment, his mask slipped—he looked younger, somehow, and just as lonely as she felt. He looked like the man she had fallen in love with, who had in truth been little more than a boy.

"You were the one who walked out of that room," he said very quietly.

Violet blinked, for a moment unaware of what he was referencing. After a beat, she realized he was referring to that terrible morning, when she had finally fled the drawing room so as not to burst into tears.

"You were supposed to follow me," she replied, her voice little more than a murmur. And then she turned and walked toward the doorway.

"Where are you going?" His voice sounded hoarse, entirely lacking his usual confident tone.

"I'll ask Diana to take me home." She turned to glance over her shoulder. "And don't follow me now. Only follow me when you're ready to admit you still love me, and to let me love you in return."

And then she swept through the room toward the doorway and let the heavy door fall shut behind her as she departed.

Much later that evening—after James had rejoined his friends' card game, after he had drunk considerably more brandy than he ought to have, after he had endured a bumpy, jostling carriage ride back to his house, without any company other than lingering traces of Violet's perfume—he found himself outside his wife's door, hesitating.

He'd raised his hand to knock, then lowered it thrice now, and he was growing disgusted with himself. He pressed his forehead against the wood of the door, relishing its coolness on his overheated skin. Violet's words of earlier echoed through his brain—there was so much there to process that he scarcely knew where to start. One part kept coming back to him, though: *When you're ready to admit you still love me, and to let me love you in return.*

Love.

Violet still loved him.

And she thought that he still loved her.

And, as usual, she was completely, utterly, infuriatingly correct.

How had he thought that he didn't care for her? How had he believed that he could go the rest of his life without the feeling of her arms wrapped around him, her lips pressed to his, their hips moving together in a perfect rhythm? The cynical part of him tried to regain control, reminding him that he had just ended a rather long dry spell, that any tumble would have had a similar effect upon him—

And yet he couldn't make himself believe it.

It had been different, and special, because it had been Violet. He didn't want anyone else. Just Violet.

And of course he'd done his damnedest to ruin it all. He winced, recalling the look upon her face when he had attacked her for the slightest cough. To be sure, one indignant part of his brain piped up, it *was* rather like the boy who cried wolf—how, precisely, was he to know that *this* cough, distinct from all the others, had been genuine?

You might have considered the timing, the more reasonable part of him said by way of reply. James winced again. The timing, indeed. There was nothing quite like making love to one's wife after a lengthy drought only to immediately attack her for having a bit of dust caught in her throat.

Not for the first time in recent days, he felt like an utter bastard.

However, one thing was clear: at the moment, he was in no condition to go barging into his wife's room, demanding to speak with her. It was the middle of the night, for one thing—she was likely asleep, and unless she'd changed a great deal in the past four years, he didn't think she'd take kindly to being woken from a dead sleep by a slightly intoxicated husband with no clear idea of what to say.

So instead he returned to his bedchamber and tried to ignore the connecting door. He undressed, trying not to think about the wife in a similar state of undress lying on the opposite side of that door. A wife who, just a few short hours before, he had . . .

Well. He wasn't entirely certain he had a word for what he and Violet had done. None of the usual verbs—*making love, tupping,* the euphemistic *sleeping with*—seemed quite right. He'd spent many a lonely night over the past four years imagining making love to Violet, but either his memory had been woefully inadequate, or what they had done this evening had surpassed any of their previous encounters.

He climbed into bed dressed only in his smalls, then proceeded to lie with his gaze firmly fixed on the canopy overhead, trying to think about anything other than Violet's breasts, the sounds of her moans, and the slight hitch to her breathing at the moment he'd entered her.

Horses. Yes, that was it, he should be thinking about horses and riding—

No, definitely not riding.

He gave up then and let his memories take over, recalling the feeling of her tongue in his mouth and on his neck, the silkiness of her hair in his hands, the excruciating pleasure of feeling her clench and convulse around him.

How in God's name had he gone without *that* for the past four years? And how could he convince himself that he could ever be satisfied with anyone else?

He was a fool. What did it matter if his and Violet's first meeting had been orchestrated by their parents? What did it matter if Violet had known about it? And the more he thought about it, the more he thought she must be telling him the truth—if the past fortnight had taught him anything, it was that his wife was not a skilled liar. Regardless, he knew, deep down, that had he been flung together on that balcony with anyone else, he would not have kissed her, would not have fallen in love, would not have married her. Perhaps being a pawn in his father's plans was all right, if it led to a life with Violet.

With that realization, at last, he slept.

❧

Violet entered the breakfast room rather nervously the next morning, having dressed with more than usual care, but the moment she saw the empty room she sagged, wishing she hadn't bothered. James wasn't here. What had she expected—that one glorious interlude on a window seat, followed by one thorough tongue-lashing, would mend all that was wrong between them?

Of course not.

She ate a rather morose breakfast by herself, then retreated to the library, as was her wont, picking up first one book, then another, casting each one aside as it failed to hold her attention. In the early afternoon she rang for tea, and the maid had just brought the tea service in when Wooton entered the room and announced, "Lady Templeton."

Violet stood as Diana entered the room, bracing herself for what was to come. The evening before, when Violet had sought Diana out and begged her to take her home, Diana had—uncharacteristically— not asked any questions, seeming to sense that Violet was in no state to answer them. Violet should have known that this reprieve would not last, however; in truth, she thought waiting a full twelve hours showed remarkable restraint on Diana's part.

"Diana," she said as Wooton and the maid departed, closing the door behind them. "How . . . unexpected."

"Don't take that tone with *me*, Violet Audley," Diana said severely, removing her gloves. "Lord, it's warm today. I really think we ought to reconsider ladies' fashions during the summer months. Wearing this much clothing is positively inhumane, I tell you." She dropped onto a settee. "Oh, lovely, tea. I see I have excellent timing."

"Don't you always?"

"I do, rather," Diana said smugly, watching as Violet poured her a cup.

"Do you have plans this afternoon?" Violet asked innocently, pouring a cup for herself as well and stirring in a lump of sugar and a splash of milk.

"Stop that at once, Violet. I did not come here for a simple chat, as I think you well know. I want to know exactly where you disappeared to last night, and why you needed so desperately to leave—looking *quite* disheveled, I might add." She gave Violet a rather beady-eyed look; Violet was suddenly strongly reminded of her own mother— perhaps the only time in her life she had thought Lady Worthington and Diana had anything in common.

"I'd rather not say," Violet said, but she could feel herself blushing as she spoke—*why* did she seem to have taken up the habit of blushing lately? It was extremely inconvenient—and she knew Diana would not leave her be.

"Well, *I* would rather not have to spend the next year attempting to get Lord Willingham married," Diana said. "And yet, here we are."

"You're the one who made that silly bet with him," Violet observed reasonably.

"That isn't the point. Stop changing the subject."

"I hardly think *I* am the one who changed the subject."

Diana sniffed. "Tell me what occurred last night," she demanded.

"James and I had an . . . interesting conversation," Violet said carefully.

"Oh?" Diana said sweetly. "Kept your mouths quite busy in this conversation, did you?"

"Diana!"

"I apologize. You were saying?"

"We were *talking*—did you just *snort*?"

"I am a lady," Diana said with great dignity.

"In any case, I thought we were making progress in the—er—proceedings . . . and then I coughed."

"Violet! If you were making progress, why on earth would you do that?" Diana looked truly indignant, as though she were a mother reprimanding an unruly child.

"Why is it," Violet wondered aloud to the room at large, "that I cannot inhale a speck of dust and cough a bit without causing such a reaction? I shall have to instruct the housemaids to be extremely thorough in their dusting, for the sake of any entertaining I wish to do."

"Oh, come now," Diana protested. "You must admit, you've

spent an entire fortnight hacking into a handkerchief at the slightest provocation."

"Encouraged by you!" Violet said, nettled. "And, in any case, I like to think I did not do any such thing as *hack*. It was far more delicate than that."

"Isn't there a children's story about this? The girl who cried wolf?" Diana mused.

"Shall I demonstrate the cough for you?" Violet asked. "Because, really, I hardly think *hack* is an accurate—"

"Violet!" Diana set her teacup down with a decisive clink. "Heavens, I wonder if this is what having children is like." She took a calming breath. "So I take it your cough was accidental?"

"Indeed."

"That was unfortunate timing."

"James seemed to agree with you," Violet said. "He took it as a sign of my . . ." She trailed off, unsure of what word to use.

"Continued duplicity?" Diana suggested helpfully.

"Something like that." Violet shrugged. "In any case, I rather lost my temper at that point and said some . . . things."

"Nothing more than the man deserved, no doubt," Diana murmured.

"I told him to alert me when he was ready to let me love him," Violet confessed in a rush. "And that I wouldn't wait forever."

"Excellent!" Diana said brightly. "Really, Violet, it doesn't do to moon over a man for too long. I think you should give up Audley and take up a lover posthaste."

"I thought you were encouraging this scheme of mine!" Violet protested.

"When I thought it was about revenge," Diana clarified. "Not love."

She looked at Violet sharply. "And that's what you're saying, isn't it? That you love him?"

"Yes," Violet said helplessly. "Though I rather wish I didn't, if this is how he's going to behave."

"Darling," Diana said. "This can't go on forever. You're young and beautiful. Any man would be lucky to have you, and it's not worth going to all this trouble for a husband who doesn't return your feelings. I don't believe in unrequited swooning," she added, giving Violet a severe look. "It doesn't do to let a man get an overly inflated sense of his own worth, you know. If Audley isn't going to rejoin you in your bed, then I say why not let some other chap?"

Violet was tempted for a moment to inquire how Diana felt about James joining her on window seats rather than beds, just to witness the reaction it would provoke, but even she was not so bold as that.

Instead, she merely said, "Ours might not have been the happiest marriage of late, but at least it is still a faithful one, and I intend for it to remain that way."

Diana sagged. "Morals," she said simply. "So tiresome."

Violet arched a brow.

"You seem to have rather a puritanical streak yourself, Diana. You've been out of mourning for how long now? And yet I've heard no whispers of a paramour."

"I'm working on it," Diana said cryptically, but before Violet could give much thought to *that* particular statement, Wooton reappeared in the doorway.

"Lord Willingham, my lady," he intoned, and stepped aside so that Jeremy could pass into the room.

"Jeremy?" Violet said, rising to offer him her hand. "How lovely. Are you looking for James? I'm afraid he's not at home."

"I was, rather," Jeremy said, bowing gallantly over her hand, then doing the same—rather more perfunctorily, it must be said—over Diana's. "But how can I be disappointed when I am presented with such charming company? Indeed, what man could resist the temptation to begin the day with two such lovely ladies?"

"I was under the impression that it was your habit to do exactly such a thing," Diana replied icily as Jeremy took a seat and Violet set about making a cup of tea for him. "Perhaps not *two*, though," she added, mock thoughtfully. "Though of course, I wouldn't know. Your stamina might be more impressive than I've been given to understand."

"I greeted the dawn alone today," Jeremy said, accepting the cup from Violet and taking a healthy gulp from it. "Which, of course, so disconcerted me that I made my way here immediately upon awakening." His tone was light, but his gaze on Diana was sharp.

"How lucky we are," Diana said venomously. "But do go away, Willingham, I was in the middle of a very important conversation with Violet and you are ruining it."

"Bedeviling her about last night, are you?" Jeremy asked wisely.

"She is, and I suspect it's the reason you called as well," Violet said. "Do leave me alone, the both of you."

"I thought you should know, Violet, that you and Audley were quite the talk of the ballroom after you left."

"Whatever for?"

"You cannot think that people did not notice Audley and Lady Fitzwilliam's dance? Particularly in light of the gossip about their meeting in Hyde Park?" Diana paused, then added delicately, "I'm surprised gentlemen aren't beating down your door as we speak."

"For what purpose?" Violet felt rather as though Diana were

speaking a foreign language; nothing she was saying seemed to make a great deal of sense to her.

"Well," Diana said, drawing out the word, "some gentlemen present seemed to think that since Audley has now made clear his intention to take a mistress, you would be more amenable to similar . . . er . . . extramarital activities, shall we say."

"Did they not notice that *I* danced with James, as soon as he was through with Lady Fitzwilliam?" Violet asked, irritated.

"No," Diana said slowly. "I believe they saw you cut in on their dance in a most scandalous fashion—and if that wasn't the action of a jealous wife, I fail to see any other alternate explanation for your behavior that seems the slightest bit plausible."

"Oh, good heavens." Violet buried her face in her hands. "I shall have to tell Wooton I am not at home to callers, if it's as bad as you say."

"I already took the liberty of doing so," Diana said serenely, sipping her tea. She focused a shrewd look on Jeremy. "Though that doesn't explain how *you* got in, Willingham."

"No one can resist my charms," Jeremy said with a winning grin. "Not even a butler of such sternness as Wooton."

"Strange, seeing as I have no difficulty in doing so."

"That is because, Lady Templeton, I have never wasted them on you. I assure you, were I to employ them, you would not stand a chance."

"In any case," Diana said, steering the conversation back to where she wanted it, "Violet, I had at least three separate gentlemen inquire about you last night. My dance card was full for the entire evening, so eager were people to hear whatever I might know about the state of your marriage."

"Your dance card is *always* full," Violet pointed out, quite truthfully.

"True," Diana said placidly, taking another sip of tea without any trace of false modesty. "But for once they didn't seem remotely interested in peering down my bodice in the most ungentlemanly fashion imaginable. All they wanted to do was talk!" She sounded thrilled and disgruntled in almost equal measure.

"You might have that experience more often if you gave them less to look at," Jeremy drawled.

"And yet you never seem able to resist the temptation to take a nice long ogle yourself," Diana shot back.

"My dear Lady Templeton, I am a *man*," Jeremy said, as though this explained everything. And, given Violet's experience with men, she supposed it probably did.

"Nonetheless," Violet said, deciding that the best course of action was to ignore this entire exchange, "I have no interest in any gentlemen who may choose to call on me, so they would be wasting their time."

"Violet, don't be so hasty," Diana chided. "Some of the gentlemen who asked me specifically about you last night were very handsome."

"I say," Jeremy said, "I don't think I should be present for this conversation."

"I couldn't agree more," Diana replied. "Feel free to show yourself out—I think you know the way."

"Did you have a particular purpose for calling, Jeremy?" Violet asked, a touch more diplomatically. "I could pass a message along for James—I've not seen him yet today, though."

"Probably hiding from any callers," Jeremy muttered darkly. "But, er, no, thank you. I just wanted to discuss—er—manly things with him. Probably wouldn't interest you in the least."

"Manly things?" Violet inquired dubiously.

"Yes, quite," Jeremy said with growing enthusiasm. "Not suitable discussion for ladies, in any case."

"What, precisely, are these 'manly things'?" Violet asked. "Horses? Mathematics? How to trick your wife into thinking you're interested in another woman?"

"Er," Jeremy said.

"Or shall I be more specific?" Violet pressed. "How to trick your wife into thinking you're interested in another woman because you know perfectly well that she's not truly ill?"

"Doesn't this give you a headache?" Jeremy burst out. "I don't know how you can stand it! I can't bloody keep track of who knows what about who at what hour of what day."

Violet and Diana exchanged raised eyebrows at this outburst. "You're right," Violet said. Diana looked as if she might fall off her chair at this admission. "It has gotten out of hand. James and I came to a similar conclusion last night, as a matter of fact." She did not mention that their accord had not lasted long—nor how, precisely, they celebrated their brief reconciliation.

"I quite agree," Diana said, which Violet thought was a bit rich, considering Diana had been in on this lunatic scheme from the very beginning. "Which is why I say, abandon the sham illness and invite one of these—very willing—gentlemen into your bed."

"You *do* realize that the man you're speaking of deceiving is my closest friend, don't you?" Jeremy asked conversationally.

"I hardly think now is the time for you to try to claim the moral high ground about deceiving a man in his marriage, Willingham," Diana said witheringly.

"I say," Jeremy said, and Violet was startled to see that he looked truly angry, a rarity from him. "I would like you to know that I have not once seduced a woman who was happily married, or whose marriage had ever been based on anything other than family connections or money." He stood abruptly, his cheeks rather flushed with anger. Diana was staring at him with frank astonishment.

"It is quite a different thing," Jeremy continued, "to speak of deceiving a man who married for love at a ridiculously young age, and then was destined to spend the rest of his life paying for it, all because his wife can't let go of some wretched argument from years past."

"I assure you," Violet said quietly, "I am not the person who is clinging to the past in this relationship. And, for the record—*not* that it's any of your affair—I informed James last night that I still loved him. I believe it is his turn to act, not mine."

At that moment, Wooton appeared at the door to the library once again and announced, "Lady Emily Turner."

"I gather you are not the only one skilled at weaseling your way past Wooton, Willingham," Diana said smugly as Emily appeared in the doorway in a state of some disarray.

This was, of course, all relative—Emily was normally so impeccably put together that even her current state, with one curl slipping from her coiffure to cling to her temple and her skirts the slightest bit rumpled, seemed startling.

Emily blinked at the sight of them gathered before her. "Did I miss an invitation of some sort?"

"Not at all," Violet said, gesturing her to take a seat with a wave of her hand. "I just seem to be the recipient of any number of unexpected guests this morning. What brings you here so early? Would you like some tea?"

"No, I can't stay," Emily said distractedly, twisting her hands. "I left my abigail loitering outside—I told her I just needed to borrow a book, because I suspect she eavesdrops on me and I didn't wish her to overhear this, but . . . I came to ask . . . well . . ." She trailed off, looking anxiously at Jeremy.

"Willingham, your presence here is decidedly de trop," Diana said with perhaps more eagerness than the situation called for.

"Diana," Violet said mildly, "kindly do me the courtesy of allowing *me* to be the person to boot guests from my own home."

Sighing dramatically, Diana desisted; before Violet could say more, however, Emily interjected, "No, perhaps Lord Willingham should stay." She cast a furtive glance at him. "A gentleman's opinion might be helpful."

Both Violet and Diana leaned forward in their chairs at that, and even Jeremy gave Emily a look that was decidedly more alert than his usual expression of amused boredom.

"Lord Julian Belfry," Emily began, and at the mere uttering of this name Diana leaned so far forward that Violet became concerned she was going to topple out of her chair entirely. Emily paused at this uncharacteristic show of enthusiasm, and Jeremy said, "Pray continue, Lady Emily, before Lady Templeton does herself some sort of grievous injury."

"Yes, well." Emily paused again. "He has asked if he might escort me to Lady Wheezle's Venetian breakfast this week."

There was a beat of silence, and then Diana wailed, "Of all the breakfasts! Why would he choose the one I've not been invited to?"

At the same moment, Jeremy asked, "Who in their right mind would want to attend *that*?"

Violet, attempting more diplomacy than either of her friends, merely asked, "Emily, how did this come about?" That was, in truth, the only question she could think to ask. She had certainly noted Belfry's interest in Emily, and indeed the difference in his casually flirtatious manner toward Diana and his more intent attention toward Emily. But she would not have thought there was anything serious in it; the man had a rather scandalous reputation, and did not seem the sort to escort debutantes to respectable society events.

Emily raised her hands. "I'm not entirely certain! We danced twice last night, and he asked me to take a turn about the room with him—this was after you two had disappeared," she added, but there was no hint of reproach in her voice. "We were chatting about nothing in particular, and he told me he had just that morning received an invitation to Lady Wheezle's breakfast, and asked if I should like to attend."

"And what did you say?" Diana asked with great interest.

"Well, I told him I was surprised he wished to attend at all, and he told me it was my company he was primarily interested in." Emily was blushing furiously by this point. "I then told him that I wasn't certain Mr. Cartham would enjoy my being escorted to the breakfast by someone else, and he told me he knew for a fact that Lady Wheezle wouldn't be inviting Mr. Cartham, and that surely I could not be expected to decline an offer of escort from another, given that I am not betrothed."

"*What did you say?*" Diana seemed with great effort to be resisting the urge to shake Emily.

"I said yes," Emily said all at once. "I was so surprised that I agreed before I could think better of it!"

"And why *should* you think better of it?" Diana asked.

"Because Belfry is a known seducer who is barely respectable?" Jeremy suggested casually.

"All men have to settle down sometime, Willingham," Diana said dismissively.

"I know you think so," Jeremy agreed. "You were willing to wager a sizable sum on that fact, if I recall correctly."

"I think it's wonderful, Emily," Violet said, ignoring Diana and Jeremy's squabbling, as was usually best. "I rather like Lord Julian. He's very handsome," she could not resist adding.

"And his pockets are *very* deep," Diana added.

"I think I agreed out of curiosity more than anything else," Emily confessed. "I've no idea how I'll convince my parents to allow his escort—they'll be worried Mr. Cartham will be offended."

"Did you mention your parents' concern to Belfry?" Jeremy asked.

Emily nodded. "He said not to worry about that—that he and Mr. Cartham run in some of the same circles, and he'd handle it." She sounded dubious at the odds of his success in this endeavor, but Violet rather thought that Lord Julian Belfry might be entirely capable of managing Oswald Cartham, and she said as much.

"Besides," she added. "Diana's right. Men have to marry eventually. Perhaps he's decided that the role of husband appeals to him."

"Speaking of husbands," Emily added, clearly desperate for a change in subject matter, "where was yours rushing off to, Violet, in such a hurry when I arrived?"

Violet frowned. "What do you mean?"

It was Emily's turn to frown. "He was departing just as I was arriving—he seemed in a state of some agitation, I must confess. Did he not tell you where he was going?"

"I didn't even know he was home," Violet said, exasperated. When had James arrived? And why had he left?

"How odd," Emily said, still frowning. "He was walking away from the hallway leading to the library just as Wooton let me in; I assumed he had been in here with you."

A cold feeling crept over Violet. What had they been discussing, just prior to Emily's arrival? What might James have overheard? She thought for a moment, and then realized, a mixture of anger and mild alarm rising within her: they'd been discussing the possibility of Violet having an affair.

Of *course* that would be the moment he chose to eavesdrop, the infuriating man. She wanted to throttle him.

Instead she said slowly to her friends, "I think he overheard us."

"What do you mean?" Diana asked.

"You were prattling on about my taking a lover," Violet said, striving to keep the irritation out of her voice. "I think that's the bit of our conversation that James overheard. Why else would he rush off like that?"

"Pish," Jeremy said dismissively. "It's not Audley's way to listen at keyholes like a naughty schoolboy."

This was an amusing mental image, but Violet did not allow herself to be distracted. "It was likely accidental," she clarified. "The door was cracked, after all, and he could have easily caught a bit of what we were saying if he were standing just outside."

"What has you so upset, Violet?" Diana asked, getting up and walking to her side.

"The man's probably gone and gotten the wrong idea *again*!" Violet burst out angrily. "No doubt he heard your nonsense and now he's gotten himself worked into a fury once more. Oh, I could strangle him!" She began to pace the length of the room—which was not inconsiderable. "How am I supposed to make a go of this marriage if he takes offense at every whispered insinuation he hears? It's infuriating!"

"To be fair," Jeremy said helpfully, "I don't think Lady Templeton was insinuating anything. She was stating it quite plainly."

Diana shot a venomous look at Jeremy, but Violet had no time for their squabbling now.

"It would be nice if I could confide in my dearest friend without her encouraging me to destroy my marriage."

Diana's face flushed with anger, which was unusual; despite her quick tongue, it was rare that she grew truly angry. She never seemed to think it worth the energy. But Violet had clearly struck a nerve.

"You've done quite enough to destroy your marriage without any help from me," she said in a clipped tone that evidenced nothing of her usual languid demeanor. "You're behaving like a child, and so is your husband." She crossed her arms. "It's absurd that you've ever tried to claim your indifference to him, in fact. People don't try so desperately to needle someone they're indifferent to."

Violet was sorely tempted at that moment to ask how that particular theory applied to Diana's perpetual spat with Jeremy, but resisted the temptation with some difficulty, deciding that it would only make matters worse.

"I'm going to take my leave of you now, Violet," Diana said decisively, gathering up her reticule and making for the doorway. "Do please let me know when all this nonsense is at an end and we might have a normal conversation once more." With that, she departed, leaving Violet, Emily, and Jeremy staring at the empty space she'd just vacated.

"You know," Jeremy said thoughtfully, "I think I might rather admire Lady Templeton after all."

Fourteen

That morning, James had done what he always did in moments of doubt: taken to his horse.

He'd felt like the very devil upon awakening, his mouth dry and head pounding, but he'd dragged himself out of bed nonetheless; he was going to feel like hell regardless—he might as well do it in the open air. And, in truth, he needed to think, and he had always thought better out of doors. He recalled his years at Oxford—whenever he had become stuck on some sort of thorny mathematical problem, a good, hard ride had usually sorted him out.

He had languished in bed long past his usual hour, courtesy of the aforementioned throbbing head, but still arrived at the park hours before five, when the *ton* turned out in force. It was, therefore, something of a surprise when he heard another rider hailing him as soon as he turned onto Rotten Row.

It was an even greater surprise when he discovered that said rider was his father.

As James had grown from boy to man, his father had seemed to shrink—he was still a tall, imposing man, but he no longer towered over James as he had in James's boyhood, nor was he a towering figure in James's imagination, one to be feared at all costs. However, he still made no effort to see the duke more than was absolutely necessary—and when one was a second son and not the cherished heir, "absolutely necessary" was rather less than one might think. Or it had been prior to West's accident.

Since that day, the duke had taken rather more of an interest in his second son. There had been the gift of Audley House as a wedding present and that frightful morning when James had returned home to find his father and Violet deep in conversation—a conversation that James was beginning to think he might have badly misunderstood. Still, despite the fact that the duke's hopes for the future of the dukedom focused rather more on James than James might have wished, he had managed to put as much distance as was seemly between himself and his father. They weren't openly feuding—they kept up appearances—but . . .

Well, but James didn't relish the idea of his father interrupting a much-needed ride. Especially on a day when his head felt as though a hammer were pounding at his temples.

"Father," he said stiffly, having reined in his horse and allowed his father to catch up. "This is rather early for you, is it not?"

"Quite," his father said dryly, with a telling glance at the less-than-crowded park around him. "I've never understood your fascination with these morning rides."

"It's after noon," James felt compelled to point out.

"Regardless." His father waved a dismissive hand.

"Riding clears my head."

"Judging by what I've heard, it needs clearing."

James clenched his jaw. "What, precisely, does that mean?" he asked, though he was fairly certain he didn't want to hear the answer.

"I heard some rather interesting talk last night at my club," the duke said casually as he spurred his horse into a gentle trot. "The general impression I received was that you and your wife have been making a spectacle of yourselves."

"And that is your concern . . . how?" James asked tightly.

"You are my son," the duke said, clearly enunciating each word, his voice taking on a sharp staccato rhythm. "If your brother is as . . . troubled as he claims, you will be responsible for providing an heir to the dukedom. What you do reflects on me."

"Then perhaps," James said, trying to keep the fury surging through him absent from his voice, "you should have considered that when you ignored me *every single day* for years." The duke opened his mouth to respond, but James wasn't finished yet. "Perhaps you should have considered that when you meddled in my life and hand-selected me a bride, assuming, I suppose, that I was too much of an idiot to accomplish the task myself."

"And yet I heard no complaints from you about my selection," his father said, his eyes on the path before them. "I rather think a thank-you is in order, all things considered." He paused pointedly, then added, "Though I understand your marriage has been less than happy of late. But that is a fact, my boy, that has nothing to do with me."

"It has everything to do with you!" James said, the resentment of all of his previous eight-and-twenty years—and most particularly the past four—boiling up within him. "My marriage—which is none of your concern, for the record—has had its rough spots only because of your interference. It is *always you*."

The duke reined his horse in hard, causing the animal to buck before settling. When James followed in kind and looked at his father head-on, he saw the duke's eyes were sparkling with anger, even as his countenance remained calm. Like father, like son.

"I have never understood, James, why it is that you think I have wronged you so terribly." Even if James had not already been paying attention, his father's rare use of his Christian name would certainly have attracted his notice. His father had called him Audley, just like everyone else, for as long as James could remember. "I am a duke. You are my son. You know precisely what that entails, what a reputation we have to uphold, and everything I have ever done to and for you has been in pursuit of that aim.

"You say I ignored you as a child. You might be correct. West is my heir; it was my duty to guide him to manhood, to make him understand the responsibility that would one day fall on his shoulders. I gave you tutors and riding lessons, I sent you to Eton and Oxford, and, when the time came and I realized the question of your marriage and children might have a rather greater bearing on the future of the dukedom than I had originally thought, I arranged them to my satisfaction. Although"—and here the duke smiled briefly—"I do not imagine how you think I possibly could have induced you to marry Violet Grey if she had not suited you. You are unlike me in many ways, but you do seem to have inherited my stubborn streak."

James felt rather as though the ground were shifting beneath his feet. He had known—had always known—that his father did not favor West out of any greater sense of camaraderie with his brother, but to hear him state it so baldly did something strange to James.

He and West were the sons of one of the wealthiest and most powerful men in the land; nothing could change that fact, or negate the numerous advantages it had always given James from the moment he had drawn his first breath. And yet, somehow, his entire life he had thought that his father's disinterest in him, his refusal to see him as anything other than a spare, had determined the course of his life; this belief had made him distrustful, even resentful at times. But West, as the heir, had suffered their father's attention; James, as the spare, had suffered just the opposite. The first time his father had tried to truly meddle in his life—with his arrangement of James being discovered upon that balcony in a compromising situation with Violet—James had been sent into a fury upon learning of it. He tried—and failed—to imagine what his life would have been like if his father had always paid him such attention.

He was certain he would not have liked it, whatever the result.

Furthermore, he was coming to realize, he had only himself to blame for the shambles he had made of his marriage. His father had meddled, it was true, but James couldn't argue with the results—he had, after all, been besotted with Violet from almost the moment he'd first seen her. It was he who had cocked everything up upon learning of his father's involvement in arranging their marriage—and why? All because any mention of his father made him lose all sense and reason.

He hadn't trusted her. It was true. If Violet said she'd not known of the schemes surrounding their courtship, no doubt it was true; Lady Worthington was certainly conniving enough to hatch such a plan with James's father without letting her daughter in on the plot.

So why had James been so quick to disbelieve her? Why had he not trusted Violet, his wife, the person he loved above all others?

Because in some part of his heart he was still the small boy watching from a window as his father and brother went out for rides without him. He was still that boy, unable to trust that anyone's love for him was unconditional and true. And yet, James realized, he had not been that boy for a very long time. He had gone to school, met Jeremy and Penvale, discovered what a difference true friendship could make in a life. He had come down to London after university and had begun to forge a relationship with his brother outside of their father's shadow. He had met Violet.

And yet, at the first whisper of doubt, he had become that boy once more—a boy in a large house full of rooms and no one within them to pay him any mind. A boy who at the first possibility someone might have betrayed him instantly believed it to be the case.

But that was not his life anymore. He would be damned if he allowed the distrust wrought in him by a childhood of neglect to write the course of his future. It was time he corrected the damage he had done, once and for all.

"I'll thank you to not interfere in my affairs again," James said shortly, his mind still working, weary of his father's presence. "I've nothing further to say to you about this, or about anything else, really." He gathered the reins in his hand, preparing to spur his horse to movement.

"If you're still so upset about this," the duke said before James could ride away, "I'm surprised you keep company with the Marquess of Willingham." James froze, and a triumphant gleam appeared in his father's eyes; the duke knew he had struck gold. "Next time you see him you might ask him how, precisely, it was that he so conveniently had lured the erstwhile Lady Violet Grey out onto a balcony just in time for you to rescue her."

His father smiled his infuriating smile at him, and then nudged his horse into a trot, leaving James, gaping like a fool, sitting atop his stationary horse in the middle of Rotten Row.

The only thing to do was to take himself home, and so James did just that. The insinuation about Jeremy had been shocking, no doubt— he had always tried his hardest *not* to think about Jeremy and Violet together on that balcony, but when the memory did spring to mind, he waved it off as Jeremy being Jeremy. Now, however, James realized that it was in fact not at all like Jeremy. Say what you liked about the man—and people had on occasion had cause to say quite a bit—but he was careful in his selection of ladies. He tended to limit himself to opera dancers, actresses, widows, and unhappily married ladies with inattentive husbands. James had never seen him panting after an un-married miss before or after that evening with Violet.

At the time, he hadn't thought anything of it. Now, he wondered how he could have been such an idiot.

Jeremy would never have lured an eligible young virgin of mar-riageable age out onto a balcony—to do so and to be caught was to be forced into marriage, and if the Jeremy of eight-and-twenty was disinterested in matrimony, the Jeremy of five years prior would have shuddered at the very word. Clearly, there had been something else afoot. It was tempting to succumb to anger—James's instinctive reac-tion to anything bearing his father's fingerprints—but he was trying, if only belatedly, to learn to trust those around him, or at least give them the benefit of the doubt. He therefore resisted the temptation to bang down Jeremy's door and present him with his accusations—and perhaps a fist to the jaw.

Instead, he rode back to the house at a feverish pace, and upon ar-riving, hopped off his mount and tossed the reins to a stable hand, en-tering the house directly from the mews and startling a scullery maid when he raced past her on the kitchen stairs. He found Wooton in the entryway, inspecting the banister railings with a white glove, in a move so entirely and stereotypically butlerish that James was, for an instant, seized with a mad desire to laugh.

"Is Lady James awake?" he asked without preamble.

Wooton straightened at the sight of him. "She is entertaining Lady Templeton and Lord Willingham with tea in the library," said Wooton, and this piece of news caused James to freeze in the act of removing his gloves. "Shall I announce you, my lord?"

"No, thank you, Wooton," James said, finishing the glove removal at a slightly less frenetic pace. "I'll just surprise them, I think."

"Very good, my lord," Wooton said with a bow, and departed—off to do whatever mysterious things butlers did all day, that all together resulted in a quietly and efficiently run house. James set off down the hallway toward the library. He hadn't counted on Violet having company, and particularly not on Jeremy being among said company. He supposed Jeremy had come in search of him and had stayed to converse with the ladies instead, though he reflected on the oddity of Jeremy paying a call just past noon; at this time of day, he was usually still abed (and frequently in someone else's company).

It was strange, too, for Diana to be here this early—she kept fashionable hours, and James was certain he had heard her remark more than once on how odd she found Violet and James's habit of early rising. He had a sneaking suspicion that Jeremy's and Diana's uncharacteristically early calls had something to do with the events of the previous evening; he and Violet had, after all, made rather a spectacle of themselves. He was sick of the games and the arguments and the interfering lunatics he called friends. He just wanted to have an honest conversation with his wife.

To be followed, preferably, by a lengthy interlude in bed.

This thought, in turn, conjured vivid memories of the events of the night before. Violet, her head tilted back wantonly, eyes shut, dark hair in disarray. The feeling of her hips tilting against his own in silent invitation. The heat and warmth of her as he had slid home, again and again and—

Christ.

How could he have ever thought than anyone other than Violet would satisfy him?

You didn't, said the quiet, reasonable voice that occupied some small corner of his head. *Not really.*

And he knew it was true. Why else had he spent the past four years as chaste as a monk, in a house with a woman who loathed him? Because he'd never stopped hoping, never stopped wanting, even if he hadn't been able to admit it, even to himself.

And that was the problem, really. Wasn't that what Violet had been saying in her roundabout fashion last night? He'd loved her, but he'd lost faith in her at the slightest provocation. He'd let his past dictate his future, and he'd never done the slightest thing to fight for that future.

He was the son of a duke, and as such, he wasn't accustomed to having to fight for much of anything. And when something didn't come easily to him, he abandoned it.

Mathematics? Easy. Wedding Violet? Easy. Inheriting his father's stables? Easy.

But moving past childhood hurts? His relationship with West? Marriage to Violet? More difficult. And so he'd never really tried.

And his life was undoubtedly emptier because of it.

So now it was time to do something about it.

The door to the library was cracked, and as James approached, he could hear voices filtering out. He reached for the doorknob, then paused as his brain registered what exactly he was hearing.

Violet was speaking. "... has gotten out of hand. James and I came to a similar conclusion last night, as a matter of fact." James felt a flash of amusement at these words, his hand still hovering above the doorknob; Violet pointedly did *not* mention the manner in which they had come to an accord of sorts.

"I quite agree," came Lady Templeton's voice. "Which is why I say, abandon the sham illness and invite one of these—very willing— gentlemen into your bed."

James froze, his arm still outstretched. What the bloody hell?

"You *do* realize that the man you're speaking of deceiving is my closest friend, don't you?" Jeremy asked, his tone casual; James thought that only someone who knew Jeremy well would have caught the note of anger running beneath the surface, and he felt a brief flash of gratitude for Jeremy, despite whatever mysterious dealings his friend might have had with his father five years past.

"I hardly think now is the time for you to try to claim the moral high ground about deceiving a man in his marriage, Willingham," Lady Templeton said, her tone scornful.

"I say," Jeremy said, and James knew instantly that Diana had gone too far, "I would like you to know that I have not once seduced a woman who was happily married, or whose marriage had ever been based on anything other than family connections or money."

James heard the sound of a chair being pushed back against the floor, and he beat a hasty retreat before he quite realized what he was doing—he didn't wish to be caught lurking outside the door eavesdropping on *this* conversation. He was irritated, even as he made his way back down the hall; he needed to speak to Violet, and he needed Jeremy and Diana to depart for him to do so. He supposed he could barge in and ask them to leave, but he didn't particularly feel like managing the awkwardness that would doubtless ensue when they realized he'd overheard their conversation. He wasn't concerned about Violet taking Diana's advice—and the realization of that unquestioning trust made him feel nearly giddy—but he still thought his presence might be a bit de trop at the moment, and it hardly seemed like a good note on which to begin a discussion with Violet.

He felt like a five-year-old who had been caught spying on his parents, which was absurd—this was *his* house, for Christ's sake. And yet, feeling like a fool, he did the only thing that seemed reasonable at the moment: he left again.

It was at his club that Jeremy found him.

"Awake rather early, aren't you?" James asked, lowering the newspaper that he'd been staring at blankly for the past thirty minutes.

"Come off it," Jeremy said, sitting down. "Did you overhear the entire bloody conversation, then?"

"Just a snippet," James said, casting his newspaper aside with a sigh. He saw no reason to lie; he assumed, since Jeremy was here, that Wooton had told Violet that he'd been home, albeit briefly, meaning that his wife now knew precisely how much of an idiot he had acted.

"And you ran away."

"I didn't want to be caught eavesdropping and have Violet get the wrong idea," James said, feeling more and more foolish by the moment.

"You might have avoided that possibility by not skulking in the hallway in the first place," said Jeremy with great dignity. It was a bit galling to be condescended to by a man who had only recently had to leave a bedroom window by way of a rose trellis, and James told him so.

"Besides," he added, "I'm the son of a duke, as my father reminded me just this afternoon. Ducal sons don't *skulk*."

Jeremy straightened in his chair, his gaze razor sharp. "You saw your father today? Whatever for, old boy? Felt like beating your head against a brick wall?"

"It was unintentional, I assure you," James said, rather testily. "I encountered him out riding in the park—the meeting was *not* coincidental, I think." He hesitated a moment, then took the plunge. "Over the course of our rather enlightening conversation, he had some interesting things to say about you."

"Did he?" Jeremy asked, suddenly very interested in the cuffs on his shirt.

"He did," James confirmed, and after a moment during which he looked at Jeremy and Jeremy looked everywhere but at him, his friend raised his eyes and met James's gaze full-on.

"He told you about the night you met Violet, then?" Jeremy asked directly.

"I'd really like to hear it from you." James had learned—rather belatedly—his lesson about taking his father at his word.

Jeremy heaved a sigh and ran a hand through his hair. James couldn't remember the last time he'd seen him look so uncomfortable; he had grown used to the lazy, always-slightly-drunken Jeremy, the womanizing good-for-nothing marquess who was amused by everything and moved by nothing. It was a very effective mask, but James hadn't realized that it was almost *too* good; those were all parts of Jeremy, it was true, but he was more than the sum of his parts, and James wondered if perhaps he had forgotten this of late. He wondered if *Jeremy* had forgotten, too.

"You recall what it was like when I'd first inherited the marquessate?" Jeremy asked. He didn't elaborate, but James nodded, understanding all that was implied. Jeremy's father hadn't left the marquessate destitute, but its coffers had been reduced by years of neglect and bad investments. Jeremy's elder brother, who had inherited the title upon their father's death when Jeremy was still at Eton, had managed, through some creative rearranging of accounts, to come up with the blunt to pay the death duties, but it had been a stretch. He had then spent his remaining capital at hand—almost all of the liquid funds the Overington family had left—on a series of costly improvements to the estate. These improvements had, over the past decade, yielded great results, and the estate was solvent once more—flourishing, even. But at the time, it had sharply limited the amount of ready funds—James could distinctly remember Jeremy grumbling at the reduction in his allowance.

Needless to say, when Jeremy's brother had died in a racing accident with West, the death duties that Jeremy had been forced to pay when *he* had inherited the title in turn had nearly bankrupted the marquessate. James often thought it amusing how carefully Jeremy had cultivated the reputation of a carefree rake, when in truth he'd had to fight bitterly—at the age of two-and-twenty, no less—to keep his family estate solvent. James had always admired him for it—and he wondered what, precisely, this had to do with the topic at hand.

The question must have been evident on his face, because Jeremy responded as though he'd voiced the query aloud.

"Your father approached me the week before that evening," he said bluntly, his gaze never moving from James's own, and James reflected that this was one of the things he liked best about Jeremy—he might hem and haw about doing what was right, but once he had made up his mind to do so, he never wavered. "He told me that he knew I'd been under a great deal of strain of late, and that he'd be happy to do a bit to alleviate the burden—for a tiny price. Just lure a certain young lady onto a balcony at a certain ball that you'd be attending." He paused then, breaking eye contact and looking down at his hands. He took a deep breath and raised his eyes once more. "I could lie and say he black-mailed me, or approached me when I was foxed, but it's not true. I was sober as a judge; he visited me at home one night. I knew how fraught your relationship with your father was, and I did it anyway." He stated this plainly, without breaking eye contact, making no excuses.

"He offered you money," James said—it was a statement, rather than a question.

Jeremy shrugged helplessly. "He must have known how desperate I was—he offered me a sum that . . . well . . ." He trailed off, looking slightly embarrassed. "It was enough to keep me afloat until those in-vestments could pay off. I wasn't really in a position to say no."

James had expected a rush of anger, but he felt oddly . . . detached.

"Audley," Jeremy said, speaking more quickly now, "I want you to know—I never would have agreed to it if I'd realized it would actually work."

"What?"

"What I mean to say is—well—we were only twenty-three! I never dreamed you'd take one look at Violet and become instantly be-sotted with her."

"I think it took a bit more than one look," James said, because a man did have his dignity to consider, after all.

"You say that," Jeremy said with a trace of his usual smugness, "be-cause you didn't see your face that evening on the balcony." He sighed, his levity evaporating once more. "I didn't mean to trap you into any-thing, Audley. The past few years, seeing how unhappy you've been . . ." He trailed off again, then cleared his throat uncomfortably. James re-flected that he had been friends with Jeremy for nearly twenty years, and yet this might be the most honest conversation they had ever had.

Violet, no doubt, would sniff and say this was typical of men. The thought made him smile—and *God*, it felt bloody marvelous to smile when he thought of Violet, rather than feel the peculiarly specific combination of anger and despair with which he had become so familiar over the past few years.

"We quarreled about that night," he said in a rush, without pausing to even consider what he was doing.

"I beg your pardon?"

"The quarrel—this . . . distance." He gestured before himself helplessly, as though his hands could encompass the four years of coldness, of slowly inching apart. "It started because I came home to find that my father had called on Violet. I overheard them discussing his and Violet's mother's arrangement of that encounter on the balcony."

"You need to stop listening at doorways."

"I assure you," James said, nettled, "that these are the only two occasions on which I have ever done so in my entire life."

"All the more reason to stop," Jeremy said sagely, "since it seems you've truly abysmal timing." He paused. "Or I suppose you could start doing it more frequently. If you listened at a doorway every day, you'd be bound to improve your odds of hearing something mundane and entirely uninteresting."

"The point is," James said, feeling that someone really ought to keep the conversation on topic, "that I leapt to conclusions. Violet seemed to already know about their scheming, so I assumed she had known all about it from the start. We quarreled over it—she told me I was being an ass, that I should trust her—which I was, and I should have—"

"You mean to tell me that this is the only reason you two have been doing a passable impression of my parents for the past four years?" Jeremy asked incredulously.

"It sounds utterly idiotic, doesn't it?"

"Dear God, man!" Jeremy said, so animated at this point that he actually leapt to his feet. This attracted considerable attention from the other gentlemen in the room; half a dozen heads turned their way, and Jeremy, belatedly realizing that he was making a scene, waved at them in a way that, far from being reassuring, made him look slightly unhinged.

"I've been feeling guilty for years for tricking you into a marriage that made you unhappy," Jeremy said, lowering his voice slightly as he resumed his seat.

"Indeed?" James arched a brow. "Yes, I can see that the guilt has truly been eating away at you. Put you off food and women, has it?"

"Well, I didn't say I was in the midst of a bloody Shakespearean tragedy," Jeremy said defensively. "But I have felt rather bad about it all. No more, though!"

"You do realize," James said conversationally, "that since our quarrel was originally about the circumstances under which we met—circumstances which you helped orchestrate, I might remind you—it seems to me that *now* is when you should be feeling most guilty of all?"

Jeremy waved a hand dismissively. "Pish. I've spent all this time thinking you two were entirely unsuited and that Violet must secretly be an utter harpy when you're alone."

"Afraid not," James said, feeling—improbably—rather cheerful.

"Indeed! It seems that it is you, in fact, who is the . . . er . . ."

"Harpy?" James suggested innocently.

"For lack of a better word."

"Well," James said, rising, "as illuminating as this conversation has been, I think it's time I took my leave of you."

"Going to grovel at your wife's feet?"

"Something like that," James said dryly. "Perhaps a bit more romantic and masculine."

"I'd stick with groveling," Jeremy said with the wisdom of a man who had soothed many an offended lady's delicate sensibilities. "They can't seem to resist it, bless them." He paused for a moment, watching James gather his gloves and hat. "Audley—we are—that is to say—" He looked up at James with a look of uncharacteristic uncertainty. "You can forgive me for this?"

James paused a moment, surprised at the realization that he could indeed, without much difficulty. "You're a good friend, Jeremy," he said, preparing to turn and leave. "I just wish sometimes you'd take things a bit more seriously."

"But then—"

"I forgive you," James said simply, and did not miss the look of relief he saw on his friend's face just before he turned and left the room.

Fifteen

Violet was in her bedchamber when James returned home.

"Is she ill?" he asked Wooton, though he wasn't quite able to muster up the appropriate note of husbandly anxiety to inject in his voice. So help him, if Violet were playing the consumptive again—

"I don't believe so, my lord," Wooton said, holding his hands out for James's hat and gloves, which he had practically torn off in his haste. James tossed them to his butler without a second glance and began bounding up the stairs three at a time. He reached the second floor and began striding down the hallway to Violet's door, at which he did not hesitate to knock firmly.

There was a brief pause, then the muffled sound of footsteps. The door opened, revealing Violet's startled face.

"James—"

He stopped the rest of her words with his mouth. While not particularly effective as a method of silencing Violet indefinitely, it certainly worked in the short term—and had various benefits to himself as well.

He half expected her to shove him away, after their less-than-warm parting of the evening before, but she responded to him like kindling to a flame. He felt her softening, melting into his arms, her mouth opening under his with a soft sigh, and he suddenly found himself being kissed with an ardor equal to his own. Violet's arms came up around his neck, her fingers plunging into his hair, and it was all he could do not to groan at the sensation, instead merely wrapping an arm around her waist and hauling her closer.

He managed to drag his lips away from hers and began planting a series of openmouthed kisses down her neck, the sound of her ragged breathing sparking his own desire even further. He felt as though he were on the verge of crawling out of his own body, so great was his need to possess, consume. Could this possibly be normal? Would this feeling never fade? Would he never be able to kiss his wife and not feel as though he were about to burst into flame?

With a herculean force of will, he managed to halt the southerly progress of his mouth, lifting his head and placing a last, more gentle kiss upon her lips. He took a step back, releasing her waist, and she opened her eyes after a moment, blinking at him in such adorable befuddlement that he was unable to resist bestowing another kiss upon her. This one would have escalated in a similarly amorous fashion had James not used both hands to bodily lift Violet away and set her down a foot or two away from him.

"Did you have an actual purpose in calling?" Violet asked casually. Her cheeks, however, were still flushed, and there was a slight hitch to her voice.

James opened his mouth, a dozen different explanations and justifications running through his head, competing for the opportunity to spill out of his mouth, and yet, in the end, the only two words to emerge were the most important ones:

"I'm sorry."

Had he been a younger, more foolish man, he might have expected these two words to work like some sort of magic spell or healing balm, causing his wife to hurl herself into his arms, weeping copiously, rending his garments, and extracting promises from him to never allow them to be parted in such a fashion again. James could not deny that this vision had its own certain appeal, but, at the end of the day, he had married a flesh-and-blood woman, Violet, *his* Violet, with her quick temper and grudges and all the rest, and so he experienced a surprising sense of relief that she did nothing of the sort. Instead, she merely arched her brow and said, "I suppose you'd better sit down. This might take a while."

She turned then, allowing him to follow her deeper into the room. She took a seat in one of the armchairs before the fireplace, gesturing for him to occupy the one opposite, which he did once she had been seated. He took this opportunity to take a proper look at her. She was wearing a morning gown of pale blue muslin, simply cut, beautiful against her fair skin. She looked a bit tired, the slight traces of dark shadows the only flaw to her lovely face, and he wondered if her night's sleep had been as hard-won and troubled as his own. Her hair was slightly disheveled, no doubt a product of their entanglement a moment ago.

He thought that she was the most beautiful thing he had ever seen.

Fortunately—as was so often the case with Violet—before he could begin any truly maudlin reflections on her visage, involving pained metaphors or, God forbid, some mangled bits of Shakespeare, she spoke.

"So," she said, her voice businesslike, "when you say you are sorry, do you mean generally or specifically?" She folded her hands neatly in her lap and shot him a politely inquiring look.

James felt as though he were back at Eton, sitting for an exam for which he hadn't fully prepared. "Specifically? No, generally?" He resisted the temptation to clutch at his own hair. "What the devil are you talking about?"

"Well," Violet said, "I was merely curious as to what you were apologizing for. Are you apologizing for our rather heated exchange last night, or for your actions over the past two weeks, or—"

"The past four years, Violet," James interrupted. "I'm apologizing for the past four years."

"Oh," Violet said, and James was pleased to see that, for the moment, she didn't seem to have any other reply. Since the occasions upon which Violet was rendered speechless were few and far between, James seized the opportunity with both hands.

"You were right last night," he said, "when you said I should trust you—should've trusted you all along." He paused, struggling for words; he was an Englishman, the son of a duke—these were not traits that led to unburdening himself easily. He had always been taught the value of a stiff upper lip, of a controlled demeanor. He had, it seemed, become rather too good at keeping one, and it was time to unlearn that skill as best he could. Never had doing so mattered more.

"You are my wife," he said simply, and these four words felt as important to him as any four words he had ever uttered in his entire life. They were, he realized, the beginning and the end of everything; she was his wife, and he loved her. "You should be the person I trust above all others. You've never given me cause not to. And I . . ." He paused a moment, the words coming too fast now, lodging in his throat. He risked a glance at her, and saw that her eyes were shining, and that there was a look in those eyes—those perfect, beautiful, dark-lashed brown eyes—that he hadn't seen there in quite some time.

Tenderness.

"You acted as anyone with your upbringing might have done," she finished for him, and he was surprised by the soft, affectionate note in her voice.

"That's not an excuse," he said. "Your parents—"

"Are frequently horrid as well," she finished for him. "I'm quite aware of that, thank you." Her voice was dry, and he could see a smile twitching at her mouth for a moment before it faded, her demeanor growing more serious. "But it was . . . different for you. My mother always took an interest in me—too great an interest, in truth," and in her voice James could hear the memory of a thousand arguments with a countess who never quite knew what to do with a willful, curious, clever daughter who never did what was expected of her.

"Your father . . ." Violet looked at him, a faint line appearing on her smooth forehead as her eyebrows furrowed slightly. "He didn't need you, and so he ignored you. And I think that that's the sort of experience that makes it very hard to trust anyone."

"It doesn't matter," James said hoarsely, and he realized he wasn't just saying it to appease her, to bolster his apology. He truly believed it. He'd been an ass, and he was beginning to realize precisely how great of an ass—and was feeling ashamed. "I was with you in St. George's; I stood at that altar with you and spoke those vows. It was . . . wrong of me to take my father's word over yours."

"Well, we can certainly agree on that." Violet smiled at him, and it was as though the sun had reappeared after a storm. After a moment, however, her smile faded. "It wasn't just that morning with your father, though. There were all the arguments leading up to those."

"We always made those up," James said, frowning slightly.

"We did," Violet said slowly, giving him a piercing look. "But I can't help but feel that they were preludes to that last fight, the one we couldn't get past. Little things, small moments when you proved, over and over, that you didn't trust our love. That you didn't trust me."

James opened his mouth to offer a hasty rebuttal, then paused, giving her words the thought and consideration they deserved—for he could tell by the slight hitch to her voice that they had not been easy for her to speak.

"You might be right," he said after a long moment. "I'd never considered it in that light, but I believe you might be entirely right."

"Of course I am." Violet sniffed, crossing her arms, and James had to fight hard against the smile tugging at the corners of his mouth.

"I would love nothing more than another chance to *not* make those same mistakes again," James said quietly, but with every ounce of feeling he held for her behind each word. Her eyes locked on his, her gaze searching, as though she were looking for some evidence of falsehood in his face. He looked calmly back at her, for once content to let his mask lie unused, his every feeling writ upon his face. After a moment, her smile returned, slowly blooming across her face, and it was so breathtakingly lovely that it made him bold, or perhaps foolish, enough to say mournfully, "Of course, it is tragic that it took such dire circumstances to bring about this realization on my part."

Violet's smile vanished once more, replaced by a furrowed brow. "I beg your pardon?"

"Your illness, of course," James said earnestly.

"James—"

"It pains me, naturally, that we will have so little time to enjoy our reconciliation," he continued dramatically, ignoring her attempts to interrupt. "But this is the hand the fates have dealt us, and we have nothing to do now but attempt to make the best of it."

"You are rather an ass, aren't you?" Violet asked.

"Oh, undoubtedly," James assured her. "And yet, I seem to recall you always found that one of my more infuriatingly attractive qualities."

"Did I?"

"To the best of my recollection, yes."

"My memory is failing me," she said sadly, looking at him coquettishly from beneath her lashes. "Perhaps you had better remind me."

"A task, madam, I am happy to undertake," James said gallantly, and then he spoke no more, for he was before her on his knees in an instant, her face in his hands, his mouth moving urgently over hers.

It was the night before, all over again—and yet somehow different, somehow more. Last night, James had been possessed with a feverish urgency, some part of him convinced it was a dream, that Violet would disappear from his arms if he paused for even a moment. And his need had been matched by her own—she had clutched him, urged him on, faster, faster.

Now, however, James deliberately slowed himself—after all, they had plenty of time. There were still words to be spoken, hurts to be addressed, but they would do so together. He no longer feared the return of the cold and echoing silence that had occupied the house for so long.

So instead of pressing her back more deeply into her chair and kissing her until she could not breathe, he broke the kiss and rose to his feet, extending a hand toward her. She stared at it blankly, looking disconcerted.

"I am as fond of this chair as any man," he explained politely, "but it occurred to me that it might make more sense to avail ourselves of the bed that is so conveniently nearby." He jerked his head in the direction of the piece of furniture in question—one that James in fact had never occupied himself.

Violet, he was delighted to see, blushed. "Of course," she said, standing and taking his hand with so blatant a display of eagerness that James had to bite back a giddy grin. Instead, he satisfied himself by leading her toward the aforementioned bed before turning her away from him and making short work of the buttons on the back of her gown.

"I don't recall you being quite so quick at that," Violet said over her shoulder, a note of suspicion in her voice as he pushed her dress aside and dedicated himself to unlacing her corset.

"It is remarkable what I can achieve when presented with an extremely enticing motivation," James said.

"So you've not been practicing?" He detected a slight hint of un-Violet-like uncertainty in her voice, and he froze, his fingers at the lacings at the base of her spine. He looked up.

"Violet."

"It has been rather a long time . . ." Her words came out as a rush.

"Good lord, woman, did you see how I nearly fled in terror when Lady Fitzwilliam so much as batted her eyelashes at me?"

"That's true," Violet admitted, and he was glad to see a smile curving the corners of her mouth once more.

"Violet, it's only ever been you," he said, and freed the lacings, stepping back so that she could fling her corset aside. "I could never even see anyone else."

"You didn't seem terribly out of practice last night," she said lightly, turning and gliding back into the circle of his arms, sliding her own around his neck, but he saw by the teasing glint in her eyes that his words had banished any real concerns.

"I shall take that as a compliment," he said, and kissed her once more.

It was an all-consuming, full-body kiss, and it seemed like only an instant later—though it must have been several minutes—that James found himself on the bed, shirtless, Violet underneath him, her chemise pulled to her waist, her legs spread wide and his head between them. He moved his lips and tongue with deliberate, torturous slowness, causing Violet's breath to hitch in her throat in a fashion that would have been gratifying had he had enough reason left to appreciate it. At the moment, however, he felt as though he were slowly being consumed by flames, and his entire world had narrowed to Violet.

Just Violet.

Violet, who was stirring restlessly beneath him, her breathing harsh. "James—" she said, and he was amused to hear the note of impatience mixed with the desperation in her voice. He raised his head.

"Too slow again?" he asked innocently.

"It is a quality I generally appreciate," she assured him, huffing a breathless half laugh. "But I must say, at the moment—"

"I've nowhere to be this afternoon," he said solemnly. "I didn't see any reason to rush the proceedings." The stiffness currently pressing almost painfully against his trousers indicated something else entirely—and Violet took full advantage, undulating her hips upward so that her leg brushed against him and smiling, catlike, at the sharp intake of breath he was unable to stop.

"Violet—"

"Since I seem to be the only one in a hurry," she said, her tone indicating that she knew perfectly well this was not the case, "it seems only fair that I control the proceedings."

James arched a brow at her, inwardly gleeful. Even more than the lovemaking itself, he had missed this. Laughing with her. Teasing her. He hadn't fully realized how much he'd missed it until he'd regained it—and he'd be damned if he'd ever give it up again.

"All right," he said, making his voice as disinterested as he could, under the circumstances—those circumstances including the fact that another portion of his anatomy was making it quite clear that he was not disinterested in the least. "If you think you can." He drew back from her slightly, giving her enough space that she might flip him onto his back, which she proceeded to do with alacrity.

She crouched above him, her chemise sliding off one shoulder, showcasing a delectable portion of creamy skin. Her hair was tumbling down in such disarray that he reached up and finished the job, removing pins and tossing them to the floor without a second glance.

"You will be picking those up later," she said severely, running her hands greedily down his torso, the muscles of his abdomen fluttering under her touch.

"If I can walk," James replied slyly, and she grinned wickedly at him.

"Was that a challenge?"

"You decide."

Her decision, though not vocalized, was evidently in the affirmative, as he found a few short minutes later when, having dispensed with his boots and trousers, Violet, straddling his legs, reached into his smalls, took him in hand, and proceeded to take him into her mouth.

His hips arched up as an inarticulate groan burst out of his mouth—he couldn't see, he couldn't think, all he could do was feel the wet warmth of her mouth around him, consuming him. She pursed her lips, sucking, and he groaned again, mingling her name with a fair bit of profanity and the merest hint of blasphemy.

Violet raised her head, a wicked glint in her eye. "Did you just mention the Archbishop of Canterbury?"

"Probably," James said, amazed that he even had the capacity for speech at the moment.

"Fair enough," Violet said, then rededicated herself to the task at hand.

Soon—all too soon—James felt the signs of release drawing near, and with a heroic display of willpower he reached down, cupping her face in his hands, drawing her upward. She slithered up his body, the fabric of her chemise doing nothing so much as heightening the sensations between them, and he pulled her face down to his own, kissing her sloppily, ravenously, with every bit of passion he had in him.

He drew back slightly after a moment, sliding his hands down to her waist and seizing her chemise in both hands as he yanked it over her head. Violet leaned back, raising her arms to assist him in his efforts, and in that moment she was so heartbreakingly beautiful that he felt as though the very breath had been sucked from his body. She straddled him, the candlelight casting a flickering light upon the expanse of smooth skin laid out before him, and arched her back slightly, presenting her breasts for him like a gift.

One that he seized, of course.

He took his time, his lips moving over her skin, and all the while Violet undulated above him until he knew with perfect clarity that if he had to wait a moment longer to be inside her he was going to explode.

"Violet," he said hoarsely, and moved his hands down her supple body until he had seized her slim waist and lifted her, moved her back. "I need—" he began, but interrupted himself with a strangled groan as Violet took him in hand, then sank down on top of him. The feeling of her, wet and warm and tight around him, was nearly enough to make him spend right then and there—but he was not a green boy of fifteen. He knew how to take his time.

And so he did.

His hips rose to meet hers in powerful thrusts, and Violet leaned forward as she moved, bracing her hands on either side of his head, her own head thrown back. He arched up and placed a series of kisses along the column of her throat, loving the way she gasped, then groaning as she inadvertently tightened around him.

He slid his hand down to the space between them, his thumb striking up a rhythm that first made her gasp, then moan. Her rhythm faltered as she became lost to her own pleasure, and in an instant he had surged up and flipped them, his thrusts becoming more erratic. He leaned down and kissed her, his tongue slipping easily against her own, his thumb still caressing her heated flesh, and in another moment she had convulsed around him, her strangled cry muffled against his lips. The feeling of her spasming around him was enough to trigger his own release; he groaned as the heat rushed through his body before he collapsed atop her with a muffled oath.

For a long moment, neither of them spoke—James, for his part, did not think himself capable of stringing two words together. All he could do was lie there and relish the feeling of his own heart pounding against hers. It was perhaps the best thing he had ever felt.

After a minute, she stirred beneath him and he quickly lifted himself onto his elbows so as not to crush her with his weight. She murmured something incomprehensible in protest, her eyes still closed, and he took advantage of the slight distance he had put between them to stare down into her face—so familiar to him, and yet so achingly lovely that he knew he would never tire of gazing at it.

He leaned down and pressed a kiss to her lips, gently at first, but with increasing ardor when her mouth opened beneath his and she flicked her tongue against his own. He broke off after a moment with a muffled half laugh, half groan, and rolled over so that he was lying on his back beside her, still winded from their exertions. He felt her arm move slightly against his, then her slim hand sliding against his own, lacing their fingers together.

"That was . . ." she said at last, but then failed to complete her sentence. He wondered if she, too, lacked the capacity for fully logical speech at the moment.

"Yes," he said, and lifted her hand to his own mouth so that he might press a kiss against it.

She turned onto her side to face him and he followed suit, so that they found themselves nose to nose, their legs tangled together. He reached out and brushed one of her sweat-dampened curls away from her face. "You're so beautiful," he said softly—not to compliment her, not because of what they had just done, but simply because it was the truth, and in that moment it needed to be uttered so desperately that he had no way to keep the words within him.

She smiled at him, her eyes overly bright. "Why?" she said, and he knew that she was not referring to his previous words.

He sighed. "I saw my father in the park this morning," he said, surprised to hear that his tone was not as bitter as it usually was when the duke arose as a topic of conversation.

Violet's brow furrowed. "Oh?" Nothing more—and he was grateful for it. He knew she was curious, he knew the questions must be about to burst from within her—because she was Violet, and that was her way—but here she was, waiting patiently all the same.

"Indeed," he said shortly, then softened his tone, reaching a hand out to trace down her impossibly soft cheek.

"Did you discuss anything important?" she asked, and he bit back a smile at her attempts to make her tone casual, to disguise the impatience lurking just beneath the surface.

He hesitated a moment—they had in fact discussed something of rather great importance, and yet he still felt that it had so little to do with the matter at hand that it was scarcely worth mentioning. He did not wish to linger upon his conversation with the duke, not when he had already allowed his father to determine so much about his relationship with Violet. "Not particularly," he said, telling himself it wasn't a lie. It didn't *feel* like a lie—his encounter with his father, to his mind, had nothing at all to do with the love he felt for his wife in this moment, and he had no desire to muddy things between them by bringing his father into it. "But speaking with him—it made me realize that I was allowing him to dictate my life. I was letting him win."

"It doesn't have to be a competition," she said softly, her eyes sad.

"I know," he said, touching her cheek gently. "I know that now."

"I missed you," she whispered. "I don't ever want to miss you that much again."

"I missed you, too." He leaned forward, kissed her forehead. "I hated sitting in the same room and feeling as though you were miles away from me."

"I'm not miles away now," she said, her gentle smile slanting into something slightly saucy, her silky foot stroking against his leg. They still had more to discuss, some small voice in his mind reminded him—he needed to prove his trust to her—but even the best intentions could be thwarted by an enticing, naked wife.

He rolled her onto her back in a single smooth motion, bracing himself on his elbows as he bent over her, smiling down into her eyes.

"And thank God for that."

Sixteen

It was some indeterminate amount of time later that the distant sound of a clock tolling the hour brought them back to themselves.

"Good lord!" Violet said, sitting up all at once. "I'm supposed to be having tea with my mother in half an hour!"

"Send her a note saying you've taken ill," James said, making no move to budge from his recumbent position. His arms were crossed behind his head, the sheet bunched at his waist, and Violet spent a silent moment casting an appreciative glance at the abdominal muscles on display.

After a moment's admiration, however, she shook her head sadly. "It won't do. She'll only make a fuss and I shall never be rid of her. It's better to go see her now." She slid her feet to the floor. "And you need to go, too, unless you wish to give Price an awful shock. I hate to think what the sight of you in all your naked glory should do to her delicate sensibilities."

"Price has nothing like delicate sensibilities," James grumbled. "She is employed by *you*, after all." But nonetheless, he rose, collected his garments from the various spots on the floor in which they had landed in his rather hasty attempt to disrobe, and, after placing one last lingering kiss upon Violet's lips, departed through her dressing room to his own set of rooms.

Half an hour later, Violet was on her way down the stairs, Price's rather choice remarks about ladies who inexplicably found their hair in disarray in the middle of the afternoon ringing in her ears. She was only a quarter of the way down the staircase, however, when Wooton opened the front door to reveal Jeremy standing on the steps.

"Wooton, old boy," Jeremy said, his voice ringing through the entryway, "did I leave my hat here earlier? I was so distracted by Lady Templeton's haranguing on the way out that I think I walked off without it. On second thought, perhaps I should just purchase a new one and send the bill to her."

"I believe you did, my lord," Wooton said, stepping aside to allow Jeremy into the house. "I would be happy to fetch it for you."

"Capital," Jeremy said, then added, "Is your master at home?"

Wooton nodded. "He is, my lord, but I fear he is rather busy at the moment."

"Still lying prostrate at his wife's feet, I expect," Jeremy said cheerfully, his smile slipping a bit when his eyes landed on Violet, who was nearly at the bottom of the stairs. "Or perhaps not. Violet, old girl, please tell me you've forgiven the poor sod."

"Jeremy," Violet said, trying to keep her tone severe, despite the fact that everything seemed to make her want to smile today. "Why would you think I've forgiven him?" she asked curiously—after all, when Jeremy had last left the house, Violet and Diana had been discussing the relative merits of Violet having an affair.

"Well, he seemed pretty cut up about this whole business of his father and your mother having orchestrated your meeting—I assume the idiot realizes he should have trusted you now." Behind Jeremy, Wooton had discreetly slipped back into the shadows, presumably in search of the missing hat—as ever, Jeremy paid little heed to who might be listening to him speak, no matter the topic. Violet felt a sudden wave of cold wash over her, as though she had just been submerged in ice water. Jeremy, who seemed blithely unaware of the effect his words were having, continued on cheerfully.

"I presume he told you about my role in the evening's events? I owe you an apology, of course—I could have damaged your reputation, and it was quite shabby of me."

Violet barely heard him, her entire being focused on one single fact: *James had lied*. He had said he hadn't discussed anything of importance with the duke this morning, and he had lied.

Why hadn't she seen it? Why had she been so ready to accept his claims that he had simply realized all at once that he should have trusted her from the start?

Because she wanted it to be true. And this, too, was true: he had told her what she wanted to hear, and she had lapped it up like a fool. But it had been a lie. James hadn't trusted her—the only thing that had brought him to her bedroom door was confirmation he had received from Jeremy that Violet hadn't been plotting with her mother all along.

So in all the big ways, nothing had changed. James still didn't trust her—from what she could make out of Jeremy's chatter, it seemed that *he* was the one who was deserving of James's distrust, and yet there was no sign of any cracking in their friendship. A surge of fury coursed through her, and Violet all at once had no more time for this.

With some sort of sixth sense that she only seemed to possess with regard to her husband, she suddenly became aware that he was near, and darted a glance sideways. He was standing, frozen, at the end of the hallway, a sheaf of papers in his hand—he had mentioned something about needing to see to a pressing piece of business regarding the dratted stables, because even in a postcoital daze, he apparently couldn't keep his mind off them. His eyes shifted between Jeremy and her, until their gazes locked.

"There you are, Audley!" Jeremy said, still—somehow!—oblivious to the fact that the temperature in the house seemed to have plummeted in the past minute. "I was just asking your lovely wife if you'd successfully groveled, as we discussed."

"Jeremy," James said, his eyes never leaving Violet's, "get out of my house." His tone wasn't angry, precisely, but it wasn't one that left room for disagreement, either.

"I say, Audley—"

"Now." James's eyes broke from hers, and Violet could see his unspoken message to Jeremy: *Please. I am begging you.* Jeremy, apparently, could read this, too, for he departed with a few murmured niceties to Violet and one last, baffled look at his best friend. Wooton rematerialized from the shadows in time to hand Jeremy his hat and close the door behind him, then wisely vanished once more.

Never had a silence seemed so deafening.

"Violet—" James said, taking three quick steps toward her. His tone was calm, soothing, and for some reason this did nothing but stoke the flame of anger that was rising within her.

"You lied to me." She barely recognized her own voice, so cold did it sound.

"I might have neglected to mention a few things," James said carefully, then winced, as though even he could see this for the evasion that it was. He looked at her directly, took a breath. "Yes. I lied."

"So when you told me that you suddenly realized that you were letting your father control your life," Violet said, striving to keep her voice calm, despite the fact that she felt as though a veritable storm of emotions was swirling within her, "that you realized that you should have trusted me, your *wife*, all along . . ." She paused, inhaling—her voice had cracked a bit on the word *wife*.

"It was all a lie," she said simply. It was not a question.

"Violet," he said again, not moving this time, though she could see how badly he wanted to. He seemed to sense, however, that a single false step could cost him dearly in this moment. "What I told you was true. I didn't mention the business with Jeremy because I didn't want to complicate things."

"Oh no," Violet said, her voice sounding brittle, as though it were about to crack and shatter. "Because of course things have been frightfully *simple* between us lately."

"Damn it," he said—he did not raise his voice or alter his tone, but the amount of feeling, of emotion packed into those two simple words was enough to nearly make her take a step backward. "I am *sick* of quarreling with you."

"Oh, I'm so sorry," Violet said, growing truly heated now, and she was grateful for the fury, because for a ridiculous moment she had been afraid that she would begin to weep. "Perhaps you shouldn't have married me, then. Perhaps you should have married one of those other insipid, simpering girls who made their debut during my Season—the ones you told me you found so *frightfully boring.*"

"There's a vast plain between boring and you, Violet," he said angrily, running his hand through his hair, as she'd often seen him do during their arguments when they'd first married, though it had been so long since they'd had a proper fight, she'd nearly forgotten the gesture. It felt oddly intimate and strange to see it again now, and she welcomed it, even as rage coursed through her.

"How kind of you to say," she replied. "Truly, the most graceful compliment I've received in years."

James swore under his breath; then, in a movement so quick Violet didn't have a chance to prevent it, he leapt up the stairs, seized her by the elbow, and began leading her forcibly down the hallway.

"Take your hands off of me," Violet said, swatting ineffectively at his fingers, which suddenly seemed to be made of iron, so unrelenting was his grip. "I am not a dog to be dragged where you please."

James ignored her, steering her into the library and closing the door firmly behind them both.

"I do apologize," he said curtly, "but I thought it best to take precautionary measures, since you were showing signs of becoming shrill."

"*Shrill?*" Violet winced at the pitch that emanated from her own mouth, then tried again, more calmly. "Shrill?"

"I can't imagine what I was so worried about," he said dryly, crossing his arms. Seeming restless, he uncrossed them, then glanced around the room. Violet wasn't certain what he was looking for until a moment later, when he moved quickly to the sideboard and seized the snifter of brandy that was stored there. He haphazardly poured a measure of the liquid into one tumbler, then another, and turned to hand her a glass.

The contents of which, of course, she promptly hurled into his face.

It was oddly satisfying, watching him gape at her as brandy dripped down his face. She sailed past him to the sideboard, where she refilled her glass and took a leisurely sip before turning back to face her still-silent husband.

James wiped his face roughly on his sleeve, then tossed back half of the contents of his glass in a single gulp.

"I believe you're supposed to savor it," Violet said, taking another small sip and examining her fingernails. "At least, that's what I recall you telling me once."

"That brandy cost a damn fortune."

"Precisely my point, darling. I don't think it should be wasted by gulping." Violet raised her eyes, risking a glance at him. His green eyes were blazing, his face still slightly damp. She curled her free hand at her side, resisting the temptation to retrieve her handkerchief, to wipe his face for him.

"But watering the rug with it is a good use instead?" He drained the rest of the contents of his glass.

Violet snorted. "Don't be absurd. I think your face absorbed the entire brunt of it."

He sighed, then set his now-empty tumbler on a side table nearby. "I suppose I deserved it."

"Yes," Violet said, sniffing and taking yet another sip. She could feel herself relaxing slightly as the brandy burned through her, her limbs feeling looser, her spine losing some of its indignant stiffness. Her anger, however, remained. The act of throwing the drink at him—something she had fantasized about more than once during long, silent dinners over the past four years—had taken the edge off of her immediate fury, but somehow she now felt even worse.

"You deserved that and more," she said, setting her glass down, the drink inside only half finished. She wondered for a brief, wild moment what her mother would think of this scene: her daughter—the daughter of an earl!—not just drinking strong spirits but hurling them into her husband's face. She made a mental note to save this story in case her mother tried to detain her overlong at tea this afternoon—though, late as she would likely be at this point, she'd be lucky to get a word in edgewise around the tongue-lashing she was sure to receive.

"I've been acting like a child these last weeks," she said frankly, because she might have been many things, but she also always tried to be fair. "I deserved any tricks you played on me, because I was being foolish. I was angry with you, and I wanted to teach you a lesson, and I went about it the wrong way. It was childish, and I apologize."

James arched a brow, looking mildly stunned. She might have considered herself an eminently fair person, but apologizing didn't come easily to her, and admitting she was wrong—about anything—was even harder.

"You don't need to apologize," he said after a moment's silence. "I believe that responsibility lies solely with me."

She could see that he was working himself up to a proper apology—one that she would likely love to hear, one that would make her soften in the face of his regret, of his nearness, of the very fact of him being *James*. And this was something that she could not do.

That she would not *let* herself do. Not when he had claimed to be ready to put their troubles behind them, and then lied to her face half an hour later. He hadn't explained anything of his discussion with his father in the park; he hadn't even *mentioned* anything about Jeremy's involvement in their parents' scheme, whatever that might have been. If these events were what had led to his apology this morning, then he had been lying when he said he trusted her, because he was still taking the word of everyone else above her own. It had hurt when he had done so four years ago, and it still stung now, even as it infuriated her.

In short, nothing had changed; she would not let him weaken her with whatever apology he intended to offer her now.

So again, she spoke. "You're going to apologize now, I know. But I don't want you to."

His brow furrowed. She wanted to smooth it, to run her thumb down the skin, feeling its warmth and firmness, watching his expression change from one of concern to something else entirely. And yet, she did not.

She could comfort this man—this infinitely precious man—over and over, but doing so would not solve their problems.

At this point, only he could solve them.

"I love you," she said simply, and felt as though a weight had been lifted from her chest, so light did she feel with this unburdening of the truth. She felt as though she had carried these three small words around with her every day for the past four years, that they had grown heavier each day for being unspoken.

"I love you," she repeated, feeling almost giddy, and she saw him open his mouth, perhaps to speak these same words back to her, and again she forestalled him, knowing that allowing him to do so would weaken her resolve. "But I don't want to hear what you have to say right now. I'm going to tea with my mother, and then I am going to dine at Diana's, and then I am going to the Goodchapel musicale with Emily tonight, and I don't want you to follow me, not unless you mean it." She swallowed, surprised by the sudden rush of emotion she felt. So often had she wished that he would trust her, love her without anything coming between them. So often had she wished that he had followed her from the drawing room on that horrible morning four years ago—wished that he had refused to let her walk away, forced her to argue with him until their issues were laid bare and things were right between them once more.

And yet, now that she thought he might follow her at last, she was turning him away. Because she realized something now—something that perhaps she should have realized long before.

She wanted him to follow her for the right reasons. She wanted him to follow her because he loved her and trusted her above all others. She wanted him to follow her without having to think twice about it, without ever doubting her word. She wished for him to follow her without her having to ask him to—and without her having to convince him, once she did, that she had been worthy of the pursuit. She was no longer willing to settle for a marriage that involved anything less, with a man who claimed to love her, but who failed to put his faith in her when it counted the most.

"I have missed you more than I can say," she said, swallowing again, and he reached for her, his arm extending halfway across the space that divided them before freezing, falling to his side once more. She saw in his face the effort that the simple action of dropping his arm took, and she was grateful for it, though she couldn't bring herself to tell him as much.

"I want this to be a true marriage again—I want us to be together. I want to spend my days and nights with you. And I think you want that, too. But I want you to trust me beyond all measure. I want a *real* marriage, and I don't think we can have that in the absence of trust. And I don't think we can have that until you stop allowing your obsession with your father to dictate everything about our lives. You were thrown from a horse less than a fortnight ago, a horse you never should have been riding in the first place. And you cannot tell me that your foolishness had to do with anything other than your obsession with showing your father your worth." She paused, swallowing around the lump that had appeared in her throat. "I already *know* your worth. You don't need to prove *anything* to me. I need for *my* opinion to be the one that matters the most to you, because I am your wife. So please, James, I am begging you. I am leaving now, and please don't come after me until you can make that true."

And, with more strength than she had known she possessed, she turned from him and walked to the library door. Deep in her heart, she knew that she was somehow hoping he would race after her, block her exit, refuse to let her leave without fixing this, once and for all. She didn't want him to follow her for the wrong reasons, it was true—but she could not help hoping he might already understand the right ones, and that he might not let her walk away after an argument once again. And yet, when he made no sign of stopping her departure, she prided herself on the fact that she left the room without once looking back.

Seventeen

After Violet left the room, James lingered. He didn't wish to— every instinct in his body was screaming at him to run after her, apologize once more, promise her that he would never lie to her again. He'd fall to his damn knees if he had to.

And yet, something held him back. She still thought him in thrall to his father. She still thought him unable to trust, to love her the way she deserved. He needed to prove to her, somehow, that this wasn't true. But how?

How could he show her what he felt so deeply? He was an Englishman, after all; dramatic declarations weren't really his forte. How could he make her trust him? Trust *them*?

An indeterminate amount of time later, Wooton appeared at the door. "The Marquess of Willingham and Viscount Penvale, my lord."

James looked up wearily from his seat by the fireplace. It was an unseasonably cool day for July, and the weather had turned gray and foggy in the afternoon; he was seated in his favorite armchair, another glass of brandy in hand. He could still feel the faint stickiness on one side of his face where he'd failed to entirely wipe away the drink that Violet had hurled at him. Despite his rage in the moment, his mouth now twitched slightly at the memory.

"You look terrible," Jeremy said without preamble, appearing behind Wooton and sauntering into the room.

"It's not been my finest day, I must confess." James gestured lazily at the sideboard without rising, merely raising his own glass. "Help yourselves."

"It will take a fair bit of work to catch up, from the smell of you," Penvale said severely as he, too, entered the room, sounding slightly like a disapproving governess, much to James's amusement. His disapproval, however, did not stop him from crossing to the sideboard and filling two glasses. He handed one to Jeremy, who had already sunk down into a chair opposite James, and kept the other for himself as he leaned against the mantel.

"Where's your wife, Audley?" Penvale asked, apparently having no time for niceties.

"At tea with her mother." James took a healthy gulp of brandy, then rubbed a hand over his forehead. "And then dining with your sister," he added, directing his words to Penvale. "And then at a godforsaken musicale with Lady Emily." He cast a dark look at Jeremy.

"You can't mean to imply that you have any desire to join her at any of those events," Jeremy said incredulously over the rim of his glass.

"Of course not. But I *did* have every intention of retrieving her from her mother's house approximately a quarter of an hour after her arrival and bringing her home again, with no intention of departing the house again for several days."

"What seems to be the problem, then?" Penvale asked lazily, swirling the liquid in his glass. James wasn't deceived by his casual demeanor; he knew Penvale was paying close attention to every word that was spoken.

James debated for a brief moment trying to explain the whole story, then quickly rejected this idea; for one, it would take too long. Additionally, he thought he might yell with frustration.

"I need to convince her that I trust her," he said shortly. "And also that I'm not allowing my father to run my life."

"So just visit him and give him his bloody horses back," Penvale said practically. He sounded casual, even disinterested; James, however, stared at him.

"What?" Penvale asked, shifting uncomfortably. "You've been killing yourself trying to manage the damn stables, just to prove to your father that you can. Why not just give them back? Won't that show Violet that you trust her judgment?"

Give them back.

It was a simple idea—deceptively so. And one that he didn't really have a strong motive for rejecting—Violet's dowry was generous, his inheritance from his mother fat. Did they truly *need* a house in the country? He suspected Violet's answer would be no, if in return she received a husband who was not spending a sizable portion of his waking hours trying to prove himself to his bastard of a father.

It seemed outlandish somehow, and yet—why not? He needed to make some sort of grand gesture, and he needed to do it fast. He refused to spend another night without her in his bed.

In his life.

He tossed back the last of his drink, then stood, clapping first Jeremy, then Penvale on the shoulder. "Thanks for the friendly advice, chaps," he said, striding for the door.

"I didn't say anything," Jeremy called after him in protest.

"Probably for the best," James tossed over his shoulder. "You can show yourselves out, I trust?" he asked, pausing briefly at the doorway.

Without waiting for an answer, he strode into the hall, bellowing for Wooton and his horse.

It was the habit of the Duke of Dovington to pass several afternoons a week at his club when he was in town. The duke was fastidious in his routine, taking great pains to appear at the venerable doors of White's at the same time on each afternoon, so that any who might have business with him would know just where he might be found. He being a duke, there were any number of men who took advantage of this predictability.

Until that day, however, his younger son had never been one of them.

James found his father in the library at White's, his head bent over a volume of Pliny the Elder. The duke did not look up as he approached, apparently so absorbed in his reading that he did not hear the sound of rapidly advancing footsteps. James, who had never seen his father read for pleasure in his life, took this for the nonsense that it was and, in one neat motion, reached out beneath the duke's very nose and flipped the book shut.

"Audley," the duke said stiffly after he had looked up to see what audacious soul had the gall to do such a thing. "I might have known it was you."

"Father," James said, but for once his voice didn't sound as stiff as it often did when he was in the presence of his father. He had taken his gloves off upon his arrival at White's, but now held them tightly in one hand, slapping them against the palm of the other with a soft thwacking sound.

"Sit down," his father instructed, gesturing to the chair opposite him rather like a king receiving visitors to court. His manner was one with which James was very familiar—and one for which he had no patience today.

"Thank you, but no," he said. "This won't take long, in part because I'm in rather a rush, and in part because I frankly don't have much to say to you." The duke blinked in surprise, but James barely even registered this small victory, so intent was he on saying what he had come here to say. "Tomorrow I am going to meet with my man of business and instruct him to start the proceedings of transferring ownership of Audley House back to you."

The duke blinked again—it was clear that whatever he had been expecting of his son, it was not this.

"Violet and I will, of course, move our possessions from Audley House back to Curzon Street," James continued, growing more confident with each word that he was doing the right thing. "I would also, at a later date, be happy to discuss with you some of the financial arrangements I have made with a view toward securing the future of the stables, as you may wish to continue with them yourself."

"James," the duke protested, "what is this about? Those stables were a wedding gift."

"No," James said quietly, and though he did not raise his voice, the duke nearly flinched at the force he put into that single word. "Those stables were a trick—another ploy on your part, because you thought that West wouldn't give you an heir, and suddenly you needed me. And how better to weasel your way into my life, to control me, than to make me beholden to you?

"So I am giving them back to you, Father. I can discuss the running of them with you some other time, but we will do so as equals. I would be happy to be your partner in this—but I'm no longer interested in being the recipient of your generosity." He could not prevent a sardonic tone from entering his voice on the word *generosity*. "Furthermore," he added, beginning to actually enjoy himself, primarily due to the dumbfounded look on his father's face, "it is my expectation that my wife and I are shortly to be reconciled, not that it is any concern of yours. It is my dearest wish that this reconciliation should result in children at some point, if we are lucky. However—" And here James took two quick steps forward, bracing a hand on one arm of his father's chair and leaning down so that their faces were very close together indeed. "—if I should ever hear you refer to our son as your *heir*, I will ensure that you never see him."

His father, for once, was speechless. James smiled, turned, and strode from the room.

And then he rode like hell.

It was, Violet decided, without a doubt the worst teatime she had ever spent in her mother's company—and that was truly saying something. Lady Worthington had wasted no time upon her arrival in launching into a lengthy lecture on Violet's behavior of late, ranging from her tardy arrival to tea to her shocking conduct at the Rocheford ball—"Cutting in on a dance! I've never heard of anything so scandalous!"—to her failings as a wife—"No wonder he's panting after Fitzwilliam Bridewell's widow! Men do have *needs*, tiresome as they may be." She even worked Violet's supposed illness into her diatribe, displaying possibly the only moment of astuteness in her entire life when she sniffed, "I'm not certain you weren't just *malingering*. Why must you always be so *dramatic*?"

While Violet was fairly practiced at ignoring her mother's words, and had perfected the look of bland pleasantness she currently wore as she spread clotted cream upon a scone, everything in her was screaming to return to Curzon Street, to fling herself into James's arms, to let him carry her upstairs, lay her down on the bed, strip away her layers of clothing until there was nothing between them but his skin pressed intimately against her own.

She loved him—she had always loved him, and she knew that now. She had thought to convince herself that that love was gone, that it had never existed, that all that she and James had ever shared was youthful infatuation and lust—but this was untrue, and she could not lie to herself. Or to him. She loved him more than anything else in her life, and to turn and leave him in the library today had nearly broken her heart. Again.

But she had done it, because she knew that she had to. She could not suffer another marriage like the one they had shared before, one where there were good days, it was true—bright, shimmering, glorious days that had seemed golden and endless and joyful beyond measure—but other days when he had vanished to a place where she could not reach him. Days when his father came to call and James retreated into his office, stewing over events from the past that he shared only bits of with her.

She wanted a true marriage again, but she could not endure more heartbreak. And she needed James to understand that.

And so she calmly took a bite of her scone and allowed her mother to prattle on, even as she kept one ear alert, out of the foolish, wild hope that perhaps James was going to follow her after all, and prove himself to her at last. She had told him not to, she reminded herself sternly—she had *thrown a drink in his face*, for heaven's sake. But still, an irrepressible part of her hoped that *this* argument would have a different outcome.

❧

Logically, James knew that he had made very good time on his journey from White's to West's house in Knightsbridge, his horse weaving in and out among the bulkier carriages and landaus that clogged London's busy streets, but it didn't feel that way to him. He felt jumpy, nervous, ready to burst out of his own skin. Each time he'd had to rein his horse in, he'd wanted to yell in frustration.

However tempting he found the prospect of abandoning his current mission and beginning pursuit of his wife instead, James knew that if he wanted to truly convince Violet that he had changed, that he was a man she could trust, he must become that man in truth—the one she deserved. He needed to manage his issues with his father and his brother, so that they did not become a problem for Violet to handle instead, something to come between them once again. He was an adult, and it was time to conduct his relationships like one.

And so here he found himself, in St. James's Square, staring at West's front door with a fair amount of trepidation. It was, after all, a door he had not knocked upon for nearly four years, and he didn't relish the prospect now. And yet, almost of its own volition, his arm was raised, the hand curled into a fist, and he knocked.

He was ushered in by a footman, then greeted by the butler, who did an admirable job of concealing his surprise at James's unexpected appearance. In short order, James found himself swept into the library and politely bade to wait—his lordship would be with him shortly.

He paced the length of the room instead, his head a jumble of thoughts. He wondered if West would keep him waiting, would turn ducal on him, but the thought had scarcely formed when the door behind him opened, and his brother's voice filled the room.

"James."

James turned; West stood in the doorway, dressed impeccably as always in coat and breeches and cravat, not a single hair out of place. He looked tired, James noted—there were dark circles under his eyes, and his forehead was more deeply etched than usual. West was thirty, but today he looked older.

"West," he said, finding himself more nervous to confront his brother than his father. Their father might have been a duke, but he was an unpleasant bastard on top of that, and one whose acceptance James no longer desired. West, however, was different.

"I apologize for dropping by unannounced like this," James added a bit hesitantly, and his brother's face softened slightly.

"You're always welcome here, James," West said, his voice quiet and sincere. He took several unhurried steps into the room. He gave every appearance of the English lord, relaxed and comfortable in his natural habitat, but James could tell he was curious.

"I came to apologize," James said without preamble.

West raised an eyebrow, then wandered toward the fireplace, where he turned to stare into the flames that flickered there, leaning on his cane a bit. "Is this about . . . her?"

James knew that by *her* his brother meant Lady Fitzwilliam—whose name West had avoided uttering at all costs over the past six years. His brother's voice was calm, carefully modulated, and with his face turned toward the flames, James couldn't read West's expression.

"In part," he said. "But I think I've much else to apologize for as well."

At this, West turned, not even bothering to disguise his curiosity anymore. "Had some sort of revelation, have you? A moment of divine inspiration?"

"Don't be an ass," James said without heat. "I merely had a rather interesting conversation with my wife this afternoon. She made me realize a few things."

"Did she?" West murmured.

"I'm giving Audley House back to Father."

West's face went blank with surprise for a moment, and James relished the feeling of having caused this, the sight all the more enjoyable for its rarity. "You can't be serious."

"As the grave," James said cheerfully. "I told Father he could have the stables back, and the house along with it. I then informed him I'd be amenable to a future discussion of us working together to run the stables as partners, but that I'd no wish to be solely responsible anymore."

"What the hell did Violet say to you?" West asked, sounding somewhere between impressed and alarmed. "I must ask her to teach me her tricks."

"Ha."

"What did Father say?" James didn't think he was imagining the note of barely contained eagerness in his brother's voice.

"Not much of anything," James said with a shrug. "I imagine he's still sitting in his chair at White's, gawking at the spot on the rug where I was standing when I told him. I'm sure he has some choice thoughts about me at the moment—likely thinks I'm an incompetent fool, at best. But I find myself unable to care overmuch. I know what I'm capable of—I'm not much bothered anymore whether Father does."

"Where will you and Violet live?" West asked, more serious now.

James shrugged again, unbothered. "We still have the house in Curzon Street—and I bought that with my inheritance from Mother. I suppose I shall see if Violet misses the country house—if she does, I expect I can find us a cottage of some sort."

"You seem remarkably unconcerned about all of this." West crossed his arms over his chest, leaning his shoulder against the mantel.

James sighed, raking his hands through his hair. "The stables are lucrative, but I've no head for withers and which filly breeds winners and all that rot. I accepted the stables as a gift from Father because I was so damned infatuated with Violet that I wanted to lay the world at her feet—I didn't trust her to continue wanting me otherwise. And I also wanted to prove to Father that I could run them. It felt like a test, one that I had to keep taking over and over again every day of my life. There was little joy in it anymore."

West was silent for a moment, and James became conscious of the fact that this was the most personal information he had shared with his brother since they were boys. And yet, it didn't feel odd. It felt . . . right.

"You said you came here to apologize?" West's voice was quiet, but his gaze—an identical shade of burning green to James's own—was fixed on James's face, unblinking.

"I've never trusted you." James paused for a moment, almost regretting his bluntness. West, however, had not offered much of a reaction; he was silent, waiting patiently for James to continue.

So he did.

"I—when we were boys . . ." He paused, took a breath, gathered himself. "Father favored you because you were the firstborn, the heir. I was always left behind." West opened his mouth, and James raised a hand, forestalling any objection. "I know it wasn't your fault, that you didn't ask for it, but it's what happened. Now I understand that growing up under Father's constant gaze wasn't a delight, either—I think I might have even had the better end of the deal. But it's hard for a boy to comprehend this.

"So, for as long as I can remember, you were Father's before you were anything else. I never trusted you not to go running to him with my secrets."

"You never gave me the chance to prove otherwise," his brother said.

"I know," James said frankly. "I'm not here to argue with you. I'm just here to say I'd like to try again."

"Did Violet ask you to apologize to me?" West asked.

"No," James said, very glad that this was the answer he was able to give. "She told me—well, she told me a number of things—not that that would surprise you, I imagine," he added with a quick grin, which was matched by one of West's own. "But I realized that I was being a bloody idiot, and I need to trust people, and that's why I'm here, telling you that I want to trust you."

James felt decidedly odd when he had finished with this little speech. He wasn't used to confiding in West—wasn't used to confiding in anyone, in truth. Even Jeremy and Penvale, two men in whom he'd have considered his faith to be unshakable, had never been on the receiving end of any confessions of this sort—and for the first time, James wondered if it wasn't so much that Jeremy and Penvale were more trustworthy than anyone else, but rather that his faith in them had never been tested in the way it had with Violet and West. He wondered what would have happened to his and Jeremy's friendship had he learned about Jeremy's role in his meeting with Violet four years ago. He thought it likely that their friendship would have been damaged beyond repair, and he spared a moment to be grateful that he was not that same man—boy, really—of four-and-twenty anymore.

"If you expect me to weep and embrace you, I shall have to tell you right away that I'm not really the sort," West said. His tone was grave, but James could see the amused look in his eyes.

"I rather think a handshake will do," James said, equally gravely, and he thrust out his hand. West seized it in his own and gave it a firm shake.

"I think this calls for a drink," West said, moving as if to cross to the sideboard, where James knew his brother kept a stock of very fine brandy. "You look rather done in by having bared your soul and all that."

"Very touching," James said dryly. "But actually, I need to go."

West raised a brow. "So soon after our joyous reunion? You wound me."

"I'd love to stay and chat"—and here, James was surprised to realize that he actually meant these words—"but I must go rescue my wife from her mother."

Eighteen

Violet was on her third scone when James arrived.

Her mother was in the midst of a lengthy exposition on the numerous ways that Violet's marital woes were Violet's own fault when the door to the drawing room was flung open. Violet and Lady Worthington turned in unison, startled, expecting to see the butler or a footman, but instead it was James.

And he was glorious.

His hair was more tousled than ever, as though he'd ridden over at great speed, and he wasn't wearing any sort of neckcloth. Violet darted a quick glance at her mother to make sure she hadn't fainted at this state of undress. After determining that the lady was still conscious, she turned back to her husband.

"James," she said coolly, clinging to the fragments of her dignity and trying—and failing—not to look at the triangle of skin that was visible at his cravat-less collar.

"Violet," he said, and her eyes shot to his at the sound of his voice, at the intensity she heard there. This was not a James in the mood for one of their games.

"I thought I told you not to follow me," she said, striving to keep her voice steady, even as her heart leapt at the sight of him, standing there as if she had willed him into existence. It was a difficult task, since he had taken several strides across the room toward her, forcing her to tilt her head back slightly to look at him.

"That's not precisely what you said," he said, and she was surprised to see the beginnings of a smile curving at the edges of his mouth. "What you said was for me not to come after you until I could trust you and make ours a true marriage again. So here I am. Following instructions."

Violet was torn between fury and—betraying fool that her heart was—hope. "I suppose you've had a change of heart and really assessed your priorities thoughtfully and carefully in the past two hours, then?" She was pleased that her voice sounded suitably frosty—but that seed of desperate hope continued to worm its way into her heart, and the part of her that had secretly wished for him to follow her was in danger of overpowering the rest of her, so great was the joy his presence sparked in her in that instant.

"No," he said, taking yet another step closer to her. He was so near now that she could smell him—he smelled faintly of horse and sweat and himself, and it made her want to tug him closer, lick his skin. At precisely the moment that these—thoroughly indecent, unladylike—thoughts were flitting through her mind at the speed of bullets, there was the sound of a throat being cleared.

"Lord James," Lady Worthington said stiffly. "To what do we owe this pleasure?"

"Lady Worthington," James said, looking away from Violet at last and offering an entirely correct bow to her mother. "It has been far too long." His tone indicated that his sentiments were exactly the opposite. "I apologize for interrupting, but I could not help but overhear a snippet of your conversation with my wife as I approached."

"You seem to be making quite a habit of that," Violet said sweetly.

Ignoring her, James continued addressing her mother. "If I am not mistaken, you were informing Violet of the ways she has failed as a wife."

"Indeed I was," Lady Worthington replied frostily. "And you should be thanking me for it, sir. If someone does not bring her back in line, how can you ever expect her to provide you with an heir?"

James turned to Violet.

"Darling, have you noticed our parents seem to have a particular fixation with your breeding organs?" James asked. Violet bit her lip to keep from laughing at the aghast look on her mother's face.

"Lady Worthington, please allow me to make something abundantly clear," James continued. "Any fault in my marriage lies entirely at my own two feet. Your daughter is not perfect, but she is perfect for *me*—and she has made me a better man than I would ever have managed to be without her. I only hope she can ever forgive me for taking such a damned long time to fully appreciate her."

Lady Worthington was gaping at him, but he evidently was not done yet. "My wife and I have rather pressing matters to discuss at the moment, so I am going to have to cut short your tea. But please believe me when I say this: neither one of us will ever walk through this doorway ever again if you do not learn to treat your daughter with the respect she deserves."

Any comment Lady Worthington might have wanted to make was forestalled by James reaching down, seizing Violet about the waist, and lifting her bodily from the settee. He executed another polite bow and then, without further preamble, took Violet by the elbow and steered her rather firmly toward the door.

Violet waved cheerfully at her mother on the way out, then paused, some of James's infectious recklessness spreading to her as well.

"By the way, Mother," she said casually, "you might want to begin keeping a closer eye on the *Times* from now on. Any letters published under the name of Mr. Viola were written by me, and I'm sure you'll disagree with every single word." Relishing the look of abject horror on her mother's face, she allowed James to lead her from the room.

Outside, James tossed her perfunctorily into the carriage before climbing up behind her and pulling the door shut.

"If you are attempting to win my favor, this is hardly the way to go about it," Violet said huffily, blowing a stray curl out of her face. "I believe you treat hounds with more courtesy than that."

"Would you mind ceasing to speak for more than three seconds?" James asked pleasantly.

Violet opened her mouth and then deliberately shut it again and settled back into her seat. As soon as she ceded the space between them, James leaned forward, somehow taking up more room than it seemed logical that he should.

"In response to your earlier question," he said in a conversational tone, "*no*, I have not come to some sort of glorious, earth-shattering conclusion in the past couple of hours. I've merely followed you to explain to you what I had already worked out."

Violet arched a brow. "James, you lied to me this morning."

"Afternoon, technically."

"The point remains."

"I know," he said quietly, and all hint of jesting was immediately absent from his voice. "I lied to you because I was afraid that you would still think I was having my actions dictated by my father. Violet, I had already realized that I should have trusted you all along—I didn't want my discussions with him, and with Jeremy, to complicate things."

"You should have trusted me to understand that," she said, her voice equally quiet. "I was mistaken four years ago when I did not come to you immediately with what I'd learned of our parents' scheming—*not*," she added severely, "as mistaken as you were in not believing me when I tried to explain the situation to you—"

"I know that," he said quickly. "And I'm sorry."

"But I understand the instinct nonetheless." She sighed. "I need to know you're not going to let your father come between us ever again. I need to know I'm not going to receive notes about your nearly killing yourself on the back of a horse, just to spite your father. I need you to think of me, of *us*, before anything else."

"I was an ass today," he said, and then his mouth quirked up at the sides. "Not just today, if we're really being honest with each other, I suppose."

"Indeed," she said, lifting her chin.

"Violet." All at once, his voice was deadly serious once again. "I'm sorry. I didn't trust you to . . . to . . ." He ran a hand through his hair, frustrated; the result was curls that were even more disheveled than they'd been a moment before. "I didn't trust you to trust me that I trusted you."

Violet blinked. "I'm sorry?"

James appeared to be running his words back through his mind, then nodded once, apparently satisfied. "I believe I had the right of it, actually."

Violet couldn't help smirking. "It sounded peculiarly appropriate."

"As convoluted as we deserve?" He grinned at her, and the sight was devastating.

"We did rather make our own beds, didn't we?" She couldn't stop herself from smiling back this time.

"Do you know," he asked conversationally, "that I'm fairly certain that at some point in the past fortnight I uttered the sentence 'She doesn't know I know she knows I know'?"

"I would mock you," Violet said gravely, "but I'm fairly certain I did the same." She paused, considering. "Changing the pronouns about, of course."

"Of course."

They sat there for a moment, grinning idiotically at each other, and it was all Violet could do to refrain from reaching out and smoothing those tousled curls. She felt as though she were standing on the edge of a precipice, hand in hand with James, ready to jump—but he'd not yet shown her the wings they'd need to fly. She wanted to jump so desperately—and yet.

And yet.

So, schooling her voice into a calmness she didn't feel, rearranging her face into an expression of polite interest, she said, "I'm sorry—you were saying?"

His own grin faded as hers did, but if a laughing James was dangerous, so, too, was the model that replaced him—gazing at her steadily, unblinkingly, his eyes full of some emotion that she recognized and yet was still afraid to believe.

"I paid my father a visit this afternoon, after you left," he said steadily. Violet tried her hardest to give nothing away, to keep her face an impassive mask. She wasn't entirely certain she was successful. "I told him I was giving Audley House back to him."

Whatever she had been expecting, it wasn't this.

"*What?*" she shrieked, nearly toppling off the carriage seat in her surprise. James reached out a hand to steady her, and without even realizing what she was doing, Violet laced her fingers through his.

James's brow creased in concern. "I—I didn't think you'd mind," he said, sounding uncertain. "I'll buy you another house in the country if you wish. Our income will be reduced without the profits from the stables, but we'll still be very comfortable, and I'm certain we can find something you'll like just as much."

Violet reached out and placed her palm over his mouth, ceasing the flow of words. Silenced, he stared at her, then slowly arched an eyebrow in inquiry.

"I don't mind about the house," she said, slowly and clearly, and watched the lines in his forehead smooth out again. "I just want to know *why*."

She started to remove her hand, but he caught it with his free hand and pressed a kiss to her palm. Her skin burned beneath his lips.

"I was doing it for all the wrong reasons," he said quietly.

"The stables?"

He nodded. "I wanted to prove something to my father. I was so angry with him—I've always been so angry with him. It's exhausting, and it's not worth it."

"I understand why you hate him," Violet said, turning her face slightly so that her cheek rested against his palm. "You don't have to forgive him—I wouldn't ask that of you."

He slid one thumb down her cheek, the smallest caress—and yet her entire body was suddenly covered in gooseflesh. How was it possible to simultaneously find a person to be entirely comforting and completely disconcerting at the same time?

"Violet," he said, and she was suddenly certain that he had never before said her name in precisely this tone of voice. "I don't hate him—I just don't bloody care anymore." His casual profanity thrilled her, singing to something deep and primal within her. "I told him I'd be happy to work as his partner, his equal, but that I didn't want all the responsibility anymore. I don't want anything he can give me, and I don't care what he thinks about that fact. He's controlled everything about my life—even when I thought I had escaped him, when I thought I didn't care about him anymore, I still let him poison the most important thing in my life."

He sank to his knees in the limited space between the seats in the carriage, both of her hands still clasped in his own.

"Violet, I love you. I will always love you. I fell in love with you approximately two minutes after I met you, and I've never stopped. The past four years . . ." He paused, his throat working. "They've been hell," he said simply after a moment. "I will do anything—anything—to make you believe I trust you. To make you trust me again with your heart. Our marriage, it is . . ." Another pause. This broken, clumsy speech was more precious to her than any smooth monologue could ever have been. "I do not care about anything else in my life so much as I care about repairing our marriage. These past two weeks have been the best fortnight of the past four years."

"Really?" Violet asked, somehow managing to find her voice, though it was a bit more hoarse than she was accustomed to sounding. "I thought you'd spent the past fortnight wishing to strangle me."

"I did," he said promptly, startling a laugh out of her. "I'd rather spend my days arguing with you than in calm conversation with anyone else in the world."

As romantic declarations went, Violet wasn't entirely certain anyone else would have found it completely satisfactory—but to her, it was perfect.

"Oh, James," she whispered, leaning down to press a gentle kiss to his forehead.

"I should be thanking you," he said, speaking more quickly now, as though worried that the words building up inside him would somehow vanish if he did not immediately give them voice. "You made me realize how afraid I've been all these years."

"Afraid?" Violet asked uncertainly, her throat feeling oddly tight.

"I was afraid of other people, afraid that none of them could be trusted, afraid that even you, you who told me you loved me—that you could be lying, or you could be taken from me somehow."

"And that day," she said softly, understanding. "That day, when you overheard me in conversation with your father—when we were discussing what he and my mother orchestrated—"

"I should never have jumped to conclusions," James said swiftly. "There's no excuse—none at all—but all I can say is that it confirmed everything I had been led to believe about life until that point. That if I loved something, it wouldn't last. You had given me no reason at all to distrust you, and I still instantly believed the worst of you. You seemed too good to be true—and there you were, proving my point."

"I hate your father," Violet said with quiet intensity, and there must have been something in her voice that had never been there before, because James drew back slightly, a look of surprise in his eyes. "I hate what he did to you. And to West," she added, because she didn't think James's elder brother had had much easier a time of it.

"I went to see West before I followed you, too," James said.

"Good heavens, did you pay a call on everyone in London?" she asked teasingly, and was pleased when she was rewarded with a slight curve of his lips.

"No, only those with the surname Audley," he said, squeezing her hands gently. "Some families take tea together, but the Audleys go in for angry confrontations instead."

"Please don't tell me you and West quarreled again," Violet said warily. The rift between James and his brother had gone on for much too long, as far as she was concerned—and it was all the more frustrating since, as best she could tell, there was no real cause for it. They had quarreled in the past, it was true, but never out of proportion to other brothers. Never so badly as she and James had quarreled during the first year of their marriage, even.

"No, nothing of the sort," James assured her. "I had rather the same conversation with him I'm having with you now." He shot her a wicked grin, and her insides grew heated in a way that only he could cause. "Without some of the displays of affection, of course."

"I should hope so," she sniffed, and he laughed out loud at that, the sound of it sweeter to her ears than any music she had ever heard. She could have listened to him laugh forever.

"Violet, please tell me what I have to do to win you," he said, all laughter leaving his voice as quickly as it had arrived, replaced instead with a tone of stark desperation. He dropped her hands, reached up to seize her face, rising up on his knees so that he could press his forehead to her own, her entire world becoming the green of his eyes.

"I've been a fool, I don't deserve you—but I want to. I would do anything, truly, if you would only trust me with your heart again." His voice cracked, but he continued speaking. "I love you so much—I want to have children with you, raise them with all the love that West and I never had. I want to embarrass them when they're older, when their father can't stop sweeping their mother off to darkened corners for scandalous embraces. I want everything I didn't think I could have—and you're the only one I want it with. So please—*please*. Tell me what to do."

Violet realized that she was crying, and didn't know how long she had been doing so. James leaned forward to taste one of her tears, his tongue darting out to stop its progress down her cheek.

"You don't need to do anything," she whispered, trying to steady her voice into something calm, strong, when she felt as though she were about to burst into a million pieces, radiant joy and a desperate urge to weep fighting a battle within her. "You followed me here. You didn't let me walk away again. You fought for us, *trusted* us."

"I will never, ever let you walk away again," he said, and even through her tears she could see the intensity of his gaze, could read the truth in his eyes. "I want to be the man who deserves you, because you deserve everything."

"We deserve each other," she said, and leaned forward to kiss him gently. The kiss slid from loving to heated in the space of a heartbeat, his head tilting slightly to give him a better angle, his tongue tracing the seam of her lips until she parted her mouth to allow him entry.

He broke the kiss with a muffled noise that sounded like a half laugh, half groan, but he did not remove his hands from where they cupped her cheeks. "I want to promise you things—everything," he said heatedly, his breathing gratifyingly unsteady. "It has to be different this time."

"It will be," she said with a certainty that she had never thought to feel about him ever again. "We understand each other now."

"You helped me understand myself." He placed another soft kiss on her lips. "I promise never to take someone's word over yours ever again."

"I promise not to let you walk away from a fight again," she replied, then kissed the tempting expanse of his throat, just visible above his collar.

"I promise never to walk away again." He slid his hand down from her cheek in a slow, loving caress along her neck to her breast, cupping its weight in his hand, rubbing his thumb across the peak. He paused, thoughtful. "And I promise to tell you the next time I'm in a riding accident."

Violet snorted. "Better yet, why don't you promise to avoid *getting* in a riding accident in the first place?"

James grinned at her. "Fair enough."

"I promise never to pretend to be dying to extract revenge for an argument," Violet continued, then leaned forward and made short work of unbuttoning his shirt.

"I promise never to pretend you're actually dying and keep you bedridden for days on end." His thumb continued its gentle pressure, and he stole another kiss.

"I promise never to cough significantly in an attempt to gain your sympathy." She loosened the collar of his shirt enough to drag her lips along his throat.

"I promise never to flirt with another lady as an act of revenge against your revenge." His hand left her breast to join his other hand in reaching around her, undoing the buttons of her frock with practiced ease.

"I promise to support you, whatever you should decide to do with regard to your relationship with your father. And West, too." She drew back from kissing him, her tone not as light. The look in his eyes was all she needed to see—the gratitude, the love.

"I promise never to spend a silent breakfast with you ever again," he said quietly, and the underlying message was crystal clear. They would never again allow their fears, their mutual uncertainties, to come between them.

"I promise never to depart in a huff in a carriage again," she said, deliberately lightening the tone. "Or at least, not to my mother's house." She gave him a saucy smile and slid her hands inside his shirt, running her palms over the smooth heat of his bare skin.

"I promise to follow you every time," he said, a wicked glint in his eye as he undid the last of her buttons and reached up to ease her dress down over her shoulders and down to her waist. "And I promise to ravish you in the aforementioned carriage once I catch you." He leaned down to place a heated kiss at the spot where chemise met bare skin, sending a shiver coursing through Violet.

"And I promise to enjoy it thoroughly when you do," she said.

And, as they rattled through the streets of London back toward Curzon Street, she immediately set about keeping that particular promise.

Acknowledgments

The publication of this book is the culmination of a lifelong dream, and I owe a tremendous debt of gratitude to a large number of people, including:

Taylor Haggerty, world's best agent, who believed in this project first and whose relentless passion and positivity have meant more to me than I can possibly express.

Kaitlin Olson, editor extraordinaire, who in addition to being all-around brilliant also helped me figure out what exactly I was trying to say.

The entire team at Atria who have worked so hard to bring this book into the world, including Megan Rudloff, Isabel DaSilva, and Sherry Wasserman.

Karin Michel and the rest of the staff, past and present, of the Chapel Hill Public Library.

The many teachers and professors who at various points encouraged my writing, both creative and academic.

My friends—from Florida, from UNC, from SILS, and beyond—and especially Lisa Duckrow and Alice "BriHo" Hayward, for half a lifetime of . . . everything; CAMEL for growing up with me; and Beatrice Allen, Kerry Anne Harris, and Allie Massey Jackson, for important support at key moments in my life as a writer.

The Shaws, who have given me a home away from home.

My family—Mom, Dad, Alice, Nan, and the Madison, Georgia, Bests—who never told me this was too big of a dream. To Mom and Dad especially: thank you for raising me in a houseful of books, and for showing me—by your own example—the value in telling stories.

And, finally—to every friend who has spent the past decade listening to me joke about consumption being the most romantic way to die: I'm sorry. I promise I know it's really not.

About the Author

Martha Waters was born and raised in sunny South Florida and is a graduate of the University of North Carolina at Chapel Hill. She works as a children's librarian in North Carolina and spends much of her free time traveling. *To Have and to Hoax* is her first novel.